2020 VISION

Where a revelation of the end is just the beginning...

Part one of the Visionary Series
by M. Owen Clark

All the characters in this book, as well as their religious and political views are fictitious, and any resemblance to actual persons, living or dead, is purely synchronistic.

ISBN: 9781514289778

Part one of the Visionary Series was first published by M. Owen Clark, August 2015
www.M-OwenClark.co.uk

Edition 2.0 was re-published in March 2018 with improved UX and bug fixes, as well as upgrades to the narrative code.

Typeset in Times New Roman and edited by Bench Press Books London.

Cover Design by Tracy Poulsom
www.lovedesignbytracy.co.uk

Printed through KDP, an Amazon.com Company. Available from Amazon.com and other retail outlets.

The ability to conceive a book is one thing; the opportunity to write one is what makes it so special.

Thanks to all of my family and friends for their on-going support, especially my parents, my wife for being so cool with me basically quitting my job and to my three wonderful boys.

Thanks also go to Petts Wood and Bromley Libraries for their original hospitality in 2015, as well as The British Library for the hot desk space and slightly less hot security pat downs.

A vote of no confidence goes to Camden Library, where on my only visit in 2015, an old man threatened me with an ivory knife… there lies another book in itself.

The new edition was created once I'd decided to commit to the sequel and as such, the narrative was updated accordingly.

"Synchronicity is an ever present reality,
for those who have eyes to see."
Carl Jung

"Coincidence is the hidden architecture of reality."
Yahweh

"Look for the dream that keeps coming back.
It's your destiny."
Orison. S. Marden

Friday January 1st 2016 – 2.56am

Hello.

Well that was weird. I've not done one of these before.

I'm 34 and in all my days I've never written a diary, so to be fair I'm not sure what the 'norms' and etiquette actually are.

What are the conventions? Do you say 'hello' to yourself? Do you even write about the merits of saying hello to yourself, or try to self rationalise about your own epic start?

Do you critique, edit, go back and proof read a diary? Do you introduce yourself to yourself? Does anyone actually write 'Dear Diary?'

Well I won't be doing any of the above. Unless of course, the above actually constitutes having done this already, so making *my* epic start a ramble at best...

Blimey, this is gonna be a long night!

I guess the age old custom has always been writing with a quality pen; gifted by a loved one for a landmark birthday, into a serious looking hard backed diary. Maybe said diary even has a padlock on it and further adorned with one of those handy ribbon type things.

Well sorry Mr *W.H Smith*, it's 2016 and as a girl of the ages, I'm starting out digital!

I'm all alone, its now 3.05am and I'm in bed feeling pretty rubbish.

Ok, maybe I've held back a bit.

I guess I can 'let go' on these pages, seeing as I'm the only one reading them.

Correction. I feel *beyond* rubbish. Bloody awful even!

If I were a man, I'd be whimpering about 'Man Flu' and resorting to breaking out a little bell by my bedside, so as to call for immediate and possibly even emergency assistance.

Alas, being alone, nobody will come to my aid, unless Valentine, my trusty cat can suddenly learn to put the kettle on and microwave a hot water bottle…

Surely, there must be some sort of App for that already... Note to self - learn how to code and write an App for that.

Better yet, save myself the bother and simply sell the rights and move to a big house in Sevenoaks before some robot does it before me!

I'm gutted to be ill.

Not only have I missed out on the New Year's party with my besties, slept through the big Midnight fireworks and run out of medicine, I'm also too sick to go on the New Years Day walkabout around Folkestone.

This is an annual event with my friends, where we all meet at the local band stand at 9am sharp, take tea at *The Grand Hotel* and then proceed to carefully traverse the perilously icy 'zig-zag' path, down the coastal cliff and head on a seafront walk, Westwards towards Sandgate.

If it's been a particularly heavy night before, sometimes such an early start is a bit of a hazy struggle. Yet the mazy path seems to hide our lack of ability to walk in a straight line, which is always handy for keeping one's pride intact.

We then head back again, but via a well deserved and all too often medicinal drink in the Ship Inn.

All very nice. Fresh air and a chance to top up the old alcohol levels, albeit this year, there will be snow everywhere!

But no...

Here I am sat up in bed typing on my tablet and even the cat has deserted me. I am however, nothing but efficient, as my first New Year's resolution to write a diary; in which to chronicle my non-fascinating life to kids I may never have, is officially underway.

Go me!

Page one in the bag - or on the Cloud, whatever the modern term is for this sort of thing. Actually I'm on page two already – even better going!

Actually, I'm starting to find this diary malarkey quite therapeutic already. That was the main aim of this exercise I think - to finally be honest with myself.

This on-going self-reflection will enable me to fully question my intentions and goals through a typical Libran kind of note taking and comparison of pros vs. cons. I may be highly organised and self-assured in public, but when it comes to my own emotions and home life, I do tend to neglect them and need someone to lean on when it all get's too much.

Steve...

LOL. I just wrote 'Steve (my boyfriend)' and then promptly deleted it, as this whole diary writing process is just so new and so bizarre to me.

I feel like I'm telling a story and almost need to introduce people along the way, and yet funnily enough, I *do* know who Steve is, hence deciding to delete it.

I thought that I would document this enthralling anecdote anyway, seeing as it made me laugh – little things eh...

Blimey, first cheesy chortle of 2016 and it's exacerbated my aching back. Ouch!

Second note to self – I must try not to make myself laugh so much! In fact, third note to self - buy a notebook, as this could be a long year...

Where was I? Ah yes. Steve. He's great, but a dreamer and completely non-committal, which winds me up no end.

Part of me has learnt to love his laid back approach to life. Any more laid back and he'd be horizontal!

Yet his liberal stance, non-confrontational outlook and general positivity are definitely a draw and a natural foil to my inherent pragmatism and stubbornness.

Damn you diary! See, the truth *has* prevailed already.

I wouldn't admit these foibles to him of course, there's too much sense of self-pride at stake, but when we're alone, he does make me feel calm and I would like to think that after five years together, he'd agree that we're a good fit too.

I just hope that he's still into me and isn't just being lazy and avoiding having to go out into the big wide world and hunt for new women in freezer isles, or worse still, swipe for a GF with a GSOH on *Tinder*. I can think of nothing worse!

To be honest, I've recently questioned my own love and loyalty to him, seeing as we still live apart and I'm probably using this diary as a way of weighing up what is actually important in my life.

So as far as I can see it, you have: love, family, friends, work and self-interest – not specifically in that order. Oh and health too while I think of it, ironically as I break into my last box of tissues.

I really do feel wretched!!!

All of these things round our lives and truly make us what we are. Who we are.

I guess if you're single with no family and a crappy zero hours job, you'd be pretty miserable and self-loathing.

Whilst I'm not an advocate of money buying you happiness, it can surely buy you security, peace of mind and the trappings of a high self worth and well-being. So long as you have perspective, I think money *can* buy you happiness – there I said it!

If I won the lottery tomorrow and suddenly had £3million pounds in my account, some would say that's not a lot of money in the grand scheme of things, especially if I suddenly wanted to swap my home in Folkestone for Fitzrovia.

It is however a lot of money to me – shed loads!

But I wouldn't go and buy a poncey townhouse in Kensington, fly Hawaiian Air or start dabbling in stocks and shares. My happiness would come; I hope, from the simple things in life.

Buying out my mum's mortgage on her little cottage in South Wales would be the first job. Then seeing my little brother right and getting rid of his student debt so he can start in life with no worries.

Come to think of it, I suppose I'd better clear what's left of my own student debt too.

Then there's the credit card(s), and I'd upscale from this two bedroom rented flat to a nice cottage somewhere looking out to sea.

I'd maybe even see if I could buy the scary looking gothic house overlooking the Old Town harbour on the hill. Then I could write my diary in peace and quiet, as everyone would be too terrified to come and ring on my enormous doorbell.

I almost played a gratuitous 'knockers' joke there, but thought better of it... a bit too 'Carry On' for day one of the diary, but I can't promise my bad, or insensitive sense of humour won't prevail in later days!

I'd like to think I'd stay grounded anyway. I know Steve would too, but would a lottery win be a catalyst for us to finally commit, or at least move in together and buy a place?

Thinking about it, I might need to meet the Lottery half way and at least invest in my first ticket, as I've not heard that they're big on donations to those who'd *wished* they'd placed their bets...

Ok, it must be a sign. The fact that I'm thinking about this is too much of a coincidence to just be of coincidence.

I love things like that.

You know, déjà vu and all things a bit mystic and synchronistic, as Steve says.

In principle I like the idea of tarot, but then my Libran head gets in the way and I start to undermine how it can possibly be true. In truth, I'm too scared to try in case I find out something I really don't like, or worse still, get turned to the dark side.

Blimey, I remember Steve going to get his palm read at a local fair in Ramsgate – well he would wouldn't he, the gullible Piscean.

They guessed that he'd recently lost a loved one – nope.

That he was in a state of flux at work – nope.

In fact he was out of work at the time...

And finally, that he was about to enjoy a holiday or a well earned break – well yes luv, it's called 'the dole'...

Three strikes and she'd have been out of there for me!

Well actually 1.7 – 2 strikes strictly speaking, as my patience is a good deal thinner than the proverbial odds.

Yet this charlatan seemed to have Steve at 'hello' and he hung on her every word, even if it was way off beam. Steve then post rationalised the session with me for over an hour in a coffee shop, trying to shoehorn in events to make sense out of this utter nonsense.

Yet Steve's positive search for hope was very endearing and I guess that's why he's religious and I'm just a practising atheist. Not a militant like Hitchens or Dawkins, just a cynic who's yet to be convinced and certainly someone who's long since lost all sense of hope.

So does that make Steve more malleable, gullible or lovable just because he's a God fearing Piscean?

I know he's inquisitive and his subsequent retraining after redundancy as a shiny new journalist for the local rag is a perfect fit for him. It's just the subsequent downgrade in pay that's been the principle blocker for us not living together.

Five years and counting Steve… Not that I'm *actually* counting yet.

Much…

All I'll say is, if I have to be a bridesmaid, maid of honour or hangeronerrer at any more of my friends' weddings, then… I think I might just bloody implode.

Anyway, rant over. If Steve can get his life back together this year, I know we'll have a more solid future together. We are good together and for all our faults. (I did just change the word 'his' to 'our' then, so I think this shows progression on my part already in 2016 – praise yay for diaries).

Maybe I need to show more outward signals and signs of commitment to him in order to obtain a similar response. Maybe doing all of the running isn't in his nature.

Ok, so I *know* it's not in his nature, but I don't want to scare him off either.

So given that it's a leap year, maybe if I propose on Valentine's Day that may not be as weird for him or quite as much of a leap of faith.

Maybe then we can focus on getting a place, as I'm tired of wasting my hard earned cash on a landlord's rent and on after work wine.

London prices are a killer! I remember paying £2 for my first alcoholic drink, now it's near enough £6 or £7 depending where we go. So much for de-bloody-flation...

Let's not get into politics at this hour though – there's plenty of time for that!

Right, so that could be something to ponder this year. An actual way to get into politics and maybe some voluntary work for a party would look good on the CV.

I guess with the US election later this year, Steve will be subjected to the usual diatribe from his father as to the runners and riders in the Grand Old Republican Party.

It still makes me laugh how spending time with his dad would allow Steve to slip into an American accent again. He may have been born here, but his ear seems to be susceptible to his dad's strong Wisconsin drawl.

New Year eh? What else can I resolve to do seeing as I am off to a flier on the old diary front?

Maybe I should stop the killer commute to London too? Ok, so the *HS1* train is pretty damn quick, but it just takes so much out of my day and for a job that's all right, but I'm not saving any lives.

I'm not sure what else I'd do though; especially in Folkestone, short of working for *SAGA*, but I'm not sure I'm ready to subject myself to the blue rinse brigade on a daily basis just yet.

I could re-train as a primary school teacher I guess. Pretty sure my degree in Political History and my fascination with all things esoteric would stand me in good stead with a five year old...? Hmm, perhaps not.

Maybe I could be a policewoman, and take a hard line on the immigrants in Margate, or I could Captain the frigate currently patrolling the town's waters. Hmm, sounds a little *too* aggressive for me. Maybe I should be a Libran librarian instead, or better still a lecturer.

I can see it now: 'Welcoming today's guest speaker Sophia Sinclair, BSC, MSC, PHD, YMCA, who will kindly be gracing us with her time to speak on Political Science and the Northern skill gap following the 'Southification' of many students, post their time at University.'

That sounds quite interesting actually, seeing as I just made that up. It would be a demographic and geographic study into Britain's endemic North/South divide. Blimey, I'm sad! Plus, I expect this great body of work has already been published somewhere.

It's now 4.52am and I'm wide-awake through feeling sooo crap - what a night!

I do hope I'm not up writing all night and finish off in some kind of weird jet lagged state, without having actually enjoyed a well-deserved holiday preceding it...

No I can't.

I need to sleep off this wretched illness.

So, tomorrow, I *need* to get better.

Get up, stand up, and find the cat, that's if it deems my presence worthy of its own.

Then maybe head into town to stock up on medicine, tissues and a lottery ticket.

Some wise man once said you have to be in it to win it!

I feel this is a bit rambling, but where else am I going to get stuff off my chest. That's the point of these things right? Goodnight diary.

Oh, I said I wouldn't do that. Sorry...

*

It would have been poetic if she could have seen the buildings instantly vaporise around her.

Just imagine watching in awe, as the age-old structures turned to dust within milliseconds of the initial impact.

The speed and ferocity of this type of destruction, playing out in her peripheral vision, could not be fully comprehended by anyone; unless, like her, they were actually in the thick of it.

Everything passed in a kind of sardonic slow motion.

The sickening sound of the resounding blast was completely deadened, as the preceding shockwaves had already burst her eardrums.

Her beautiful brown eyes, now streaming and bloodshot from the original flash of light, widened in anticipation of life's final act.

What had started as a calm evening amble, utterly inverted in an instant.

It simply became the most wild and wicked image to behold. An unapologetically apocalyptic scene and one that literally took her breathe away.

The blinding light. That searing heat. Wildfires seemed to spread like touch paper.

She witnessed the faint submission of once proud buildings that not so graciously bowed under the power and majesty of unrelenting waves of pressure and sound.

A series of unrelated explosions went off, seemingly in every direction and there was an unnerving judder to the ground in the very spot that she was now crouching.

Just take a moment to envisage such an awesome spectacle and try to comprehend the time it takes to complete its catastrophic course.

A moment, was all she had.

You'd want to lift a hand to cover your face from the fast approaching furnace. Perhaps, mutter an instinctive expletive or even contemplate what might have been.

If only she could have enjoyed time enough for one last turn to her only daughter.

A solemn smile and a reassuring grip of her hand, not least an array of goodbye kisses.

'I'll love you always.' she would whisper, as she knelt down beside the unsuspecting and innocent looking child.

Yet her last teardrop would surely evaporate before it had time to fully well up within her saddened eyes.

These eyes would now reflect the impending abomination that was to engulf their ending embrace.

The night sky quickly re-blackened. A calamitous column of smoke grew on the horizon and with thick, acrid and choking dust quickly filling the air; she feared their bodies would soon be fused as one. Their love was 'never ending' and they held on tight for the impact.

Yet, time doesn't allow for romanticism or heroism.

Time marches on apace, and in the case of an atomic-like blast, it simply stands still for the first nano-second and then absolutely and unequivocally overwhelms you.

The roar. The power. That supreme raw power.

She looked up, still in a state of disbelief and saw a light in the night sky for one final time. A deep emerald hue, cast a shadow on an otherwise neon moon. This was the malevolent splendour her brain would never have time to appreciate, or fear.

She saw the sky light up for one final time and just like that - they were gone.

*

Friday January 1st 2016 – 3.15pm

OMG!

Holy mother of God and all his extended family.

Ok, so that's if God actually *is* a 'he', there *is* an extended family bobbing around up high somewhere, or *even* exists at all - but that's another subject entirely!

Whatever the theological and celestial state of affairs, I've immediately grabbed for the sanctity of my new diary, but now I'm here, I'm utterly speechless! Wordless, or type-less even.

I literally have tears streaming down my face and I'm covered from top to toe in sweat. It's disgusting!

I think I just had a dream or more likely a friggin' nightmare. In fact, I really hope I just had a dream - wait a minute...

Ok, so I am going completely mad. Well more manic than normal anyway.

I just checked out of the window and the flats next door are still there, which is re-assuring. I even saw my bloody Valentine knocking over a snow-covered bin, which considering my relationship with the neighbours; is the least of my worries.

Yes that was definitely just a bad dream. No, funnily enough bad, doesn't really sum it up sufficiently.

This is hard to fully encapsulate, but the strength and intensity of this dream is like nothing I've seen before.

It had to have been real, or was it my brain re-living a scene from a movie? It's not a film that I can recall seeing before, but I felt like I was there.

I know I was there!

It was like I was seeing the destruction through my *own* eyes, but I had a daughter too...

I remember feeling an immense sense of love and then an unerring pain for losing her.

Good grief, I'm still crying as I type!

It was me, I had to be me. I *know* it was me.

So is that my version of a tarot reading?

Am I going to have a kid, forge a bond, create some memories and lose it all in an instance? There's no way that can happen. Not to me!

You see this sort of thing on the news in Syria and Iraq. Terror atrocities combined with war and conflict in conveniently far off places.

This must be what it's like for them.

The horror! The horror!

Perhaps I was simply channelling someone else's pain, from somewhere else on the planet…?

My mum's a bit witchy, but she's not admitted to this sort of heroic ability before. Where in the world could something like this be happening?

Those feelings - just so real!

I love Steve, but I've never felt such a strong sense of love for *him*, as I felt for my child in that dream.

Just incredible!

Neither have I ever experienced that gut wrenching or foreboding feeling of loss before.

Nor would I want to again!

I can't have been channelling someone. It had to be my daughter and I, but why?

Where? When?

To think I will bring a child into this world and feel anything like that sort of love is scary and a thing of beauty. How is that intensity and sense of possessiveness even possible? Just nature I guess. Alas, I wouldn't know.

I just felt an unnatural urge to embrace and protect her, but maybe that *is* absolutely natural. Maybe that *is* my evolved instinct coming out.

Flight or fight, and if all else fails, just flipping well duck and run for cover!

I know it's nothing more than flu, but my heart rate's hit the roof. If I felt bad before, I feel at a crazy low now. I'm still teary. I can't seem to stem the flow, or console myself. It's ridiculous.

I feel like I‘ve just lost a loved one. Still grieving and unable to understand their loss, believe it or let go.

Yet the most bizarre thing, it's my *own* life that I mourn and that of someone I'm yet to meet that I yearn for, and that's the sickest part of this twisted dream.

What the hell do I do now?

I think I'm going to be sick...

3.50pm

I've had a shower, I've got nothing left inside me to be sick with, and now I just feel cold. Pardon the graphic nature diary, but I can't remember the last time I felt this way.

If ever…?

I now feel a real sense of dread and apprehension.

This is crazy, I actually feel as if someone *has* actually died, if not just a little part of me.

I just want Steve to come over and hold me, but I know if I tell him why, he'll just bloody laugh at me.

If I ring my mum, she'll just worry and Welsh Wales to the snowy Kent coast is no easy ride for a retiree.

For goodness sake, sort yourself out woman!

The fact that I'm still tapping away on this stupid tablet is more odd than the dream itself, but I've got nothing else to do, as I feel like crap and look a whole lot worse.

Is this still a cathartic process now, or just a constant stream of consciousness?

I am however, reticent to put into words exactly what I just saw in this most damned of dreams.

People will think I'm bonkers... it was just too real, that's what I can't get my head around.

I felt in total control of my actions in the dream, and strangely viewed through a first person vantage, rather than a third person voyeur looking in.

Sometimes I'm not in my own dreams, they're just my brain's way of processing life's events and making sense of the otherwise mundane.

This time, my brain didn't know what'd hit it, bless her cranial cotton socks. Just crazy!

I can't decide if the dream was really fast, or if I was somehow able to hold or control time, to allow me to make more sense of it.

It did seem slow, and there was some sort of explosion and the sound and smell were sickening. It was a mixture of a deafening distant blast, interwoven with screams from all those around me. I think I was silent and even my daughter seemed cool under pressure.

There I go again. *My* daughter...

This is just too much for me to take in.

I felt that she was my daughter and I would even go as far as to say that subliminally I *know* her name to be Rebecca, albeit she did not say as much.

Mad as it sounds, it's like I just know somehow…

And yet, to dream about someone that doesn't exist with such love and devotion is just so strange! Let alone naming the poor girl…

I may have to book myself into care at this rate, with a padded cell - the whole nine yards. Either that or put a bet on that I have a daughter, call her Rebecca and that she dies before she is ten. That would then save on the 'lottery' aspect of buying a get rich quick ticket.

WTF? I'm a rambling mess!

How the hell can I contemplate betting on the demise of a daughter I'm yet to conceive?

I feel like death and all I want to do is sleep, but I'm afraid to go back.

'Go back' ????

Bloody hell, I sound like an advert for a Hollywood horror flick or something, but I honestly couldn't bear to see any more. Enough's enough!

This is *not* real, everything's fine, breathe and sleep.

You're not crazy. The world is still spinning, albeit slightly off kilter, despite what Steve's stupid flat Earther friend says and it's just the illness.

Surely?

With all that's going on in the world, I'd be surprised if it's not just my subconscious trying to make sense of Turkey shooting down that Russian plane. I thought they and Syria were all on the same side and merrily syphoning off ISIS oil over the Turkish border?

Blimey, I think Steve's been spending too much time with that Tim Osman fella, his theories seem to be getting to me via osmosis. I guess you hear enough of the same drip, drip message, you start to believe anything right?

Right then, time to sleep this off.

*

Life couldn't get much better, she thought, as she sipped on her mocha coffee and watched her beautiful daughter Rebecca playing on the slide.

Well, much better considering the shitty circumstances surrounding the divorce anyway...

A faint breeze was a relief from an otherwise blisteringly hot day in the city and this urban London oasis was respite indeed, from what had otherwise been a hellishly hectic week.

Rebecca never let on, but she loved 'one on one' time with her mum.

Her younger sister somehow seemed to take the limelight since her mum and dad had split up. She now had few opportunities to spend the quality time that she used to take for granted as a younger child.

Now it was just all about dodging her parents' arguments at handover time.

Her parents never seemed to be able to view her as the priority and look at situations objectively. There was always point scoring to be had and as the eldest, Rebecca was always the key pawn in this game of one-upmanship.

Sophia closed her eyes, unaware of her daughter's true hidden feelings. Content to be there with her, she breathed in the not so fresh city air and contemplated the turbulent six months that had seen her seemingly normal life unravel so epically.

Although it was on her terms, her stubbornness would never allow for mediation or compassion.

The death of Steve's father had been the catalyst for change, reversing his once jovial outlook on life into a more introspective and cynical one.

Let down by God and let down by his own family.

The couple grew apart, and all of a relationship's niggles that would normally be overlooked, were suddenly personified and gradually cascaded into a petty game of cause and effect.

To an outsider, the end came suddenly and not for any major misdemeanour, but simply because neither party had the energy, nor the stomach to save a relationship well and truly in its final throws.

It's always the children that suffer and Rebecca had even been put forward for counselling in the earliest stages of the split; such was the detrimental effect on her schoolwork.

Sophia's eyes meandered around the park, just looking without actually seeing.

Everything she took in was simply subliminal, whilst she pondered a meeting with a divorce solicitor booked for the following week.

She had let the relationship fade.

It was not *all* down to her, but it was arguably broken before Steve's father's passing.

Sophia was in a reflective state and felt sad that Rebecca had to grow up in such a state of flux. Flitting from parent to parent and not being able to call one house her home was never ideal. Moving around so much had obviously taken its toll on her own childhood, but perhaps she'd never forced herself to face her *own* demons before.

Rebecca and her sister shared a room at Steve's new flat on the coast, whilst Sophia at least had some resemblance of a family home in her rented three bed Victorian terrace in Bermondsey.

Her move back to South London came to be one of necessity. Having taken stock of the new situation, she felt more at ease putting distance between her and Steve and she always felt more at home here.

They'd never actually bought a place after the wedding. The savings went on chasing Steve's ambition to visit Machu Picchu, which whilst being an amazing sight; in Sophia's mind, the money could and should have been better spent on a deposit.

That was Sophia all over. Ever the pragmatist.

She was worn out.

Worn down and it was only her time with the kids that kept her feeling alive.

Work was better since she'd moved – new house, new job, 'new me' she promised herself and it was all about *her* after all.

The children's needs and those paternal requests from Steve would always come second and this sense of resentment grew ever deeper on his part.

His last bastion of positivity meant that he tried to take the moral high ground, hoping that; in time, the children would recognise that he remained loyal, true to himself and with his dignity held intact.

However, Sophia knew how to 'play' him and he really had to stop himself from biting - especially on those already stressful changeover days.

The situation is not good for any party, but it is what it is and as far as *Rebecca* was concerned, she was outside, having fun and spending time with her mum – even if mum was just watching rather than *actually* playing with her.

As Rebecca slowed, she suddenly noticed that mum was no longer looking at her at all.

She shook her head, despondent.

Sophia's graduated gaze had fixed on one point - the newspaper belonging to the old suited gentleman that was sat beside her. Why save Sunday best for the weekend, especially when a week day could be your last, her own dad used to say. Must be a generational thing.

The man neither noticed, nor cared that she openly read over his shoulder, one of few social taboos left in London. Faster and faster her eyes skimmed down the lead article, her mouth agog to what she was reading.

Her work and busy personal schedule had meant that any interest in politics and current affairs had taken a back seat, so it was ironic that this news, was in fact *news* to her.

Rebecca started to well up. She couldn't understand why her mother had just run off, with a level of gusto she'd certainly never displayed before.

Mummy didn't even look back.

She didn't even turn her all so sudden exit into a joke, or a game and this immediately confused and then, after a few more seconds waiting, started to worry young Rebecca.

Mummy had dropped her coffee and left her handbag on the weathered wooden bench. For all intents and purposes, it looked as if she'd forgotten Rebecca too.

Rebecca ventured over to her mother's bag with a view to safeguarding it, as she guessed mummy would be back shortly to collect them both.

But she never did...

Rebecca's tears started to fall in earnest as Sophia disappeared fully out of sight and a subsequent wrenching feeling of emptiness hit the pit of her stomach.

Complete helplessness and fear gripped her tiny frame and with that, the old man looked up from his broadsheet and simply smiled, solemnly.

'Sorry,' he said calmly. 'Mum's had to run'.

'What did you say to her?' asked Rebecca reeling in confusion and anxiety. It shouldn't be that a seven year old is left alone in the city.

'I can't lose her too!' she sobbed, acutely aware of her inability to contact her own father.

'She's not lost,' said the old timer, gently stroking his thin white goatee beard, 'Just the opposite my dear, she's taken a different path. She's just been found'.

Rebecca didn't understand and assumed he was a little barmy, so held her mother's bag even tighter, more as a defensive barrier than a precaution. Then she was suddenly struck by its possible contents and started feverishly delving into its seeming depths to find her mother's phone.

'No Service' said the icon in the top left hand corner. In London? Really?

She flicked through the phone contacts to try calling her dad or nana, yet strangely there was just one contact in the whole of the list, which seemed odd, even to a seven year old. It just read:

'MABUS'.

Rebecca didn't know a Mr or Mrs Mabus, but out if desperation, and despite the apparent lack of network service, she tried to call the number anyway.

The mobile surprisingly connected and went straight to the bleep of an answer phone. No pre-recorded message of instruction, just an impersonal monotone.

'This is a message for Mr or Mrs Mabus. I don't know who you are, but I am Rebecca Sinclair and you know my mum Sophia Sinclair. Can you please call me back please. Thank you.'

Rebecca put the phone back in the bag and expectantly surveyed the park once again, hoping her mother had suddenly reappeared.

She had not.

'As I say my dear she has found herself and it's not up to you to get in her way' said the old man slowly.

'What do you mean? How can you say such a thing? She's my mum and *I'm* now lost!' cried Rebecca.

'Unfortunately my dear, we are all lost until we are found.' The man started to fold up his newspaper and inadvertently revealed the front cover for the first time.

Rebecca's eyes darted down to read the five-word headline and she immediately turned cold.

She knew exactly where her mother had gone and where she could find her, but it was not somewhere she could ever go.

Not because it was outside of the *Oyster* card zone, or even that hard to reach. It was simply because *time* itself would not allow it.

Rebecca replaced the handbag on the bench and turned back towards the bright orange swings where she sat down and reflected on what seemed too big an ordeal for her tiny mind to fully comprehend.

Her tears had long stopped, her resolve had hardened.

She somehow knew her mother wouldn't be back and that the phone would never ring a return call.

Rebecca sniffed, wiped her eyes and looked back up to see that the old man had also now disappeared, leaving her totally alone in the small urban pocket park with just her fluffy white stuffed owl for company.

To think, one minute she was innocently playing with a naive joy in her heart, and the next didn't even bear a comparison.

Again she slowly shook her head.

Where the old man once sat, laid in his place was an oversized and slightly crumpled newspaper.

The ominous words of its leader article were left in plain sight, and conspired to compound her issues further:

'YOUR WORLD IS
BREAKING APART'

Saturday January 2nd 2016 – 8.15am

Morning! I've come out of my slumber slowly today, smugly stretching and safe in the knowledge that I now have the whole weekend to get myself right.

Hooray for Friday Bank Holidays is what I say!

I feel a little more human and dare I say it, re-energised today. I'm also glad to report that I've not had any more apocalyptic premonitions or visions again, but instead a rather odd dream, that was like something bizarre from *Twin Peaks*.

This time I was an older, and rather stylishly dressed I might add. Sat in a city somewhere, assume London, but again with my daughter.

Yet this time, and this is where the dream all went a bit ayawaska, I was *also* my daughter! Seeing and feeling how she felt, which was pretty lonely from what I remember.

Again this dream was so clear, so intense, vivid and visceral. I could touch things and feel them, say things and mean them, whilst also connecting and conversing with people, just as you would in real life.

I think I ran away from her.

Yes, I remember reading something. A newspaper I presume and then just bolting. Not only that, but the dream then span in on itself with an action replay from another angle, as I then witnessed my departure through my daughter's eyes.

High strangeness, but that's all I got on this one.

The rest of the dream is just a hazy fog, like most dreams are when you first wake.

Why would you run from a child? These dreams just get more curious! But do they mean something? Are they linked, other than the presence of a young girl?

My young girl.

Is that my lot in life now? Am I to be a postmodern prophet, but more of a modern day, OCD, insecure, indie feminist version? I'm not sure about being a prophet.

I'm more pathetic than prophetic!

It's too early to recall exactly what else I saw, but I'm sure from the feelings that I have now, that I don't want to go back to *that* place either.

I still feel achy, but not as bad as yesterday. That was a freakin' horror show, not least that crazy dream. Well, the first dream mainly.

Just sick – no one should witness something like that, I just simply cannot put into words the emotions running through my brain at the time. It was like I woke up on something like speed!

Not that I've ever done speed Your Honour, but I would imagine it can get quite intense and you hear about feelings of paranoia and all sorts. Not a good place!

I'm gonna brave the five minute slip and slide into town and I think, after all this sleep, the fresh sea air might do me some good. Finally blow some sense into me!

Suppose I'd better call the clan, to let them down gently about the walkabout too.

Laters diary!

8.20pm

Early night tonight me thinks. I do actually feel pretty exhausted, considering the vast amount of sleep I've had.

I've worn myself out today, almost going arse over tit on the treacherous walk to the shops and also been thinking about these dreams. I've not really made any sense of any of it yet, other than I am going to have a daughter, see the end of the world, and presumably before this finale, at some point, run away from her to a destination unknown...

Fancy leaving your bloody daughter in a park! You must be quite desperate or deluded to even consider it.

But hey, this is my head, so in retrospect, I'm not overly surprised by the tripe that it churns out.

Despite the chilly air and the snowfall, I'm once again reminded why I actually live in Folkestone and not London.

It was quiet.

Those people who had ventured out, were all polite and friendly and it's the historic nature of where I live that I love.

I was even half tempted to meet up with the gang for the walk. I'm really gutted to have missed out, but in a sad kind of way, I may actually do the walk by myself tomorrow, just to allow me to contemplate this strange start to the New Year.

It's pretty weird why I should start having hallucinations day one into 2016. It must be some kind of inner awakening for me, to sort my shabby life out.

Too early...

No scratch that.

WAY too early for a mid-life crisis!

So I've been moping around the flat before mopping it clean. I finally got around to opening the back door (well the flats' back bedroom window anyway) and then welcomed in the New Year through the front door. Albeit the neighbour thought I was a little bit mad, as she came home just at the point I flung open the door, shouted 'Good Morning 2016' in my best manic Robin Williams voice and then, just as quickly, shut the door in its chilly New Year face.

I did my duty and spoke to my mum, wished her a happy New Year and heard all about how ill her best friend's, son's partner's father is. Think that's right, son's partner's father. Yeah, but basically some random I don't know…

It's scary how quickly our lives become punctuated by other peoples misfortune or illness and chaptered by births, marriages and deaths.

I see enough of this life sapping information on *Facebook* from people I *do* know, so I'm not sure I need to know about the equally tragic lives of others too.

I really should remove myself from this most antisocial time waster, but it can be strangely compelling to see how people bare their souls on social networks and check that their life *is* in fact worse than my already sorry existence.

Speaking of which, I finally got around to speaking to Steve today. I thought that of all the people I could soundboard and confide in with my story about the impending end of days, true to form, I was right.

The bugger laughed at me.

He told me to stop being so melodramatic and to man up!

Well: One, I am a woman, so I'm physically unable to 'man' up and in any case, I still have the remnants of a bad bout of what he terms 'Bird Flu', the sarcastic sod!

Second, and to be honest, I only shared the more rational facts of the dreams; I was NOT being melodramatic!

I didn't mention the emotional connection or the whole 'daughter' thing, just in case he totally freaked and it was *he* that did a runner! So it *could* have been ten times more dramatic for him…!

I just chose to play it down a little.

To be fair, he did make me feel slightly better about the whole thing, as when I mentioned that I had two random, really vivid dreams, he deducted that I had more than likely been experiencing 'Fever Dreams'.

Sounds like the name of a 1970's erotic novel, but apparently, according to t'internet, a fever is induced by the body releasing certain chemicals, which in high doses, also stimulates sleepiness.

We also experience more REM sleep when we're sick, to help the body repair itself, however the release of these chemicals perversely, as part of a fever, reduces the chances of lasting REM.

This is something to do with REM sleep producing muscle stiffness or a similar state to a motionless coma and so not allowing the body its ability to shiver and manage the changing temperature as part of a fever.

All very intense I know, but REM *fever* sleep is therefore inherently fragmented, to allow the body to keep reacting to core temperature changes. Apparently around 90% of fever dreams are remembered if you are woken during a state of REM fever sleep, as opposed to waking naturally.

It sounds like one would normally wake during REM as part of a fever and I also read that a higher body temperature can also evoke a higher, or at least an altered state of consciousness, whilst asleep.

Spacey! It seems I can finally release my inner shaman.

This may explain sleepwalking or sleep talking for example, but in my case, it does give me some mild relief that I'm not about to be carted off to Bedlam.

So without wanting to sound like a sleep bore, I think that my crazy dreams were simply due to circumstance and my illness, rather than any sort of lasting mental disorder or pre-ordained power to see into the future.

However my sense for a little melodrama, may in retrospect, have manifested itself in a few choice words being used in Steve's direction, such as 'Modern Day Visionary'. So maybe it's unsurprising that he thought I was getting all David Icke on him.

Steve promised he'd come over tomorrow, having submitted his last article to finally put the paper to bed.

I'm proud that Steve has kicked on following redundancy. This role as a reporter suits his inquisitive nature and allows him to get out and about to talk to people, rather than being tied to a desk. That used to drive him potty when he was at the insurance company.

Anyway, looking forward to his visit and I may divulge a little more of my dreams to him... if he plays nicely.

Sunday January 3rd 2016 – 9.25am

Day three in the fever house and my temperature and aches have all but gone - just a bit of a headache and still a bit groggy, despite a good night's sleep.

No new dreams to report thank goodness. The more I think about them, the more they worry me. Fair enough if I'd had a dream about falling onto a pavement and bashing my head in, or a public argument with a random person, but to dream so specifically about two comparatively distinctive events, is what really bugs me.

The first was more of a night terror than a dream. A vivid intensity where I could feel the heat on my face, but the location and my companion were a mystery to me - other than it was my unborn daughter...

I just remember how there seemed to be a thick dust that rained down, like during the impromptu evacuation after the first of the twin towers fell.

Those poor souls.

If I felt anything like 10% of their pain and anguish in my dream, as they would have experienced that day, I cannot comprehend what that situation must have been like.

Minding their own business and scurrying around like ants in the financial district, then suddenly boom! They witnessed and experienced the tipping point that changed the face of the modern day political landscape forever.

And what must it have been like for those in the buildings that escaped and that sense of ultimate relief, not to mention those who had to call their loved ones, knowing they wouldn't make it out alive?

It all just beggars belief, despite what Tim Osman told Steve about what '*really*' happened that day… douche!

I was at work and in that one moment, the world was united in collective consciousness, watching the chaos unfold.

Steve told me that post 9/11, his dad Patrick was going to try and sign up to the Territorial Army and go straight to Iraq; such was his immediate disdain for the Muslim nation after those horrific events.

He felt it was an attack on his own sovereignty and he really did show his true colours that day - how blindly nationalistic we can all be in duress. Steve directed his energy into talking him down, but even now, his dad pathologically links all of the world's ills to somewhere in the Middle East.

I have no other new clues from the second dream either, albeit it was strange dreaming from multiple perspectives.

Quite a talent if you ask me...

I have since remembered digging around in a handbag and some old codger irking me, but other than running off and then seeing myself run off from the perspective of someone not as yet conceived; I can't remember, or explain much else.

Figures why I haven't told Steve much about the dreams, as I don't actually have much to go on myself, other than the apocalyptic vision – maybe *I* should be the one to stand on street corners, with a sandwich board exclaiming that 'The End is Nigh!'

I best not tell Steve's dad, as he'd have me repent; being such a God fearing man himself.

Oh that was odd. A pronounced chill just went down my spine then when thinking about Patrick.

Perhaps I should suggest that we meet up with him, as Steve said he'd been unwell over Christmas.

Steve does dote on his dad, but he's such an old fashioned kind of fellow.

Mostly harmless, when he's not kicking off over Islam, but at the same time; he's just completely lifeless. He just seems to exist in his retirement, embracing the sort of routine that you'd expect of a toddler. It's a wonder how his Pam puts up with him? At least she throws herself into the grandkids I guess.

Yes, I think I'll suggest that we meet up with Steve's brother Seth and his family too – safety in numbers me thinks!

That does mean a trip to West Croydon though. As a certain Mr Lucas once deftly described it: 'You'll never find a more wretched hive...'

Right then Miss Sinclair, breakfast and a bath before your man arrives! I'll report back later.

Quite liking this whole diary thing, I may publish it one day. Ha ha!

10.30pm

Shit the bed I'm jumpy! This whole saga has made me a nervous wreck.

So I'm strolling down the Old High Street towards the harbour and looking at my phone, as you do, when suddenly there was this almighty bloody explosion that came seemingly from the middle distance.

Now the Creative Quarter in town is quite insulated with tall buildings rising up each side of the narrow road, so it was hard to gauge where the horrific noise came from, but I thought that was it! That's the end, the 4th July and November 5th all rolled into one singularity of a Big Bang.

Now the fact that I'm writing this proves (spoiler alert) that the world has not ended, but oh my days did I get a fright!

I was rigid! My brain had neither the context nor the comprehension to compute what was happening. Having already witnessed the end of he world and replayed the somewhat finality of the incident in my head just a few times, you'd have thought that I'd be on my game, fleet of foot and a natural leader in the darkest of times.

I'd have gathered the woman and children, huddled them into one of the small independent clothing boutiques and still had time to save the men *and* appreciate the competitiveness of local pricing compared to the fashion houses of the capital.

Alas I was shit!

Ok, so maybe I'm doing shit an injustice and at least that gives off a smell. I pretty much just stood there. Mouth ajar, completely static and still holding my phone aloft, complete with a half written inane tweet, primed to enlighten the world as to my mundane musings on the state of the local pavements.

I do lie somewhat. Despite being frozen to the spot, I *was* able to swivel my eyes to notice that the rest of the misfits that tend to frequent the streets of Folkestone during the day were totally oblivious of the impending doom.

I gradually looked up, the terrific sound of the impact still ringing in my ears and the sky blackening above me. Holy shit, it's happening! It's really happening! I shivered, briefly flashing back to my dream and almost immediately snapping back to reality.

It was only now that the instinct to flee finally transcended the tissue of my very slow brain.

Yet life went on.

The local drones continued to bustle past me, parents continued to push buggies up the inexplicably steep hill towards me and I continued to exist, albeit a motionless moment captured in space and time.

Breathe, sigh of relief, compose and restart.

I deleted the *Twitter* post and went to the search bar. *'Explosion Folkestone'* I typed clumsily, through my electrostatic enabled woolly gloves (Think that's what the tech is called, Tesla I'm not!).

'Sorry no results for this search.'

Damnit, they're all dead already, there's nobody left to report it in, I thought...

'Nuclear attack UK'.

Nada.

My heart was just starting to normalise, I just wished my life would too! What in hell was that noise? I tentatively started to edge closer to the bottom of the hill, peering around the corner towards the old fishing harbour.

There I found a crowd of people congregating close to the harbour arm. As I moved nearer, the blood fully returned to my legs and I felt slightly more at ease about the future of our blue marble. On face value, it looked like an incident, rather than a planetary disaster.

Pushing past a few of the onlookers, I could start to see the crumpled shell of a rather sorry looking and charred yellow digger, presumably once sporting a jackhammer on its arm.

'Looks like it's gone straight into a bomb buried in the beach luv.' said a tall, smartly dressed middle-aged chap.

He looked like an authority on the subject and so I nodded in somewhat bemused agreement. He then drew in slowly on the cigarette hanging from the side of his painfully chapped lips, 'Either that or a gas main.'

'Would it not be advisable to put that out then?' I mooted, nodding towards his smoking appendage.

He looked me up and down with a look of disgust, as if I'd just asked if he liked being tickled at weekends with a feather duster. I moved in for a closer look.

Now in hindsight, if I'd thought about my dear beloved, I may have considered snapping the action on my mobile so he could get a live scoop, a byline and a bonus.

Instead I simply Tweeted to my fan base of four: 'It's all going off at the old nightclub!' (Apologies diary, I know you don't get out much, but there used to be a ropey nightclub on that very spot).

Now there was just a smoldering wreck, scattered beach shingle everywhere, a few broken panes of glass and a chip in a windscreen of an old Ford Capri, double parked on the front.

That'll learn them!

The crowd started to disperse and then I got to thinking. If my first reaction to every loud bang is going into shock and checking social for an update on global meltdown, maybe that's no way to live.

Short of hunkering down in my own personal bunker, it may be more prudent for future quality of life to nip this in the bud quick smart.

I'm going to report this in. My dream that is, not the Capri's parking misdemeanor.

Nuclear Armageddon aside, on reflection this has been a nice day. Lovely to see Steve in the flesh and after convincing him that I still hadn’t got bubonic plague, get the sort of afternoon post-traumatic support that only a time of intimacy can provide.

Why am I dressing it up all coy for you diary? Not like my mum’s going to read it!

Having lost out on three days holiday through no fault of my own, Steve convinced me to take a 'duvet day' tomorrow and meet in town for lunch. On him!

I'm not one for pulling sickies and don't actually think I've had a sick day at all last year, so I'm sure I won't get a reputation at work just yet. That said, being off the first working day of the year does seem a little suspect, but sod it, as I've just witnessed in my dreams, you only live once!

Carpe Diem and all that jazz!

Speaking of a dream, that's all I seem to have done today – speak about them, that is.

Steve suggested that I go for a walk tomorrow morning and try to place myself in situations that may remind me about other elements from the dreams. I wasn't planning on walking into the arms of the apocalypse just yet, but I know what he means. I'll just keep away from the harbour!

Also, I'm not sure I should be hanging around any kid's playgrounds on my own. Could be viewed as being a bit too Operation Yewtree-ish for my liking...

I even Googled the word 'premonition' earlier, in the hope of drawing some clarity or ruling it out. There were millions of entries and those that I read went from the strange to the extreme, yet after today's action, I do now feel like I have some sort of perverse or nihilistic sense of civic duty to report it to someone in authority.

Do you report these sorts of things? You always hear on the news that someone comes out of the woodwork after a tragic event and says: 'Oh yeah, I had a feeling that might happen, but thought nothing of it'.

Well thanks! Hundreds of people are now dead because you didn't fancy picking up the phone.

I don't want to be 'that gal'.

But do you trust your gut, or self medicated feverish brain functions and where the hell do you start?

Do I call the operator and say 'Premonition Report Line please'. Is there even still an operator to call?

Do I call MI5, Interpol or The Police? I'm not sure Sting would be that fussed anyway… and he's a legal alien!

Maybe I should do some more Internet research first, before I go baring my soul to the powers that be and give them a good laugh at my expense.

It might be *them* booking me into *West Ryder*, instead of me, if I'm not too careful.

Maybe this is my destiny - the woman that predicted the end of the world. And what did she do about it?

Well she took a sickie', went out for a nice spot of lunch with her, obviously handsome boyfriend, shot a bit of pool and then boom; that was that, too late.

Goodnight sweetheart, goodnight world…

That's the trick you see. The first thing someone will say to me is: 'Ok, so you've had a premonition, when will it be? Tomorrow, five or fifty year's time?'

'Not sure Sir.' I'd reply, head bowed and cowed, like a scalded little schoolgirl.

'And where will it take place?' he would press with an officious voice, his half mooned glasses on the tip of his beaky nose, peering over at me like the *Demon Headmaster*.

'Again, apologies I can't be specific on that. All I know is it all goes tits up somewhere, at some time in my lifetime and possibly within my daughter's lifetime.' I would answer, shifting slightly in my seat; possibly even sitting on my hands and biting my bottom lip in embarrassment.

'Ah ok; now we're getting somewhere. So how old is your daughter madam?' he would enquire, thankful that he may finally have a solid line of enquiry, or at least someone else to interview. 'Oh, I've not conceived her yet, but my boyfriend and I have talked quite a few times about starting a family, if that helps at all?'

I would then beam confidently, gripping Steve's knee, as he magically appeared at my side, as if for moral support.

The thought of actually publicising this nonsense fills me with confidence…obviously…

There must be some sort of X-File office in Whitehall, as I can't be the only nutter to have ever had dreams like this. Maybe my case would have to take its place in a bureaucratic queue behind those abducted by aliens and those with special powers of levitation like that Dynamo fella off the tele.

I may miss my slot!

The blast might go off before they even get to my Top Secret file, such is their slow and out dated raffle ticket system, like you'd find at a shoe shop or the cold meat counter in the supermarket.

My case may yet get reviewed, but the sky might light up before I've even had the chance to remove my coat, let alone before they interview me, regress me into hypnosis and water-board the damn information out of me.

I may be flippant, but I did mention regression to Steve and even *he* was sceptical. Maybe I'll research that too. Doesn't sound like much of a day off tomorrow then after all, but someone has to save the bloody world!

Wonder Woman signing off...

Monday January 4th 2016 – 7.30am

A nice early start for me! Work to be done don't you know?

Plus I don't want the end of the world to come before lunch and our best of three game of pool!

That would be most bloody inconvenient!

I'm not sure that I should take this premonition thing so lightly really, but if I write too seriously about it, I think I may turn into a neurotic nutter by default.

I'm simply keeping my feet on the ground and my head from entering my own posterior.

If my first dream is anything to go by, it looks like I'll burn up as part of the destruction anyway, so I'm sure I can afford a little light hearted entertainment, to keep any ensuing depression at bay.

I may have to put my earnest game face on though. Once I'm at the police station that is!

Yes, that's right diary….

I've decided in my infinite wisdom to report it in. So if it does all go Pete Tong, it can officially go on record, that a very willing and girl next door type, glamorous good egg called Sophia Sinclair of Springvale Close, Folkestone, *did* actually tip us off after all and it was the wheels of a Government in austere times that were to blame for not processing her statement in time.

That is, as opposed to that selfish Sophia keeping her seeming madness to herself.

I'm shaking my head as I write this, as who knows what I'm going to say to them or how to position such a tall tale?

'Oh hello, you don't know me as I've not been here before, but I had a dream about the end of the world - well what looked like the end of the world, or a *significant* event at the very least.' I would say, nodding, whilst all the while, still secretly trying to convince myself.

And so it would go on from there in a similar vein, I guess – totes awks!

I'll have a clearer conscience at least. Think I'll have to speak off the cuff. Just tell it how it is, and maybe level with them and say: 'Look, I know how crazy and insane this sounds, but...'.

I also think it would be best to do this face to face rather than on the phone, so they can see I don't have two heads or a lazy eye. At least if I'm there in person, then I can ensure they're filing a report, as opposed to simply filing their nails.

Unfortunately, a crime number will be of no use to man or beast should the worst happen!

I'll also do my belated New Year walk today, albeit on my own, so as to work up an appetite before lunch and maybe buy a newspaper and see what I've missed out on.

Oh and I'd better call work too, and put on my best croaky voice. I am feeling better today though, thanks for asking!

12.20pm in the *Ship Inn*, Folkestone

Well I made it to the pub.

Four days into the New Year and I'm having my first liquid lunch. Only joking.

I'm not meeting Steve until 2.00pm now, as they had some last minute issues at work with the Editor or something, so his lunch break has been delayed.

Suits me, as I've been able to enjoy a lovely seaside stroll past the *Dolphin Café*, heading west towards Sandgate and I now find myself sat in the *Ship Inn* with a steaming bucket of black coffee.

Despite its historic appearance, the pub itself is relatively modern inside and its best feature is the panoramic views over the Strait of Dover.

On a clear day you can see French France and sat on my own, I find watching the waves just as entrancing as watching a flickering flame. It was odd walking along the sea path covered in snow. I'm not used to it.

The snow was patchy on the pebbled beach, having been thawed in places where the tide had come in, but thick enough elsewhere to stay in one piece, frozen I guess, by the bracing sea air.

I've not made it to the police station as yet – think I'll brave that after lunch and maybe with a drink inside me.

Work was fine when I called them.

I couldn't speak to my boss Lucy, so I left her a message via dippy Dawn on reception. I'm half expecting a text later from Lucy asking where I am, but to be fair, I doubt they'll even notice my absence...

I've not been out for a seaside walk for a while.

You'd think that living on the coast would mean that you couldn't keep me off the old pebbly beach, or even the sandy parts down at the old town fishing port.

Well I may live here, but my South London roots ere me on the side of a landlubber. I just like to see the sea, rather than actually going in it. Also, last time I went out east of the old town towards the Warren Conservation Area, I ended up getting a text message saying '*Welcome to France*' and that made me long for London even more.

We're close, but not that close surely?

You may get the impression that I'm killing time. Far from it, I'm learning to love the diary and like all my obsessive compulsions, this is just the latest in a long line of short lived whims. I'm just hoping that I continue this particular fancy, as I quite like talking twaddle to myself.

I guess that if I invest the time in it, as I have done to date, I'll feel more enthused and devoted to continue the entries.

I just might find that work, housework and *Corrie* might get in the way of it, that's all…

Not sure I should turn down any invitations though.

Say Steve invites me out and I say: 'No sorry, I've got to do my diary tonight.'

It would be like the new 'washing my hair' line. Nah, don't be daft. Anyway I can't afford to blow him out if I'm going to do the running for this impending wedding!

"Wedding"???

Well, if I'm going to have a daughter, I'd better meet her half way and get married and convince her father that her conception might actually be a good idea in the first place!

Maybe I'll drop 'Rebecca' into our chats at lunch. Like the proverbial conversational grenade and see what goes off. I could say that the sea air made me remember her, or seeing the kids playing in the Millennium Park below the Leas sparked me off into a series of regressed and emotive flashbacks.

Cue the melodrama ☺!

Not sure I should have bought the newspaper – It's all doom and gloom, but I'll record the goings on for future posterity and as a reminder of the prelude to apocalypse, should it all suddenly go off!

The not so shiny and new slimmed down Government still can't organise a piss up in a brewery, or decide which football team it supports.

The Russians have flown yet more bomber runs off the coast of Bournemouth. Not sure if they're testing our military reaction times, or are just voyeurs looking for skinny dippers on a *Carry On* type of nudist beach?

Either way, this has been going on since late 2014 and it feels more like the Cold War each passing week. At least the whole Ukrainian invasion has settled down – a bit. I'm not sure the Russians could stand the sanctions much more.

They still seem to be there from what I can gather, just not shelling the shit out of each other. Their currency has probably gone so low that they have resorted to firing clusters of melted Roubles at each other, as the next best economical thing to an actual mortar.

Maybe my dream is timely and it's the Ruskies that spark WWIII?? Thinking about it, Turkey shooting down one of their planes is never going to help tensions either.

And yet, they both bomb different parts of Syria…

I just can't keep up anymore!

Excuse me for sounding like *The Economist*, but once a Political Scientist, always a Political Scientist! Maybe it'll be the harsh winter we're experiencing combined with the UN sanctions that exacerbate problems internally within Russia. Maybe civil unrest will ensue and their leaders put the skids on energy supplies to their neighbours, so leading to a lack of supply and rising energy prices across Europe.

Maybe this would then see an over reliance on Middle East oil and gas and the West being held to ransom by a new axis of evil – OPEC!

Maybe none of the above, but I always wondered if the end of the world might just come down to who has the energy supplies and who has the nuclear capability.

And those with both would probably prevail.

I note that the main towns being fought over in Syria have transnational gas pipes going through them…

No wonder the Government has been carrying on with Trident, despite not having two brass farthings to rub together elsewhere. Not so much a deterrent, but an overt show of power from what is otherwise a glorified triangle of a country, well, according to Steve's dad anyway.

Although he lives here and pays his taxes, he has no love lost for UK PLC and described it as a series of jumped up triangles or a 'glorified triangle' when he refers specifically to the crude shape of England. He thinks we like to involve ourselves in everything, so as to keep up the pretence that Great Britain still matters in the world.

A size injustice that this American just can't get his head around. I think that's why he and Pam still live so close to Heathrow. Not just because he's a former pilot, but so he knows he can get out within a moment's notice.

Patrick probably thinks that world standing should be in ratio or direct proportion of the land mass to power.

No question of population, history or GDP, that's all just detail. USA, China, Russia – all the superpowers. But if size really did matter (in this instance), Australia would be a superpower and I'm not sure they could give a XXXX for such responsibility…

Patrick's politics baffle me sometimes.

I know that the Democrats and Republicans are both centre, or right of centre on the political spectrum, despite what Bernie Sanders is standing for. It may be hard for a Brit to distinguish the difference, comparing the Dems to our newly radicalised leftist Labour Party, but they seem to differentiate from each other on such polarising policies.

Abortion, gay marriage, gun control, slavery in the past and more recently, over the strength of its foreign policy. What happened to good old fights over the NHS and immigration?

Hillary Clinton's Democrats are positioning themselves as the sensible World Police, overseeing and consulting where necessary, whilst concentrating on domestic issues that Obama has been unable to push through the two Republican dominated houses or Speaker Ryan's impenetrable beard.

The Republicans on the other hand seem to be getting back to their good old rooting tooting ways of picking fights with anyone that doesn't tow their party line. Whether that's good Christian values at a domestic level, or on the international stage - especially with ISIS seemingly picking on Christian victims in particular.

I read a nice article in the *Guardian* today about the forthcoming primaries as part of the US election – the famous Iowa caucus no less!

It seems that despite so many Republican candidates throwing their hat into the ring, there hasn't been one outstanding candidate, unlike for the Democrats.

Sounds like a long shot from Patrick's own state of Wisconsin is making a noise in what is otherwise too level a playing field.

'*A young principled black man standing out from the otherwise white, middle class male runners for the Grand Old Party*' cites the paper.

His strong Christian beliefs seem to have placated many of the less moderate sections of the party and he appears to be particularly vociferous about foreign policy and '*getting the job done*'.

Sounds like re-opening old war wounds to me, but what do I know or care what happens across the pond.

I have my own issues!

Anyway, I'm sure I will hear all about this when we meet up with Patrick...

Best I wend my way to the next pub on my mini crawl then. Onwards to meet Steve outside the white render and empty hanging baskets of the *British Lion* pub at The Bayle.

3.15pm in the *British Lion,* Folkestone

The pub was quiet, which was good, as we didn't have to speak in too hushed tones.

The original fireplace was lit and a welcome relief from the bitter cold outside. We sat by the window in 'book corner' and I ordered more coffee along with a pint of the black stuff for Steve.

You can't beat gammon and eggs the day after being ill. Steve was in a good mood today, not that he isn't normally, but I thought that he'd be more stressed or pre-occupied following a morning at work.

He was in fact, very attentive and despite being slightly side-tracked by the football news on the TV screen behind me, he offered some good advice about how to play my impending visit to the police station on nearby Bouverie Road.

'Be yourself 'cos that's all you know how to be.' is what he said, and of course, he was right.

Whether they believe me or not. Whether they choose to entertain my fantasies, and whether they deem it necessary to question me, I still have plenty of my own questions that I daren't ask myself!

The more I self rationalise as to whether I should even be going to the police, I just keep coming back to the same thing.

It's more a sense of civic duty and if I *am* going to become the proverbial 'watcher on the wall', then I don't want the end of the world happening on my watch!

Here goes then Lord Commander.

For the Watch!

4.00pm Folkestone Police Headquarters

Well I've done it. Well got here anyway. Steve's gone back to work and I'm sitting in a rather small and sterile holding area.

A few chairs, a table with the usual array of waiting room essentials – car magazines, *Woman's Own, Golf Pro* etc, etc.

There's a pin board on the wall opposite giving colour to an otherwise white and stark looking utilitarian room. Flyers promote the usual nanny state and Police guidance.

Don't drink and drive. Breathe in, breathe out.

Apparently, they have the 'network' to tackle Cyber criminals and the benefits of the new and improved Neighbourhood Watch scheme are 'there for all to see'.

All inspiring stuff, but this situation was alien and left me with an unsettled feeling of growing unease.

I've done nothing wrong, so how must those with a guilty conscience feel, stewing alone in this dreary environment?

You can tell I'm padding whilst I'm waiting... Even in hospital, I'm never the most patient of patients.

I've not been here before and outside, it's a massive sixties looking block with a long ramp leading up to the blue arched entrance.

The snow covered open space alongside the imposing building accentuated its white linear rendered lines and white windows that both offset its otherwise brown brick exterior.

Four or five stories high, I can't recall now, but it really is much bigger and busier than I envisaged. Especially for a simple town like Folkestone.

I guess they must serve a wide catchment area from here these days, since the cutbacks.

Maybe even France?

'Won't be long dear.' said the old WPC on reception, following my arrival fifteen minutes ago – she looked like she'd been put out to pasture long ago and re-recruited to fill in the part time gaps left by the redundancies of the recent cuts. It's a wonder they cut back on policing, after the simmering social unrest has looked close to spilling over again.

I did bottle it a bit at reception though. Not giving too much away to the old crone, in case she judged me; the bitter cow. I played my cards very close to my chest so I did. Paraphrasing my bumbling introduction slightly:

'Hello. I wanted to make a statement to document a vision that I've had. I know that sounds odd, but it's something quite awful that could happen and I really need some help or advice as to what to do next.' or something along those lines…

She looked at me a little in shock: 'Not had one of your kind before dear, bear with me whilst I speak to my Duty Sergeant. Take a seat in that room and we won't be long.'

The old sixties style clock on the wall ticks slowly.

It was Scandinavian looking, with a light wood veneer to its thick outside and an oval shaped edge. Thickset black hands ticked softly inside the dusty looking face, prolonging my agony with every agonising stroke.

It was a style somewhat out of character with the rest of the room, due to it possessing, well, a sense of style, but it is in fact, in keeping with the original age of the building.

I wonder if it's adorned this room over 50 years?

I wonder if anyone's had to wait that long to be seen?

Golf Pro?

That's quite a niche market to appeal to in this sort of place? Maybe I'll enquire if and when someone does finally come by: 'Get a lot of golfers in here do you? Do they swing by often? Do they get tee'd off for waiting for so long?'

Maybe I'll just keep quiet…

'My Kind,' the old bint said to me. Blimin' cheek!

I read 'My kind' as being a 'raving loony'. More like a natural mystic who can see divine futures good and bad and whose destiny it is to report back to the Elders, the echoes of these distant futures?

I'd love it to be the latter, but the former looks more likely, judging by the sort of people that roam the streets of Folkestone during the working day.

Good grief – that scene could be on a Jeremy Kyle meets Benefit Street Christmas special. They are a special kind of people, my neighbours!

I'm such a snob! But seriously these people must come off an identikit production line. I'm sure if I went to arbitrary places; the first that randomly come into my head - Crawley, Bromsgrove or Wigan, it would be the same. Just loads of chavs wandering around in a daze.

Enough said you bloody bigot!

Tick follows tock, follows tick, follows tock…

I can almost feel the hair on my legs growing; I've been in here so long. The paint is physically degrading on the wall; such is the time that ever so slowly passes here.

Species yet to be discovered in deepest Amazonia are gradually dying out; in the time it takes to… oh hang on, movement!

5.25pm

Short but sweet! Well about an hour all told.

I didn't get frisked, no prints taken, no swabs, no full cavity search – more's the pity.

I did have a slight fantasy about a 'man in uniform' taking me into a cell. He'd pin my arms against the wall above my head, whilst he set about tearing off tights with his teeth. He'd then draw his shining truncheon and…

Back in the room, I'm now sitting in a coffee shop in town, as I thought best to get this down whilst it was fresh in my mind. The story of my visit, not the fantasy.

OMG, how sad am I?

I've literally turned into a literary bore!

To be fair, I've never done this sort of thing before, so I'm wanting to note it all down just in case I become a lonely spinster, drink myself to oblivion through societal rejection and regret not being able to remember the details.

I didn't see the WPC again, but PC Howard - assume that was his surname - took all my details.

He was not fantasy material!

I had to describe both dreams to him in as much detail as I could and this was tricky. Not just to remember them, but to also describe the feelings involved. I tried to appeal to him that it was the sense of emotions that made it so real and *that* alone gave me the strongest sense of responsibility to report them in.

He said it was probably nothing, but thanked me for the information, which he would put on file and share with the 'relevant departments'. File under 'U' probably. Not for 'Unexplained', but for 'Unequivocal Nutter'.

He did seem quite thorough though and asked about my family, how I came to be in Folkestone and other seemingly non-related items, constantly jotting down entries into his tiny notepad. Presume this is part of the cutbacks too!

His hairy hands crept down to his knuckles and matched his thick, dark set hair.

I would've thought it would be more efficient to type straight into a report, seeing as he would obviously need to compile a whole dossier on me, but maybe he is one of those slow, self-conscious, two finger typer types?

Maybe he just can't listen and type at once.

Yes that must be it.

After all he *is* just a man...

On reflection, I'm not sure how useful that exercise actually was for either party.

I didn't remember any more than I had previously and was guarded about every detail for fear of being banged up for wasting police time. But it did force me to focus and re-live the experience more so than I've done on *these* pages.

Hairy hands Howard made me go through my mobile phone and see if that reminded me of the contact on the phone in my dream and although I couldn't recall a name, I was drawn to M or B. Not that it helped him...

Having just regaled the first dream in particular, it's ironic, if not slightly coincidental that *House of Dust* by *Everything Everything* just popped up on my randomised *iTunes* playlist, now as I write. The beauty of typing onto a tablet is that I can be wired for sound at the same time!

Why should it pick that apocalyptic inspired song of all songs out of a shuffle of 3,793 tracks? And to play it now of all times - how does that work in a world of coincidences?

Anyway I've jotted down the emotive lyrics at the end of the song, which seem pertinent to the present time:

I wish I could be living, at the end, of all living.
Just to know what happens, just to know what happens,
I would know, every answer and just how far we all made it,
This is all my life, this is all my life.

I guess that's how *my* life is going to roll this year.

Is everything happening for a reason and do I just need to open up my receptors; my senses and soak in all the information that I may otherwise ignore?

How many times have I been driving and the place name that's marked on the signpost that I notice on the motorway, is then mentioned on the radio at the exact same time?

I'd say, more than 5 and less than 10, but still enough to make an impression and be of statistical significance.

I always did like the bit in *The Matrix*, where they described déjà vu as a glitch in the Matrix. The film gives me more answers on that subject that we have in reality anyway.

So that said, maybe I need to become a 'Yes Woman' and take advantage of situations or invitations, as they may have an unknowing benefit to me in the future.

Are these situations to become something else that'll assist my quest or my calling, or will they simply be clues, to help me remember my dreams?

I think the coffee may be too strong, as I am off again!

Delusions of grandeur perhaps, but hey, I know come tomorrow morning, I'll be back on the 'dreadmill' of life:

Eat. Sleep. Crave. Repeat.

I did sit in front of the box the other night and literally not move for three and a half hours. My mouth was agog, with a little bit of dribble falling onto my TV dinner lap tray.

Ok, so the last one was a lie, but I do wonder, are we being conditioned to consume TV dinners full of crap to suppress us? Conditioned to consume TV with an 'edited' or partisan view of the news, so as to cause a nationwide slumber?

Do we only see the tip of the iceberg?

The masses wouldn't be so revolting if they were hooked up to addictive concoction of *Celebrity Big Brother* or The Only Way is Chelsea on Ice...

Smirnoff Ice too… now that would be worth taping!

Yet we can be quite easily moulded into a national outpouring or an outcry over certain subjects. It amazes me how the press whip up such a storm over certain individuals. They love to build people up and then knock out the pedestal from under them.

Operation Yewtree is a case in point, which is a bit of a witch hunt, quite rightly for those who were in the wrong, but those celebrities who were called out for wrong doing, only to be found not guilty, had a scar on their reputation forevermore.

Other subjects also seem to catch the imagination of the press and suddenly there's a fear of panic among the people.

Immigrants. Terrorists.

Or worse still in the *Daily Mail* - Terrorist Immigrants!

I might add at this juncture that I was *not* one of those to change my Facebook favicon to a French flag last year, just because *that* atrocity was conveniently close to home.

Anyway, I'm sure it was simply a ploy or poll to see how many sheep there are online and how far a particular agenda can resonate with the populous at large.

Everyone's becoming so polarised, so nationalistic, so divided on so many issues. It's like there's a national undercurrent bubbling away, I'm just not sure where or how it might actually manifest itself.

We see so much bad news at the moment, I'm almost becoming desensitised to it. Or maybe my emotional empathy has been stripped so much that I simply don't care or notice anymore…

Oh, I could submit this as an article to the Economist. Bit deep for a diary I guess, but it gets it off my chest.

Anyway, I digress and not for the first time! You can't beat a brain dump within the confines of your diary. Love it!

I think I'll chill out at home tonight, catch up on some fun stuff like reconciling the credit card bill and some ironing, whilst watching TV - of course.

This is living right?

Work tomorrow!

'The fear' has set in already…

Tuesday January 5th 2016 – 7.30am

I'm on the train up to London and it was ten minutes late.

It's amazing how a few days off and a couple of minor premonitions can change your outlook on life!

I'm so over this damn commute already! Going back to sleep now, see you later and hopefully not in Bedford!

1.30pm

I was right. a) Dippy Dawn never passed on my message and b) Lucy didn't notice I wasn't in the office anyway, so I had to log my *own* absence with HR.

Grr, useless bunch of tools!

Otherwise a quiet start to the year on the email front with some clients still not back – that *is* the way aha, aha I like it!

I'll await their bidding in due course, with positive anticipation and a large smile, both inside and out. NOT!

There may be no 'I' in team, but there are actually FOUR in 'ironic musings of a pissed off drone...'

10.40pm

Sod 'Blue Monday', how about 'Cold Hearted Tuesday' – ok so it wasn't that bad, but I just don't seem to have my get up and go anymore.

I think it got up and went!

Since I found out that I'll lose a daughter and have now returned to my mundane routine and even more mundane colleagues, I've developed a general malaise about life.

It's almost like, what's the point in getting married, buying a home, getting pregnant, worrying about everything that goes with that... will I be healthy, will the baby be healthy… And to think that all the fun stuff up to, whatever age she was in the dream; will all be for nout.

Why me? This isn't fair to witness such a catastrophe, let alone have an emotional carrot of a child dangled in front of you, only to have it incinerated.

I need to put it to the back of my mind if possible. Take my usual pragmatic approach to life, none of this soppy stuff.

Man up, as Steve said.

He really is starting to add value to this relationship! I think it's through the diary that I am finally able to appreciate what he does and *has* done for me in the past.

Wow, am I really that self-absorbed?

I guess seeing as I put my health before that of the baby in my list of concerns above; that may give an insight for some shrink somewhere.

Ok, so maybe it's *me* that needs to get my life together this year. I enjoyed my job last year, I think, or was that just because I had a different outlook on life?

How fast things change eh?

Our minds are delicate things and although I don't claim to have anything like depression, I can appreciate how people could spiral out of control, ever downward if they're not mentally tough enough, or have a good enough reason to climb out of the pits of despair.

I'll erect my mental ladder now then and just live for the weekend. Live one day at a time.

Right, I've got nothing planned, I'll text Steve about seeing his family, as I forgot to mention it to him yesterday and see if I can't get me some brownie points. I'll also see if he wants to come over tomorrow night, as I can't spend another one blobbing around in my *Duran Duran* onesie.

A vision in *Gold*, I am not!

Hmm, I feel this is a bit of a short entry today, compared to some of the others. I don't really want to document everything I have done each day, so let's just assume for future entries that unless I say otherwise, I've breathed in, breathed out, cleaned my teeth, showered, eaten three square meals and had the odd drink here and there to survive.

Oh baubles! I still need to take the Chrimbo tree down too! I don't want any more bad luck! I can't afford it!

Wednesday January 6th 2016 – 11.11pm

Blimey it's late and this is going to hurt tomorrow morning, but I've got to get all of this down because, basically - wow what an evening with Steve – no not like that saucy!

Where do I start? Work was average. Better than yesterday, as I was busier, but I just seemed to have meetings about meetings today, which in my state, is just depressing.

There's planning and then there's planning to formulate a plan of how we will plan the master plan, fulfil the plan and then carry out a post-mortem of the plan, so as to inform the planning phase of the next plan.

That's how we roll in Project Management - apparently. That and huddles, scrums and goalposts.

Sounds like I work at Twickenham!

My boss asked me if I wanted to train to be a Scrum Master – so she wants me to be a high class hooker – great, there's something to be proud of on my CV.

Anyway I digress again. I notice I'm good at that, so much so that when I read this in my dotage, I'll no doubt be confused into thinking that I'm reading the 'Ronnie Corbett Chronicles' at this rate.

So anyway, Steve came over for dinner and we got talking about my dreams – shock I know!

I've still not mentioned the whole 'daughter thing', but I took the conversation to a more macro level and he agreed to help me do some research.

Where the hell do you start eh?

Well this is how it went down, again paraphrasing, embellishing and adding oodles of melodrama where appropriate, so that post apocalyptic book clubs can appreciate how events actually unfolded…

He arrived promptly, wearing an open neck white shirt and smart blue work slacks. His thick blonde hair freshly gelled, and aftershave recently re-applied to his seven o'clock shadow, which I immediately noticed following our lusty embrace and subconsciously scored him a perfect 10 for trying!

'Good evening Steven, welcome to my humble abode, my name is Sophia Sinclair and yes. I'm naked.' – ha, just joking!

What really happened was, he strolled in, dumped his bag, pecked me on the cheek and went straight to the loo…

'Alight luv?' he called loudly, despite the door being wide open behind him.

'Yep,' I said, or something equally eloquent. I do hope that other couples have just as stimulating moments as us…

We sat in the open plan living/dining space in my flat at my small table for two, had dinner; blah, talked about the price of fish; blah. He confirmed we'd go to his brother's on Saturday and their kids and his parents Patrick and Pam would be there too – swell! Blah, blah, cut to the good stuff...

Well, we started surfing the net, as you do at our age. Looking for generic watchwords related to my dreams and seeing what would come up. So pretty much your normal Wednesday night's entertainment then.

'Let's search for "apocalypse" and see what the old *Google* spits out.' said Steve, feverishly typing and excited by his extended journalistic role on my behalf. 'Excellent, just the 95,200,000 entries then. This could be a long night...'

I couldn't be doing with this, so I brushed his hand away from the mouse pad and looked him in the eyes and said: 'Ok, so rules of the game: Look at the first page of each search term, maybe pages 2 or 3 at a push, but no more. Take crackpot websites with a pinch of salt and please stop getting distracted by looking at images associated with the chosen search term, like that one of *Madonna*, and wondering how some of them made it into such a niche search.'

'Aye Captain!' said Steve, leaning closely into the laptop screen and clicking off the images tab.

I think his eyesight may be going. I also think he'd look sexy in glasses. Sorry, I digress again!

'According to this poll, 37% of Brits thought apocalypse would be down to nuclear war, 13% climate change and 8% unspecified cause.' he said matter-of-factly.

We deduced that this unspecified cause might include an asteroid impact, alien invasion or possible self-combustion after succumbing to either a solar flare, or just a final post curry wafer thin mint.

Steve ran his index finger down the screen to aid his appraisal: 'And then there's 5% that think the apocalypse will be down to a worldwide revolution and just 3% on zombies'.

'Zombies?!? Really? They're probably the same people who polled in the National Census that they're following the Jedi religion too.' I said, sarcastically.

'Woo,' said Steve as he opened his fourth internet window, so as not to lose anything, I guessed: 'An '*ELE*' is an Extinction Level Event – like an asteroid impact – can you believe our Moon was once part of the Earth and got blown apart during an asteroid impact?'

'I just thought that Ele was the elephant that packed his truck, and said goodbye to the circus.' I replied innocently, conscious of the time and just keen to get him back on track!

Also I'm not entirely sure how the Earth and Moon both became rounded again after this catastrophic separation. Probably something to do with spinning and friction – who knows and Steve couldn't explain how all the water didn't pour out of the Earth at the time either – maybe it *was* flat back then after all?

'Then there's the Fermi Paradox.' said Steve, really getting into this end of world nightmare: 'It looks to be a study into the size of the Milky Way and the wider Universe and the associated probability of extra terrestrial life being out there as paradoxically high, due to the amount of planets in the galaxy, when compared to the lack of evidential sightings of ET that we have recorded here on Earth.'

I did ask him to repeat that last one TWICE, as there's a reason I am not a proper scientist!

'Hence the paradox you see,' he said, hands behind his head, as if it were *he* that just hypothesised the thing in the first place. You know, just chillin' out in my living room, cooking up a theory or two.

'There should be aliens out there, but where are they?' he asked, to no one in particular, and certainly didn't wait for an answer! 'Aren't they advanced enough to visit us, or…' he paused for effect, a knowing look shot across his wide expectant eyes.

'Are they in fact, too advanced to bother annihilating us? Maybe they've seen what a bunch of self destructive dickheads we are as a race, and so just carry on flying by. Safe in the knowledge that we're already on our own path to Armageddon and it would be a futile waste of their deadly ammunition?'

He has a point!

'Christ, it says here that it's estimated that there's 200-400 billion stars in the Milky Way alone, each probably hosting its own planetary system. Pro that up for the visible known universe as a whole Sophia, and what do we have?'

'A headache?'

'No babes, paradox aside, the chances of life being out there must be like, 'odds on' at least! The mind boggles! Any of them could decide to take a pop at us at any time!'

Is it bad that I checked my watch as he spoke and my immediate concern was that I might miss two key episodes of *Coronation Street* tonight, unless ET could conveniently plan its attack for after the weekend! That would help.

Steve laid on the sofa, as if to reflect on his discovery. He likes a bit of the old Sci-Fi does Steve, but I'm not sure he'd ever looked into the nitty gritty of how the universe actually works and the sheer scale of it. I remember being taught about the nine planets and that's about it. And now we're at eight!

I still can't comprehend that you can fit the equivalent size of over one million Earths inside the volume of our own Sun. It's that chuffing big!

If the Earth were the size of a marble, the sun would comparatively be the size of a two-man zorbing ball. No wonder its gravitational pull is quite weighty...

Steve then got back on the case, and his journalistic researcher side came to the fore: 'The Carrington Event was a solar mass ejection recorded in 1859, which is basically a solar storm that hit the Earth's atmosphere and caused all sorts of electrical problems. That could cause an apocalypse right? Maybe your dream was a solar flare, they're quite common,'

'What if we had one now and that lit up the sky and knocked out the whole electricity network! No email, no Internet, no job, no Corrie!' I said, worriedly.

'Things may be looking up...no work *and* no Corrie,' said Steve with a wink: 'The Aurora Borealis is normally seen close to the poles, but back at the time of this particular solar storm, it was seen across the globe; including equatorial places like Cuba and Hawaii. It even woke up miners in America and they started making breakfast, thinking it was time to get up!'

'Maybe that's what I saw in my dream then, as the night sky did light up, but having said that, the ground shook, buildings fell and there was an acrid dust and smell. It sounds like it could be a solar flare, massive earthquake and a thermonuclear strike, all in one.'

My head was in my hands, reliving the shocking mental image, forever scarred on my ruined retinas.

'The *BBC* has quite a scary timeline of celestial events over the next quintillion years – amazing how they concoct this stuff!' laughed Steve, tracing his finger on the screen, following the winding timeline through deep space.

'A quin-what?' I said, not having heard of anything higher that a Terabyte.

'Quintillion, one level up from a quadrillion – get it? Bi-llion, tri-llion, etc,' said Steve, literally walking me through the math.

'It puts a date on when the sun will run out of gas, when the poles will melt, when each landmass will have completed its tectonic journey to reform the original Pangaea, before then starting to break apart again.' he started making some notes, as if somehow this was relevant to my dream.

'Fascinating,' I replied scornfully: 'Can we get back to the job in hand please?'

'Ok, so I've got a reference to Wormwood, which is a star or angel that appears in the *Bible*, in the *Book of Revelations* that causes a third of the Earth's rivers and springs to go bitter. Interpretations vary greatly, but this could be an asteroid lit up by the atmosphere, rather than an actual star and similarly it could be a person. Does this name ring a bell? Was that the one in the phone?' he asked, looking at me expectantly, as if I'd suddenly recall an entire dream, on the basis of one word...

'No idea.' I shrugged, 'Only Wormwood I know is of the Scrubs variety and it sounds like something out of Dr Who.'

'That was Torchwood,' said Steve, rolling his eyes: 'And I still can't believe John Barrowman was gay!'

'He probably still *is* to be fair. What else have you got?'

'Well, other than the fact that the word 'Wormwood' in Russian is apparently translated as 'Chernobyl' of all things; nothing on this line of enquiry Captain.'

Steve continued to search down the page and I trusted him not to miss anything, albeit I do find it hard to let go of my control freakery at times.

Ok, so all of the time.

Steve pointed to the screen, leaning back; so maybe his eyes aren't shot quite yet: 'Right here we go with the most nutty website. I know we said it's against the rules, but this one looks interesting for the benefit of broadening our own knowledge. I've not seen this one myself!'

I bowed to his better judgement and he continued in a hushed tone for some reason: 'It looks like the airport in Denver covers up a hidden bunker for the big knobs within the New World Order. Or maybe that's a fake conspiracy theory, that's actually a Government smokescreen for something else even bigger. Something far more nefarious! Eh? Eh?'

Steve's eyes widened in anticipation and he promptly tried to extract my opinion, or possible approval on his latest and greatest bloody conspiracy theory.

Steve's one of those classic, modern day conspiracy 'researchers', first raised on a staple diet of the *X-Files* and provocative or thought provoking output on the *Discovery* and *Sci-Fi* Channels. It all started with an Arthur C Clarke book, moved onto the Internet and now the endless podcasts and *YouTube* output from some guy called Alex Jones, doesn't help dampen his flames either!

The day after 9/11, he was apparently the first to jump on the bandwagon that the towers were actually detonated to facilitate a law change on terrorist activity. He was convinced it would allow war mongering in the Middle East as a cover story to secure oil, Israel's wider protection and eventually oust the CIA patsy that was Saddam Hussein. All in all, the creation of a law that allows them to go to war on terror, wherever, whenever and one that they still dine out on today.

I won't even get onto his 'distraction theory' on the whole 9/11 event, where he thinks it may have been used to mask the destruction of WTC7 building and facilitate the looting of underground gold reserves… I ask you!

I've called him out on some of his rantings, but to be fair he just likes to keep an open mind, be aware of this 'hidden world', outside of the main media and I did just have to *Google* this, but he often quotes Aristotle to me:

> *"It's the mark of an educated mind to be able to entertain a thought without accepting it."*

To be fair, having listened to Steve evangelise on the subject of 9/11, I'm still not sure how the 58,000 word Patriot Act was drafted so damn fast, or if George W Bush could've looked less shocked, as he was whispered the fateful news by some Alphabet Agency staffer in that school classroom.

Then there was that missing plane at The Pentagon, the strange way that the two towers came straight down in a cloud of dust and the relatively new evidence of nuclear explosives at ground zero and high levels of cancer sufferers within the surviving first responders. And breathe!

I can't get on board with all this though.

As interesting as hearing the counter arguments are, part of me just doesn't want to believe this could've been perpetrated in the name of politics and not just religion and I almost shut down my sense to it.

Yet Steve often reminds me, much of what he believes, is hidden in plain sight, whatever that actually means. Maybe it's just so they can avoid Karma or something, but in this instance, Denver airport being an apocalyptic hideout seemed a little *too* hidden in plain sight, so as to only be hidden by the virtue of being underground…

Anyway, back in the room! Again.

'Something else bigger and more nefarious like??'

My eyes half closed, face wincing and wary of what might just come out of his lips next…

'Something else bigger like an extension of the local chemical weapons factory, also located in Denver, or the development of the former Stapleton Airport into housing, when in fact there might be a bunker under all of that land as well!' he said, gripping his fists with excitement. 'Or maybe that's what Area 51 is in Nevada! The alien thing's just a smokescreen for it being a black-op bunker where they opened a portal and accidently let a load of entities in.'

'Right…' I said slowly, starting to wonder exactly what it was I saw in Steve and why I was asking for his help in the first place, 'ok space cadet, we're not here to debunk every one of your bloody theories from Kubrick's moon landings and The Rapture to the Moloch sucking Bohemian Grove and the supposed depopulation Agenda 21 of the New World Order.'

'Wow, kudos! You got that down pat!' he said, almost proud of my inadvertent osmosis, or simple ability to absorb his left field propaganda.

'We're here, looking to enlighten my dreams. That's all!'

Steve winked at me and carried on regardless: 'Just wait a bit, this one's a doozy! There's a series of freaky murals at the new Denver airport that depict a solar flare of some kind, a mass killing and then the world's children coming together in unity to preside over the new world order.' he said, pointing out the massive and colourful images of the murals that are dotted around the baggage reclaim area, for all to see.

'Will you stop going on about the New World bloody Order!' I demanded, keen to curtail his constant conspiracies.

'Well, to be fair I didn't actually mean it like that. Freudian slip or force of habit I guess, but it says that it's not fully known who funded the construction of the airport. The capstone, symbolically laid as the final stone by local Freemasons, says that the airport is run by - wait for it, *The New World Airport Commission*. A body, according to the author of this article that does not actually exist. And, just to compound things, Obama was in Denver in 2014 when the Comet Elenin passed the Earth within a cosmic hair's breadth. Seems coincidental that he was there on that day of all days, ready to be whisked underground in case it went KABOOM!'

'My God, you've gone full blown Fox Mulder on me! Maybe The President had a meeting there that day and like there's buildings hidden under the runways anyway! Fool!'

I was now mindful that this exercise was taking way longer than I had ever envisaged and my beauty sleep would be suitably impinged.

'Ok lady, stick this in your bloody tablet, there *are* friggin' buildings under the runways. They apparently constructed five buildings that were 'in the wrong place' or some old bullshit. So they then decided to '*sink*' them under the ground for storage and save wasting the time and money. What sort of crappy Scrum Master did they have on that project unless they simply wanted plausible denial?' lectured Steve defiantly.

'Seriously? That's just one website we've seen, you'd need to verify and check that crazy story out on others too!'

I looked over onto the screen, to witness the subsequent search myself: 'Argh, why are you skirting around on so many tabs, what a mess. Stop looking at that one! What is that, The Philadelphia Experiment? Come off that one too, go back to the airport.' I said hurriedly, trying to tidy the mass of tabs and windows on the screen.

Steve opened a few more tabs in relation to the Denver airport: 'Yep seems to check out, but who knows? They're not exactly going to have a case study and testimonies from the architect to verify that they messed up and had their buildings sunk are they?'

Steve gave me a knowing look and switched back to the original apocalyptic search: 'We've still got our jolly friends at ISIS of course. Islamic State's hastening the apocalypse by continuing to slaughter Christian people in Egypt and Syria. They're still destroying and selling historical Christian artefacts, as a way of stirring up hatred and almost teasing The West into action for one final biblical face off. How does that sound for an impending doom?' he said mockingly.

‘Sounds inspiring, I hear Damascus is lovely this time of year, single or return Sir?’ I said, jokingly proffering an imaginary flight ticket towards his hand.

‘I think if you’re going *there*, a one-way ticket would suffice. Highway to hell in my mind.’

Steve yawned, it was getting late and he had to be up first thing to interview a pensioner about an incongruous gas bill.

Hard news stops for no man in Folkestone!

Steve made his excuses and intimated that we could have another thrilling instalment later in the week. I still can’t believe those crazy murals in Denver.

So odd, yet needlessly and overtly explicit! Hardly what you’d want your kids to be confronted with anyway.

Each animal depicted on the murals had a deeper symbolic meaning within them. People within each image had symbolism within their clothing, jewellery or the item that they were holding. To have so much symbolism about apocalyptic scenes and religious allegory seems at odds with being a secret hideout for a secret society – Dan Brown would have a field day with this one!

Maybe that *was* part of the wider plan.

Hidden in plane sight in this instance, pardon the pun!

But it really is a bizarre project. The runways are seemingly laid out in the shape of a swastika, which finds its roots as a symbol of auspiciousness, rather than the Nazi connotations that have seen the symbol more recently hijacked.

Then there’s the sunken storage buildings, the miles of tunnels for apparently transferring baggage reclaim – why not just the normal tried and tested, or arguably cheaper process?

How could a project, originally budgeted at $1.9 billion, end up costing over $4 billion and counting - especially one that’s privately funded? Somebody, somewhere wanted that thing built - literally at all costs!

So it seems from our short sojourn on the net that the apocalypse is increasingly in the public’s consciousness - well the mass media and alternative blogosphere anyway.

I may do a straw poll at work. Just something subtle, not: 'I've had a premonition, have you?'

Something subtle, classy and scientific - nerd alert!

Speaking of apocalypse, I've just seen on *Twitter* that North Korea's hydrogen bomb test today might just raise a few heart rates globally. Now *there* is a nutter with a trigger finger!

OMG it's like 1.40am!

Think I best go to sleep, or I may be next to useless at work tomorrow – in fact that might be an interesting social experiment in itself, to see if they notice any change in me...

Thursday January 7th 2016 – 7.30am

Bleep, bleep, bleep.

No, not my alarm. I'm on the train now and the doors just closed. Almost on me!

The train was on time, but I wasn't, and had to peg it down the road in these stupid heels that society says I should wear as part of my 'office uniform'.

I might write to my Ombudsman about it you know.

No one should suffer in silence!

Things *are* looking up though, as not only did I make the train, but I now also have a coffee from the buffet cart!

So this is just a quick check in really, to state for the record, Your Honour, that I feel officially shattered, but dedicated to the cause as ever, I will make it to work on time.

10.50pm

Late into bed tonight as I've been out with Steve at the flicks and then I started to watch *Question Time*, but it's set in Scotland and they keep banging on about Trident.

Not the toothpaste neither!

In principle, I'm against the idea of it, must be my Liberal left leaning, but it would surely cripple the local economy in Scotland? Yet knowing what I know from my dreams, and with ISIS running amuck, cutting off more heads than the Queen of Hearts, whatever it costs, it's probably a sound investment to be fair.

What's more with Russia, Iran and North Korea still playing stupid isolationist games, it may be the best inheritance to pass down ever! Just probably best to meet the kids half way and have actual missiles in them, eh Mr Corbyn!

Anyway, back in the room. So the results of the work straw poll are in. They have been counted and verified!

Yeah I actually did one! Sad eh?

I asked ten unwitting colleagues, in independent locations the following five questions. Their insightful answers are in brackets, together with my immediate reactions or conclusions.

1) **What does the word 'apocalypse' mean to you?** (Eight of the people got the overarching meaning of destruction, some aligning it to religion and others to warfare. Interestingly no one mentioned natural destruction like climate change or a comet. One said 'don't know' and one said it was a computer game! I ask you, kids today…)

2) **Do you ever think about the end of the world?** (Two said 'yes', usually after consuming a related film or book; six said 'no never, why would I?' Two asked me 'why', like I was some kind of weird zealot and questioned my motives for such a bleak and downright depressing survey - guilty as charged!)

3) **If the end does come soon, what do you see as being the main catalyst?** (Some had already answered this as part of question one, but two said 'religion' and the Lord commeth- really! Six said 'warfare' and one said 'disease or some sort of man-made virus/pandemic'. It was at this point I thought back to my bout of 'Bird' flu! One person, said '*Electronic Arts*' – does he not know what's at stake?!)

4) **Do you think we'll see this life-changing event within your lifetime?** (One said 'yes probably, the rate we're going', eight replied 'no' and various derivatives of it, and one said: 'I already played *Apocalypse* last week, it's the bomb!' - #facepalm)

5) Lastly and before they thought I was some kind of MI5 agent or something worse like a weirdo... **What could we do to prevent the end of the world?** (Interestingly this gave the most varied array of answers) – all 10 verbatim here for posterity:

a) Task the UN with greater powers to act as a World Policeman and use NATO as an even more aggressive military arm that is tasked with defending the undefendable (I quite liked that one, sounds like a legalised A-Team meets UNCLE)

b) Tell the UK and America to mind their own and stop standing up for Israel the whole time and let them all just blow each other up. Let the dust settle and then go in for the oil (I think this was slightly tongue in cheek – I hope – but the sentiment was simply one of autonomy and self destruction, almost like enacting God's supposed freewill on other countries. Some sort of perverse Manifest Destiny if you like. So if they all commit genocide, we'll let them get on with it, until all the fundamentalists are gone, or inadvertently worse still, it's only the fundamentalists that are left!)

c) Nuke the fockers!... (Short, but sweet from Stuart in IT, but it does exactly what it says on the tin! I guess he means to end the aggressor's ability to strike first, before they end the world for us. Truly insightful and it's all in the delivery!)

d) We just need to learn to get along together and live in peace. How hard can it be? (Lauren in Accounts, bless her, she's only 18, but she makes a good point. Perhaps a little naive to think that some 2,016 years after supposedly sticking God's boy on a cross for getting too big for his sandals, we can suddenly put eons of warring and prejudice behind us. However I like the simplistic ideology in her argument. As she says…how hard can it be?

We're all human. Just one race divided in the most part by colour, cultural differences and a religious doctrine set down way before anyone in over 50 generations of your own family were even conceived. Why would you trust so implicitly an ideology so old? Safety in numbers I guess. The age-old adage of 2.2 billion Christians can't be wrong… A discussion in its own right me thinks!)

e) Ban nuclear weapons outright and/or trading any key ingredient like Uranium, so rogue states don't suddenly end up as being the only nations still proliferating. (My preferred route in principle; not that any country would agree to give them up, having spent so much money on researching and developing them in the first place!

It's like the US gun law - if they ban guns, there'll be no gun crime right? People will always be able to get hold of a gun and similarly on the world stage, there'll always be some cunning country, hell bent on profiting from the situation – surreptitiously selling off stockpiled warheads, built under the table after Hans Blix had been in to tally up the arsenal.)

f) Start again with the UN and update it to create some sort of New World Order – (Someone actually said that and the irony is his name's Mason! I shit you not! Again this is much like point (a), in that it would give the UN special powers to police and it seems to make sense, but the chances of getting all 190 odd countries to buy in and tow the line is almost impossible. And who then watches the watchers?)

g) We can't, nature will get us even if we don't kill each other off first (probably true given enough time. How do we prevent all diseases, the 100-year floods, the 500-year comet strikes, the 1,000-year Mount Etna's, the 5,000-year solar flare or the 10,000-year earthquake?)

h) Simple. Put women in charge of each country! Not only will we be able to get more than one thing done at once, we won't have to worry about if our country's proverbial penis is bigger than our neighbours. (I did laugh, but the sentiment here I think is that the pragmatism, empathy and the ability to take no rubbish off stupid bickering white middle to upper class men could be the way forward – Imagine Thatcher, Sturgeon, Merkel, May, Lagarde and Hilary Clinton on the same UN netball team – scary even for someone with feminist tendencies like me!)

i) Invest more money into NASA so they can be on the lookout for meteors and asteroids or even alien invaders. Step up investment in research and stamp out killer diseases in the third world that already have cures in the first world. Also, we should invest in education, so the next rounds of leaders don't turn out to be self-absorbed overlords. (Lots of investment required here in a world generally short of cash – Most of it went on Denver airport by the looks of it!

I always wondered who all of these indebted countries owe their money to exactly, as everyone seems as skint as the next. Apart from those sycophantic Swiss types – they're always too quiet and they must have splinters up their arses from all the fences they've straddled over the years.

Switzerland could be seen as the international wallflower at the UN party. Quietly waiting for all the boys to get drunk, have a fight and then take their chance to make out with the Prom Queen. Maybe they're just biding their time, lending their money and one day; just as we are all high on aspartame, hippy crack and THC, they'll strike down upon us with great vengeance and furious anger, those who attempted to poison and destroy their brothers. And we will know their name is *Illuminati,* when they lay their fiscal law and escalating interest rates upon thee). Greece, take note, IMF has you by the balls!

j) Eat more veg and give peas a chance... (I'll ignore this one – stupid kid!)

So there you go, report format and a qualitative research exercise undertaken. There can't be many diaries that go to this extent of obsession to prove a point!

But what is the point?

What can I actually glean from these water cooler conversations with a disparate group of *Diet Coke* addicts?

Well, the end of the world is simply not on *their* radar. Where their next meal out and glass of wine are coming from, are probably the main things they concern themselves with.

Thinking back, I'd never consider the end of the world as part of any everyday existence. I'd not sit on the train extrapolating how many ways there are to die en masse, or what to do in Denver when everyone else is dead.

The sad thing is that since those two damned dreams, I don't think about much else...

I mentioned that I'd been out earlier tonight and I managed to skip out of work early and get back to hit the local multiplex to see the keenly awaited new *Star Wars Force Awakens* film… better late than never and O.M.G, how good was that!

Finally going to see the movie was something exciting for Steve and I, and when Han Solo walked back into the Falcon, well - Goosebumps! Who am I kidding? I proper welled up!

There was a much darker aspect to the film though and not just the gratuitous slaying of villagers in the opening scenes.

The Nazi connotations depicted within the First Order's rally were just a little too overt!

Red and black flags formed a stylish, yet less than subtle backdrop to the assembled mass of troops, who were all-listening to an impassioned orator and then dutifully saluting with raised arms into the air.

The nationalistic undertones were palpable; perhaps it was a comment on the state of American identity politics?

Steve then pointed out the symbolic similarities between the Knights of Ren and the Empire's First Order to the historic Germanic First Order of Teutonic Knights, itself a derivative of the secretive Knights Templar.

Steve also tried to explain that the esoteric themes of duality play out through the whole of the *Star Wars* saga. Despite light and dark sides of the force, there's no real definition of good and evil. The supposed 'Goodies' are actually rebels and we end up feeling sorry for the lead 'Baddie' Darth Vader, as he redeems himself by killing the Emperor. As they say in the movie, life's about finding a balance to the force and not necessarily good overcoming evil.

Deep for a diary I know, but an interesting life lesson and analysis nonetheless and he also noted how strange it was that, at a time when I'm worrying about the 'end of times', the movie trailers seemed to be unnervingly prophetic…

X-Men Apocalypse, with the tag lines '2026 prepare for the Apocalypse' and 'Only the strong will survive' are, ominous to say the least!

I do hope there isn't a 'coded message' within these films, as if the new *Avengers Civil War* and the frivolously named *London has Fallen* have anything to do with this theory, then I may stay in bed and watch the new American sitcom *You, Me and the Apocalypse,* with a rather more *keen* eye in future.

So, maybe the apocalypse *is* in the public consciousness after all… or otherwise, Hollywood and the mass media are making damn sure it's in our subconscious at least…

Friday January 8th 2016 – 7.40am

Steve's coming over for round two of the Internet search later. A gruelling rematch no doubt, with me taking up the reins this time, seeing as we ended the other night so badly off-piste.

I need to buy more wine and I'm doing a takeaway this time, to pay him back for the New Year lunch, so we'll have more time to get on top of this.

That wasn't a euphemism by the way. If he wants to keep abreast of the situation, that's up to him...

I'm starting to regret going to the police.

Not only the self sponsored degradation of it all, but also I had an email this morning, which made me feel proper daft.

Basically, it said they: '*Did not have enough information or evidence to constitute a viable line of enquiry, or the necessity to pass the limited information onto any other sections of Government that may cover National Security. But if I do have any more information, to contact them...*' on some generic email address, giving my case number.

So PR fluff then for 'Piss off you nut job'.

To be fair they have a point.

I *was* pretty limited on my description and whilst the dreams were emotionally intense, they didn't leave a massive impression on me in terms of the exact detail that the police deal in. For example, times, dates, locations, protagonists, etc.

Maybe I should look into hypnotherapy.

Hang on I'll *Google* it.

Arse, signal dropped. Going through a tunnel. Bear with...

Ah here we go, past life regression.

Not thought of that angle, maybe I was a prophet in a former life? Anyway, I stumbled on this interesting article on *Uncommonknowledge.com*:

'Hypnosis is no longer permissible in law as a tool to uncover 'facts' about witness reports, and hypnosis certainly shouldn't be used as a tool in psychotherapy to 'discover' memories. Because memory doesn't work like that. However much it may seem so, human memory is not just like a tape

recorder that you can use to record, rewind and accurately replay events exactly as they happened.'

Bugger! Back to the drawing board then Sinclair.

7.15pm

Ok, so I'm going to type this as we go tonight, as it was way too time consuming to make physical notes and then type them up last time. I'm all for efficiency you know!

Steve probably thinks I'm just making notes, little does he know my innermost intimate thoughts are within these pages...

Scary!

Well not that intimate anyway!

Note to self; take my tablet to the loo! Just in case.

Anyway, the boy is here.

I say the boy, as he's six months my junior. We've just ordered an Indian version of a Tapas starter to share, including spinach potato, some vegetable samosas, onion bhajis, or however you spell it, as well as the usual poppadoms and dips.

Num, num, num!

Main course will be a prawn curry for me and a vindaloo for Steve – standard.

Rice and a naan bread to share. Forty minute wait, no washing up and time to get the vino out, Boom!

Dessert – hopefully me, but if that's not on the menu, all deserters will be shot with a look; not of love, but with the ferocity of a 1,000 year solar flare stare!

'So research time and we've done the apocalypse to death, if you pardon the pun.' I said, rather pleased with my supposedly 'inappropriately bad' joke.

'Yes quite, but even if we do stumble on some additional information, it won't be the end of the world.' retorted Steve, laughing and holding up two index fingers to denote the score as being tied to 1-1. Cocky sod!

'I thank you. I'm here all night!' he smarmed, leaning back in his chair, arms behind his head with a look that said spent satisfaction and smug, all rolled into one.

'I hope not, I've got to go to the gym in the morning and your snoring is enough to bring on a localised natural tremor, or set off the car alarm at least.'

Ha, I promptly parried and reposted, obviously up for a highbrow intellectual fight and a bit of sabre rattling.

'Ouch!' Steve feigned to be mortally wounded by the blow, the perfect foil to my fencing analogy. He gripped his heart and almost spilled his glass of red, 'And to think, the only reason I came over was on the promise I could stay over.'

Steve and I were both sat at my small white *Ikea* dining table. Its 'fold-up-ability', as I like to call it, is perfect for the otherwise tight space and it was nice to be able to eat at the table for a change.

Too many TV dinners or drinks after work that lead to missed meals completely. Then there's the occasional pizza and DVD in bed on a Sunday night - everyone does that right?

'So what are we searching tonight mein fuehrer? How to scrub a hammock or the sex life of a Mars bar?' Steve was obviously in a playful mood, having lost the first bout 2-1 away from home.

'I'll be searching for the word 'premonition' and/or 'vision' and *you* can search for Spock for all I care, you sarcastic little sausage.'

The fuehrer's patience was wearing thin already!

'Right for those of you in the room that don't already know this verbatim: Premonition is defined thus: "noun – a strong feeling that something is about to happen, especially something unpleasant." So that is pretty much the right word to search then I think.'

'Agreed!' nodded Steve, feeling suitably chastised and struggling to hold back the urge to do something equally unpleasant to me.

'Are you sitting comfortably? Then we will begin,' I think I missed my vocation as a Head Mistress after all: 'So what's first up on the *Google* search? Sandra Bullock's film *Premonition*, yep seen that.'

'So did she!' scoffed Steve, trying to revive his spirits, if not just the score line.

‘Bloody hell, it’s all about the film on the first page of the search and dictionary entries. Ah here we go, ‘Ten unnerving premonitions that foretold disasters’ on *Listverse*. This might be good, not that I really know what I’m looking for. Just to see if it’s normal I guess, how commonplace they are, if there’s a central directory of visions that I should be tapping into with my own entry? Is there a community or blog? Or is there actually an international Quango, set up to record and investigate visions or dreams that I should be subscribing to?’

I’m convinced that despite the lack of detail in my dreams, there must be more people in the world having similar dreams at a similar time. And if all accounts could somehow be both pooled and policed by say, an ‘International Dream Investigation Committee’, or ‘iDic’ for short, then researchers within the organisation would be able to cross check the detail, triangulate an expected time and location and then warn the relevant authorities. Simples.

Makes sense to me, although maybe that’s what’s going on in Denver airport – the *real* ‘Mile High’ Club, for those at the top of the tree of knowledge.

I continued looking at the top ten unnerving premonitions that foretold disasters: ‘Number 10 then. Some chap had the same nightmare about a plane crash for 10 nights in a row in 1970 and informed the authorities, but what else could they do, short of grounding all flights? Suffice to say on the day of his last dream, flight 191 crashed shortly after take-off, killing all 273 passengers – blimey, what if my dream has already happened somewhere?’

‘I think you’d know if the world had ended luv...’ he said apologetically with a half smile: ‘Anyway, I thought you were in the thick of the action when it all goes off?’

‘Er, yes thanks, but what if it’s not the end of the world after all, but just a bomb blast? It could have already happened in one of the less fashionable and less news-worthy war torn countries that they don’t bother reporting on, you know!?!’

‘Well you’d think they’d report that, unless it was a cover up or something?’ the continuing thought of insidious conspiracy lifting his spirits further still.

'Let's not get too far ahead of ourselves just yet boyo. Lynyrd Skynard's plane crash was dreamt the day before it occurred by the band's vocalist. Another short lead time then!'

I skipped a few other tenuous entries: 'The Titanic almost collided with another boat as it left Southampton and the cat and its litter had a premonition, so left the ship, which was apparently bad luck on ships. So even felines have feelings. It also says that some passengers had bad vibes about the trip and refused to board.'

Steve raised his hands, as if to make a point: 'Ah here's one for you. Did you hear about the story of the 'unsinkable ship' that hit an iceberg and then sank in mid April?'

'Well, that's what we're just talking about. Hello, McFly?' I knocked myself on the head with my knuckles, confused.

'Gotcha!' he said smiling, 'My story is about a work of fiction. A novel in fact, called *Futility*, and written some 14 years before the Titanic sank! But don't worry, you won't go home empty handed. For the chocolate gilded Cartwright chequebook and pen; Sophia, what was the name of this fictional liner that suffered the exact same fate as the Titanic?'

I shook my head. More because I wondered why he'd suddenly turned into Jim bloody Bowen, but I had no idea where he was going with this anyway: '*The Cameron*?'

I could tell Steve was about to tease me, but on my answer, he drew his breath slightly: 'Oh. Well, it's not right, but I see what you've done there. James Cameron right? Ladies and gentlemen, it's a clever try nonetheless, but the answer we're looking for, and the name of the ship that was termed 'unsinkable' in the novel 14 years before the Titanic also hit an iceberg was…'

'Yes?' I said expectantly, picturing half of the *Monty Python* crew coming in stage left to shout: 'Get on with it!'

'The Titan.' he replied softly, as if for added drama.

Steve sat back, eyes widening, awaiting reaction.

'Is that it?'

I remember not really absorbing the answer at first.

I'm not sure what I was expecting, but not *that*.

'Is that it? Is that it?' he asked baring his open palms in astonishment, 'Don't you think that's a bit of a coincidence?'

I shrugged: 'I guess??'

'The Titan!' he repeated, as if to make a point.

'I'm not bloody deaf.' I replied, screwing up my nose.

'Two ships, same story, same month, pretty much the same name. Well, if you ask me, its pretty insane! The odds on that happening are like…'

'Higher than a one!' I replied in my best (or worst) Bruce Forsyth impression, trying in vain to continue his lame TV quiz show motif.

I blew air from my puffed cheeks, time was marching on rapidly, so I got back to the list: 'Here's another one for you, Reeva Steenkamp's painting'.

'What she do? Paint herself hiding in the loo?'

'She painted it when she was 14, and it depicted her as an angel with a dark figure in the background holding a gun.'

Steve was getting increasingly sceptical about this line of search: 'Well that's every other bugger in Saffa isn't it? I remember going to Jo'burg airport and there was a sign about giving up your guns before you go through passport control. And you'd take your gun to the airport why? Aged 14 huh, that must have been a nice surprise for her parents. 'What did you do at school today Reeva?''

'Yes I get the picture!' jumping in, not wanting him to finish saying such a nasty thing.

'Yes, so did her parents...' said Steve unscrupulously.

I shot him a look of frickin' laser beams that not only put him back in his box, but also gift wrapped it with a bow, and then stuck him on *eBay* for someone else's entertainment.

The search continued: 'Littleton School shooting in Colorado. A gunman walked in and opened fire, but no one died, with just one lad in critical condition.'

'So what, the gunman had a premonition that he'd walk in and start shooting?' he mocked sarcastically.

'No, the boy who was in critical condition was said to have predicted it months beforehand.'

Steve laughed: 'Well there's an advert for playing hooky if ever I've seen one!'

Shaking my head: 'This top 10 has to be American, here we go again, Sandy Hook school shooting. A boy left the school two weeks before the shooting that killed 20 kids and six adults. He had panic attacks saying it wasn't a safe place and started freaking out, so they took him out of the school.'

'Sounds like there's always someone that's going to come out of the woodwork or have a tenuous link to make it sound like a prediction,' supposed Steve: 'A premonition is only as good as the next disaster. Anyway Sandy Hoax was a false flag. Neocon gun grab apparently, with crisis actors bussed into a disused school.'

I shook my head again, his seeming ability to link any subject to a conspiracy was frightening and I almost wanted to close the book on this conversation, seeing as I knew exactly where the next subject might take us.

'Number two.' I drew breathe: '9/11.'

Steve thumped the table: 'That's what I'm talkin' about. Anyone in the world could come out and proclaim divine sight on that one, when it was obviously the CIA and Mossad for God's sake. I've been directing my energy to this for years. World Trade 7. Deception theory, look it up lady! Look it up.'

See, I told you! Prize prick, but someone's gotta love him.

'Good grief, where's my dinner already?'

'Patience is a virtue' I replied assertively.

'Yes, one I don't have!' he sniffed, venturing for a tissue in his oversized shoulder bag, man sack or 'boy bag', as I liked to call it.

'9/11...' I continued, overtly clearing my throat like a jumped up newsreader, much to Steve's annoyance: 'Actually this one's a goodie, some dude worked in the towers and he had a premonition in 1993 whilst on the train to work, whereby he had a bad feeling and so went home. That was the first bombing, the original one and then he did the same in 2001, but this time returned home to see the towers were no longer there when he turned on the TV.'

I then played him at his own little game of deception theory: 'Sod that. I guess when your number's up, it's up right? He got hit by a bus a week later.'

'Shut the front door!' said Steve, jumping out of his seat to view the screen.

Tears started to roll down my face and my shoulders convulsed in spasms: 'Only joking - sorry couldn't help that one. My bad!' Steve's reaction was classic. I've never seen his lanky frame move so fast. 'I was just making sure you were listening, my petal.'

'Piss off!' he mumbled, brushing the crisps off his trousers, that were disrupted during his sudden fright. The crisps that is, not his trousers. Can you imagine disrupted trousers? Sounds like the result of something quite disgusting!

'Ok, last one then I'll top you up.'

'I'll top you off if you do that again!' he warned with a mock clenched fist and a broad toothy grin.

'The Great War. Carl Jung saw the sea turn to blood with bodies drowning in yellow waves in 1914. This was a few months before war broke out and it doesn't say it, but I bet the yellow waves are mustard gas. Spooky! Ok, enough of that one now, back to the search.

The *Mystica* website, that looks more like a blog entry. This makes it sound like a premonition is a bit more of a gut feel and it's actually *precognition* that I experienced.'

Steve was topping us both up, embracing his new role as sommelier, as opposed to lead researcher: 'Not heard of that one before.'

'Ditto, actually this one's quite deep, it has a few examples of disasters, but this bit's interesting. It says here, premonitions are more often experienced whilst one is awake and that dreams are often symbolic. It also refers to the Titanic again and says that it only had 58% of its passengers on board. Maybe they'd all read that Titan book a few years before…? WOW look at this one! I just hit the friggin' jackpot!' my hands pumped the air in triumph.

'Bloody hell did you just swear?' almost missing his glass with the neck of the bottle.

'Yes, I Effing, Geoffing well did. Take a good look at this journo boy and put this in your research pipe. Following a disaster in Welsh Wales a British Premonition Bureau was established in January 1967. I knew it! They'd be mad not to have something like that wouldn't they? All that data out there to collate and collude. I just didn't think that I could *Google* such an official sounding body, or I'd have tried that already. Classic! Ok, so we know where to search next – like Ghostbusters, they are just a phone call away!'

Steve moved across the room. Slowly. Gradually. Deliberately.

He was half waiting for me to spring another joke on him and not wanting to be caught out as being gullible again. He looked into my eyes and once confident that he could not see an ounce of sarcasm, or a hint of a malevolent streak, he then snuck a peak at the screen, nodded and confidently replied: 'Bloody hell! Now we're really cooking!'

Ironically, as he said it, the intercom suddenly rang and I pressed the rectangular red button for entry.

The door then swung open to reveal a beaming driver, two small brown bags in each hand and a dusting of snow on his flat cap and shoulders:

'Or *not* cooking, as the case may be. Dinner is served!'

8.30pm

Ok, so meal over, refreshment breaks done, wine topped up and laptop charging. Albeit, I was slightly delayed by my loo roll OCD, which Steve obviously doesn't fully appreciate.

I can't abide a roll with a few binds left on it. It looks so unsightly, so I tend to use the last ones to randomly blow my nose or something – nutter I know, but it's like opening a packet of crisps at the bottom so the label is upside down!

Just why would you do that?

Imagine my predicament at the petrol station recently, where I couldn't decide whether to put a round £40 in the car, or have the litres say 45 rather than 45.2. Somebody sound the anal klaxon and end my misery now!

In my pre-meal excitement, I seems that I stopped reading the Premonition Bureau blog mid entry, so pleased was I with my newfound revelation.

Right, back to the moment at hand, as the British Premonition Bureau would be awaiting its next hero. Sent to save the world from itself. Sent not to judge or rain fire, but to warn of an impending thunder. I can see it now…

The woman who saved the world!

Too much?

Meh…

'Did you actually read this babes?' Steve ventured softly, as if to break some news, as he retook his turn in the hot seat.

'What do you mean?' I shrugged, laying back in the sofa, so that I was comfy enough to take my plaudits.

'Well, if only you read the very next sentence, rather than going off cart wheeling, it says that a year later, the Central Premonition Bureau was formed in New York.'

Arms aloft again, wine glass beckoning a toast: 'Blimey it was catching on across the Atlantic. Superb! Good on them Yankee doodles!'

'Yes, but not for long, I quote: '*Both bureaus did not progress too far because of low budgets, poor PR and so much inaccurate information.*' Unlucky sweetheart!'

Steve pushed his tongue into his lower lip until it bulged like a child at kindergarten.

Covering my face in my hands and biting my lip I was somehow able to muster a mutter, despite self evidently having placed my whole foot in my mouth, possibly even halfway up the shin bone: 'Ah piss, sorry.'

I did half wonder if it would still be worth searching for those terms anyway, to see if there is actually a modern day equivalent out there, or if there was any evidence of it now being an underground movement, or an Above Top Secret department in Whitehall.

'Ok, the page 3 searches on Google are all spurious and it then says related searches: 'Premonition Dreams', so I'll try that first. Crikey, there's a load. 'Real meanings of Dreams'. It has a Doctor who says that some dreams...'

'*Dr Who*'s on there? Which incarnation? The 10th? I love the 10th, Tennant's super.' I simply couldn't let that one go!

I then received such a look that would distil the armoury within the *House of Daggers* and launch them broadside with an express intent to harm: 'It has a Dr, comma, *who* says that some dreams, especially in *women* are the, 'media announcement type', so this is where you would see the future announced through the media by way of TV, radio or a well researched and written newspaper article in the local *Folkestone Herald* for example.'

'Wouldn't have been one of your articles then!' I quipped, acidly. 'Interesting though, as that checks out on my second dream, as now you mention it, there was an old man with a newspaper, but I'll be buggered if I can remember what was on it. Enough to make me run off I guess.'

'Exactly!' said Steve, slightly backing off: 'It also refers to pregnant dreams here too.'

There was then a long pause. A pregnant pause, you might say; followed by a rather quizzical look: 'You're not...?'

'No I'm bloody not!' boomed my foghorn, as I hurled an unsuspecting scatter cushion at his head. Such was the ferocity of my throw; he had little time to scatter himself!

Then after regaining my equilibrium, I replied softly: 'I'm just naturally hormonal, thanks very much for asking.'

'Figures...! Ok, so dream symbolism search up next. It says most premonitions come true very quickly, so if something unpredictable happens in the short term, your dream may well be linked to it.'

'So what you're saying is that whatever I've dreamt should've happened already, so basically we're just wasting our time?'

I think I retorted defensively, obviously still peeved by his pregnant pause and what follows is paraphrased when I wrote it later in the night, as I was unable to take notes from that point on - it got a bit fractious, to say the least!

'What I'm *reading* is what it says here, that's all. Moving on, it says *here* that a dream about a nuclear explosion, for example, could symbolise a terrible event and may not be specifically a bomb. In this case, the bomb represented his grandma's death. It also says that these dreams capture the reality of our emotions, as opposed to the actual reality of our lives – again symbolism in dreams.'

I started to think, and apparently my inner monologue mischievously manifested itself aloud, as I pondered this latest information: 'Ok, I see, so the intuitive feelings of loss and bereavement are the symbol and there could consequently, be a death forthcoming to someone I know. And it may not be the girl that was with me in the dream that may be dying specifically, so even if she is our daughter, she's a symbol, so it's not necessarily *her* that perishes right?'

'Daughter?' asked Steve innocently, as if mishearing.

I laughed embarrassingly. A false 'ha, ha, ha', combined with a maniacal grin across my face. I visibly squirmed on the sofa – crikey, crumbs, bother and blow!!

'Yes err, did I not tell you?' I cringed inside, stomach unceremoniously imploding, with awks off the Richter scale.

He then proceeded to toy with me, the bastard:

'Oh no darling, you may have accidentally failed to mention any sort of *wider* family in the dream. You may have failed to mention some information of key relevance to our relationship. Information that, despite its chilling end; actually gives me some hope and something to aim for in this shitty life. To think that one day I'll have children, may actually be a nice thing to know! You know?'

'Maybe this is why I forgot to mention it before, as I knew that you'd freak out.' I continued, defensively.

'That *I'd* freak out? Was that one of your fabled premonitions too? Freak out at what? You haven't actually told me anything yet, other than we have a daughter in your pretty perverted head!'

‘Well the girl that was with me in the first dream, it felt like she was really close to me. You talk about the manifestation of emotions and this particular emotion was so *very* strong that she *has* to be my daughter. So naturally, I assumed her to be *our* daughter. Then in the second dream, I’m in the park watching what I guess is the same girl playing, and then I run off. Suddenly I’m seeing the situation through her eyes and again that same strong emotional bond is there – the feeling of separation was just awful!’

Ok, so the whole truth was finally out. And breathe…

‘Right, so what you’re telling me is that the person in the first dream, that may or may not be you, in a place that you don’t recognise, is cradling a girl, who may or may not be your daughter, or the daughter of the person you are freakishly channelling. That is assuming you’re channelling and not just having a nightmare like the rest of us mere mortals anyway? How and what makes you think she’s *our* child anyway?’

I looked down at my feet, ashamed of not telling him, but still searching for a way out: ‘Yes, I see your point... She may have had your nose.’

Steve stood up as if to exert his authority in the situation, which was rapidly spiralling south from my perspective:

‘And what you’re also telling me is that the person in the second dream may be the mother of the little girl, rather than some park pervert, despite legging it after reading the newspaper and not looking back or showing any concern. Pardon me if I’m just a man, but that does *not* sound overtly maternal now does it? It’s probably just the handbag that’s left laying on the bench that’s the symbolism here for some sort of impending loss, or as you say, the message via a newspaper with no actual bloody message to impart. Talk about tenuous dreams for Christ’s sake! Maybe this *is* all a waste of time!’

I tried to take back some of the initiative, albeit very badly: ‘I was *not* just some nonce in the park you insensitive prick! The feelings I had were of love and admiration for the girl and as I say, the emotional ties we had were stronger than I’ve ever felt before. That’s what brought me to tears and why I’m going through all this bullshit with you. But pardon me if I'm wasting your time, you douche!'

'Well remind me to never have kids with *you* then, if you're this liable to run off at a moment's notice!' he turned away, shaking his head.

'She could have been *your* kid you idiot, don't you get it? That's why I didn't tell you! You're too emotionally immature to understand!' I was getting irate myself now - Fore shields up, maximum power and not just my underwear set to stun!

'Piss off!' he spat, 'Bloody lunatic. If that's how you're going to be, then I'll just go now and you can stew in your own ridiculous pot of make believe shite. Maybe *that* was the loss you predicted in your second dream – *me* leaving *you*!'

Steve started to mumble under his breath and reached for his phone, as if to pack up his things, including his laptop with the many tabs of research still live and open.

'Arrggh! Why do you have to be so bloody-minded? Listen, I had a couple of dreams right, I know as much as you do. I have no idea what they mean, or how to interpret them. Funnily enough, I don't have this happen to me often. What am I supposed to do? Make myself look like a fool by saying that our daughter is going to be annihilated, then time travel so that I can then leave her on her own in a park? Do I need to caveat it for you that it's not necessarily in the correct order and it may contain nuts!?!'

'Full of nuts if you ask me! Right from the proverbial nutter herself. I *am* freaking out, as I'm trying to help you and you've not even told me the whole story and now it's you that's freaking out, as you know you're in the wrong and can't bear the thought of it!'

Steve started to don his heavy black leather coat, ready to embrace the snowy night sky.

'Look, I'm sorry I didn't mention the whole 'daughter' thing. I just watered down the description a bit, to save my own sanity.'

'So I'm on a need to know basis right? Fan-bloody-tastic.' His boots were going on now.

‘What do you want me to say? I said I’m sorry, just come and sit down and maybe we can carry on searching. Searching for answers to what all this craziness means.’

‘Oh great then everything will be fine then. I think what this means, is that you need to sleep on it and I’ll speak to you tomorrow. Maybe.’

The door closed behind him. No kiss. No goodbye. No apology from his side. Just the sound of my latch closing and then the communal door down the corridor slamming shut.

Well that went better than expected.

NOT!

Why didn’t I just tell him? It’s now 11.15pm, I’m in bed re-writing this sorry shower and it amazes me how things can just escalate so quickly!

One minute, it’s just banter and then it’s a barrage. I think I may have some making up to do, but it would be handy to go back with something concrete from my research to reel Steve’s interest back into this supposed lost cause.

I really think he’s lost faith in this whole exercise, let alone me. A right royal balls up!

So I got back to researching, albeit on this tiny tablet, seeing as the luxuriously large laptop was now gone.

My laptop has long seen better days in fact; it may not even have a modem in it? Not so much a laptop, but a Leviathan fit for a winch or a museum.

So, from my current tablet research, it seems that precognition relates to extra sensory perception (ESP) and the scientific community doesn’t accept this, as it can’t be reconciled as to how the effect of something can come before the cause. So, case closed in their eyes.

I’m currently reading some reports of premonitions attached to the 9/11 attacks which, as Steve said, could’ve been made up, but they’re a pretty convincing read!

An article from the *Mail* in 2015 says that “Sometimes premonitions allow the person to pinpoint a specific time and place, leaving the dreamer enough time to alter the course of the disaster.”

Is that what I am supposed to do?

I don't have any clue on the date though. If only I could remember what was in the newspaper. That would be the key.

It also alludes to animals being the first to know of an impending natural disaster, like the Boxing Day tsunami in 2004. Maybe Valentine knows something is up, as she's been gone for bloody days!

None of these articles have a note at the bottom to say "If you have been affected by any of these issues, call 0845 blah blah." No 50/50 and no phone a friend available either.

I'm now searching random words: premonition Islam, Russia, Korea, British Premonition Bureau, dreams and bombs, nuclear dreams, fusion, ISIS on Facebook and You Tube. The list goes on and on, as does the time.

However, I'm in the zone now and hungry for some success to act as a pseudo olive branch for Steve.

There is no new Premonition Bureau to report to and the police would have put me onto them anyway...

So I started searching "vision". Not so easy to do this research and typing on my tablet at the same time, but them's the breaks I guess.

Still no word from Steve, no text to say he got home safely. In fact how did he get home? It's a good half hour walk to mine from his, let alone by foot, in a foot of snow.

Maybe he just did it. I know he won't pay for cabs out of principle, let alone leave a tip. Think it goes back to his student days and the *Reservoir Dogs* factor – he found Mr Pink's argument quite compelling.

Great, another page full of random entries - *Vision Express* and a map to show my closest branch. I wonder if they do advice services too. I can picture the scenario now:

'Good afternoon madam, can I help you?' the kindly optician's assistant would ask me.

'Yes I've had a *Vision* and I'd like an *Express* consultation with regards to the symbolism involved.'

The potential look on her face would be actually worth doing it I think.

Otherwise, I may report them to the ASA for advertising mis-descriptions. Would you also believe that *Selfridges* don't actually sell fridges? The greatest retail advertising travesty, OF ALL TIME!

Vision London, East London vision, vision 2020 for London, Diocese of London's Capital Vision 2020…

Sorry. I've not been typing for a bit.

2020. I'm looking at that date now and I've a funny feeling that could've been the date on the newspaper in my dream.

I guess I must have subliminally absorbed it either on the inside page, or on the cover, but that date does ring a huge Big Ben with me.

Maybe I just *want* the date to be linked with my dream and I'm jumping to convenient conclusions.

Yes, this must be too much of a coincidence, seeing as I'm looking at it next to the word 'Vision'. I'll sleep on that one, as I can just imagine Steve's cynical response now!

Ha, I just searched for: '*What do I do if I have a dream about the end of the world?*'

Seemed a sensible approach at the time!

There are loads of entries, descriptions of people's dreams and their own interpretations from the sublime to the ridiculous. According to the *Mail,* end of the world dreams are in the top five most common reported dreams.

Blimey! What a prat do I feel now, going to the police like that! At least they were polite in their email, bless them.

'Dream interpretation' - death dreams, featuring the end of *the,* or *your* own world symbolise an ending or transition in your life. This apparently could be a significant change to job, family, relationship or something else.

In this instance, I guess the "something else" could just be the end of the world...?

So basically I'm not alone. It looks like this is common and if it's in the *Mail* online, it must be true!

There are just so many articles. Ones about natural disasters in dreams, but I'm not sure what mine was. It felt like a nuclear blast, such was the speed and intensity.

Well my interpretation of one anyway, as I've not survived many nuclear blasts in the past to regale actual first-hand knowledge and testimony.

It also says: 'An end of the world dream could be the end of a relationship'. Yep, figures! After tonight, this could be the worst self-fulfilling prophecy yet!

Maybe that's it; I had a vision that my vision would lead to the end of my relationship with Steve. Maybe it was a coincidence that I started writing this diary, at a time when I had doubts about the relationship come into my mind in the first place.

But if anything, this evening aside, the vision has actually brought us closer together. A shared interest to talk about, other than just soaps and the rest of the state sponsored output that Steve lectures me on...

I even sound like Steve now!

Oh I do hope that this isn't the end!

So not only have I got to pick up the baton and propose to him, I have to meet the relationship halfway, swallow my pride and at least get us back on speaking terms first!

So much to do, so little time!

Hmm page 3 of the search and lots on here about Dr. Martin Luther King's 'I Have a Dream Speech'. Goosebumps!

Ha, I just remembered about my GCSE mock exam for Religious Studies and the question was something like 'Who was Martin Luther?' Suffice to say I got zero marks... and did not take the main exam!

Black power wasn't on the agenda at the time, nor the plight of the Panthers or the Malcolm X factor!

I've never been a religious person. It can't just be me that sees the Bible simply as a good book about the rights and wrongs of man and how to lead your life?

An instruction manual on life if you will; just a little too long and not really necessitating all the deities, miracles and constant visits and hand-outs in church. Let alone the continual

Christianisation of countries, communities and clans over the last 2,000 years.

Sorry that's just the cynic in me. Or the devil, some would say...Wasn't it the venerable John Humphrys that wrote 'In God we Doubt' as part of his personal search for faith?

Needless to say, his search failed...

I then tried searching "prophecy" - sounded good, but it *is* 12.19am.

Ah sod it, I saw a lady in the canteen at work today with a mug that said 'You have the same amount of hours in the day as Beyoncé. So use them!'

So here we go then. One final push.

Fix bayonets and cry: 'If you want it, then you should have put a ring on it' for Harry, England and Saint George!

Wow a website called *Prophecy News Watch*! This apparently keeps me informed of world events from a biblical perspective. Joy of joys and sing Hosanna to the king of kings!

'10 Signs that Russia is preparing to fight a nuclear war with the US' is a scary read for the dead of night...

Published in 2014, it's amazing how much this wagon has rolled on since then. It cites Russian research into cloaked bombing planes, continued buzzing of European boundaries by bombers, which we have seen here in Blighty and the sizing up of NATO's not so rapid response rate.

It reports that Russia has created an anti ballistic missile system to deflect any attacks, whilst also test launching submarine-based intercontinental and cloaked ballistic missiles from virtually undetectable and equally cloaked submarines.

A silent assassin awaits its prey.

This technology is also for sale to the highest bidder, so roll up despots throughout the world!

It also says that Russia has more strategic nuclear warheads deployed than the US for the first time in history. So all in all, the Russian strategic agenda seems to be that of preparation. But preparation for what exactly?

Blimey, if I were in charge of the US, I'd build a massive underground bunker in the centre of the country in Colorado and hide!

Oh yeah, they did that already and called it an airport ...clever bastards!

Ok, so who else is going to screw up the Blue Planet?

A Jewish Temple being built on a sacred site in Jerusalem, which will host ritual sacrifices and has not been in operation since the Romans sacked it in 70 A.D. Sounds intriguing if a little macabre...

This Biblical temple has been predicted in various parts of the good book and is essential for the second coming and the fulfilment of the Bible's prophecy.

So is this why Israel gets so much protection from the Western world, so they can expedite the ability to meet their Christian maker?

Next up, a war with Islam, or a war within Islam. Well, I think that may just be on the horizon since the Bataclan attack.

Iran and ISIS both believe 'end days' are upon us and are trying to hasten the arrival of their Messiah Mahdi.

Well, I'll be sure to get the best china out if he does turn up. Front row seats for the next calamity!

As a Political Scientist, the way I see it, is that this is a Muslim problem, which the Muslim world must face up to and reclaim the true word of Islam. I'm sure the Koran doesn't preach genocide? Whether it's a radical or apocalyptic form of Islam, it's up to the Muslim nation to defeat this abhorrent rising itself, not for the already tarnished West to put their size 12 boots back in the sand.

That really will exacerbate the problem and is what I think ISIS really wants. It seems to be a race to the end of time and a question of who can dupe who into the final apocalyptic move.

Knight to B6. Check mate, Boom!

Am I just a pawn in a game of international strategy, and once I've been 'taken' out of the game, that's it?

The International Armageddon Committee moved the Doomsday Clock to 'three minutes to Midnight' in January

2015 and we await the 2016 update. This is the closest it's ever been to 'doom' since 1987 and the height of the Cold War.

The final game seems to be afoot and I just hope that the four knights in chess are not symbolic themselves for the four horsemen of the apocalypse!

Scriptures also predict end days are coming, when a group of unnamed nations attack Israel. I do seem to recollect Benjamin Netanyahu getting het up by the Iranian nuclear deal with the US recently. He knows the prophesised danger!

And so it goes on…

The more I read, the more conflict I'm exposed to and it beggars belief how people bringing children into the world now, are able to educate them in current affairs.

How do you explain the tipping point of the 9/11 attacks to a seven year old?

The US isn't mentioned in scripture by name and some say that by the time of 'end of days', the US may have been defeated, not relevant or maybe misread completely, but thinking outside of the box, what if the Antichrist that brings about end of days, is just an atheist like me?

Someone that is simply anti religion, or anti Christ as it were and not anti Christianity per se. If so many people want to take a literal reading of the Bible, how about that as a starter for ten?

Maybe the Biblical Antichrist is only seen as a false prophet by Christian hardliners, as this Antichrist speaks of uniting nations, but not under a God?

Maybe he'll be the non-secular puppet for the New World Order? Maybe *he* will be a she?

The article also says that the Antichrist signs a seven-year deal with Israel, which triggers the final countdown. Could this be a future treaty to get them out of Palestine or Gaza that sets the doomsday clock ticking ever closer?

The article mentions a prophecy of a 10-headed beast, symbolising ten kingdoms. Maybe this too, is a misreading and a treaty of 10 nations simply signs up against some future evil tyranny to protect the Holy land?

Then there is a 7-headed red beast in the *Book of Revelations*, with crowns, also symbolising kingdoms. Is the red beast Russia soaking back up 6 of the former USSR countries or Turkey and Syria?

It seems the scriptures allude to the Antichrist as being 'The Assyrian' – I'll have to look up where that actually is…

Luckily for me the only country I've not read about as yet is good old Blighty, so sounds like I'll not have to fight them on the beaches just yet then, with my lone friggin' frigate...

The other country that doesn't get a mention is North Korea, albeit they've gone quiet following their release of news reports showing the White House exploding in 2014. Maybe it was just them posturing for privacy and to secure their isolationism. It seems to have done the trick...despite the Hollywood movie release that is. That country is also a ticking time bomb to watch! They write their own destiny…

As interesting as it is to read all this, I'm having to take copious pinches of salt given the nature of the website this is all on, but if it means that I stumble on a clue, or an answer, and then so be it.

Ok, so I just searched for Assyria and it was an advanced Christian country that ruled for 19 centuries and looks to lie in Mesopotamia within lands now occupied by Iraq, Syria and Turkey – an inviting Middle Eastern mix for a potential Antichrist and geographically ISIS strongholds.

That said, the eagle on the ancient Assyrian flag has a close likeness to that on American federal documents and is apparently a phoenix, which is symbolically linked to Nimrod - a once great Assyrian leader of his time.

It says here that the Assyrians do still exist on the Kurdish border north of Tehran in Iran and they are Orthodox Christians that are perversely respected and accepted by Muslims in Iran.

This is apparently because the Assyrians are the original Iranians and are actually related to Nimrod. He built Babel in modern day Iraq, and is also mentioned as being the Antichrist *himself* in some scriptures.

As a race that I'd assumed to be extinct, the Assyrians are global. There's 50,000 of them in Northern California alone!

So an Assyrian could come to power somewhere in the world, including the US, and arguably be the only race that could possibly unite all major conflicting religions – Christian, Catholic and Islamic, due to their mutual respect from each religious faction.

Why am I doing all this? It's so late. My fingers ache and it's not like I'm ever going to read all this crap again.

Surely some self respected theologian or classical historian will have worked all this out by now. I think all this typing just reminds me of my student research days and the ability to come to my own conclusions, but I'm struggling to find one article that encompasses everything that I'm looking for.

But what is it exactly that I *am* looking for?

There's plenty of prophecy websites, all purporting to be the 'watcher on the wall' for all our sakes, but they all cover the same sort of things as the above. Does that add fuel to the arguments, or just prove they're all just as mad as each other?

Last search of the night and it could be a big one!

Nostradamus…

Boy, lots of websites and articles, maybe this is not such a good idea... No I can't face it. My brain's awash with conspiracy and conjecture. Whether we find ourselves in end times or not, it certainly is the end of my day!

Toodles.

Saturday January 9th 2016 – 11.40am

I dared not look at the clock last night when I finally turned out the light. I also forgot we're supposed to be seeing Steve's family tomorrow. So one way or another, I have a bit to do today and fast, if we're to play happy families and all...

I'll check my phone first, make sure that he's not got all *Star Trek* on me and made first contact.

Ha! I knew he would!

Here we go. He really doesn't do confrontation well - not that I want him to. The message read:

'Are you the third Antichrist after all? Call me you stubborn wench!'

How rude.

Topical - but still rude.

Ok, so I'll call him, it's not too early is it? What's the time again? Ha, no not exactly. Right, I'll report back in five.

12.05pm

Sorry diary. I got waylaid and put the washing on.

Whoops. Said I wouldn't do that!

Speak to the diary that is, not washing my clothes.

That conversation went well. I climbed down off my Babel like tower of stubbornness, held aloft the mystical symbol of an olive branch unto my beloved and...

... He laughed.

'I didn't realise you actually had the capacity to apologise.' he said sarcastically, but he took it in good spirits and admitted that he understood why I'd watered down my dream for his supposed benefit. Steve did make me promise though, wait for it, on our unborn child, that there would be no more lies. More than a little creepy, but I agreed all the same.

On reflection the fact that he's able to entertain the idea of *our* unborn child is what really intrigues me and got me thinking, whilst loading the washing machine - as you do...

Jeez, I'm like an emotional swing-o-meter at the moment, one moment I'm left wing, being socially and emotionally open to Steve and the next I'm in a kind of right wing isolationist state of mind.

Let's try and take the centre ground then, seeing as I have already conceded the moral high ground to Steve this morning... afternoon; whatever it is at the moment.

We're around to see his brother Seth at their family home in Croydon for lunch tomorrow. Patrick and Pam will be there, as well as Seth's wife Mel and the two girls Isobel and Chloe. Oh and their little fluffy ball of a dog, Mr Snubs.

Talking of animals I may have to find my elusive and presumably emaciated moggy at some point. The allure of dried food and water must not be to her taste anymore.

2.15pm

I'm back from the gym. Just wanted to record that, in case it all goes off before now and tea time and I won't be judged as being a lazy mare!

5.00pm

It's been a doing day! Well, what I have seen of today anyway, seeing as I got up so late.

Housework, shopping, hanging up the washing. All the fun things that up to now, I've taken for granted and not recorded in these pages, but seeing as I've little else to report from a day that'll go down as a waste of my 'Beyoncé' hours; I've at least achieved a few of life's little necessities!

5.35pm

My Lord, it really is the Second Coming!

Battlecat has returned from her latest crusade. Did she go east in search of spiritual enlightenment?

No she went next door for salmon again, the ungrateful little fleabag!

6.45pm

I have just watched the news, it's only January and the wall-to-wall US election coverage has started already. Really...? I swear this gets earlier than the onset of Christmas.

Cards in the shops in September I ask you! It's not right.

I've decided to have a quick 'Nostradamus' peek online and then an early night, so I can be up with the lark tomorrow, as I'm driving - apparently…

Good start to the search. It seems that most academic sources say that any associations made between Nostradamus' predictions and actual world events are tenuous at best and either mistranslated or just misinterpreted.

Well, that saved a night's worth of searching then, but with Steve on my shoulder, *they* would say that wouldn't *they*, to distract us from the scent. The swines! Lols!

I must say, my first viewings of the famous quatrains seem to be quite ambiguous. From what I briefly read, not only were the quatrains coded, they were split apart from their original running order, so that their *mystical contents* didn't fall into the wrong hands.

It also sounds like Nostradamus has begged, borrowed and stolen from old premonitions of the 1500s, as well as older prophetic texts than that. He's then forecast similar events into the future, according to the comparable alignment of the stars.

Genius!

So if a King were crowned under a Sagittarius constellation on a certain date, Nostradamus would extrapolate that same event into the future and prophesise that a future King of note would come to reign around that celestial time.

So no quatrain has ever been known to predict an event before it happens, just retrospectively attributed where it fits…

Basically, he's pretty much discounted out of hand, but his name's one of the few non-religious prophets I've heard of. I guess that's because of the films made, the general interest in his works and that as world events unfold, they do sometimes throw up undeniable arguments for his work.

I tried Nostradamus.org – he's got his own website you know! I wonder if he's on Facebook too? Maybe I'll poke him, seeing as he's even more old school than me.

Ok, so this is strange. I was hazy on whether 2020 was the date on the newspaper or not, and in retrospect that date can't be right, as that's only four years away and Rebecca was older than that in my dream. However, my hair is officially standing up on the back of my neck.

Atop of this website is a list of articles related to Nostradamus and towards the end of the list is one word.

Mabus.

No wonder my hairs are on edge! I'm almost scared to click on it, to see what it links to, as I swear down that's the name on the phone in my dream!

Whooa. It just came to me as I saw the word, as if I'd opened Pandora 's box and it came flooding out.

A flash in front of my eyes and I can feel the same fear I faced before.

The same feelings as in the dream!

Those feelings of pure dread, panic and confusion that I swore I'd never forget. Could not forget.

I feel sick. That poor girl, what on Earth could lead me to leave her alone like that? I don't want to know!

Mabus.

Yes, I remember. The one, the only number on that phone and thinking about it, I think I left him a voicemail too!

Hope I was polite...!

Ok, I'm gonna to click the link.

I've got an awful feeling of foreboding, like I know what it's going to say, but I can't *actually* think what it might be.

My heart is pounding.

This is ridiculous; it's just a name, just a website!

What's the worst that can happen?

Sunday January 10th 2016 – 6.15am

I've not been able to write until now.

I was so emotionally tired and after clicking on the website it sent me into a spiral of confusion and melancholy.

It sent me to a point where I was *actually* physically sick and I fell asleep wondering why it should be me that would have such a dreaded dream.

I think if I'd mentioned the word 'Mabus' to the police, they may've taken slightly more interest.

Well here goes, the only cathartic way I know, is to get it all down, and boy do I have a car journey for Steve. A full debrief on my own findings.

He was out with 'the lads' last night, so he'll be in no fit state to drive, but hopefully listening will still be a strong suit.

The first Nostradamus website that I was on paints a vision of a person called Mabus, whose death causes a cataclysmic world event. Super start.

Mabus is actually mentioned in one of the famous Quatrains. By name for goodness sake and linked with being the Antichrist himself!

What the hell he's doing on my mobile phone contacts; I can only begin to guess, but reassuring to know I mix in such highfalutin circles.

The website lists out a host of people that could *be,* or could've been Mabus before their death.

Obama, Bush Junior, Bush Senior, Bin Laden, Saddam Hussein, the terrorist Abu Masub al-Zarqwi, Palestinian leader Mahmud Abbas, Yassar Arafat, the deck of cards of possible A-list culprits goes on and on...

It seems Nostradamus had a thing for mixing up letters as part of his code you see. He describes three Antichrists in his prophecies: Napoleon, who was coded as being '*Napaulon*', Hitler as the second, who became '*Hister*' in a relevant quatrain and the third name, yet to be officially claimed, was '*Mabus*'. The list of names above all contain some semblance of that word and so it has been inferred that one of these people could be him, just based on the similar method of rearranging the letters.

I know this all sounds tenuous, but there are websites, upon books, upon blogs devoted to debunking this subject and seeing as I've seen this specific name in my dream, with no previous detailed exposure to the subject, this obviously strikes me as just a little suspicious. I really don't need this!

So his actual translated quatrains, according to the website and relating to the mentions of this third Antichrist read verbatim:

One who the infernal gods of Hannibal,
Will cause to be born, terror to all mankind:
Never more horror nor the newspapers tell of worse in the past,
Then will come to the Italians through Babel.

On first glance it's all a bit flighty, but what interested me is that it mentions newspapers, i.e. my second dream.

Not sure of any link as yet, other than Babel, which as I found out earlier links to Nimrod, the ancestor of the Assyrians, who are foretold in the Bible to produce the Antichrist. Still with me diary? Good, 'cos I'm struggling…

An online reading about this verse indicates that the last line alludes to Italy being the place of entry of some sort of invasion from Babel, in what is now Iraq.

It was reported in 2014 that ISIS wanted to bring terror to Europe and Rome in particular, which seemed odd at the time, but I do remember that, so maybe that is somehow linked too? Maybe they've been attacking Syria in order to clear a direct geographical path to Italy, Rome and wider Europe? Is that why ISIS are making their way across North Africa too, to gain easy access to Bari and beyond? Could the thousands of migrants pouring into Greece, simply be a Trojan horse?

It also mentioned Hannibal, who I've now discovered was a Carthaginian General who died around 200 years B.C. The Gods that these people worshipped included 'Baal Hammon' and Baal worship took place in an area not too dissimilar to ancient Assyria.

Are the first two lines simply saying that Mabus will be born of this former Assyrian land? If so it pretty much mimics the Bible's predictions of the Antichrist, but as I did read online about this visionary, Nostradamus did pilfer some of his best ideas from much older prophecies.

For all Nostradamus's famous mistranslation, it does seem worth further examination. The Quatrains go on:

Mabus will soon die, then will come,
A horrible undoing of people and animals,
At once one will see vengeance,
One hundred powers, thirst, famine, when the comet will pass.

So to me, it sounds like Mabus' death is a catalyst for change, a tipping point in its own right and for some possible future apocalyptic cause and a subsequent uprising of one hundred powers, possibly the UN??

Could the comet that he speaks of actually be a modern day missile, or is that too literal a reading?

The online reading indicates Mabus' death, a great undoing that he created as part of his tyranny and then a counterstroke around the time of a comet. This reading also cites that the Romans sacked the city of Carthage in 146 B.C and built their own city in its place called Thurbo Majus.

So could "Majus" in this case, actually be Mabus like Hister became Hitler? The ruins of Carthage are in Tunisia, North Africa and the scenes of terror last year no less, so maybe Mabus is actually a *place* that dies and this Tunisian protagonist plays regional havoc and serves up an ISIS linked apocalyptic end...

The same players seem to be mentioned across multiple texts and it worries me that real life events are aligning in such a way as to be almost prophetic.

The Third Antichrist very soon annihilated,
Twenty-seven years his bloody war will last.
The heretics (are) dead, captives exiled,
Blood soaked human bodies, and a reddened icy hail covering the Earth.

Really makes you want to get up in the morning eh?

So, it stands to reason that after Mabus' death, if he is a 'he' and not a *place* after all, there will be a 27-year conflict, which will lead to a 'finality'.

Maybe the Rapture after all!

The online reading is taken from 2002 and talks about possible Middle Eastern threats including Saddam Hussein of Iraq, Yasser Arafat of Palestine and Colonel Gaddafi of Libya.

Strange that all three of these leaders were all subjected to a media hate campaign and are now long since dead...

No wonder the West was so keen to get in there and the race for 'oil and weapons of mass destruction' may've been a weapon of mass distraction to allow for the 'removal' of these three potential Antichrists?

I think this Nostradamus stuff might be truer than we're led to believe.

Maybe the *truth* is hiding in plain sight.

I guess I'm just as guilty of indoctrination. I've already described Nostradamus' work as 'ramblings' and anyone who believes otherwise is to be outcast by society as a dreamer or worse - a nut bar!

So, maybe Steve's not such a tin hatter after all and it's me that's been duped into thinking he's stupid for believing in such wild conspiracies.

Oh what a tangled web we weave, when first we practise to deceive!

Well, I didn't think I'd be quoting Sir Walter Scott in here, but hey: *A lie told often enough, becomes the truth*. V.Lenin.

Thinking about the whole Iraq invasion and the 45 minutes debacle, maybe Dr David Kelly knew this truth after all? After his death, the police found his home riddled by bugs, just the spooky type, rather than the creepy crawly ones in the bed.

Yet what strikes me now is the last line of that quatrain. At first I thought it could allude to blood soaked snow or ice, or nuclear winter. But what if this is another 'sounds like' game from Nostradamus?

What if "Icy" is actually ISIS?

And the word "hail"?

Not the white stuff that falls like ice, but instead a synonym being the word 'summon'.

What if it actually means that people are summoned up by ISIS across the Earth in the name of jihad and blood; resulting in vengeance against the West?

Up out of Syria, Libya or Tunisia and into Italy, as the first port of call and a symbol of Christendom. They've already threatened the taking of Rome or the Vatican in the press - what if all this is for real?

The mention of a one hundred-nation reprisal could be the vast list of countries that denounced the 9/11 atrocities or the recent Paris attacks. Yet, there's some debate as to whether Mabus and the third Antichrist are actually one and same person anyway.

So just one final thing for me to debunk - the 27 year war.

If Mabus has already died, then the war may actually be on already...waging under our noses like a ticking time bomb!

The original Gulf War, which incidentally may've kicked all this off, was in 1990 and the Iraq war was 2003. Clinton brokered a Middle East peace deal in 1993, all of which puts us in date ballpark that could be between 2017 and 2020, before the end of this war and associated conflicts.

I can't seem to find anyone of note that died around the early 90's that sounded like 'Mabus', but again with the coded letters, it could be like finding a needle in a giant haystack.

So if the prophesised war *is* on and the clock's ticking, then what will happen when we reach 2020?

Is that when my first dream kicks in?

I need to speak to Steve about this. I'm no detective, but as a researcher looking in; it does beg a host of questions. As a researcher himself, I think he may be impressed.

Diary, don't take the wedding hat back just yet!

9.30am

Just about to leave for Steve's and then onto his brother's house. Should be an eventful day!

Why I feel the need to constantly check in, I don't know. It's like typing into a silent companion. Informing a faceless host of my innermost thoughts and movements, despite a lack of encouragement, approval or vilification.

I guess that's what it's for and to be honest, it's very addictive and I'm a bit gutted I've only just started a diary.

Yet this is the first time I've seen drama, so better *now* than my previous customary conveyer belt of mind-numbing news. Brain dump complete, thank you for your patience!

11.30am

We're here and I've snuck into the loo to get this down, whilst it is fresh in my mind. They'll think I have an upset stomach or something, so best be quick!

It turns out that Steve recalled we'd not searched for Nostradamus and in the spirit of a problem shared is a problem halved, found time yesterday to do some research of his own.

He too had stumbled on the word Mabus in terms of being the Antichrist, but hadn't fully researched this aspect, as he didn't appreciate its massive importance.

I brought him up to speed during the drive, albeit from memory, but he made me stop at the services so that I could then read my notes to him verbatim.

'You're kidding me,' he said, gripping my hand and almost taking me out of gear when I finally got around to telling him about Mabus' number being on my phone.

'No way, that shit is not possible. Jesus! Seriously you dreamt that name and you've never been exposed to it before? You said you'd heard of Nostradamus.'

'Yes, but only because I saw a bit of the film back in 96', but I had no idea of the specific word Mabus.'

Steve just sat there shaking his head for a good few seconds. He started a sentence a few times, stalling his first word, almost realising the enormity of the revelation and then searching for a more compelling, forthright and memorable word or phrase, more befitting the dramatic situation.

'Shit a brick' he said.

Yep, that would do it. I smiled, knowing that we may finally be getting closer to an answer.

But an answer to what exactly?

What is it exactly I'm searching for? It's like I need to keep reminding myself.

I had a dream... So what?

Millions of us do every night.

But this dream was different. Well it felt different and that's the key for me. I have this inner compulsion to find out its meaning. I can't put my finger on why and I've no illusions that I'm going to be some sort of saviour or Earth mother, but too many things keep happening for it to be just left to chance, or a trick of the mind.

I heard the other day that if we slow down, we notice more things. We see things that we'd not have seen before and the more we see, the more these things seem to link together somehow. It could be coincidence in motion, six degrees of separation, or the ability to control our own perception of time.

All this, just to prove once and for all that maybe there *is* a design for life after all.

Whether that is some fateful coincidence, a cosmic coercion or some higher power, I don't know, but now I'm starting to see things clearer. I'm starting to understand and maybe appreciate my role in this life.

Maybe I *am* here to see, learn and eventually warn.

Blimey I'm starting to sound like some sort of religious zealot, but perhaps I've found my faith, my calling?

I'm not interested in the religious doctrine or dogma that goes with it, but if pure faith in itself is simply a complete self-awareness and a moral inner conscience, then surely I'm half way there already? I have faith in myself, my ability and faith in others. Is that not my own holy trinity?

I wouldn't have remembered the name Mabus unless I'd been searching for something. Anything. Any sort of a clue, and that's the whole point. I'm finally looking.

Eyes open, senses heightened. I'm starting to see things, those little idiosyncrasies of day-to-day living that combine as the small almost indiscriminate linkages of life. There is a lot in the six degrees of separation notion, whereby you will know complete random people through the entangled relationships of just six people, including yourself.

When I embarked on 2015's New Year's resolution to become a 'Yes' woman, inspired by Danny Wallace's classic novel, I met two people independently in two differing social circles and it turned out they're married and we now meet up and go out as a four-ball, as Steve would say.

Life's weird like that.

It brings people together and if the fates collide, as they will, and for some reason friends are not drawn together; future partners don't happen to meet eyes and the unemployed don't happen upon the self-employed looking to hire; then they will.

Just not yet.

Yet repeating evidence points to the fact that they'll meet one day – albeit all in good time.

Blimey, this diary has turned me into a self-reflective theorist, or maybe just confirmed me as the opinionated and self-interested narcissist that I already knew I was.

Ok, best example to prove a point to myself.

How Steve and I met.

He shouldn't have been in that club in Maidstone, as there was a mix up with his friend's stag night booking and I was only there because I was visiting a friend and she wanted to show me a 'good' time.

A good time in Maidstone. You know right!?!

The rest is detail, but suffice to say the fates allowed for us to both be there and for an opportunity for us to meet. It subsequently turns out after conversations with Steve that there have been a couple of other places that we've both been to in the past, but not met.

Glastonbury Festival about ten years ago and then on St Patrick's Day in *O'Neils* pub in Leicester Square the year before we met. On that basis, maybe he *is* the 'one'?

Crikey, I've been up here ages!

I need to make my apologies before they think I have flushed myself away...

9.30pm

Long old day, but a good one in so many ways! Me and the boy are back on track. His family weren't too painful and

I'll go into that more in a moment, but Steve also took me through more of his own research on the way home, using his loosely cobbled together notes in his traditional spiral bound journalist pad.

'Well you have well and truly trumped me on Nostradamus! I found it all a bit mumbo jumbo, but looks like you really got into that one and Mabus obviously gave you the hook to look for!' he said sincerely.

Not once today did we joust, cross swords or intellectually fence – well not with each other anyway.

It was almost like we were both on best behaviour, but not in a false, staged and silent kind of way. Just a natural calm, an inner peace of being back together on equal terms, with neither of us having a point to prove or an agenda to push.

This continuation of his sincerity on the drive back gave me the licence to open up to him a little more and we talked about *us*, the future – not just the bleak apocalyptic version, but the much more fabled day of reckoning when we will go to see a mortgage advisor.

Steve was up for it in principle and said he just wanted to get a bit more saved for the deposit, but for every month of saving, there's another month of haemorrhaging the majority of his cash on the rent, so it's the lesser of two evils for him.

Steve likes his space and time, hence the reason we've not already pooled our resources and rented a flat together. Being religious he didn't want to be seen in his father's eyes as sharing a rented flat 'out of wedlock'. Yet as time has passed and the ring has failed to be put on the finger, it's got increasingly 'normalised' for us to be together in Patrick's eyes, so I think Steve will be less paranoid about us moving in together prior to being engaged.

Relationships can be complicated for little or no reason sometimes. To think we're wasting cash so as to appease the biased and out-dated views of Patrick.

Mental!

So I think we've managed to get over this hurdle now and I offered to lend Steve the deposit, or just put in *more* of the deposit in reality, but ever mindful that like all great modern relationships, what's his is ours and what's mine is mine, unless I deem it to be in my interest.

Although he was a little weird about this at first, he soon came around to the idea, as a means of getting out of the rental trap. That is to the idea of me putting in more money, so I win again, yip, yip!

Steve got us back onto the original discussion and how the Internet research spawns pages of information and how hard it is to stay on track and not branch off down a rabbit hole.

Anyway, Steve duly strayed *deep* inside the rabbit hole...

'I can't recall how I came across it, but I did a bit of digging into the United Persian Empire' he said, revelling in his journalistic calling.

I laughed and almost swerved into the middle lane of the M20 looking at him, 'The United what? How the hell did you get onto that?'

'Oh don't ask, but I didn't find anything until page five of *Google*, which I know is against the rules, but it was a bit of a tricky fish to catch. There is an old article on *The Trumpet*, which insinuated that Iran was expanding and helping in the fight against ISIS in Iraq and Syria to gain local support for a wider Persian nation that once embraced all religions of the region under King Cyrus. It also hinted that Saudi Arabia may have been keeping oil prices at a low, so as to put financial pressure on Iran, so reducing its ability to pay off its own debts and also subdue payments for the nuclear expansion and state sponsored support elsewhere.'

Being the driver, I was struggling to take all this on board, but couldn't bare the thought of him repeating it to me.

'Fine, but what's that got to do with the end of the world?' Middle Eastern politics was never my strongest suit.

'This was and still is having a knock on effect with Russian oil prices and the ability for them to pay for their defensive re-armament.' he said, almost in a whisper.

'I see,' whispering back, so as not to cause alarm: 'So win-win for the US then – two for the price of one? Russia and Iran both shackled without having to commit boots on the ground, eh?'

‘Well yes short term, but the US won’t want Iran to become too powerful, even if they have just lifted sanctions. If they expand geographically, as Russia has been trying to do, it’ll almost negate last year’s work in trying to stop Iran developing nuclear weapons. Their sphere of influence in the region will give them power that a simple nuclear deterrent cannot.’

‘It’s all a bit messy,’ I ventured, slightly confused: ‘But how does this save the US getting directly involved in the Middle East all over again if Iran is expanding?’

‘Well apart from the US air strikes against ISIS, they’ve been reticent to get too involved, particularly with the impending election. That’s why they wanted UK and France to pile into Syria, using the Paris attacks as a supposedly legitimate excuse. But it looks to all intents and purposes that the Islamic world is trying to get its own house in order…’

‘It’s just that Iran is also apparently using the situation as a way of exploiting trade routes in Yemen and Libya. This was rumbled by Saudi and stopped in its tracks, but if Iran can’t pull the strings on the local trade themselves, then they can affect trade routes to the West and cut them off if necessary. Oil passes out of the Middle East through the Gulf in Yemen, so he who has the key to the sea, holds the key to the trade route. Hence Iran’s on-going exploits in Yemen and a proxy war against the Western backed Saudis.’

Steve looked slightly pleased with himself, even if he had just read it on a website, which was out of date already, but he continued to layer the cake:

‘I have been totally switched off to Middle Eastern politics, especially with our own election and the fallout that brought. Bahrain apparently hosts America’s 5th Naval Fleet, and Bahrain has been trying to unite the predominantly Shiite populous with the Sunni leadership, which is like having George Galloway over to tea in your local Synagogue.’

Steve’s irony was lost on me there, but he went on to detail how the whole Middle East conflict seems to boil down to which reading of the Koran you believe and it’s sectarian violence, not too dissimilar to that in Northern Ireland, that is the main cause of the bloodshed.

Sunnis and Shiite Muslims are not easy bedfellows and their religions are polarising a region into a state of flux, not seen since biblical times.

'Lebanon hosts Iran's terrorist group Hezbollah, which has been attacking Syria and northern Israel over the last few years. Iran also continues to harass Israel through its tentacles in Palestine and Gaza, allegedly arming much of the region to arguably reform a Persian Empire and take back the Holy lands in Israel. That's why Isreal had a shitfit over America lifting some sanctions in Iran, it just plays into this nihilistic narrative.' He paused, as if for effect: 'Deep, but deeply interesting!' he concluded, feet up on my dashboard.

'Deeply worrying! So Iran has basically been trying to take over then and the US has been, by and large, standing by watching?' I asked incredulously, shooting him a look and a nod aimed at his ankles on the dash that would surely break his prostrate pose.

Steve seemed to take the hint and removed his feet: 'You got it, or so it seems anyway. Worth keeping an eye on the news in the future with this in mind now, to see if it affects either your dreams or I don't know, wider world security? The US can't police everyone. Leader of the free world they may be, but the 'catalyst of catastrophe', they would prefer not to have on their international C.V.'

Keep an eye out, I pondered and then thumped the steering wheel: 'Well I'd assume that the powers that be will've someone watching for us. Well I hope so, for the 3% Council Tax increase, the unscrupulous bastards!'

The rest of the trip was pretty low key in comparison.

Just general chitchat and neither of us seemingly wanting to confront the elephant in the car, which was the minor question over our future commitment. Softly, softly they say...

So going back in time, as is my want. We had a good ol' time with the family and this question of commitment came up immediately!

We pulled up outside Seth and Mel's 1970's semi-detached house. Its white rendered frontage is offset by a red tile roof and out-dated, and if I may say within the confines of this diary, shabby looking wooden window frames. Inside the rooms are all open plan, as was the fad back then, but everything in terms of decor is now mostly contemporary.

'Sophia. Steve!' said Pam in a slightly false, over excited tone of greeting. Her open arms were enough to take us both into her ample bosom in one hit and the overriding smell of perfume left a lasting legacy in our ill prepared nostrils.

It was not even her house, but Pam was ever the hostess. You can take the woman out of Bolton, but her Northern gregarious nature could not be shaken, despite numerous trips on the London Underground...

Her tumbling red dyed hair betrayed her years, but her bulk soon reminded me that she's not that young and active anymore – despite the grandchildren.

'Come and sit down Mum.' said Mel over the din of the squealing children, who by now were clambering and keen to show their Uncle Steve what they'd got from Father Christmas.

She called her 'Mum', which always irked me. I'd never do that, seems an old fashioned thing to do, but I know it comes from a good place.

Mel is pretty plain. Pretty, but plain.

She hides her beauty within scruffy, baggy clothes and I'd imagine that she'd blame the kids for the lack of time and investment in her own wellbeing. Her blonde hair straight and tied back in a ponytail, her thick rimmed black glasses offset by her chipped black nail varnish.

I'd imagined she might have dressed up for the occasion, but obviously not...

'So no ring Sophia? Steve when are you going to do the deed?' piped Pam playfully.

'The deed'. Bloody cheek. It seems that we've been together for so long now, that it's more of an overdue chore, than a declaration of love to be looked forward to.

I'm sure it'll be an anti-climax for all, if and when it does come to pass! More of a shared feeling of relief that they've two more 30 something's finally off the shelf.

We must be starting to make the place look untidy!

Steve looked down at his feet like an immature and embarrassed schoolboy: 'No mother. We now want to move in first anyway and then see how it goes.'

Patrick scoffed: 'Ha. Well if you haven't noticed how the relationship has gone in all these year's son, I'm not sure what living with the girl will accomplish.'

'I *am* here.' I reminded them, almost apologetically.

I'm one of the most outgoing people I know, but for some reason in front of Patrick in particular, I do tend to clam up. Maybe it's because I can't get a blessed word in!

Like his sons, Patrick is tall and mousy blonde, but broader and fuller. Middle aged spread has capitalised on his capitulation for keeping fit and has advanced unchecked, across the borders of his belt into an apparent no man's land stretching out, so as to cast a shadow over his creaking knees.

Unlike Mel, Patrick was always smartly dressed. Today he had a shirt and tie. Old school, I thought and he'd probably already been to church, so was still sporting his Sunday best.

'I'm only kidding my love.' re-affirmed Patrick, his hand stretched outright, awaiting an equally strong gripped shake.

I'm not sure what came over me, but I remember thinking, 'ah sod it'. So I went in for the kill. I slapped his large hand aside and went straight for a cheek peck.

'Well hello to you too Sophia.' he said, obviously taken aback by my forthright greeting.

'Put her down Pat.' said Pam, clipping him around the ear; her gaudy bangles clanking on each other around her wrist, which made Patrick jump, just as much as the clipped impact.

'She...' Patrick stopped himself and I laughed, as for all the world, it sounded like he was about to say 'she started it,' and had then thought better of it.

'Hey Soph.' said Steve's brother Seth. A half shoulder cuddle with a quick peck out. That was all that was needed. It was honest, heartfelt and not over the top. Textbook greeting.

It still amazes me how similar Seth is to Steve. Well in the looks department anyway. Tall and slim with a similar gelled back haircut, just with a parting and lighter blonde hair, compared to Steve's slicked back darker blonde locks. They have the same brown eyes, slight nose and full lips to go with the strong jaw line that attracted me in the first place.

To Steve that is, not Seth– just to be clear... he was already taken LOL.

Dress sense is another thing. Steve is quite preppy, with a designer polo shirt tucked into jeans or chinos most of the time. He just doesn't go for the no socks and boating shoes look – a step too far for his age...

Seth on the other hand is like Mel. Hoodies and low slung jeans, presumably to fit in within the Croydon massive... Snob klaxon alert!

Mel's belated greeting then followed suit, despite her struggling to rein in the two kids, who by now had already made base camp, climbed up Steve's trousers and found great first foot holes in his two front jean pockets.

Mel and Seth had lived in Croydon for the last ten years, for as long as I'd known them and more. Their house must have doubled in value in that time!

They'd morphed from fun time, to family in just a few years. Something that comes to us all I guess...

All nighters and lock in's had taken on a totally new aspect since the two girls arrived. Now, they're up all night trying to appease teething trouble and picking the toilet lock from the outside when Isobel trapped herself in there over Christmas lunch, I'm told!

There's an advert for contraception right there...

Isobel had returned back to school this week and took pride in showing Steve her latest and greatest handiwork. We'd both missed them at Christmas, having gone west to see my mum and my not so little brother.

Chloe conversed as best she could, bless her, but she was having the same trouble getting a word in as me, what with Isobel's seemingly verbal diarrhoea.

It was good to see them all. It had been a while.

The conversation was polite without being small and everyone had something to say. Even Patrick, despite keeping half an eye on me, following my 'Kissgate' exploits.

I knew that would throw the old codger off his perch. He's holier than thou and to have his future daughter in law 'throw' herself at him amused *me* anyway.

Mel had put on a great spread. It was as if she was mindful that we missed them at Christmas and that only an equally epic feast would be appropriate for the latest reunion. Just no presents to open or crackers to pull, mores' the pity.

Steve clapped to raise attention: 'So...' he announced.

I had not really appreciated the intentional incendiary device Steve was about to lob his father's way.

Steve was and still is to this day, what some may describe as, a 'right bugger'!

Just when you think things are rolling along nicely with his family and maybe to take the heat off him a little, he would throw a curveball, drop a grenade or simply a throw away remark, just to see what would happen.

'So Pa, you gonna vote?'

Patrick almost choked on his chicken: 'You know very well that I'm unable to vote anymore. Been in this blasted country for too long and can't represent my forefathers. They died on the battlefields against this mob handed rule you lot are loyal to. King and Country. Pha. In God we trust. One nation under one flag I say!' His southern drawl seemed to take on a new parochial dimension.

I closed my eyes. A slow intake of breath, knowing what was coming.

'We fought for our independence, the bell tolled for liberty and freedom son, more than you'll ever expect here under this tyrannical dictatorship.'

'What? The Queen...?' said Steve coolly, knowing exactly where this line of attack was going.

'The Queen is just a puppet,' said Patrick pointing his finger across the table: 'A puppet for a shadowy set of masters that would have her own daughter in law killed for shaming the monarchy. Dark actors, all of them!'

Patrick looked at me, as a possible daughter in law, I presumed for effect, which did give me the creeps a little: 'So yes, I'm going to follow the election campaign from start to finish. The primaries, the caucuses, the gerrymandering of votes if necessary until the Grand Old Party is returned to its rightful Presidential Office.'

'Redneck.' breathed Seth, veiled in a muffled cough, but audible enough to make the point that we were all thinking.

Pam included.

Mel and I kept well out of it, but Steve loved to take his dad to task on his red state beliefs and knew that his UK citizenship, his inability to vote in the US and make his democratic right count, would wind him up no end!

Patrick shot Seth a look of redneck rage, who disguised his smirk by stuffing a potato into an already full mouth.

'I'll have you know young Seth that your great, great grandfather fought and died at Gettysburg.'

'What? That was because he wanted to keep his slaves, not because of any higher ideology.' Steve retorted, forcefully defending his younger brother, whilst his mouth was still full.

'Ah, but the *right* to keep slaves son. The freedom to choose.' said Patrick obviously unnerved.

'What rights did the slaves have? I can't believe that it was still only 50 odd years ago that black people were segregated on the back of the bus in the land of the free?' said Steve provocatively.

'Yeah!' chipped Seth in support and solidarity.

My eyes caught Mel's and then Pam's who rolled hers, having heard this not so civil war too many times before in various guises.

And so it went on, the Confederate kin and adopted UK taxpayer trading metaphoric blows with his own royalist blood, who had both tactically, if not unwittingly formed in a pincer movement, sitting either side of their father.

The death throws from the argument of a dinosaur soon came to a head and so it came to pass that his only way out of the situation, was to remove himself from this not so grand old party completely. Patrick soon beat a hasty retreat to the bathroom; the wounded old animal scurried from the table, his stained napkin still tucked into his massive trousers.

Steve knew this was the time to lay off the old dog, but one last jerk of his choke chain wouldn't hurt...

'At least the Democrats have a clear leader and contender for POTUS, your lot are in disarray.' he said launching the final arrow to the King's eye.

The thick rhinoceros skin of the sixty-year-old timer took the mortal blow and traded no more.

It merely turned and proceeded back to the privacy of its cave. He refused to resort to name-calling or a public slanging match and knew when his sons were both being provocative on purpose. Done just to get a rise out of him and it worked like a charm every time!

A good ten minutes later Patrick returned.

Not skulking like a scalded schoolboy, but quite cheery as if nothing had happened. Maybe he spoke to God on the big white telephone, who'd reminded him that he could take a moral and religious high ground.

So back he came, returned to his pedestal of power. Confidence now flowing and he was seemingly unmoved by the preceding exchanges.

'So I've been following the first primaries and the news is, as you quite rightly allude to, that there is not just one obvious candidate for the Republican presidential running. There are a number of equally strong leaders and it's up to the people of the party to decide as to who will take the party forward.'

This reminded me of the rhetoric coming out during the old Battle of Milliband.

Patrick continued calmly: 'God has ordained that the party should have an abundance of riches to choose from'.

'Did he just say that?' I thought... physically wincing.

'An abundance that'll bring like-minded people together. United in voice for the greater good and a greater America.'

Yes, he'd been watching those preachy shows on channel 815 again hadn't he! Religion and politics going hand in hand – a dangerous cocktail if ever I've seen one!

Anti gay. Anti abortion. Anti pasti.

Those homo loving, child killing, mushroom eating Democrats! God fearing, tunnel visioned, wall building, warmongers, now that's what you need to lead a great nation!

Thank goodness for our multi-party system. At least you can spot the Monster Raving Looney's a mile off!

As predicted, Patrick did then set off into a diatribe of denial. Coercing the argument to his creed. Avoiding the political pitfalls and managing to divert with dignity all viewpoints contrary to his own, with the deft prowess of a Republican orator in his own right.

'Now,' he whispered, as if he had the inside track on the winner of the 2.35pm at Cheltenham: 'The one to watch...'

I thought I might have been right! Bookies here I come!

'The one to watch, is black!'

Pam spluttered on her Spumante and all eyes were now on Patrick, if they were not already.

'Now I'm not a fan of people of colour per se, especially those purporting to lead my party, but there's something about this fella. Something almost, spiritual!'

'It's not the second coming is it?' mocked Seth, unaware that Steve and I would both look at him shocked at the same moment: 'Something I said?' he queried.

'Hmm? No mate.' said Steve, pretending to go about his business and load an already overflowing fork with even more crumble and custard.

'I'm not sure you can say 'people of colour' anymore Dad.' said Mel innocently.

Sweet sodding Cydonia, now she just called him Dad and my skin just crawled off and left the room!

'Why the hell not?' boomed Patrick defensively: 'I can say whatever I like in my own home' he protested vociferously.

I'm sure Seth considered for a fraction of a second question, whether this meant that Patrick would be prepared to pay *his* mortgage as well, but thought better of it.

‘There is a sense of integrity, confidence and empathy to the people – his and ours.’ said Patrick emphatically.

Steve laughed out loud shaking his head. How amazing it is that racial tolerance has come so far in just one generation.

Patrick continued, undeterred: ‘This confidence is almost palpable, it breeds respect for the man.’

‘Blimey!’ said Seth: ‘He must be the Messiah for *you* to respect a black man.’

‘He’s a good Christian boy naturally. Faith is what will keep our good nation together in these dark times.’

Patrick was oblivious to how prophetic his melodrama actually was. Steve’s eyes darted to mine.

Amazing how innocent some phrases are, until one is said in and around an apocalyptic context.

‘His name is Orlando Johnson and he happens to be running for my home state of Wisconsin.’ Patrick then paused for effect, as if someone from the table would heckle his newfound faith in a ‘man of colour’.

All he got was a burp from Chloe, which seemed to break the unnecessary silence, much to Isobel’s amusement.

We all looked at each other. It was not a name that we knew and to be fair, none of the other Republican hopefuls would have resonated much with us either.

With the lack of retort, Patrick got back into his stride and extolled Johnson’s virtues as to how he’d stood up to the unions for fairer pay and working conditions.

‘I’d be more worried about how his Christian leanings and presumed foreign policy go down on the coasts if I were you.’ said Steve, slipping back into serious mode: ‘Radical ideas won’t hold much traction on the East and West sides. He may appeal to the Bible belt; the farming contingent and the ‘black’ vote to a lesser extent, but what about where it really counts? What will he do for healthcare, banking reform, lessening the poverty gap and the balance of payments deficit, as well as repairing foreign relations in the East?’

‘Ah he’ll do all that for sure.’ quipped Patrick, almost sweeping the more political points under the carpet, so he could get back onto the front foot.

‘What interests me and many fellow Americans is that, as a Christian, he is committed to defending the nation and the annihilation of ISIS and the rest of the axis that Obama failed to clear up. What’s more, he won't play politics either, trying to trump his opponents by denigrating minorities for example.’

‘That’s nice dear.’ said Pam, taking his bowl away.

I’m not sure if she was being ironic or was *actually* on autopilot? So used to going along with her husband’s radical ramblings, so as to become completely immune.

‘Exactly dear. They come to our country, take advantage of our democracy and then throw it in our face. Sons of bitches, flying planes into buildings I ask you! It’s a liberty! A liberty on *our* liberty.’ he concluded, suitably pleased with his own wordplay.

‘It’s time to take the power back I tell you. Too long now have we played second fiddle to this political correctness and fair play agenda. It’s time we stood up for our own values and take the initiative back from them. Going around butchering, raping and beheading in the name of religion. We need our own crusade in the name of *our* religion. The religion of the just, the noble and the one true God.’ Patrick banged the table with his glass.

Well if *this* newly recruited ‘Johnsonite’ is this militant and full of this much rhetoric and hate; then Lord only knows what the real McCoy is like.

I’m sure the Deep South will just love him! I’m just not sure about the UN, NATO, G8 and the IMF.

Even the WWF should be worried...

Being half American, Steve has always defended his patronage in the past, from those in the pub that have rubbished the country’s historic gun-toting policies.

The fact that Blair took us to war too, almost overshadowed how gung-ho the US actually was. Fair enough it was in the wake of 9/11 and in times of heightened tensions, but are things in 2016 any less fraught?

Especially in that region.

I almost wrote the word ‘theatre’ there out of habit talking about war. Is that what all this is going to come to – the final curtain and no chance of an encore, let alone an overpriced tub of ice cream?

Say Johnson *is* voted in as President and the US takes a much more abhorrent stance to Islamic terror and what cannot be understated as modern genocide of Christians in Egypt and Syria, to name but a few places.

What if he is anti Iranian expansion? What if he gets in and forms a unilateral alliance with Israel to defeat this 'terror' once and for all? What is he recognises Jerusalem as the capital and causes ructions in the region?

What if he takes Russia's lead and starts to re-arm?

How will Iran then feel having negotiated with the US in Vienna last year? They will put their nuclear programme into overdrive and although this all seems highly probable, I can't see the US backing down this time, no matter what the stakes. Principle may come before politics, especially when you're new to office...

Knowing what I now know about the significance of Israel to the US and the region as a whole through their Biblical and apocalyptic importance, it's going to be a doomsday bun fight.

Last man standing stuff...

Let's just hope this glorified triangle keeps its pointy nose clean this time. There's enough chance of thermo nuclear disaster at Sellafield, let alone from Jihadists looking for vengeance in our High Streets and Pound stores.

I could spend hours worrying about what might happen. He's not even the confirmed candidate for the GOP yet, let alone inducted into the Oval office...

Patrick then continued and this is pretty much when my world started to fall apart!

'We need to arm the 5th Fleet under General Mabus and take out this threat once and for all.' said Patrick defiantly, fist thumping the table again.

The sound of my glass falling to the laminate wooden floor made everyone jump.

It made Chloe scream.

Mel leapt up, first to react, as only a mother would to gather her children from the impending shattered glass.

I observed in slow motion just how the maternal instinct kicks in so quickly and smiled inside that I had felt something similar, even if it was only in a dream.

I quietly watched the glass fall in slow motion, its claret contents spiralling asunder.

The scraping of chairs was shrill to my ears as Seth and Pam then immediately reacted to the spillage. It was like time had just stopped and was ticking along so slowly that I could notice finally the minutia.

There'd be muffled, stop animated shouts for paper towels, an absorbent cloth and I'm sure someone, somewhere cried for a medic!

There'd no doubt be reassurances in time that I shouldn't worry about it: 'At least it wasn't on the carpet dear', they would say.

But I was not worried.

I was watching.

Seeing.

Eyes open and senses heightened...

That such a moment of tiny chaos around a table could come from the utterance of just one word.

Yet that's all that it took.

It was milliseconds between the words General Mabus, passing Patrick's lips, the slip and the shatter.

The red wine glass had dropped at the very same time as my first tear.

My watery eyes passed slowly to Patrick's mouth. I think he'd just finished saying the words 'once and for all', and only now had he started to rise in reaction to the wine going over.

My eyes then slowly passed to Steve and bless him; he was already looking at me.

Absolutely still, with a solemn, knowing look in his eyes. Those eyes I love and now need so much for support.

My tears were now in full flow and my head had finally caught up and caused my breathing to labour and convulse.

Steve's index finger simply rose to his pursed lips.
I knew. He knew. That was it.
That was all that we needed from each other.

The slow motion suddenly came to a halt and life sped up once again through my mascara stained outlook.

Mel had the kids in front of the TV. Pam and Seth were on their knees cleaning, absorbing and self medicating. Patrick supervised, as only he could, pointing out which bits had been missed and denouncing the use of so much white wine going on the red wine stained rug.

Life continued apace whilst Steve and I just sat still.

'No need to cry dear,' said Pam looking up at me: 'It was only an accident. At least it was not on the carpet, isn't that right Mel? Patrick you made her jump, pounding the table like that, you silly old sod.'

Mel wasn't listening; she was faffing around with the remote, frantically looking for *Peppa Pig* playbacks that would appease the still crying Chloe.

Patrick looked completely nonplussed.

Steve finally rose and the same index finger, stiffly pointed at me and then to the front door in a quick and overt jabbing motion, but surreptitious all the while.

We met on the other side, two non-smokers, feigning a fag break and leaving the workers to attend to the wreckage.

Steve had his own wreck to attend to.

I was then promptly pinned to the exterior wall of the house by Steve's forceful palm against my right shoulder: 'What the hell is going on Soph?' he demanded in hushed tones, eyes darting left and right to ensure we were alone: 'This has just escalated from belated Christmas lunch to DEFCON feckin' Red!'

Steve released his arm, aware that I may have taken his frustration as an attack on me and held his head in his hands: 'This name! This pissing name keeps cropping up, what the hell is going on? Who the hell employs the Commander of their Navy with the same name as the Antichrist?' his hands dropping to his side, limp upon realisation, as he looked me in the eye, 'unless of course...'

'...he *is* the bloody Antichrist?' I ventured meekly, finishing his sentence for him.

Steve started to pace the length of the lounge bay window, his shoes wet from the melted snow: 'So your Nostradamus chap said Mabus would die right? And it would all kick on from there with massive reprisals. End of days shit.'

I merely nodded.

'Well that's just great isn't it and there's me with my big break and it's all going to be for cock all!'

'Big break? What big break?'

'I was going to announce it *after* dinner, but it doesn't seem worth it now. I've got a new job!' he said semi proudly, but understatedly; as is his way.

Normally, one would announce such a thing *over* dinner, but not Steve. He was quite happy reporting it in dispatches, so as to avoid the limelight.

'Bloody hell Steve, I didn't even know you were looking. Wow, congratulations, I think. Where? Where is it? Please for Christ's sake say London and not Lebanon! What is it? Same sort of thing, but who with? Wow, how'd you keep this so quiet, that's amazing? So you got the job right, or are you still in negotiation? Did you get a raise? Oh no, it *is* away isn't it! That's why you were being so bloody evasive earlier about buying a place together. Well that's just great isn't it! I bare all and tell you that I want to move in with you and all along you're moving abroad. And who with, what's her name, the slut, I'll punch her in the throat!?!'

'Finished?' he asked quietly.

My tears were still drizzling down and I'd started to hyperventilate in between talking *at* him.

'Maybe...?' I slightly raised my voice at the end of the intonation, denoting the possible question, or just a general feeling of indecision, confusion and childlike embarrassment.

'Good. Well now you've calmed the hell down, and I can't promise to answer all the questions in the right order, but: Yes, I've accepted a job *in* London, with *Thomson Reuters* the news agency. Yes it's more money, no I don't have to go to Lebanon; not that they mentioned anyway. Yes I can still move in with you, but for your information Little Miss Stressball, the bank will need at least three months of pay slips before they commit any money to us, hence me covering my ass saying that we'll need to save a bit more first. Was that everything? Oh and her name is Shelley by the way.'

I was now in a state of double shock, but I computed this news within the blink of an eye - my female brain works that fast! Crikey, a new job in London I thought to myself. *Reuters* eh? Very reputable, hasn't *he* done well for himself? More money, good ok, although much of that will go on the train fare, but we can work with that. Pay slips. Yes that figures. Good thinking Steve, and Shelley, yes thought there might be another woman involved and she sounds just like the skanky barmaid type he would go for too...

'Wait a pissing second there. Who the hell is Shelley?' I demanded, as the emotional side of my brain caught up with the analytical department.

'Sorry babes, but she's the new love of my life.' said Steve, slowly backing away, hands out in front defensively, as if expecting the impending clout of a clutch bag.

'Like hell she is!' I shouted, ready to fight for my man: 'Where is this stinking harlot?'

I never swear and now I'd turned into some sort of sobbing potty mouth!

'Wow, do you know her already? She is quite stinky. And a little dishevelled, but nothing a good bath and a brush down won't cure.'

'What the hell are you talking about man? A good brush down? Who is she, a hobo you found outside Kings Cross at Christmas?' I demanded, holding back any further tears until I'd got my answer and pinning *him* back against the same wall.

It had never seen so much action!

Steve could tell that I'd had enough, that I was past the end of my tether. The bugger even told me after the event that he was a moment away from landing a needless final punch about needing new pussy in his life, but thought better of it...

'Shelley's my new rescue kitten.' he said calmly.

I did cry after all. Half out of relief and half from the confusion as to what the hell was going on.

That name, Mabus again!

My head felt like it was going to explode.

'Well with all you've been going through this year, I just kept it on the down low. I'd been looking for a new job back end of last year and I was in a pub recently and overheard some American guy saying to their pal that *Reuters* was hiring through a local firm. So that was that. Unbeknown to them, I was straight on the recruitment consultant's website behind them, checking it out and stone me. They were! They did! Talk about being in the right place at the right time eh?'

'Yes,' I said finally composing myself: 'I was thinking about that situation earlier, funnily enough. Small world!'

'Yes and the chap that was doing the talking in the pub only did my interview too. And his name is Steve and he looked at my CV and said to me: 'Oh I live in Folkestone as well, small world'. If only he knew how I came to know about the job.' Steve chuckled to himself, pleased with his deception.

'I'm just bemused by this whole situation.' I said to him, feeling, well... bemused.

'As you say, this name keeps cropping up and the linkages to the dream are getting stronger. Does that mean that time is running out or that we've got our man and now need to report it in again?'

With that the front door opened and it was a smiling Mel, holding a damp, dripping cloth in one hand and a replenished glass of red in the other.

'You ok Sophia? Did you get lost?' she asked innocently and with genuine concern.

Steve looked at me and laughed:

'No Mel. I think Sophia has just been found.'

Monday January 11th 2016 – 7.30am

Back on the old rattler with the chattering classes.

I'm bushed still and I note that the word 'work' comes first in the term 'work/life balance'.

Steve getting a new job has also reinvigorated my idea of looking for something new!

Well we are what, eleven days into the New Year?

Eleven days into a clean slate and already I'm looking to jump bail and start afresh. But more importantly, eleven days after the dream and nothing has come true.

Well, as yet and not to my knowledge anyway, but that's good right? We're still here…

What a burden to carry around. I am either deluded that I may have some sort of sway on destiny, or I do in fact hold the key to averting what could be the worst kind of self fulfilling prophecy of all time...

A ridiculous notion!

Yet, what are the chances of me having a dream, researching it, remembering a name and then hearing the same name on the same day in the same context of a warlike situation? Coincidence or something bigger?

Of course we never explained anything to Steve's family. We didn't let on as to why we went outside at all.

Steve made his announcement about his job and his acquisition of Shelley, including his gratuitous pussy joke, much to Seth's liking and Patrick's condemnation.

'A cat?' proclaimed Patrick pompously: 'You couldn't even keep my fish Peyton and Eli alive when we went away, how can you be trusted with a proper pet?'

Steve never did answer that one. I think the look said it all.

We made our apologies about the wine, were grateful to Pam who allowed us to blame Patricks' ranting and we exited stage right, more emotionally and physically shattered than the poor wine glass.

Naturally I asked Steve to search for this 'US Navy' Mabus on his phone on the return drive home.

Ray-bloody-Mabus, the United States Secretary to the Navy. Crazy stuff that simply defies belief!

I think I'll have an early night tonight; a night off all this madness. But something Steve said yesterday did make me feel a little odd inside. A flag went up somewhere.

It was just a throwaway line, something about me being found? Random I know...

And now I'm home, I've noticed that Steve has been leaving the loo roll down on its last knockings again! Arrrrgggghhhhh!

That's one thing I'll have to get straight when we do move in together. Who leaves a few last binds of paper on a roll?

Especially when they know how much it grates me!

Tuesday January 12th 2016 – 7.40am

Here we go, Groundhog Day, off to work again and I'm not sure I'm feeling this diary thing anymore. It's just a bit all encompassing, but hey I've come this far. I think I'll give it 'til the end of the month and if the end is not so nigh after all, then I'll give it a swerve and get back to looking inanely out of the window and catching up on kip.

I was too tired to write last night. I needed some mindless entertainment to wash over me and then I headed straight off to bed – out like a light.

I see that in true coincidental form, our friend Orlando Johnston makes the *Metro* front page today.

He looks tall, slim and charismatic. Not unlike Obama to be fair, just darker skinned and no hair. Oh and a *red* button on his lapel.

'The race for the White House', the newspaper headline announces, as if we're really interested over here. Just let me know who's in the semi finals and which glutton for punishment ends up policing the world.

There's also an article today about the State of the Union address, but I didn't bother to read that. Sorry Barack…

Great just read an article about a US boat that's strayed into Iranian waters in the Gulf and been accused of spying.

It's all falling into place some might say…

9.45pm

Work was ok. Starting on a new project with a new client at the moment, so that might spice up my day a bit - or just add to the pressure pot!

Steve called tonight and he said that he's going to do some digging around Ray Mabus and sell in a possible apocalyptic expose as his first story in his new job.

He only has a month's notice, but he said it'd look good if he can get ahead. Sounds like setting dangerous precedents before you even start working there, if you ask me. And quite a niche subject to work on as your first assignment, but hey, what do I know?

Also I've been thinking, Mabus is not new to the US Government, so I would presume that this sort of research work would have been done before, but I trust that Steve will sense check this at the time of writing.

Petty I know, and I'm sure a diary is not the place for my OCD to manifest itself; or maybe it is, but Steve denies leaving my loo roll almost bare, which is odd.

I'm not sure why he'd lie over something so trivial like that, but maybe he knows that it's my pet hate and it'll annoy me! Grrrrr!

Wednesday January 13th 2016 – 7.35am

I am going out tonight with a few people after work. Yesterday afternoon, Kate and Jo both suggested going to a gig in Brixton, but I left them looking into the finer details, as I slipped out of the door after work.

I then forgot about it to be honest, but I've had a text already this morning saying that it's a goer and I'm wearing a trouser suit! Typical...

I've quite a varied taste in music, but they say it should be quite rocky tonight. And boozy I expect - on a school night!

So I'm now mentally preparing myself for another trip to the dry cleaners, this time to remove the *Sailor Jerry* stains from my trousers... or worse...

Speaking of worse, the news in the Middle East goes from bad to, well for want of a better word, worse. You couldn't make this up given the context! The Iranians are kicking off with Saudi over the killing of a Shia cleric and both of these nations are pissed with the US for flooding the market with cheap oil, which the commentator speculates could be to drive down prices and cripple the Russian economy.

Will everyone please stop playing politics and just play nicely. Don't you know Mabus has an itchy trigger finger?

Then you'll all be sorry!

1.15pm

Lunchtime already, where does the time go?

A morning of meetings as usual and the emails pile up unanswered – it's a joke.

What happened to the good old days where you wrote a letter, posted it and that gave you a fighting chance to catch up on other stuff, before the client then received the letter and replied via post – much more civilised, but not that I ever got to experience that fabled lost system…

Now, I have clients emailing me at night, as they catch up on their own workload, so I then email them back to clear out my inbox, before the impending deluge in the morning and then they only bloody reply...

And so it goes on, the balance and boundaries between work and life are ever closing in favour of 'the man and the machine'. I don't have to be on call, but anything that helps me the following day shouldn't be sniffed at.

Suffice to say since these dreams; extracurricular stuff has been going on, so I haven't really had time to do any work of an evening. This now means the days are quite fraught.

At least I can work on the train home, but I think after tonight's gig, the notion of work tomorrow might be a bit of a write-off.

I'm in the canteen at the moment. I'm sitting on my own, so as to be able to write a little. I look busy, head down, so colleagues are tending to ignore me, which is good. It may be a bit of a short entry tonight as I'll be home late.

I sound like I'm managing my mother's expectations, not a stupid diary, but I feel like I'm cheating if I leave any gaps, otherwise what's the point?

I should be able to at least record my emotional state - and for the record it's slightly stressed, due to the fear of checking emails later and the joy that will bring for the rest of the day. Can't I just hide in here all day or curl up on the floor of a toilet cubicle for a nap? Please...?

Oh, here we go, I may have to pack up now as Jo's coming over to sit down, presumably to expand on tonight's drunken exploits to come.

Thursday January 14th 2016 – 1.15am

I bloody luv you dairy! I love Jo and quite like Kate, but less so now though - the biach.

Got too go bed night now ....

7.50am

OMG, I still feel pissed!

I've kept last night's entry exactly as I typed it for posterity, seeing as I apparently lost all ability to spell or see what I was writing. LOL,

I don't even remember doing it - classic.

It's a wonder I remembered the password on my tablet, let alone taking a tablet to lessen the ensuing hangover too.

I somehow dragged my sorry carcass out of bed this morning, my alarm bleeping like an air raid siren in my ear. I'm now a little bit travel sick looking at this screen.

I don't think I'm going to be ill, but I just have the strong taste of cola in my mouth from drinking rum and *Coke* all night. Thank goodness I didn't mix drinks, or I may still be under my warm, plump and delectable duvet. Hmmm!

No word from the girls as to how they are feeling...

I saw a photo on FaceyB from last night that Jo'd posted of our three sets of feet around three handbags - random. Presume it was funny at the time, hence no 'likes' as yet...

Well to sum up the night, the main band, *Fort Hoxton* were noisy. Not heard of them before, but they had two drummers and two singers, as well as three people on guitar, so I felt that I got good value for money!

It's a great sound they have at Brixton and we avoided the wreckage of clashing bodies up the front and just hung around at the top of the sloping floor, for a good view and easy access to the bar.

I dare not check my purse to see how much money I went through – it's scary how quickly hard earned cash suddenly transforms into 'rum tokens' so readily.

I do love it at the *O2 Academy*; the feeling of excitement as you approach the venue and the scary sight of the queue of people stretching down the side road – mostly keen to get up the front.

We had a quick one in the *Dogstar* with a pizza meal - awesome pizza in there! And I think I may have actually mixed drinks, as I do now recall drinking wine in there. Great!

Then the three of us went into the venue to see the band. We didn't fancy the second support act *Ambient Cassini* and we'd already missed *Shirtsleeve Order's* slot, so we stayed at the bar at the back of the slope.

The queue was a joke, about 10 people deep. It was like getting a pint at half time at the rugby - not that I go a lot.

Needless to say I had my invisible coat on, so I had to text the girls to get them to barge their way through the throng and then we hit the bar with an ingenious three-pronged attack that Napoleon would've been proud of.

A triumvirate of giggleheads, each desperate to get served and including, I might add, the best dressed person in the venue – C'est moi!

Ever efficient, we bought two drinks each and so it went along a similar vein all night. Maybe that was why the handbags were on the floor, as we had no hands left to hold onto them...?

It was around this time that I decided to tell the girls about my recent scary conversations with Steve and our exciting future together.

I told them about his new job, our plans to move in together and that I was thinking about proposing to him on Valentine's Day. Just thought I would see how that idea went down in principle.

Sound boarding them through the sound check so to speak.

From what I remember Jo was cool about it, gave me an embracing hug and seemed really excited for me, well both of us. Kate? Well Kate was nice…

Polite and said all the right things at the right time, but I'm not convinced that she's totally on board with the whole proposal thing: 'If he loves you, *he* should propose.' she said loudly, to compensate for the background filler music.

'I know, but I've been waiting years already, not that I specifically wanted to get married even a year ago, but I've been thinking it might be nice and the right thing to do for a while now. I know Steve, and he's too laid back to even think about doing it.'

Looking back, I think that I was trying to convince myself that this was the right thing to do, more so than the girls.

The band was now on and we had to shout even louder at each other to be heard, covering our mouths with our hands to help amplify our strained voices and direct the sound to the two strategically placed ears that seemed to converge in formation before me.

Then the next person would speak and the other two ears duly leaned in. It was almost like an odd looking dance for the almost deaf. A continuously pivoting huddle centred around three handbags and a coat, whilst people danced around us, or performed their own similar and intriguing looking huddle shuffle to the actual music.

Jo chipped in: 'If that's what you want to do babes, then you go for it. At least you're in control of the proposal then and he's bound to say 'yes' isn't he!'

'Well I hope so. Yes. Yes he must do, otherwise he's wasting his time isn't he?' I boomed back to her.

Kate looked thoughtful, as if weighing up whether to comment, or not and then she dived in anyway: 'What if he's just as laid back as you say? Lazy even and if the pressure is suddenly applied to actually get married, he may well end up freaking out?'

'Yeah cheers Kate. Thanks for the support.' I threw back at her, looking at Jo to back me up.

She obliged: 'Yeah Kate, what's all that about. Just because you and Craig will never get hitched.'

'Craig doesn't want to get married again, I already know that. He's been through all that before and doesn't see why a slightly weightier left hand and an emptier wallet will change anything between us.' said Kate defensively.

I laughed: 'That's Craig talking right there babes. Tightwad! An emptier wallet I ask you!?! Last of the romantics he's not. I'm simply trying to tie Steve down on my terms. Power to the women!'

Jo beamed at me: 'You go girl. I think you should consider having a Spice Girls theme at the wedding and you'd be Scary Spice of course!'

'By the time Steve would get around to proposing to me, I'd be Old Spice!' I retorted laughing and aware of a sudden commotion on stage.

The hipster bearded lead singer started to bay at the crowd and they loved it. He raised his heavily tattooed arms in the air and proceeded to bounce them once fully extended. He wanted to see the crowd jump and even way at the back where we were; we started to leap to the beat.

Fort Hoxton was in full effect and all three of us embraced in a tight trinity, jumping up and down just as the crescendo bass riff kicked in.

'I love this one!' screamed Jo: 'Tuuuuuune!'

Kate and I didn't know the words, but it wasn't hard to sing along to the catchy chorus: *'Nothing beside remains. Round the decay!'*

I can hear it in my head now. It was pretty good to be fair and the two singers would take it in turns to shout the two halves of the chorus, whilst the other pulled off some frenetic dance moves.

By this time, there were feet up in the air at the front!

Five, maybe six kids all being pulled down by the burly and surly security men at the very front by the railings. The tall skinny vocalist then started to climb up the ornate, almost Grecian set to the left side of the stage.

It was a permanent set, with stark white columns and green creeping ivy, like something out of the *I Claudius* film and most out of keeping with the venue.

Security was then trying to get the vocalist down and the mob started soliciting him to plunge into their mass of sweaty outstretched arms. Almost a test of faith on his part, but one that he didn't look unduly phased by...

Anyway the mentalist only went and did it and dropped backwards into the raging horde below. He was only about four of five feet above them, but it did look good and he even seemed to fall in time with the climatic beat at the end of the song; a timing that was not lost on the crowd, which then erupted in delight.

Jo voiced her excitement at the spectacle and Kate and I just laughed. It was turning into quite a show!

We were all quite well oiled by now and Jo, who is 'perpetually available', started to dance next to some poor unsuspecting teenager. He must have thought it was like dancing with one of his mum's friends!

Kate turned to me and shouted into her cupped amplifying hand. 'I'm so glad that I don't have to do this still!'

I nodded as I watched Jo playing with this 'kid', like a cat with a new toy mouse.

She danced up close to him, and then bounced away in time with the music, offering a curled index finger that said 'come get me, not so big boy'.

The poor child looked bemused.

Jo's almost 40; she looks good for her years, but must have been double his age at least. It was funny to watch and yet at the same time, a little depressing...

'She's all mouth is Jo,' I shouted towards Kate, trying not to spill my drink as the mass of clammy adolescents crossed into my personal space: 'If he actually started dancing back with her, I think she'd be out of her comfort zone. A rabbit in headlights and that's probably why she's still single.'

With that, the house lights went up, so for an instant, everyone in the room could see exactly who or *what* was in front of them and then they faded back down again.

Whilst we'd been watching Jo cavorting, the band was of course cracking on in the background and having seen Jo in the cold light of day, as it were, the pubescent minor quickly scarpered off back to his spotty mates.

Kate and I pissed ourselves laughing and Jo returned, feigning a mortal wound to the heart. She could see the funny side of it too and I assume she'd not really intended to take it any further than a playful dance...

The band played silly buggers doing two encores. So much so that we picked up our bags and started going out, before they came back on again and we were then forced to stop in our tracks; the crowd roaring their constant appreciation.

When *Hoxton,* as the 'cool cats' apparently call them, finally did finish, it was a crush to get through the two sets of doors either side of the bar and then out into the main open reception area, with its tiny little merchandise stall.

There was just a sea of people.

Constantly being topped up by those streaming down from the two sets of side staircases leading from the seated balcony area, up above where we'd been dancing.

Naturally, we all got split up in the pushing and shoving of the throng and that was that...

My phone battery had all but gone, as I'd left too many apps running and I was too short to see above all the heads of the predominantly young male crowd.

So I ended up getting the last train - just!

Despite Kate's beef about the proposal, I think I'll run it by Beth and then just do it. You only live once and judging by my wacky dreams, I'm not sure how long that will be...

The train's pulling into St Pancs' now. Think I'll have to catch up with the girls at lunch to see if there was any other drunken gos'. Feeling better now, despite the typing!

10.40pm

Question Time's on in the background and they're talking about whether we as a nation, have any right to interfere in the Middle East again, despite so many young people still managing to go out there to fight for either side.

Stay well clear I think! Don't stir the hornets' nest.

On the panel it will be the pacifists vs the pragmatists, watched all the while by an auditorium of pessimists.

We all met up at lunch today, still looking a bit worse for wear. I almost told them about my dreams when we met last night, but I think that was the drink tempting me to commit social suicide.

It's still only Steve that knows.

Well, he and Folkestone police, but they don't count.

I do feel like I should have a second soundboard and probably a female perspective would be good too.

Maybe I'll speak to Beth about that and the proposal too. Trouble is, with her being in Aussie land, I never remember when to call her. I'll email her and set up a video call! Job for tomorrow then and another note to self - still need to buy that notepad by the way!

I picked up the paper on the way home.

ISIS is being accused of selling more treasures from the desecrated Nimrud site on the black market to fund their expansion, by who else, but O.J Johnston?

Looks like the writing's on the wall for his stance on the Middle East then and presume this will go down well with the Defence Department, so that they can ensure their annual budget increases.

Steve is coming over tomorrow night to stay. Maybe I should broach the whole moving in thing again, and see if we can't set up a meeting with a mortgage advisor.

I'm tired now after last night.

Laters x

Friday January 15th 2016 – 7.35am

Just checking in...

I must have the Friday feeling!! It's nearly the weekend and wine o'clock!

7.05pm

Steve's coming over shortly for takeaway, wine etc. So I doubt I'll be able to write anything tonight, as hopefully it won't just my soul I'll be laying bare!

Work was good today, must have been my jovial mood. First time this year I think I've felt happy there.

Maybe it's because I've not poured over the dreams in the last few days. I may not actually write it down, but I do think about them a lot. Always before I go to sleep for some reason. Maybe I'm subliminally trying to trick my brain to 'go back in' as it were, so I can get some more clues.

Oh well, maybe I can hope to preoccupy myself with something else tonight as I say...

And I booked a call with Beth for Sunday afternoon.

The notepad system works, even without an actual pad!

Wish me luck!

Saturday January 16th 2016 – 11.15am

Steve's gone to the shops to pick up breakfast and is going to cook for *me*, apparently! So now's a good opportunity to catch up on life's reflections in the mean time, until he returns laden with bags that is. Can't have him know I pour my every living thought into these pages: 'Why are you writing all this?' he'd say: 'Nobody writes that much in a diary' he'd protest.

Well I do. Well until the end of the month anyway, or until I get distracted onto something more sparkly and exciting.

We had a great chat last night reconfirming what we've learnt about my dream, what we've found on the internet to date and generally put the world to rights, including the dangers of fracking, which he's also been researching for yet another article.

Reuters had emailed him the brief the day after the job offer, so as to get him started on the report asap, but Steve had no idea about the subject or the pitfalls involved: 'What the frack is fucking?' was his not so eloquent response, after he skim read the briefing sheet.

We then talked about Steve's new job, his own Mabus research assignment and needless to say, he's very excited about the opportunity, bless him.

I brought up the subject about the mortgage advisor and he's going to see if anyone at The *Herald* can recommend a local contact, as I've no idea.

We're getting close now in more ways than one!

I suppose I should sound the landlord out about notice periods and then we should start looking for our first home!!!

Exciting times!

9.15pm

Absolute Power? Absolute fucking liberty!

Or not as the case may be…

I honestly can't believe it, it just beggars belief, there *is* no bloody liberty! There I said it. Well typed it, as I can't say it aloud. Why? Because diary, as it turns out, I don't know who may be listening to me, that's bloody well why…

Oh my days, I'm shaking, I'm still so mad!

I pay my taxes, I abide their laws and for well, what? Those unscrupulous, bloody bastards!!!

They, whoever "they" are, have stuck some sort of device in my flat, and I don't mean one of those stupid *Alexa* contraptions. I've only found one, so goodness only knows how many others there are dotted around...

I didn't think that anything could be more shocking than those dreams, but this just takes the biscuit!

What the hell do I do now?

Steve helped me change a light fitting that's been on the blink lately and inside the fitment that came away from the ceiling was a round metallic dot. It's the size of one of those small batteries you get in the old electronic Donkey Kong game, but with a little tail, like a tiny antennae.

'What the hell is this?' he asked, bending down from the ladder and passing me the device.

'How should I know?' I replied shrugging: 'What is it? Where'd you get it from?' I'd guessed that it'd broken off the light, hence the reason why it wasn't working properly.

'It was magnetised to the inside of the light fitting and...' Steve stopped himself short.

He climbed down the stepladder, and carefully placed the offending device delicately into my handbag.

'Oh help yourself.' I said muscling him aside, paranoid that he was after my diary.

He shot me a look.

A look I'd not seen before and it frightened me.

It was then the same routine as last time, at Seth's house. He took his index finger, touched it to his lips to imply 'hush' and then pointed to the door.

'What the hell are you doing you weirdo?' I questioned, as he crept to the door, carefully turning the latch, as if not wanting to wake a sleeping baby. He was white, like he'd seen a ghost. There was that look again, so I fell into line and followed him outside.

I stopped at the top of the communal stairs, but he continued on outside, so again I followed, expecting to find him outside the door.

This time he'd carried on walking out onto the main road and was looking back up at the three-story block of flats that we just vacated.

I jogged after him to catch up with his quickening pace: 'Will you please tell me what you're doing. Was I supposed to lock up and I assume I was meant to leave my bag right?'

'Do you know what that thing is?' he whispered.

'Eh? No and why are you whispering, what are we doing out in the road, in fact, move over there's a car coming now you loon.' I said, shoving him to one side to save his bacon.

'I've seen one of these before when I did some work experience at the *News of the World.* This sort of stuff was right up their street. It's a listening device!'

'Shut the front door!'

This was my immediate and somewhat stone-faced reaction to this otherwise ridiculous conclusion.

'Yep, someone has been listening to all we've been chatting about and more. And who's to say that it's the only one? They could be in every room, the communal areas and your car. There could be cameras in the shower and bugs in your bed – need I go on?'

'Don't be daft. I think you're over reacting slightly.' I tried to be a calming influence on the situation.

The tables had turned.

It now seemed to be Steve in a mild state of panic and it was *my* flat he found it in, not his: 'Why are you freaking out? It's my flat, it's nothing to do with you.'

He cupped my face in his soft warm hands: 'It has everything to do with me you silly sweet little flower. They are listening and have me on tape talking about a myriad of conspiracy shit including my first assignment for *Reuters* and I haven't even started working there yet. What if this all blows up and I screw up my chance to work there? What if I get indicted for slander? That's Journalism 101!'

‘What if what blows up? We’ve done nothing wrong. No crime has been committed; nobody’s hurt and why am I able to stay calm? This is my problem, in my flat. In fact, it may be old. It may be something left from years ago? Cold War era? It’s not *my* flat after all, who knows it’s history.’

‘It looks new to me. It’s too small, too refined to be an old model. The previous models are quite cumbersome in comparison. Great. I’m going to get implicated in this mess. I don’t need this!’ he then reeled away in visible distress. Almost verging on a stroppy flounce.

I then grabbed him by the arm and stabbed my finger into his lapel to shake him up: ‘Er, excuse me Mr Solidarity? Partners? What exactly have *I* got you into?’

‘You still don’t get it do you?’ the tone of his voice incredulous: ‘I don’t know why I didn’t think of it before, but I’m guessing that all of our internet searches for conspiracies, New World Order, Nostradamus, Mabus, ISIS etc, etc, etc have hoisted every red friggin’ flag on GCHQ’s watch list and someone is suddenly taking an interest in what we’re doing. Particularly as we might be onto something! And you had to get onto the pissing police about it too didn’t you! Why’d you have to do that?’

I laughed out loud and as the laugh petered out it turned to a nervous laugh, as I slowly realised that good old laid back Steve was actually being really, really serious for once in his life: ‘But that’s all stuff off *Spooks* on the tele. It’s just for show right, surely they don’t actually *do* that in real life?’

‘Well for one, you live in a rented flat, so ‘they’ may not actually know who lives there, as you can’t trust the electoral role or the tax office records. None of the databases sync or talk to each other and it’s too big a job to holistically integrate everything, so they just keep patching up and bolting on new systems. So I presume they instructed boots on the ground to see who exactly has been watching ISIS videos on *YouTube* and searching for Ray Mabus. You could be the next Muslim schoolgirl about to abscond to Syria for all they know.’

Silence fell as we both contemplated what we’d found: ‘Why were you in my handbag?’

‘I was looking for a pad and pen to write ‘go outside’, but couldn’t see one. Why does nobody use pen and paper anymore?’ he smiled kindly, trying to reassure me.

‘So do you think this is the police then? They do know me, my address and about my dreams after all. Also if they’re listening, they’ll *now* know about the Mabus reference on the phone in my dream, which *will* be news to them?’

‘I don’t know. Not sure if MI5 has the manpower to go breaking in and planting bugs in this day and age, or if they do sub it out to the local police, or even a third party. *Rentokil* I guess.’ he mumbled under his breath.

‘So are we allowed back in? Do you think there’ll be more?’ I asked tentatively, slowly shepherding him back towards the flat.

‘Well we’re going to have to go back in now, as it looks a bit dodge to suddenly both vacate like that, but you’ll need to act normal. Well as normal as a neurotic, motor mouthed feminist nut job can be.’ he said smiling and gently gripping my hand.

‘My life just goes from one mental thing to another. Wow, me bugged? Bugger me! Looks like the diary will be going a bit longer then.’

‘What diary?’

‘Eh? Oh nothing, I said diarrhoea. Yes, awful tummy, I’ll spare you the details.’ I pulled a face and could feel myself sinking on my feet: ‘Anyway, must be all this excitement!’

‘I don’t think it’s something to be proud of babes. We could be in danger. There may be some dark forces that think we’re onto something above our pay grade?’

‘I’m not aware that I *am* onto anything and as I say, we’ve done nothing wrong. Yes I’ve been on a few dodgy Internet sites, but who hasn’t right? I’m not selling arms or sex slaves on the Dark Net and me innocently searching for ISIS doesn’t necessarily mean that I’m going to be the next Jihadi Joan.’

‘Right, let’s get back in there then. They’re probably already suspicious that we might be onto the fact that they’re onto us.’ he said, quickening his pace.

‘But if what you’re saying is true, it’s the fact that we’re onto them, that has resulted in them getting onto us in the first place. And now that we know they’re onto us, for us being onto them, isn’t it fair that we just hand the device back to them and admit that we *are* onto them being onto us for being onto them in the first place?’

‘Piss taker!’ he said, fiercely holding back a slight grin.

We walked back to the flat and I wasn’t sure why I wasn’t more paranoid or angry at the time. It was as if I *was* excited. Nothing like this ever happens to me and I was, well slightly flattered.

Steve strode ahead and turned just before the entrance door: ‘Normal ok?’ he demanded, pointing to his temple.

I nodded in acquiescence.

Once inside he asked in an overtly posh tone, well posh for him anyway: ‘Cup of tea my love?’

‘Oh, yes please darling, that would be super. Thank you for asking. Most obliged kind sir.’

He shot me *the* look again, which made me laugh.

Steve seemed to be looking around the flat, as if he’d lost his car keys, but I knew what he was up to.

Peering inside table lamps, under the edges of tables, under the sofa, but to no avail. Inside the kitchen cupboards, behind the picture frames on the walls and on the window ledges, the deep search went on.

Yet still nothing.

He stood in the middle of the room, hands on hips. ‘This place could do with a good sweep.’ he muttered to himself absentmindedly.

‘Yeah, subtle!’ I said, shrugging at him.

This situation was just too bizarre. I’m a prisoner in my own home, unable to speak my mind for fear of being arrested, but for *what* exactly, I’m yet to comprehend.

I’m unable to get undressed, for fear of being spied upon, so I opened the notes app on my phone and typed in a message for Steve: *‘We can go to yours/out for dinner/pub to talk???’*

He looked at me thoughtfully, grabbed the phone and typed underneath: *'Mine may not be safe either...??!! If they know who u r, they'll go on your Facebook and c me as your partner... Pub!'*

I nodded and absentmindedly picked up my handbag and keys: 'Shall we go to *The Chambers* for a quick one instead? Turn the kettle off, this one's on me darling.'

We drove in silence to *The Chambers*, a half pub and half coffee shop; as I knew he'd need a pint - or a brandy, and I just really fancied a high fat, high caffeine cappuccino.

We were too scared to talk in the car, apart from the odd: 'No, left here darling.' from him, for added effect of our supposed Middle England normality.

Once inside, we were both able to finally physically relax.

We made our orders and slumped in the tatty brown Chesterfield sofa in the window: 'It'll be interesting to see if we're being watched too. We can see from here.' said Steve, not so subtlety craning his neck into the bay window and mentally noting each parked car and van, so that he could spot any changes.

'Ok Poirot,' sipping noisily from my frothy coffee: 'So now what? We can't just go on pretending to be normal. I don't do normal; it's doing my head in already. It's like living in *Ever Decreasing Circles* and that's how I feel my life is spiralling right now. I want to be able to prance around in my giraffe onesie, listening to Aha and not have to worry about being watched or judged.'

'Strictly bedroom eh? Do you think you'll finish your onesie routine and Len Goodman will dive out of the wardrobe with a big "7" for you?'

'Not that sort of judge you prize plum! I just mean that I want to do what I want, when I want and not feel like I'm living back with my parents. The sooner we move out the better! That place is starting to give me the creeps now.'

'Blimey! Of course, that was them wasn't it! They used and abused my loo didn't they!' slapping my forehead in a brilliant realisation.

‘What? How you figure that one out?’ asked Steve, supping his pint of stout, leaving a white froth on the end of his nose.

‘The loo roll. That’s how! I told you it was on its last legs.’

‘You *accused* me of leaving it on its last legs, you didn’t just tell me. I assured you that it wasn’t me.’ he defended, hands raised with palms showing, as if caught red handed by the local Sherriff.

‘So it’s not an old bug then. It’s brand frickin’ new as of...I guess...last Sunday when we were both out.’

A similar look of realisation hit Steve’s face. He nodded slowly and checked the bay window again.

The blue *Meganne* had gone.

I pondered the situation, rapidly trying to compute exactly what we could be implicated in and why Steve was so worried: ‘Last Sunday. Ok, so they’ve not heard a lot then. In fact I’ve only been there last night and this morning, so everything they know is really what we discussed last night.’

‘Which was pretty much everything. My report, my job, your dreams, our plans to move. Anything else?’ he sighed: ‘Who’s to say my place isn’t rigged too?’

A feeling of helplessness now overtook the original excitement, as the enormity of MI5 snooping in on me finally took hold: ‘Well if they *are* listening, at least they know I’m not going to abscond to Syria.’

Steve seemed to be continually distracted.

A white van had pulled up in the spare space; two men had got out and were loitering. One of them was on his phone, the other touching a Bluetooth device in his ear and muttering to himself in what looked like hushed tones.

Steve looked widely at me and rolled his eyes towards them, directing my gaze, in a less than subtle movement.

‘For goodness sake, will you just chill out. They’re just a couple of plumbers, or something.’

‘Ah, that’s what they’re supposed to look like. Good aren’t they!’ he said raising his phone in selfie camera mode, so as to see the live footage unfolding behind him.

Steve quickly buried his phone between his legs: 'Hold up, they're coming over. Just pretend I told you a funny joke and laugh, but make it sound real right.'

'Yeah, as if. That's funny enough on its own Steve.'

The men both strode in, heads facing forward, seemingly disinterested in us: 'Watcha Trace, two teas please luv and the pot of sugar.' said the shorter of the two men. His large hands and his black trainers were all speckled with white paint.

'See, they *are* just a couple of decorators for goodness sake. Will you please just stop now.' I said pulling his shoulder around to stop Steve leaning back out into the bay for his next sortie.

'There's a black car out there now.' he reported.

'Oh really?' I whispered back, leaning in towards him: 'Is it a black *Sedan*, tinted windows and does the license plate read *FED5 R U5*? Grow up!'

'They might say FED UP', he replied shifting in his seat: 'They'll have been tracking your IP address too you realise. So anything you search for now will be monitored. And your mobile. Calls and searches will be tapped. The house phone, emails, new and historical will all be scrutinised, your post will be pre-vetted at the Mail Centre. It's all compromised!'

'My God you sound like Jack Bauer. Tell you what, I'll buy a SIM only contract, just get £10 credit a month until this all blows over.' I suggested, downing the last of my drink.

'Yes ok good, I'll do the same and we'll have just one number in each phone - each others.'

As he muttered those words my mind immediately shot back to my dream.

Just one number on a phone!

I remember thinking who the hell has just one number on their phone and here we are talking about it. I may as well just go and save his number under 'Mabus' as a code name now shall I? This is getting too weird now and my emotions were up and down like a jack in a box.

'The black car's gone now.' Steve updated me.

I ignored him and snapped my biscotti in two, which seemed to make him jump he was so on edge: 'Half?'

‘No ta. You know we can pick up the SIM cards from the supermarket. Let’s do it now and then I can check up on you tonight by text. Act normal on the text though just in case.’ He said forthrightly.

‘You not staying over with me then?’ shocked to hear that he was planning to leave me to fend for myself within the infestation. Fend off the Feds.

‘I need to do some research on this Mabus fella. Nah, they don’t scare me. I’m gonna take the establishment down and Mabus too if I have to. If it’s all set to kick off when he dies, society needs to make sure that he’s wrapped in cotton picking cotton wool! Pop him in a bunker and close the blast doors, as there’ll be *nothing* to do in Denver if he’s dead!’

If Mabus’ survival is key to stopping the impending global carnage, then surely the less people that know about it, the better. That’s how “Above Top Secret” works I guess. A need to know basis and the populous don’t need to know!

‘So plastering a story about him across the news wires is going to help his safety how exactly?’

‘It’s a test. A trap. Let’s see if he suddenly stands down or something and then we’ll really know if we’re onto something and that he *is* the known catalyst for catastrophe.’ he said rubbing his hands together, like a newshound with a sniff of the scent.

On that note, I made my excuses to powder my nose and as I closed the toilet door behind me, I rummaged through my bag for my lippy and found a little metal disc with a tail...

I shut my eyes and slowly looked to the ceiling in anguish! ‘Super-friggin-duper.’ I sighed, as I dropped the bloody bug into the toilet and flushed it away.

So much for privacy and it was a boring one-sided conversation anyway.

I popped my head out of the door and shouted across the busy room: ‘STEVE!’

He looked up, the final bit of froth from his pint still sat on his stupid nose.

‘We’re gonna have company!’

Sunday January 17th 2016 – 9.40am

Steve did stay over in the end, but he was being strange and rather distant, like he had stuff on his mind. He didn't say as much, but when we watched a soppy Rom Com about the end of the world, I think he enjoyed the escapism of it, despite the rather raw subject matter.

Anyway, he's gone to do his research now and is planning to do it in a coffee shop, using *their* wifi and *their* IP address according to his text, which just came through to my new SIM, which is in my clunky old *Nokia* handset. It came up simply as the contact MABUS.

Well I couldn't resist could I?

Going to catch up on chores today. Thrilling for a diary I know, so I'll spare the detail of micro home economics.

3.00pm

I'm sitting at the back of my local coffee shop. Walked here in case I was followed and sat at the back so I could observe everyone coming and going - Steve will be so proud! Oh and I've video called Beth from here too.

I've known her since we were five and although there are miles between us, we have a kinship that transcends both space and time – yuck – that was a bit pukey!

I told her about my plans to propose and she reacted just as I'd hoped. She screamed at the top of her voice and then went quiet: 'I have two words for you girl.' her adopted Australian twang was even more noticeable since I last spoke to her before Christmas time: 'HEN NIGHT!!!!'

I laughed out loud, drawing attention from those sitting not so close by: 'Yeah as if you'll come over.'

'Too right I will mate. If you can stage it so it's say two, three weeks before the wedding, I'll take a long trip over and bring my 'L' plates and my best Ascot hat.'

I never expected this of her. We've not seen each other for must be eight years or so. It was now my turn to scream, which produced several ironic tuts from the dissenting division of yummy mummies, supervising their equally noisy offspring.

'Seriously!?! Wow, yes of course, I'll sort that out for you. In fact, I think I'll organise my own hen night to ensure it.'

'Control freak! You got a Gantt chart running already Soph?' she teased.

'Maybe...'

She knew me too well and if only she'd been living here, she'd be the only one I'd fully entrust with the duty of Maid of Honour.

'Listen Beth, I need to run something by you. Make sure you're sitting down, please don't laugh or tell me that I'm crackers, as you can be sure as hell that I already know it...'

I proceeded to quietly tell her. Chapter and verse about both dreams, the research, the names, the phones, the small little linkages that we had spotted, the flashbacks that I had to the dreams and lastly, that the walls do in fact have ears.

Beth sat there visibly aghast and listened.

She listened intently like I'd not known or thought she was capable of. I normally can't shut her up: 'You still there?' I asked at one point, even though I could obviously see her.

'Yes Sophia, I'm just listening. Glad you asked me to sit down! You couldn't quite make this up!'

'Quite! This is not for repeating right! Not for email, not for text, not for friends, not for family, not for FaceyB! Not until I can work out exactly what's going on. I'm living in a state of paranoia now, fuelled mainly by my fella, but I now understand the gravity of the situation. I fear the Police, the Establishment have gone to a lot of trouble to bury my fears about my first dream in mysticism and conjecture and it now turns out that ironically my worst nightmare *is* in fact, my worst nightmare!'

'Yes Sophia.' she replied. The pleasantries had gone. No 'Soph' anymore. No jovial 'mates' at the end of her replies.

Was my story really that mad? This is exactly what I'd been dreading - social suicide!

I could envisage my friends dropping off one by one, as each either saw me as a loon and a liability, or not wanting to associate with me for fear of being implicated by default.

We finished up and I'm just about to head for home - not that it feels that homely anymore!

10.50pm

I'm ready for bed and just received a text on my 'SIM' phone. Only one contact in there, so who else could it be, except a random and ever hopeful robotic PPI caller?

The text not so simply read:

'*I've swept my apartment and no sign of dust mites here! Your allergy may be better suited to staying at mine? Call me from work tomorrow on my work phone x*'

The secret spy in all of us has started to manifest in Steve more overtly than some.

I may have sat surreptitiously at the back of the coffee shop, but I'm certainly not resorting to texting in code!

Ok, so I do have a phone with just one number saved on it – seems pretty spooky to me I guess.

I'm thinking of moving out to Steve's tomorrow and remind him to get onto a Mortgage Advisor pronto! Or at least, we both give a month's notice on our respective flats and rent together in a 'clean' property with no sweeping or pest control required.

Even if it's just for six months, what Steve doesn't know is that by the end of that time we should; assuming he says 'yes', be engaged to be married!

Yip yip!

Monday January 18th 2016 – 11.15am

What no morning entry Soph? To be honest I was too busy reading the paper.

Russia is provoking the NATO defences again, with a bomber almost colliding with a US plane over the Black Sea. And with the UN and US either unable or unwilling to stand up to them, their posturing continues to be a distraction from the ever-disturbing news from the Middle East.

Anyway, I just called Steve and I'm only bloody moving into his place - tonight!

He's finally officially accepted the job at *Reuters*, despite starting to work on a brief already and so handed in his notice, despite protests from his current boss.

And he's even booked an appointment with a Mortgage Advisor without me reminding him!

I told him that I don't feel safe at mine and unless there are other bugs in the flat, it will be pretty obvious to the listeners the reasons as to why the flat has suddenly gone quiet.

I'm scared they'll come for me at the dead of night. Scoop me into a side door of a van, hessian hood pulled tightly over my head and then water-board me until I promise not to reveal my revelations about Mabus, Denver's covert cave system or the prelude to a prophetic Armageddon currently counting down in Israel.

On the other hand, I wouldn't expect a safe house from the powers that be - Just a bullet behind my ear probably. Cut backs and simply silenced by those insidious insiders, who do not speak aloud themselves.

So I may be a little melodramatic, but seriously, I don't know what's going to happen next.

I feel a little out of control.

At least Steve and I are in it together; if I were on my own, I'd have given myself up already.

'Don't be absurd,' I keep telling myself. I've done nothing wrong! I didn't ask to have that stupid dream and that's exactly what it could yet turn out to be – just a lousy dream after all and not an Earth shattering prediction of Earth's shattering.

I'm just so confused, these seemingly constant references to Mabus must be more than just coincidence and here I am creeping around, forced out of my own home because of a man who may, or may not be part of the US hierarchy.

Who am I kidding; life's just a series of coincidences and disappointments right?

Maybe I'm just reading into things way too much...?

10.35pm

I am hiding! Literally...

I'm hiding in Steve's bathroom, sat on the toilet seat in my dressing gown and writing my diary, as I don't want him to know that I've one on the go.

A diary that is!

I'm also *in* hiding from dark forces and I was wrong.

Not a few hours ago, I was postulating as to whether I was mad, paranoid, deluded or just all three. Turns out someone *has* been watching us, but maybe not for the reasons that we first thought…

Steve went out to lunch for a walk around West Cliff Gardens, as he normally does. He walked up to the amphitheatre at the bottom of the zigzag path and sat down to eat his packed lunch.

He normally sits alone, lots of people passing by, but not many choose to sit on the bare grassed areas on the stepped seating around the amphitheatre. Particularly now the snow's melted and left a glistening surface in its place.

Old habits die hard I guess and this habitual process may have been his undoing.

Steve sat, minding his own business, looking out to sea through the semi circle of white Grecian-esque pillars behind the 'stage' area of the amphitheatre.

There was a disturbance in the water.

Something was blocking the lapping tide, so forming a crescent shaped area of tranquil water with a lip of foaming ripple protecting its border against the incoming tide. Suddenly there was a crash of waves in this otherwise still section of sea.

A dolphin! It wasn't the first time he'd seen one off the Folkestone coastline and presumably wouldn't be the last, but its playfulness distracted him enough from noticing the two people sitting down either side of him.

At first he thought it odd that they should sit with him, considering the amount of other grassy steps they could've sat on, let alone how close they both chose to sit next to him.

They almost looked like a group of friends, a threesome enjoying their lunch together.

And this was exactly how it was supposed to look.

The elder gentleman on his left was dressed in a dark suit, beige overcoat and dark sunglasses on an otherwise cloudy day. His greasy thinning grey hair glinted in the sunlight and the pale complexion to his long, drawn face was clean-shaven, so further accentuating his sunken eyes and high cheekbones.

He tightly gripped a manila file in his begloved hand. The man to his right was heavier set. Younger, also dressed in a suit and equally prone to sunlight as his colleague. His hair was thick brown, which added to his bear-like appearance. Behind his left ear was a curled wire disappearing off into the collar of his dark overcoat.

'A nice spot you enjoy here Mr Cartwright.' said the slighter man to his left.

Steve took a double take at the man and then eyed up his adversary to his right, before looking left once again. He tried to stand, but was 'restrained' by the heavy man; his strong left paw outstretched and wrapped around the front of his stomach, like a seatbelt with no give.

'Finished your lunch so soon? You usually stay for an average of five or six minutes more on a clear day like today Mr Cartwright.'

Despite the harness that he now found himself temporarily wearing, it was the use of his surname that unnerved Steve more, coupled with the fact that the older man seemed to know his lunchtime movements better than he did.

'What? What do you want?' stuttered Steve, gripping the wrist of the goon next to him, trying and failing to release his burly limb.

'It's not so much what *we* can do for you Mr Cartwright, but what *you* are willing to do for our country.'

The older man's accent was American and his irony was not lost on Steve.

The more he spoke, the more Steve's attuned ear recognised the East coast twang and the more he spoke, the more Steve wanted out of this situation.

Thank Christ he was in public. Whoever these people were and however much they wanted him to remain seated, at least they'd not accosted him in a back alley somewhere.

'I'm fairly easy going,' said Steve with a false calm: 'I'm sure we can come to some sort of arrangement, you know?'

Steve then described to me how it suddenly dawned on him, who these people might be and how his greatest fears were now starting to unfurl in front of him.

'An arrangement sounds quite palatable Mr Cartwright. As palatable, say as your usual ham, tomato and cheese sandwich for example.'

Steve looked at his empty wrapper: 'How did you?'

Steve quickly gathered that his sweep of his flat might not actually have been as thorough as he perhaps should have carried out and it was not just sounds that 'they' were listening to. A full heads up display of exactly what he was prepping for his lunch was also available!

'Let's cut to the chase Mr Cartwright,' the older man patting his right hand on Steve's left knee somewhat jovially, given the situation: 'We all know why we're here today, so let's quit the niceties, as I'm sure your impending print deadline looms even larger than my friend Mr Channing here.'

Steve looked again to his right, to see a wry half smile on Mr Channing's pursed lips.

They curled up ever so slightly, so as not to afford a full smile or any evidence of emotion, yet there was enough of a movement to prove Channing took great pleasure in his work.

Mr Channing's nose looked to have suffered a number of breakages in the past and made a backstreet bare-knuckle boxer's sorry schnoz look positively perfect.

The older man continued: 'My name's Lennox and you've got something that you'll be able to help me with.'

Steve's mind scurried back and forward, frantically filtering through filing cabinets of information stored away within the 'easy access' and 'deep thought' libraries of his brain. His head spun as he racked his cranium for clues as to what exactly these people could want.

Could it be a mistake? Well they knew who he is, where he lives, what he eats for lunch, where he eats it and how long he tends to chew for. So perhaps they've been watching for longer than the relatively short period of our recent escapades.

The reason for the meeting still eluded him, other than the obvious one surrounding the set of dreams and Police visit.

'Let me make this easy for you Mr Cartwright,' sighed Lennox, leaning into Steve's left ear: 'Shall we go for a walk?'

'Oh, not sure I fancy a walk. It might bring on heartburn you know.' protested Steve, but with that his torso was whisked up from underneath him. His legs followed and floundered for a footing on the floor below, as Channing lifted his comparatively skinny frame with just one hydraulic arm.

Lennox was apparently quite tactile and overtly brushed the damp grass off the back of Steve's coat almost touching below his waistband, which threw Steve off kilter even more.

He'd heard of good cop, bad cop routine, but never the bad cop, bent cop version!

'A lovely day for a walk, don't you think Mr Cartwright? Perhaps we'll walk towards your office, so you've easy access for your return to work, once we're finished.'

Steve relaxed slightly after hearing that their intention was in fact to safely deposit him back at the *Herald* and not off the top of the Leas Lift for example, in some 'tragic accident'.

The trio continued to walk the coastal path, heading east, back towards the old harbour and access to the town centre via the Creative Quarter and the Old High Street.

Steve considered running, but thought this futile, seeing as they knew everything about him.

He considered asking questions, but again he was indifferent to this idea, pre-judging their silent responses.

No, the power was definitely in their hands. They held the cards, whatever those cards were, and he hoped for a deal to be struck rather than just folding – especially seeing as they'd just upped the ante.

'Mr Cartwright, you've stumbled across some information. This information seems to be highly classified and we're not entirely sure where you got this from with your contacts in the press. We have knowledge of a new venture that you will shortly be embarking on in London and an unsolicited assignment that you're considering writing. I strongly suggest that this assignment should be viewed as non-viable, both from the point of view of potential liable litigation from the main protagonist of your story, a certain General Mabus - not the best way to get off in a new job Mr Cartwright. Then there's also the safety of Miss Sinclair to consider in all of this.'

'Are you threatening me and my girlfriend?' hissed Steve under his breath, his right arm suppressed from rising by the ever-alert Channing.

Lennox didn't break step, didn't seem annoyed by Steve's subordinate challenge or swayed in any way: 'What I'm doing Mr Cartwright is stating facts. Facts of life and a laying out a series of hoops that I fully expect you to jump through with such vigour that you'll have wished you'd joined the circus - such will be your proficiency at diving through them.'

Channing laughed heartily which made Steve physically jump: 'Christ, it speaks! Sort of...' he said pushing down on Channing's vice like grip that had formed on his right forearm.

'Correct assertion. My friend is a man of very few words Mr Cartwright.'

'You're telling me!' said Steve, still not so subtly fighting for his freedom until Channing finally relinquished his grasp, obviously bored of the feeble fight being put up by poor Steve.

'My friend is simply here to aid my delivery. Listen Mr Cartwright, I'm not threatening you; I'm simply explaining how things are going to be and how they will play out. You will take your new cover job as planned, but your first assignment will be set by us, not by your misguided agenda.'

Steve was stunned silent.

‘Cover job? What the hell are he talking about?’ asked Steve confused and staring into the eyes of the older man.

Lennox placed his hand on Steve’s shoulder, his tone soft and relaxed: ‘You’ve been chosen, somewhat fast-tracked for my liking, but that comes from above me.’

‘Chosen? For what exactly? Talk sense man, what are you talking about?’ Steve’s voice raised, more animated, a slight sense of worry detectable, as you would expect.

‘Easy Sir.’ breathed Channing in a deep, dulcet tone, re-affirming his hold on Steve’s arm.

‘Oh for goodness sake Mr Cartwright. We’ve been monitoring your research. It seems that you’ve quite the penchant for conspiracy theory, but the specific nature and uncanny sequence of your searches has flagged your *potential*, more so than you being a threat to us. You have recently got a new job yes?’

‘Yes...’ said Steve slowly, suddenly aware that they must have overheard him talking about it via the listening device.

‘And you found this job in which agency, newspaper or website?’ Lennox questioned, his eyes widening in expectation of the answer.

‘Well funnily enough I overheard this chap in the pub and...’ Steve’s words tailed off as he realised that this fateful opportunity may not have been as lucky as he’d first thought: ‘A friggin’ American too…’ he nodded, as it finally dawned on him.

‘Ah congratulations, that was lucky for you Mr Cartwright. Right place, right time and all of that, eh?’

Steve eyed him once again, looking closer at the file in Lennox’s hand for the first time. All that was written on its cover were the words, ‘*Project Mabus*’.

His eyes widened, like a rabbit’s in headlights: ‘Who are you?’ he demanded.

‘We’re here for help Mr Cartwright. Your help. You really think you’ll go from a year at a provincial newspaper to working for the foremost news agency in the world quite so easily?’ he quipped curtly.

‘Well, I presumed it was the quality of my work that got me through.’ replied Steve, asserting himself and unhappy that Lennox could be quite so condescending about his big break.

‘Mr Cartwright, really? What you don’t know is that you were in fact, the only applicant for that job. And what *Reuters* also hasn’t told you yet, is what your first assignment will actually be. Inside this folder is everything you need to know. Read it. Absorb it and return to this very spot tomorrow morning, 06.00 hours please, sharp.’

‘But my girlfriend is coming over tonight, she’s moving in you see, we’ll be busy unpacking and stuff.’

‘May I suggest Mr Cartwright, you get your Goddamned priorities in order. Instruct Miss Sinclair to stay in her apartment and please assure her that the ‘dust mites’ as you so affectionately call them, will be gone by the morning. You have some important homework to attend to this evening that will take precedence over your housework and her sorting through piles of junk.’

Junk I ask you! The bare face cheek!

Well suffice to say this freaked Steve out no end.

What he now guesses as being the CIA in Folkestone, and they’re following his Internet habits.

It turns out his history had enough radical red flags to create an interest and even put him on the No Fly List, before he’d even started searching for Nostradamus, Mabus et al.

Shit a brick, as Steve would say.

OMG, I’m starting to lose the feeling in my legs sitting down on this plastic toilet seat for so long.

So basically Steve went back to work, white as a sheet and quiet as a mouse.

He kept his head down. Did what he had to do, stashed the envelope into his bag, not wanting to even open it until he got to the sanctity of his flat, not that it seems to be much of a secure shelter after all...

I came over anyway, but he text me on my Mabus phone; which may not even be secure either, to say not to bring my stuff after all and he’d explain when I got here.

Not sure how I'm to trust that the bugs and devices will be gone by the morning, maybe they'll leave a calling card?

I'm also not sure I can trust Steve, as he has totally clammed up, especially about Operation Mabus, I mean what the hell?!?

We went to the pub for some privacy and he explained his eventful afternoon, but he'll still not share the contents of the envelope.

He's reading it now and basically told me in no uncertain terms that I can stay if I want, but he has some reading to do – on his own and for my own sake, I can not know its contents!

Believe me diary; short of beating the information out of him, I've tried every trick in the book. Pleading, fluttering of eyelashes, a hissy fit and even an overtly melodramatic apology and the promise of full on sexual sex!

Damn this kid is hard to crack.

They have proper turned him, those Yanks!

Other than what I know above, I know no more.

Were they actually CIA? How long have they been tracking him or us? Why have they gone to such lengths to get him a job? Why have they warned him off the Mabus assignment? What was it he has stumbled on exactly and what does this have to do with him?

He's no spook in the making that's for sure!

Or thinking about it. Is he?

He's level headed and fairly calm under pressure. Worldly wise with a good general knowledge and research is *totally* his thing. He's got a massively inquisitive mind and speaks Americanese, or understands their lingo anyway.

Blimey, has he really been co-opted into the CIA?

Steve, a spy?

Either way, I really need to get out of this pokey room before my legs totally cease up!

Tuesday January 19th 2016 – 7.45am

Ok, so I did stay over. The conversation was strained, the sex almost apologetic, our minds clearly on other things...

I tried to get information out of Steve about the contents of the envelope. He buffeted me at every turn, citing my safety as the main reason for not sharing.

This may be massively magnanimous, but it's totally not fair for a knowledge hungry jealous type like me.

It was my bloody dream, so why's he getting in on all the action?!?

He says he'll be out tonight – a likely story!

He also left at stupid o'clock this morning to go to this stupid meeting with the stupid CIA on the beach, so goodness only knows what that was all about.

I can but try, but fully expect him to not tell me.

I'll message him now and see:

'Dear Mabus...
You been swimming yet, as u forgot your trunks?!
Seriously what happened, you ok?
Can we talk later?
I Love you btw.'

Well let's see in some real time social experiment whether he comes back to me. I wonder if anyone else does this sort of stuff in their diary?

They must right?

Surely those who are vacuous enough to write how many calories they've burned, what they've drunk, eaten and who and what they've done at work certainly will. What Lily said to Lenny and what Hattie said to Henry...

Updates on celebrity culture, like the diary even cares!

I guess a diary only has the intellect of the author though. It doesn't know any different.

If I were to jot down my feelings on Nietzsche or Hawking, Kant or Sagan, Plato or Milton, would my diary be suitably impressed?

If you gaze long enough into an abyss, will your diary conclude that what doesn't kill you will only make you stronger? Ok, that was cheap. A Nietzsche aficionado I'm not.

Oh, my handbag just vibrated. Text from MABUS... *'I Know.'*

I know? I know what? I know I love you? I know I forgot my trunks? Oh for goodness sake, why does this have to be so friggin' hard?

'?? You know what...??' I replied immediately, fingers furious and no answer... in real time or otherwise.

9.15am

Just got into work, trains delayed, and still no reply. I do hope he's ok! It's fine, no news and all that...

8.25pm

Those canny buggers!

I did joke about the possibility of them leaving a calling card and whaddya know...

So, I return home to find everything in its right place, except a yellow *Post it Note* on the kitchen worktop with a short message and an '*x*' for a kiss written on it. Then placed next to the note was a lone quilted toilet roll:

'Sorry, had to go for a Jimmy! Riddle not Choo x'

Well nice to know the CIA has adopted our East End sense of humour and quilted too! Ambassador, you spoil us!

I still can't quite believe that my flat's been bugged, let alone de-bugged. How can I really be certain that I'm not still being watched, or my emails being read? Am I just supposed to let sleeping dogs lie and take their word for it?

The fact that I've simply been tracked and not been asked to 'come in' for questioning – can I assume that my dreams are about nothing significant at all?

Has all my worrying and research been for nout?

I need to sleep on this.

I feel so very tired.

Wednesday January 20th 2016 – 8.15am

Still no reply from Steve and he's not taking my calls, dammit!

Well, I'm going to do the next best thing and call his receptionist at work and ask to be put straight through to him. No officious secretary or receptionist will stand in my way!

11.15am

What the hell is going on? I'm in yet *another* toilet cubicle writing this bloody diary like some sort of paranoid obsessive. A ridiculous habit I feel is both odd and unclean, both in terms of my current location *and* how often I now type on this tablet.

It's taking over and I've bigger things to worry about now! But I've come this far and it does still help me to collect and make some sense of my thoughts.

I've just called Steve's office at the *Herald*, asked to be put through to him and they apologised and said that Steve no longer works there and he started a new job yesterday!

Yesterday? I repeat - What the hell is going on?

'What happened to his statutory four week notice period?' I demanded. I really gave the receptionist short shrift on reflection, which was a bit wicked considering she sounded like a lovely old dear, but HELLO?

'Yes madam I wondered the same, but apparently according to our group memo, he's been allowed special dispensation, due to unforeseen circumstances. Are you Sophia? He talks about you a lot. To be honest, I'd feared something terrible might have happened to you, dear.'

'Terrible to me, why do you say that?'

'Well the speed in which he left and the "unforeseen circumstances" scenario. We had a chap leave last year just like that; his wife was taken seriously ill and I guess I just put two and two together...'

'Yes, well it just so happens I'm still here, thanks.'

'But, if you didn't know Steve had left, where is he now?' she asked innocently.

'That my lovely is *the* question!'

I hung up.

Thursday January 21st 2016 – 9.45pm

I had nothing to write last night. Nothing left to give...

I ate alone, somehow managed to iron the bedding without scalding myself and stupidly checked the flat for bugs, such is my on-going paranoia!

I also spent half the night on my sofa pressing redial for Steve's phone.

No answer. Voicemail and not even his voice.

Should I be worried?

Confused more like!

What *is* the next logical step to take after being told your boyfriend, partner, or future husband (touch wood) is absent without leave?

So, it seems the next logical step was to call *Reuters*. Yet I don't know which office he's going to be working out of, as we never got that far into the conversation at the time.

There are multiple offices in London and I studiously called each one this morning, asking for him by name, but either he's so new that they've not got his details, or this is just another lie.

This is doing my tree in. I have two phone numbers for him, a personal email and Skype account. All are met with silence. I drove to his flat after getting back from work and his car was still there, his curtains both pulled shut. His neighbour said she hadn't seen or heard him today.

He likes his music loud, so that was the 'tell'. So that's it then. My detective skills pretty much end there.

I've text Seth to see if he's heard from him, to which he answered: '*No, why should I have?*'

So that's great, I've probably got him worried now, as I've not replied back to Seth as yet.

What do you say exactly?

'Your brother's gone AWOL with the CIA, but try not to worry yourself' Oh what do I do?

I very much doubt he'd go to Pam or Patrick in a time of need. He's only been under the radar for a day, maybe he's *not* in a time of need? Maybe he just needs more time...

I don't even have a key for his flat to see if his passport is still there – what's going on?

I feel like my world is breaking apart!

10.45pm

Just had a text from Seth: *'Mum and Dad haven't heard from him either and he's not answering his phones. What's going on Soph?'*

Well what do you text back? '*Oh he's been surfing some dark stuff on the net, flagging up danger signs along the way and been kidnapped by the CIA.'*

Yeah that would go down well and make me sound sane and the perfect future daughter/sister in law, wouldn't it!

Maybe I should report it to the police, but after my last visit, they might as well just laugh me out of reception.

I'll sleep on it.

Seems to be my stock phrase for when I don't know what the hell to do!

Friday January 22nd 2016 – 7.35am

Still no word. I should've beaten that envelope out of him - stupid woman!

Maybe I'll try all the *Reuters* offices again; another day may've given them more time to put his name on their system.

I don't even know which department or desk he works on though. Note to self, ask the next logical question, as you never know what might happen. Oh, and always get a key to your partner's place!

8.00pm

I *am* conscious that this diary is becoming more of a log now, rather than a true diary.

I've only been interested in one theme, rather than my holistic life, but to be fair, it has taken over my life and is slowly eating me away.

Ok, so in the spirit of diaries everywhere:

Work: Thrilling, thanks for asking...

Emotions: Scared. Shit scared, as I don't know where the love of my life is and I can't get hold of him. He could be in a ditch somewhere for all I know? Coated in concrete, hurled off Harrowdown Hill or "brushed" over Beachy Head?

The not knowing is the real killer here!

Dinner: I can't eat.

Booze: Yes please.

I've bought a few newspapers to read, as I figured that there might be a clue in the press as to where he's gone.

What if he *has* gone to work at *Reuters* already and they've sent him off somewhere straight away?

That's it, Jeez, I'm so stupid - the clue was written in here, by me days ago. Lennox said that everything Steve needed to know was in the envelope. Everything about his assignment or perhaps something bigger than that?

Maybe he had to leave early as he'd got a flight to catch! Maybe he hasn't got a phone signal or simply couldn't take his phone with him.

Ah, I'm just guessing, but what else do I have?

The newspapers...

10.45pm

Nothing. Nada. Neit.

Well plenty of news, views and opinions, but nothing that says in big bold letters 'STEVEN CARTWRIGHT IS HERE...' with a nice map and contact number for emergencies.

I even went through the small ads on the classified pages to see if there was a secret message in there.

Such a nerd!

Either the message was too subtle for me to notice, or I'm too clever, thinking that someone would be equally cunning to place an advert in there in the first place.

Watched too many old Hitchcock movies I think!

This is just getting ridiculous, so if I don't hear by the morning, I'm going to the police.

I've no more avenues *or* alleyways of enquiry left to search, let alone being at my wits end!

One minute I'm planning my proposal and now he's gone. I can't take this anguish, the pain of not knowing!

How must wives, husbands and children of soldiers feel when their loved one goes off to war? They don't really know if they'll come back in one piece, if at all, but at least they know *where* they are and their cause is just...

I'd *just* like to know where Steve is...

Saturday January 23rd 2016 – 9.00am

Right, I'm dressed and ready.

I'm ready to take that walk of shame to the police station. AGAIN....

I'd never been before and here I am, twice in a month. Not exactly how I imagined *my* New Year to start!

So I've tried all his phones to no avail this morning and I finally replied to Seth's text to say...well what can you say?

The truth...

'I've not heard from your brother for 4 or 5 days and last I heard he was fraternising with the CIA. Yes Seth, the CIA in Folkestone. Home of dolphins, earthquakes and now the CIA, as it turns out...'

No? Maybe not then.

But I did say that I've simply not heard from him for days and was going to the police this morning to report him as a missing person. The reply from Seth was short and sweet:

'We're on our way!'

6.00pm

I've made my excuses from Seth and his family and gone for a walk, as I'm tired, deflated and emotionally unstable.

I've left them in a nice family restaurant finishing the kid's left over ice cream and sorting the bill.

I spent the morning in an interview room and I feel like it's me that's the cause of all this turmoil.

I feel like I was quizzed like a common criminal.

Now, I'm sitting on a surprisingly comfortable wicker chair inside the *Dolphin* café, looking out to sea with a hot chocolate cupped in my hands. That is, when I'm not typing...

It's quite quiet for teatime here, despite the constant shrill cries of the gulls, but it's cold today. The bright blue winter's sky offers seaside walkers no protection from the chill and the sea breeze doesn't help. But that works in my favour, as I can have some peace and a chance to think things through logically and thoroughly.

It was nice to have company over an early dinner, to take my mind off things, but now I need to reflect on this morning.

Make some sort of sense from the day's events, even just for my own sanity.

I arrived at the police station on my own. It didn't look quite as bleak as before, now the snow has melted. The green open space to the right of the building brought colour to the otherwise monolithic structure.

Being a Saturday I was met, once again, by my old friend, the retired Juliet Bravo:

'Oh hello dear, do I know you?' she enquired innocently, the quiver of half recognition in her aged eye.

'Yes I was in here a few weeks back. The one with the dodgy dreams.'

'Oh yes. That's right, I heard all about those. We're all still here then. No big boom just yet then dear?'

Yeah, bet you did, nattering in the canteen, laughing over some poor soul who came in thinking she was the next Messiah, prophesying the end of the world. 'Still here,' she said to me knowingly, the cheeky old bint!

'No, not just yet, although I'm starting to wonder if *I'm* all there. Anyway I'd like to report a missing person please.'

It looks quite a nonchalant kind of statement when you write it out. Yet, given the fantastical nature of our preamble, saying it didn't actually feel that weird, for some reason.

I did feel crap on the inside. I never thought I'd have to report someone missing, let alone the love of my life and I assumed I was going about it in the right way...

'Oh I see,' said the old crone, taken aback by the sudden unpredictability of my second visit: 'Didn't see that coming, did you?' She laughed out loud, pleased with her quick, if not wholly inappropriate prophetic wit.

I decided to let her off the hook and play her at her own game. Well she was never going to out pun me!

'That's right; I never dreamt that the love of my life would go missing.'

She visibly caught her breath as the true situation became apparent to her – finally.

'The love of your life you say. We're a bit thin on the ground today, if you'd like to wait in this room, we won't be long dear.'

Now *this* is the déjà vu of the worst kind!

Oh, how I was glad to be back in such comfortable and familiar surroundings. The rusty old clock, the magazines for the masses, the messages of public warning, they were all still there, just with a little more dust. Oh, how we whiled away the time together, but this time I had company.

An older gentleman, about 65, I don't know, I'm awful with ages, particularly men.

He wore a thick and slightly beige tartan overcoat that looked a bit moth eaten. Then there was the obligatory flat cap, smart black shoes and thickset reading glasses.

Naturally he was engrossed in SAGA magazine, whilst the other protagonist in the room was also male.

Younger this time, 24 maybe 25 at a push. Short cropped blond hair with an equally short beard shaped around his face like a rider's chinstrap. He wore a white T-shirt publicising the 'second coming' of the band *Faith No More*, as well as dark grey leisure trousers and white, and I mean *white* trainers. No coat, which was odd considering the temperature and he was head down, playing on his mobile.

Apart from the odd cough, there was silence.

In the movies we would've all been conversing.

Up north, we would've at least said *hello* or acknowledged each other's existence.

But this is South East England.

We revel in silence and a mutual respect for each other's space and time.

Despite being last in, I was thankfully first out – much like Steve was at the local newspaper…

I was ushered into 'Interview Room 4'. A small enclosed space, with an equally small square dark wood table, two matching chairs and an old tape recorder built into the thick wooden plinth or dado rail that surrounded three sides of the dank, windowless room.

There was nothing else adorning the wall, no piped music, no waiting cup of tea and certainly no cold finger buffet.

More Tory cuts!

'DI Rees will be with you soon,' said the young PC who showed me to my seat.

Not five minutes passed by and a jovial looking chap strode in confidently. Not a day older than 45 (I'd hope), a good six foot and dark hair in a groomed and greased parting. Greying slightly at the temples, he was not unattractive, which on reflection, may be my prudish way of saying that for a 30 something like me, he was in fact quite hot...

His plain clothes belied his rank. Blue shirt buttoned up to the neck, dark blue jeans with a few scruffy parts around the pockets, old tatty *New Balance* running shoes and a security lanyard around his neck.

'Good morning Sophia, my name is Detective Inspector Rees and I'm going to be on your case today, as it were.'

His nod to humour and immediate impression of a mild manor were a welcome sight in what was otherwise a traumatic process. Rees' thick accent from the Welsh valleys also added a sense of soothing nature to the proceedings: 'Has anyone offered you a drink? Can I get you a drink my lovely?'

I was convinced that he obviously felt an instant and fatal attraction to me too. That's what diaries are for right?

An expansion of the truth?

I nodded and asked if they had cappuccino, which didn't seem too unreasonable. I wasn't exactly expecting chocolate shakes on top.

He laughed to himself: 'Unfortunately not presh. The good Mr Cameron would have us drink black tea, white tea, black coffee or white coffee. Austerity is as black and white as that these days, I'm afraid.'

I gave my order and he disappeared. In your own time, I thought, there's been no question as to whether *I'm* on the clock today... which I'm not, thanks for asking diary... but it's the principle of the point!

DI Rees popped his head around the door: 'Sugar, sugar?' chuckling to himself, which also sounded classically Welsh in its tone. I'm not convinced he was fully briefed as to why I was there and whether this sort of question was appropriate, but it did perversely put me further at ease.

Three minutes later, he was back and sat in his chair, comfortable in his own surroundings; both confident and strangely alluring.

'Is this thing on?' I asked, pointing to the old fashioned tape recorder.

'That old thing? God no. It's not worked since the turn of the century. Oh that sounded odd didn't it. I'm so used to referring to the turn of the century as 1900, not the Millennium. Anyway where was I?' shaking his head quickly as if to re-gather his thoughts.

I did hope that he wasn't one of these absent minded professor types that keep going off on rambling tangents…

Pot, kettle eh?

'You were discussing the latest in audio technologies at your disposal, despite the recent cuts.' I reminded him.

'And you're right. We don't need tapes you see, it's all hidden in the walls. Well you won't see, because it's all hidden in the walls, but you get where I'm going?'

I'm not sure I did.

And I'm not sure if it was a rhetorical question, but I nodded anyway, so as to keep him on track.

'Lovely, lovely. So Sophia Sinclair of Flat 4, Ellis House, Springvale Close, what brings you to my office?' he sat back expectantly, pristine notepad at the ready.

'Well, I wanted to report a missing person please.'

'Missing you say. How long has this person been missing and who might they be?'

I explained about how I'd not spoken to Steve since early Tuesday morning, I didn't choose to expand as to why he was up so early, or why I happened to be at his flat though.

The CIA and bugs didn't seem appropriate for the light-hearted pre-amble. I felt that he'd need to probe a little first, before I gave up my entire crazy story.

Plus I was intrigued to see how the process worked.

'I see, so just to confirm I will talk you through how the process is going to work. I will take down all Steve's personal details, which I assume you have to hand?'

I nodded again, pleased with the conversation's progress.

'So I will pop his details onto my computer and then circulate him as 'missing' on the Police National Computer. Once that flags up, any Officer in the country or internationally can contact me for further details. Hence being 'on your case' you see. Do you have any or all of the following information please, my lovely?

- Contact details of any friends or family.
- Places that Steve is known to frequent.
- Any medical conditions he may suffer from?
- Details of his financial accounts so we can see if he's been withdrawing money from any specific locations?
- Is he on any sort of benefits that he may still be claiming?
- Can you let us have some recent photographs of him for me to circulate?
- I will need some DNA from him, for example a toothbrush or a comb, both of which we can pick up from our search of his property.
- Do I have your consent to publish this in the media for an appeal, first locally and then on the wider stage?
- Lastly and most importantly, are you aware of any events that could be linked with his recent disappearance?'

Rees pushed his crib sheet towards me and continued: 'Now I must also point out, that many people that go missing have simply gone somewhere for self reflection, time on their own and may actually *want* to remain anonymous.'

I cut him off in his tracks: 'I don't think that's applicable in this case.'

'Oh you don't? How can you be so certain Miss Sinclair?' he asked, leaning in towards me.

'Well I was just about to move into his flat you see, well sort of and well, he just wouldn't ok!'

I was getting a little flustered and annoyed and remember thinking that the next thing Rees would throw at me, is that for all he knew, I may have murdered Steve and be using this as an ingenious cover story.

Luckily, he did not.

'I'm going to leave you with some forms to fill out for me with his details, some tick boxes to tick relating to his health and benefits status and if you have anything missing, not to worry; we can pick those up at his property.'

Rees scooped up the empty cups and vacated the room, leaving me alone with my thoughts and a four-page A4 white form. I'd heard of a P40, a P45 and an E111 form, but an MP14 was a new one on me.

All of this was.

I filled out his contact details and those that I could remember of his brother and parents.

Medical conditions, none.

Benefits, none.

Photo, yep got one I can email and I consciously decided there and then not to supply one of those grainy, odd looking photos that you so often see of missing persons on the news.

I then consented to publish his name, details and a photograph in local the media? Blimey that'll be a little weird for his old boss.

One day, he's told that he has to let Steve leave his job early for whatever reason and the next day, he's re-writing a Police press release about their lead staff writer going missing.

This is such a bugger's muddle! I wanted to come clean.

Tell the truth, the whole truth and nothing but the truth, but what if I was supposed to keep quiet?

I've not actually been formally, or 'informally' informed as to whether our involvement in - whatever we are actually involved in, is secret or in fact, a free for all to publicise.

Is Steve even in trouble?

Well I can't contact him and it seems he can't contact us either, so that doesn't sit well with me.

I feel out of control!

This was my dilemma at the time, which I still can't reconcile, even *after* the visit to the police.

Anyway, for better or worse at the time, I decided to just go with the flow, act dumb and again, see where the process took me – us...

I was torn.

Should every second count? How do I know his life isn't in danger, or how could I be sure his life wouldn't be put in more danger, should I tell them the whole story?

Just a ridiculous situation to find yourself in!

So I filled in the form, as best I could and five minutes later, DI Rees again popped his head around the door like some comedic mime artist.

'All done pet?' he asked cheerfully, that lovely smile putting me further at ease.

I nodded – again.

'Super, smashing, great. Right let's take a gander at this here form then. Mr Cartwright of Folkestone. Apart from you my lovely, the next of kin all seem to reside in Surrey and Buckinghamshire. Well thank goodness for that. We wouldn't want to have to drive to Wales or somewhere like that would we?' his eyes widening, expecting my polite chuckle at his supposed irony.

I duly obliged, awkward smile added for his instant gratification. I also felt best not to mention that I have family there, in case that opened up a whole Pandora's Box of Welsh anecdotes and stupid questions like, does your mum know Mrs Jones of 45 Cwmbran Avenue?

Rees thumbed through the form, his eyes scanning the contents quickly: 'No benefits, no health conditions, lovely. No friends?' the cadence of his voice raising higher, his head tilted ever so slightly.

'Well I hadn't filled that out really, as most of his friends are our joint friends, so I was going to fill those out or call them myself. I'm not sure what to do really. And his friends from work and old school friends, I don't really know that well and certainly don't have contact numbers for them. Most of them aren't local, you see?'

'I see. Well don't you worry your pretty little head about your *joint* friends; you make it sound like you invite them over for a good smoke session. We'll do the old ring around for you.' He made it sound like he was organising a secret 40th birthday bash.

'Media relations. Oh I see. Hmm, might have to treat that one a bit sensitively. Where's his new work place?'

'*Reuters* in London. That's all I know. He started this week and I've tried to call them, but there are a lot of offices up there and the receptionists didn't have his name as yet, so as to be able to put me through anyway.'

'I see. Yes, may be a bit early to make yourself known on the database, but a big company like that with today's technology?' He nodded at the tape recorder, as if to insinuate that even *Reuters* don't use them anymore.

'Right first things first, how you fixed for another cuppa whilst I donk all this into my database - no time like the present and then we can go for a bit of a drive.' His hands then mimicked being at a steering wheel, over zealously driving from side to side like a crazed B.A. Baracus.

I nodded, slightly wary of his impending driving style and he left the room.

I did wonder at the time if he might think it strange that a person on the cusp of moving in would not know where their partner was actually working, but hey, who knows how a detective's mind works?

The young PC kindly brought in my tea and that was that.

Next thing I knew, myself, DI Rees and a 30 something short brunette WPC introduced as Miss Allen, all clambered into their Panda, or whatever it was, and we headed towards Steve's flat, takeaway tea still in hand.

At the time I was impressed with their speed and efficiency. Not of the driving specifically, but I think I thought I might have to wait days for an answer or any sort of action. Yet, not only did they react straight away, but they also took me along for the ride - Result!

'Right then Miss Sinclair,' he said, looking at me in the rear view mirror. I could've sworn he winked at me!

'Sophia, please.'

'Right then Miss Sophia, do you have a key on you or at your house or wherever you live?'

I shook my head.

'Then we'll have to go in the old fashioned way,' he said, rubbing his hands gleefully: 'Roger will be pleased of the early New Year's outing!'

Roger, as it turns out, was a red steel ram that lived in the boot and obviously only came out on special occasions like dawn raids and when long term girlfriends still don't have a latch key...

The wooden door splintered around the bolt and bounced back off the inner wall, such was the force that Rees put behind it: 'Ooops, you never know how many locks and bolts are on there. Easier to go in hard from the outset I say,' his single eyebrow raising as he looked at me, knowingly: 'We'll fix that up later my little chickadee.'

Rees strode into the two bedroom first floor flat, as part of a converted maisonette. The front garden was Steve's, which suited him, as it was gravel and easy to maintain and park on. The tenant below had the back garden, which Steve could access should he want, but the tenant had been there long term and had invested in flowering shrubs, decking and copious pot plants, despite it technically not being their own.

'Ok Miss Sophia, rule number one if you could - don't touch a thing. I want to speed up this process by you simply pointing out to me where Steve would keep his personal effects. Contacts, banking records, that sort of thing, oh and a toothbrush would be tidy.'

I directed Rees around the bedroom and bathroom mainly, with him ticking off the items on his sheet and placing Steve's 'effects', as he called them, into clear plastic bags. WPC Allen had another agenda, which I was not privy too and she busied herself in the kitchen and lounge area.

'Can I ask that you wait in the car now please Miss Sophia, WPC Allen will lead the way and once we've finished our first sweep, we'll take you back to the farm and leave the flat in the hands of forensics, oh and a locksmith I guess.'

Rees had obviously found a spare key in a drawer somewhere and proceeded to wave it at me, as if rubbing my nose in its very existence.

So, there I sat. In a cold car catching up on my diary - that was, until Rees reappeared at the car window with a rather more stern expression. His full lips were pursed, the crows' feet around his eyes, even more pronounced.

'There seems to have been a development Miss Sinclair.' he said curtly, reverting back to formalities.

Fantastic, I thought, perhaps the mainframe had spat something out already. An APB out on the airwaves had struck gold and Steve was now on the radar once more!

I was wrong.

As I walked back into the flat, there was another man there with long protective gloves tending to the door. I hadn't seen him arrive.

'Mr Rand says there's evidence of a forced entry,' said Rees, straight faced for the first time today.

I turned to look at the splintered door, half hanging on its hinges and promptly laughed out loud.

'No, other than mine.' he said, equally seriously.

He then clicked his fingers and WPC Allen appeared out of the second bedroom and lifted up a clear bag. Inside was a small round metal disc with a tiny tail.

Rees' dark eyebrows both raised, causing a ripple of fine lines to cascade upwards along his forehead: 'Any thoughts as to what this might be Miss Sinclair?' he asked and I was surprised, if not a little disappointed that the pleasantries had gone, after all, I *was* the victim here.

'I, I've never seen such a thing.' I defended, lying through my teeth and trying to look and sound normal.

This was no easy task and I had to improvise.

'Fair enough Miss Sinclair, I think our work here is done; if you could let yourself out Mr Rand, we'll be back at the station. Jasmine, you carry on with your search, see if you can't stumble across any other evidence of infestation.' Rees nodded to WPC Allen, who then turned to continue with her thorough investigation.

We then drove back to the station and it must've been lunchtime, as I was famished, but still no cold cuts were forthcoming, let alone scones.

I then found myself back in Interview Room 4, a welcome cup of tea waiting on the table, if not a little cold.

So this was a slight improvement on the time before.

'Let me just get a few things together Miss Sinclair and I'll be with you in a minute.' breathed DI Rees. This must have been quite a day for him, for a quiet Saturday in Folkestone.

After what must have been 15 minutes stewing with my already stewed tea, Rees strode confidently back in.

He was more officious now, the humour had definitely passed and it was as if my case was keeping him from the end of his shift. Which might have been the case, for all I knew...

'Interview with Miss Sinclair, 2.21pm. So you came to see us, not too long ago did you not?'

I nodded.

'For the benefit of the tape, Miss Sinclair just nodded.'

This *had* officially turned official.

Maybe he *was* going to pin me for murder after all!

'You came to see us, to tell us about your fantastical dreams Miss Sinclair. Dreams that we duly noted down, investigated to the best of our abilities and we emailed you to confirm our conclusion that there *was* no conclusion.'

'Pretty much.' I said, leaning towards the tape recorder, unaware where the microphones actually were.

'And presumably Steve was aware of these dreams?'

'He was yes.'

'And despite our very best efforts and subsequent closing of a case on the basis of there not being a case to open, it seems Miss Sinclair that someone *else* has taken an interest.'

'If you say so Detective Inspector Rees.' I said acting dumb, like the blonde I am.

'You see Miss Sinclair, that little round wee disc with a tail we showed you, is in fact not just a Tamagotchi.'

'Oh yes?'

'Oh yes. It is in fact a listening device. Do you have any idea who might be trying to listen to you and your boyfriend Miss Sinclair?'

I stupidly shook my head.

'And, for the benefit of the tape, Miss Sinclair just shook her head in the negative,' shaking his head subconsciously: 'So we've got a bug in your boyfriend's flat and he's gone missing. This seems a little suspicious to me, don't you think?' he said, stroking his hairless chin and strong jaw line.

'I agree,' I piped up, thinking best to defend myself: 'So what are you going to do about it?'

'Well in the first instance, why Miss Sinclair, if he has been missing since Tuesday the 19th, did you wait until today, the 23rd to report this incident?' checking his notes for the correct dates, his dark brown eyes looking directly into mine.

'Well I didn't think it an incident at first.'

With that the door cracked open and PC Howard beckoned Rees with his finger, to which he stood up and spoke: 'Interview suspended by PC Howard at, 2.24pm.' he said, checking his watch and leaving the room.

Ten minutes later he returned.

The pressure was a killer, even though I'd nothing to hide.

Well I say nothing...

'Ok, Miss Sinclair, it's 2.35pm, here we go again. It seems that despite the fact that you didn't think his absence to be a potential incident, for some reason you called Steve at his place of work.'

'Yes, I told you that he was starting at *Reuters* and I didn't know which one and...'

Rees cut me off.

'Pardon me Miss Sinclair, his previous place of work. You called the *Folkestone Herald* on Tuesday. Why would you do that if you knew he was starting at *Reuters* this week? The day before in fact? Seems a little odd does it not? Almost as odd as someone moving in with him to be totally unaware of exactly which London location he was to be working from and not having a front door key.'

I shifted nervously in my seat.

The bugger was picking holes in my story, which is never ideal: 'I was just checking in with them that they hadn't heard from him, you know old work colleagues and all that?'

I smiled to try to break the fast frosting atmosphere.

'PC Howard has been so kind as to take the trouble of speaking to Miss Kaplan, the receptionist at the *Herald*, who distinctly remembers speaking to you and she also remembers that you not only asked for Steve by name, but you were surprised that he wasn't there. She described his departure as immediate and under extraordinary circumstances. She also described your reaction Miss Sinclair, which didn't sound like that of a 'loved one' that, knew what was going on.'

Rees' lyrical accent bobbed and faded in a rhythmic dance and I was on the cusp a few times of letting the proverbial cat completely out of the bag.

Blimey, talking of which, I've still not seen Shelley! Maybe I should report her as missing too, as she certainly wasn't in the flat?

'Yes I was confused I think, it's been a very traumatic week you see Mr Rees.' I pleaded, my arms inadvertently folding and I leaned back in my chair.

'Quite.' He replied suspiciously: 'PC Howard *has* been a busy boy. He has also taken the opportunity to note a very one-sided text conversation with a Mr Seth Cartwright about Steve going missing. You did not seem overly in a hurry to get back to a worried brother Miss Sinclair and there's no evidence of you calling him to allay his fears.'

I didn't know what to say. I was amazed with the speed of how all of this can unfold. I guess it's just a quick check of phone records etc, but still, do they not have lunch breaks?

'So Miss Sinclair, just to confirm for the benefit of the tape and my befuddled mind. Your boyfriend has been missing for four days. He was to start work at *Reuters* on Monday, but to your knowledge he never arrived. You checked out the *Herald* just in case he had any last minute nerves, or a change of heart and went back there, but to no avail. He left the *Herald* under strange circumstances, not normal statutory procedure of working his notice anyway. We have evidence of a listening device found by WPC Allen within Steve's property and now a mysterious disappearance. Is there anything *I'm* missing at all?'

'I wouldn't say that I called the *Herald* simply to check out if he had returned, as I say I called just to speak to his colleagues.'

'But Miss Kaplan said that she never put you through to anyone, so you never spoke to a colleague. And what's more, you were shocked that Steve wasn't actually there. You asked for him by name after all?'

I put my head in my hands.

I must have looked guilty as sin: 'I don't know what I know anymore.'

'Listen to me Miss Sophia, if there's anything that you're keeping from me that could in any way help find your boyfriend. All I'm going to say is that the introduction of a listening device is never good news for us and it won't be long until the 'Nationals' are all over this case and all over you. Let's break for some sustenance. I'm not going to arrest you, but I suggest that you stay a while, so as to help us with our enquires throughout the rest of the day. We will also need to have permission to access to your flat too please.'

'And what if I don't?'

'Then I shall simply obtain a warrant and let Roger come out to play again.' He said eyeing me strangely, as if trying to read my actions, my mannerisms, my eye movements.

I acted fast to defend myself having failed in my fishing expedition: ‘Sorry, I meant what if I don’t have any more information, not that I won’t allow access.’

He laughed, which was a welcome relief: ‘Ah Miss Sophia, if you cannot think of anything else, then I’m sure the Nationals will be able to ask some more pressing and pertinent questions that a kindly local detective such as myself would not be able to even think of.’

Again he read me for my reaction.

I could read him too now.

He was trying to suggest that the ‘Nationals’, as he referred to them, would swoop down all heavy fisted, no doubt to break me into submission and life would be much better for me if I ‘fessed up now, to this more ‘kindly’ Welshman.

Yeah sod that, I’ll take my chances with the big boys!

I figured that if they’d had time to check my phone accounts, someone else would‘ve been onto some database somewhere or straight onto MI5 to see who’s listening to Steve and why exactly. I guessed, knowing what I know, that this came up blank, seeing as it’s an American device, but it was *what* exactly they wanted with Steve that stopped me coming completely clean with Rees.

We’ve not *done* anything. If Lennox wanted to ‘take him out’, they would’ve done that in their first meeting, let alone before that if needs be.

So why did they have to meet so damned early on that Tuesday morning?

Rees left the room on the promise of food. These natural breaks, if not pressure situations, did allow me to make notes on my tablet and review the proceedings to aid my alibi.

There I go again.

Alibi for what exactly.

Well possibly perverting the course of justice for one, wasting police time for another.

Food soon followed, but again I was still confined to the interview room, so they knew where I was. However, I was unaware of course, of what was, or was not, going on behind the scenes.

How much manpower did they have on the case? How long would it take them to detect the detector wasn't British? Where was Steve when I needed him?

It was 4pm before I realised and Rees came back in: 'Ok, if you could please sign this form to allow us entry to your flat, a key would be nice and you're free to go, but please stay local in case we need you. I'll call you personally to let you know when your flat is ready for handover.'

I shook my head, it sounded like they were a hotel concierge changing my sheets, turning them back and leaving a mint chocolate on my pillow: 'A goodnight kiss from Kent County Constabulary.' it would say on it.

Scratch that, they would be riffling through my drawers and my best draws for all I knew.

So here I am, back in the present, back in the *Dolphin Café* and finally caught up with what has been a very long, tiring and somewhat confusing day.

I'm still not sure if I'm doing the right thing.

Be sure the truth will out, is what they say, but to what end? To what end exactly?

7.15pm

I just checked my phone.

It's still on silent! Whoops...!

Missed calls x 3 from Seth's mobile and one from a Folkestone landline number.

I just called Seth and they'd returned to Surrey, but he promised that he'd be on call, should I need anything.

I told them that the police would probably want to speak to them and he then confirmed that a WPC Allen had already made contact shortly after I left the restaurant.

Blimey she's efficient!

They were going to expect her visit tomorrow to make a statement and answer any questions.

I then called the random landline number and it just rang and rang. Odd, I assumed that it would be Rees to say that I could return home. No voicemail option either.

Strange!

So in the absence of a call from Rees, I think I'll wend my way back to the flat. Amble it and hopefully by the time I get there, they'll be done.

Oh, what if they're already done and take my key back to the station, seeing as they couldn't get me on the phone?

Ah, let's just see what happens.

I'll no doubt report in later…

10.46pm

I've just got back in now.

I've just chosen to take a break. Feels like I've been writing on and off all day. No hard feelings diary!

I just imagined it replied: 'Bygones,' - diaries are pretty cool like that.

Blimey, I really am losing it. I'm going to bed!

Sunday January 24th 2016 – 8.30am

I'm lying in bed, fresh sheets and new PJ's, still with that distinctive clean smell of washing powder tempting me to linger longer.

The sun is blazing in through my window and I even awoke to find the cat on the end of the bed. Today is going to be a good day; I can feel it in my water!

I have black coffee, two croissants and a Saturday paper that my neighbour kindly posted through the door, after they'd finished with it.

Let's see what's happening in the world.

Trident makes the front page, the Scottish Nationals proclaiming, 'not in our back yard and not on our watch'. Fair enough, the port at Folkestone needs some love, so we may as well have a nuclear submarine posted here instead – it would make me feel a hell of a lot safer!

Unless the town then becomes a strategic military target ...

Well, it took until page five to find American election news; even the press seem to be fed up with it already - only ten months to go fellas, get used to it!

The headline reads: 'OJ set to pip Clinton in US election race.' Genius punage and a 'Steve special' if ever I'd seen one! He'd have been so proud, if a little jealous. Blimey, why am I writing in the past tense?

Apparently, Orlando Johnston leads the polls, not only within his own party to become the chosen Republican presidential candidate, but his hard line seems to be galvanising views across America and he's picking off floating voters and faltering Democrats who are less enthused by Hillary's more 'stable' domestic policies.

He promised to: '*...be judge, jury and executioner and the Axis of Evil should know now, that they'll be found and brought to justice. All of them.'*

Oh joy. Another gun-toting, war-mongering zealot on our hands and the trouble is, his words resonate with the electorate and appeal to their insecurities. Surly populism won't last?

It looks as if he's promising an international shit storm that's just as likely to cause nuclear war, as Clinton's lack of opposition to Russia and Iran would do.

Keep your head down Sinclair; you've got your own issues to contend with!

Rees finally did call me, just as I was walking around the corner onto my road as it happens.

He placed my keys back into my hands softly and played down the search, saying that nothing of interest came up and that he and his cronies had now left. Not even so much as a mint on the pillow!

He said he'd call me if he had any other questions or leads and seemed a little annoyed for some reason. There was this intensity to his face that I'd not witnessed before and it was, well, kind of sexy!

The thought of this authoritative figure coming down hard on me... I could only imagine what he'd be like if he was in uniform too! So seeing as he's got nothing to stick on me, I'm just going to enjoy my coffee and paper in bed.

Alone.

Not sure what else to do today... I would normally meet with Steve.

I do miss him!

I've just tried calling his numbers again and if they *are* tracking my phone records, it at least shows willing on my part! I also tried that odd landline number again, but still no answer. Strange…

9.00pm

Well apart from a sunny, if not cold stroll around the Leas, I just spent the day, well – spending...

Bought some food, clothes and toiletries in town and played my consumerist role in society, dancing to the tune of the state, by purchasing things I don't actually need.

The elites will be pleased!

Retail therapy at its best - it keeps someone in a job and also keeps me sane on a day that I should be with my man!

No calls from the Police, which although is good, is slightly disconcerting. Does that mean they've absolutely no leads on Steve, or just no more dirt on me?

I'm so paranoid sometimes, but this is all such a mess, even sleeping on it has not helped as to which way to turn! Should I tell them about the CIA, or whoever they are, or not?

Ok, I'm going for an early night, if I've not heard from the police by 11am tomorrow morning, I'm going to call them and let them know the whole truth.

I just text Steve from my Mabus phone, as I know they can't be onto me for that number, as the SIM isn't registered to me and I paid cash. Just thought I'd keep it simple:

'Hope u r ok. I love you!'

Monday January 25th 2016 – 7.40am

Well Kent Police, the meter's running, chop friggin chop - the clock's ticking to find young Steve and I don't just mean my biological one!

You have exactly 3 hours and 20 minutes to solve it, or I'm going to give you a clue, or maybe just string myself and possibly Steve up in the process.

Maybe I can supply this diary as evidence as to my pre-meditated subversion for the right reasons. Or maybe they'll assume I've written this just to create a technological alibi – How very postmodern!

Despite Steve not being around, I quite enjoyed the freedom and lazy lifestyle that yesterday served up. It's not often I get to read the papers and chill and that's without having kids or *Netflix*.

Who knows how those poor souls cope. Families and farmers both! Spare a thought for the farmers with families – when do *they* get to sleep? And what if the farmer with kids is also addicted to *Candy Crush*? The mind boggles and the eyes redden at the thought of it!

Are diaries supposed to be a medium for just venting and rambling? I guess they can be used for whatever. I'm 25 days in and the novelty hasn't worn off just yet, but do I still stick to my self-imposed cut off at the end of the month?

With Steve missing and the police involved, this might actually be the most exciting chapter in my life to date – apart from that fling with a holiday rep in Greece I guess, but I can't possibly divulge that filth in these pages! What if the police do use this diary for evidence? Then they'll know exactly where the sand gets. Everywhere!

Where are you Steve? If you ever read this, it's not funny! The relentless waiting, the inability to contact you and the bizarre nature of your sudden disappearance, it's all so hard, but what else *can* I do? Just wait; hope - cry...

This is when my decision for a life of atheism is either fully verified, as there's nobody out there to help me from a higher plain, or am I just being punished for my obtuse lack of faith? If the signs of God's greatness are supposedly all around us, I could do with one right now, that's for sure.

Ok, so as a test case in point, I just looked out of the window and the first sign I saw was 'Men at Work'. Great... that either means my life, my faith and my hope are under construction, or is that in fact a sign to say that 'the Man', or the Establishment is working to help me now, via an on-going police investigation?

I'm reading into this way too much!

Bloody train journey. Maybe I'll just get a job at *Boots*. Make life simple. Simpler anyways...

10.40am

Twenty minutes to go for the police investigation deadline, but I've just had a game changer! It's only a bloody reply on my 'Mabus' phone: *'Where are you? We need to speak!'*

Thank you God, if in fact you are there listening to my doubting mind and if not, thank you cosmic oblivion for the change in fortune! Either way I'm chuffing well chuffed to say the least!

So maybe I'll hold off on elaborating on the police case for a while. See if I can arrange to meet Steve and see what the hell's going on first. What am I talking about? If I can meet with Steve, then I can drop the missing person case outright!

I just tried calling the 'Mabus' phone, but it rang and rang and ticked over to a generic voicemail, but I didn't leave one.

I just text back, trying to set up the meeting.

"Where are you?" it asked. Where does he think I am? *Hello,* some of us have to work you know. I can't just lie about all day playing detective and victim. And "we need to speak". He's telling me! I replied on the text that I've involved the police, so maybe that'll jolt him into some action!

11.10am

Just had a call from DI Rees. He asked where I was and was I available to pop in? I told him I'm at work in London and that his cold, stewed tea was not overly inviting or convenient at the moment!

Typical parochial police, not everyone works at their local *Boots* you know and can be around in five shakes of a Welsh lamb's tail!

He seemed a little agitated and apologised for any inconvenience, which was odd. Ok, I've a job of work to do and felt that I've spent most of the morning on personal calls, texts and diary entries, but apart from that, no harm done.

10.10pm

Famous last words and how the day can spin and capitulate in on itself so easily!

I'd come out of a meeting, got back to my workstation and there was a sticky note on my screen that said in jaunty red handwriting: 'Scarper it's the Rozza's!'

I assumed this was code for a missed call from Folkestone nick for me, so I ventured over to reception.

'Oh hi Sophia, you got my note then?' said Holly, looking up from her screen.

I was glad it was Holly and not the other dippy lass.

'Yes very witty, but I've chosen to come quietly.' I replied with a laugh, sticking the note to her blonde fringed forehead.

She grimaced, thinking it would affect her foundation and threw it back at my face: 'Get off! Yes, someone called for you earlier; they said there was no message. You still up for lunch in the park?'

'Was it a man, was his name Rees?'

'No, sorry that doesn't ring a bell. I never was that good at remembering the names to be fair.' she said.

Great. And she's on reception!

Then seemed like as good a time as any to pop out for lunch in the park. Well, I say park, it's more of a glorified square with children's play equipment around the corner.

LOL, lots of glorified shapes going on in this diary!

I can remember giving my fullest address as a child. 64 Acacia Avenue, Bermondsey, London, England, Europe, The Earth, The Milky Way, The Universe. We've all done it!

Now here I was some thirty years later in a Glorified Square within a Glorified Triangle, part of a Glorified Sphere, orbiting a Glorified Star somewhere in the endless and dark unknown matter of what could be a three dimensional and ever expanding glorified Omnigon of a shape - itself with an infinite number of sides, edges and points.

Deep!

Deep breath anyway... I digress, as only I can under the circumstances of my predicament.

Anyway, Holly and I went to lunch and sat on a park bench watching the young children playing with their grandparents or carers. No parents at this urban park.

The small playground seemed out of sorts amongst the tall buildings of the city, almost dwarfed and insignificant, yet standing out as an oasis against development. A last bastion of greenery, in this ever-expanding urban environment - which seems to be expanding upwards in the most part.

Despite its close proximity to the office, I hadn't been there before and Holly was talking *at* me about some puerile piffle on the tele.

'I know it's not really real, but can you believe that she dumped him for that? To me, he's a keeper no matter what! With his looks and money, I'd do anything to have a boyfriend like him! Anyway, so I told Abby earlier what happened and she was like: "Shut up", and then I was like: "Yeah tell me about it". You know what I mean Soph? It could only happen in Essex right?'

I obliged the banal conversation with the response it deserved: 'Aha,' for I was busy.

Not doing anything specific, but just busy looking. At what exactly, I was unsure. I was just seeing rather than focussing and in doing so, I had a sudden feeling of déjà vu - to my second dream.

The park wasn't exactly as I remember it from the dream, and as I say, I hadn't been before, so my mind couldn't have constructed it - one assumes? Yet that same feeling of looking without focussing and seeing without knowing came over me.

The children were there, just not *my* child. I darted my eyes looking for an old man with a newspaper, but that would've been far too easy. Far too obvious.

'You alright babes?' asked Holly, suddenly aware of my preoccupied state. Suddenly there was a deep male voice from behind me: 'Miss Sinclair?'

The hairs on the back of my neck stood on end, a cold chill went down my spine out of surprise and also foreboding as to whom might be there after my, sort of out of body experience.

I was relieved.

It was two kindly looking police officers. Not the old man with a newspaper that I was half expecting or an agent with dark sunglasses and holding a hessian hood for me.

'Sophia Sinclair?' probed the taller of the two PCs. It was a deep booming and guttural voice that must have come from the depths of his 6'4" frame.

Dark haired under his flat peaked police hat and broad shouldered - he looked like a rugby number '4' I used to date, so I quizzed him as such.

'Oh, you took me by surprise, sorry, yes that's right. That's me. You play lock by any chance?' I winced, thinking my comment wasn't overly relevant or appropriate at the time.

The two officers looked at each other slightly confused. The smaller man was around 5'8", with a wiry build, good looking and probably a number '9', I presumed. He had a proper constable's helmet on too, probably to gain a few extra inches on his lofty mate. Small policeman syndrome!

'Miss Sinclair, whether I play rugby is of no concern to you, but seeing as you asked, I played at 8.' he said, sternly.

'Oh yes, at the back of the scrum, that would've been my next guess,' I replied jauntily, smiling at Holly with a knowing look: 'Yes, I dated a number 4 for a number of years, very big lad in more ways than one I can tell you...' I joked nervously, raising a suitably dirty pitched laugh from Holly.

'Miss Sinclair,' said the scrummy half PC: 'May we have a word in private?'

'Sorry, yes, is this about Steve? I spoke to DI Rees not long ago. You guys come up from Folkestone?'

Maybe Steve had been in touch with them too, seeing as I mentioned having gone to the police on the text I sent to him.

Holly looked at me quizzically.

I'd not told anyone at work about Steve being missing or my dealings with the police - let alone the CIA.

'This way Miss Sinclair,' said the wannabe lock, directing me away from the bench, his giant hand parting me from Holly's side. I guessed the information to be private and at the time, I was quite pleased for their concern and consummate professionalism. After all, they couldn't assume that I'd shared Steve's situation with Holly.

We duly walked away to a clearing by a small sapling.

'Miss Sinclair, I'm arresting you on suspicion of perverting the course of justice.' whispered the tall man, not wanting to make a fuss in public.

'Arresting? *Me*?' I asked, probably too loudly as Holly immediately caught my eye. She bit her lip, shunted her chin to the side and gave me a look that totally said "totes awks!"

'You don't have to say anything, but anything you do say will be taken down and could be given as evidence...'

I cut off the suddenly not so scrummy one in his pompous prime: 'Evidence for what exactly?'

'...in a court of law.' he continued unflinchingly.

The impish officer looked up at his towering counterpart and asked if cuffs were necessary. The lanky lock then assured him that the car was only "over there" and that he'd rugby tackle me if I tried to get away! The shorter officer laughed out loud. Amazing how quickly you can go off someone!

Anyway so in the car we went, leaving a horrified Holly in our wake and this is where I now reside. Paddington station - and I don't mean the one of the chuff chuff variety, with the pet Peruvian bear. I mean Paddington police station, a holding area and waiting to see the Duty Sergeant to have my possessions removed. Including my tablet!

The wheels of justice, or injustice in my case, haven't moved as fast today. It was in fact the Met that caught me, incarcerated me and that's it.

No charge, no questions and certainly no answers.

Tuesday January 26th 2016 – 10.40pm

Ok, so I'm out and on a train home – finally.

What a friggin few days! It was an emotional joyride, just without the joy, and definitely with the feeling of being totally out of control. I was a mere passenger to someone else's plan and one without a seatbelt, airbag or insurance to boot.

I was taken to see the Custody Sergeant, a meek, middle aged man, who looked run down by life and saw me as a major inconvenience to his plans to rest his aching legs, let alone complete the last few remaining years until retirement.

He took my name, contact details and even my fingerprints – how degrading!

I was photographed, swabbed and awaiting the obligatory full cavity search, when I was advised that I'd got a phone call to take. I took the black old-fashioned handset, suspicious of who exactly would know my whereabouts and muttered timidly: 'Hello?'

'How are you Miss Sophia?' said Rees in a reassuringly jovial Welsh tone.

'How do you think I am Rees? Living the dream, I'm just living the friggin dream!'

In ironic hindsight, this is neither how my actual dream had transpired, nor how my general hopes and dreams for my life had played out in my head either.

'Hang in there pet. A few key things moved on the case yesterday morning, which I wasn't aware of. People then got involved over my head, starting playing stupid games and I'm now trying to resolve the situation. However being down here is proving difficult and Scotland Yard are now all over it, as I feared they would be. Sorry!'

'All over what?' I asked innocently, actually not entirely sure where and how this so called case had suddenly escalated. Had they found Steve? Was he ok? There were all sorts running through my head and none of it liquorice!

'Listen, I can't update you now, but I'll debrief you tomorrow. Sit tight, hold on, hang tough, stay strong and...

I can't think of any more, but you get the gist. Oh, got one. Take it easy presh!'

'Easy? Easy for you to say, you're not the one about to be strip searched and showered off at distance!' I was short with him now, as his seemingly false friendly manner was starting to grate. How can I do anything *but* sit tight, when I was about to be put in a cell? How can I stay strong, when I've not even been officially told why I'm here, let alone allowed to eat my poxy lunch in private?

Anyway, he rang off and the Sergeant continued, looking at me over his glasses that were professionally perched on the end of his nose. His lank, dark and greasy comb over annoyed me, as much as his officious attitude.

He snapped, clipped abrupt questions at me. He was curt to the core and revelled in his role. In a matter of what seemed like ten minutes, I was placed unceremoniously in cell six. No possessions, no belt; in case I chose to hang myself I presumed and there I stayed until I was taken to an interview room.

Now I can't recall the absolute ins and outs of the whole conversation, as I had no means of keeping a running note, but this is pretty much how it went:

'So Miss Sinclair, my name is DI Campbell and...' to be fair I can't actually remember the other person's name, something like DI Schofield I think, but it was a real blur.

Campbell was late 40's I recon, close-cropped hair, fair complexion and small hands. He was dressed in a dark suit with an ill fitting white shirt, gaping at the neck and a dishevelled looking tie just sort of, hanging there.

DI Schofield, Scowcroft or just DIsco, as I now refer to her as, was overtly feminine. Good skin, lovely large hazelnut eyes that you could dive into; if you were so inclined and a rather stylish and extreme comb over half bob type thing. One side above her left ear was shaved short and the rest of her light brown hair, with a deep reddy tinge, was swept over her right eye and tucked behind her right ear.

She was probably early 30's and dressed in plain clothes - one of those 'cooler' looking Officers that wouldn't look out of place in Shoreditch or Brixton and her dark hoody and jeans, were both tight enough to hint at her athletic physique.

Campbell broke my admiring gaze: 'I'll cut to the chase Miss Sinclair if I may, as I know you've been waiting a long time, so apologies for that.' his East London accent was more apparent now, no heirs and graces in this nick: 'We've 'ad a busy day today, all sorts of maddens comin' out the woodwork! Not good for my 'art!'

I trusted he was not referring to me as being just the latest mad person to pass his desk, but I appreciated his direct approach. I too, just wanted to get this over with!

'So, we've been speaking to Rees and Allen down in Folkestone nick, as well as some others to do with this case. Has anyone actually explained why you've been arrested today?' his eyes widening for an honest answer.

'Not exactly. Just perverting the course of justice, to which I'd like to make a statement on.'

'Well let me just update you on a few things and we'll gladly take your statement Sophia. Ok to call you Sophia?' he looked up from his notebook, wholly expecting an affirmative.

I nodded. I'm good at that in police stations.

'Ok good, so Rees made you aware of a device found in Mr Cartwright's flat, yeah?'

I nodded again.

'So although this is odd in its own right, what's really odd is, when we checked it out with GCHQ and other interested departments, the device, well, it's not theirs. It's actually American origin. GCHQ's aware of your boyfriend for some unusual or unsavoury activity on his Internet searching, but nothing they saw as incitement to terror or potential to cause a 'situation', let alone feel the need to bug him.' His face creased as he tried to comprehend the situation, his nose wrinkling as he sniffed and tried to clear his blocked sinuses.

'I may be able to elaborate...' I said almost apologetically, meekly raising my right hand.

'As I say, you can make your statement in due course Miss Sinclair. Sophia sorry,' he cut himself short: 'As you're also aware, Folkestone nick's been looking for Mr Cartwright and naturally it came to our attention via the internal wires. They've been tracking your phone calls. Tracing numbers, not necessarily listening in, but one of the numbers flagged as being odd too.'

'Oh?' I interjected, still unsure as to where all this was actually going.

'Yeah, it was a landline, a Folkestone number to be precise. First incoming to you and not answered. Then multiple calls out to the same number, but no connection ever made. We looked into this as being potential for contact from and to the missing person you see ...'

'He has a name you know!' I hissed.

'Potential contact from, or to *Steve*.' he corrected, tilting his head to the side: 'And then there's his mobile phone.'

I looked at Campbell confused. A frown developed on my face and he must have sensed my honest bewilderment.

Campbell looked me in the eyes: 'His mobile was found in his flat, but the funny thing is, it's just got one number on it. Someone called Pris?'

'Pris!' I blurted, screwing my face up in shock.

'As far as I can see, Pris was a replicant in the film *Bladerunner*. A *"basic pleasure model of the Nexus 6 variety"* - according to the Internet, and what I assumed was an odd nickname for a girlfriend. Well I assumed it was his girlfriend as the replicant, I mean recipient, was very keen to find out where he was and express their affection for him. Any ideas?' he looked up, this time half expecting to be stoned walled.

Campbell smiled at me knowingly and continued: 'So, we text the number back to see what happened. A sort of honey trap for his honey you see. To your credit and at the moment Miss Sinclair, I'm assuming you were the recipient; your reply was consistent with your story, so you seem to be tellin' the truth as to the mystery surrounding his disappearance. But the outgoing Folkestone landline number I spoke about was traced to a public call box on Albion Street in Folkestone. However, from BT's records, no credit was activated for that number and on further inspection a call from the *US* of all places, has been routed via that number to you. Why do you think you're getting calls from the US Miss Sinclair?'

A rhetorical question it seemed, as Disco then jumped immediately into the conversation.

'That got us thinking Sophia and we're currently making enquiries with our American counterparts as to whether it was them making that call and them planting a device in Steve's flat. From our search of your flat, it came up clean, but there is forensic evidence of traces of adhesive in a number of places where we may 'expect' listening devices to be placed. So basically we've reason to believe that your flat has also been bugged and then subsequently cleaned, which usually notifies that something has happened or gone wrong, as the cost to send people out to 'clear up', far outweighs the cost of leaving the devices hidden.'

Her soft voice belied the hard edged look of her haircut, which again, she tucked behind her ear, as it flopped out of place during a turn to face Campbell.

I just sat there absorbing all they said. Things *had* moved on apace and I was now a little bamboozled!

Campbell shuffled his paperwork and took control once again: 'We've contacted *Reuters*' HR department and they confirmed "officially", they don't 'ave a Steven Cartwright on their books as yet, but he *is* due to start work in about 3-4 weeks time. They stated that his appointment was odd, in so much as HR had been kept in the dark and no official vacancy was ever officially advertised. So we've got a situation where your missing boyfriend has left one job unexpectedly and not joined his new job as expected, even by your good self.'

Disco looked me in the eyes: 'He has a phone with one number on it, in the drawer of his bedroom and we assume a phone with multiple contacts on him at the moment, wherever he may be. Albeit that phone is off, as we are unable to GPRS track its current position.'

I just sat there aghast. What the hell was Steve up to? What was in those documents he had from the Americans?

Ok, enough was enough; they were almost there and back again, so I put my hands up again.

Literally...

'Ok, some of what you say is definitely news to me, but I wanted to add for the record that Steve told me on the day before he disappeared that he'd been approached by two Americans. He wasn't sure, but guessed they must be alphabet agency of some kind, possibly attached to Langley. They warned him off publishing a story he'd earmarked as his first freelance assignment and basically intimated that they'd engineered the *Reuters* job for him.'

Campbell and Disco both looked up from their respective notebooks: 'And you didn't think this to be salient information for Folkestone nick because...?' Campbell enquired frowning, his mouth left slightly open in surprise.

'Because I couldn't be sure it was true and I almost wanted them to do the digging to corroborate my story, so I didn't look daft. It wasn't the first time I've been to that nick this year you know.'

'Yes, we heard.' smiled Disco, re-fixing her hair. Again.

Jeez, I couldn't be doing with the faff of that all day every day, no matter how good it looked! Proper faff factor. Oh and remind me to update you on that theory one day diary – The Faff Factor by Sophia Sinclair.

'I'll give you that. It does sound slightly fantastical that the US Government makes contact with Steve and creates a job for him, but to what end? What story were they trying to suppress anyway?' asked Campbell, leaning back in his chair and dangerously close to tipping it over.

'To cut a long story short, having been offered the job, Steve earmarked a breaking story linking General Mabus of the US Navy, to being the third Antichrist of Nostradamus' prophecies, who obviously goes by the same name.'

I physically winced, as the statement sounded so crazy.

Campbell laughed heartily, sitting back upright in his chair: 'Pardon my French luv, but what in shitting hell are you banging on about and what's a US Navy General gotta' do with my case?'

Disco smiled at him: 'The Antichrist is basically the devil right?' and she looked back at me for affirmation.

'You got it Makepeace.' I quipped.

This was another reason why I decided not to tell the whole truth, as it *is* just bonkers!

Disco looked at me confused.

Too young I assumed, but it amused my *Dempsey* who seemed to look at his colleague in a 'different', more amorous light: 'Right so this long story that you've cut short makes no sense to me right! So maybe I need the long story, especially as you *are* technically under arrest. I'll make the call to shorthand anything once I know all the facts first, right?'

I paused, not for effect, but simply to compose myself.

'You asked for it...'

I then proceeded to fill them both in on the last 26 days, from the fever dreams they would've already seen in the police report and about how the word Mabus kept cropping up. Also how the Americans had intercepted Steve and provided him with some documentation that I'd not seen and how they'd arranged to meet the following day and that was that.

A long story short for diary purposes, but I laboured the point about holding back the information for fear of exposing Steve and possibly putting him in even more danger.

Campbell expelled air through his lips so they made a fast flubbering sound, as they rapidly reverberated against each other: 'Jesus. Emma we'll need to get Section 4 to ramp up their comms with Langley. I'm wondering if Steve may be working for them in some capacity, you know?' Disco Emma nodded slowly, still trying to comprehend what I'd imparted.

With that, the door cracked open and a short lady with long black hair and a trouser suit walked in: 'Moment Guv? We're into her old *Nokia*. It's the other end of the line alright. Only one contact though, someone by the name of Mabus??'

She looked at me with distain, as if it was the phone of a convicted paedophile and then left the room abruptly.

Campbell looked me in the eyes questioningly and frowned. So I just simply shrugged one shoulder innocently: 'What can I say? Seemed a good idea at the time…'

'Ok, we've now confirmed that the second phone in your possession is the other end of the honey trap conversation with Steve's phone. This leads me to believe that you *are* in fact unaware of his whereabouts. Nice touch with the contact name by the way.' Campbell half smiled, exposing yellowing cigarette stained teeth below.

Again I shrugged, embarrassed: 'So now what?'

'Now you get to go home Sophia.' said Disco kindly. We'll carry on with our enquiries, see where this "Special Relationship" has taken your boyfriend and report back either directly or via DI Rees with any other news.'

And that's where we're at. I was released without charge.

Turns out the fantastical truth was perhaps too fantastic to make up after all, but this doesn't really answer any more of the questions that I have - such as, where is Steve?

At least I know he only has his main phone with him now and I don't have to keep texting both phones, but his lack of contact is still alarming nevertheless.

Wednesday January 27th 2016 – 9.45am

Back to work today, tail between legs as I was sure that between Holly and HR, my arrest would've caused more hilarity, rather than genuine distress.

I was wrong and immediately called into the boss' office to update them on what was going on. I reported that Steve had gone missing and that the police wanted to eliminate me from their enquiries, which they had now done, once and for all.

They were of course relieved, if a little disappointed that I didn't have more juicy gossip to impart.

So the day goes on. Back to reality, back to waiting - waiting for a call to possibly say: 'Yes our fears of Steve's defection have come true and he's in fact working for a covert US agency, trying to undermine the UK political establishment from within. Or, our fears of Steve's passing have sadly been confirmed.'

Either way, this is agony!

2.15pm

Just got off the phone from DI Rees and he confirmed that the CCTV images show Steve around the *Herald's* offices and heading towards the Millennium Park at around 6.00am. It also corroborates him being 'escorted' back towards the direction of the office with two men.

The footage then shows Steve arriving at the bottom of the Leas Lift area and a black car arriving, with black diplomatic plates, subsequently confirmed to be registered to the American Embassy in London and that he proceeds to get into the car, which then drives away.

They are currently following up the CCTV footage to track the final destination of the vehicle. Apart from that and a lack of cooperation from Langley over the listening devices, that's their only outstanding line of enquiry.

All of our friends have come up short of answers as to Steve's whereabouts and Folkestone nick has held off on the media announcements for the time being, much to Seth's distain. Until, that is, the research of the CCTV footage can be completed anyway.

Seth text to ask what was going on and I finally called him last night to confirm that I'd been in police custody in London, but was ok now.

Seth's no mug and I think he smells a rat. I think he rightly assumes that I'm not coming clean on everything. In this instance, he, Patrick and Pam are all on a need to know basis. Who knows where all this is going and I don't want to implicate or involve them if it all blows up. Steve may find himself being blackmailed; after all, he did tell me that they threatened him with *my* safety.

I'm going for a late lunch break now in the canteen, not the park - shudder!

Oh and the girls have persuaded me to go out for dinner – on them… They don't want me to stay at home, stewing on my own apparently.

They'd rather I sit and stew with them instead, it seems.

Thursday January 28th 2016 – 12.10am

I didn't drink. Well, much anyway...

I wanted to keep my wits about me, should the police call and not be that person that starts blubbing to any impending bad news, seeing as they've got themselves so drunk.

We had a nice three-course meal in a little Italian off Sicilian Avenue in Holborn, which seemed appropriate. A low fat salad to start, followed by linguine with feta cheese and bacon pieces. Then it was onto the crème brulee and coffee.

The conversation was mainly that - conversational.

Jo was there, as were Kate and Holly, as well as Rachel, Laura from Accounts and Spencer, who's always one of the girls on a night out.

When the conversation did come around to my plight, Holly took delight in regaling the parkland arrest in full *Technicolor* and *Dolby* friggin' surround sound.

Up until then it'd been like the elephant in the room. Nobody wanted to be first to mention it and *until* then, everything seemed like a pre-amble. Before, that is, they were able to get to the crux of what had actually happened.

So rather than stay at home and try to forget the last few days, I was made to go through yet another line of questioning, this time from the fools panel.

'And she was like "oh my fuckin' God",' said Holly in her inevitable way: 'I swear down, I've never seen Sophia so flustered. Talk about resist arrest, she was squirming all over the place, kicking her legs and shouting her potty mouth off as she demanded that they release her shackles! I thought she was going to deck the smaller of the two officers!'

I threw my napkin at Holly's head, again furrowing into her fringe: 'I did nothing of the sort! I just went quietly and they didn't even *use* cuffs.'

'I bet they did, you saucy minx!' she laughed out loud: 'Oh, sorry you're right, they didn't need cuffs love, 'cos they freakin' tazered your ass first.' Holly's shrill laugh filled the restaurant and the other hyenas followed suit, as she proceeded to feign electrocution, convulsing uncontrollably in her chair until she shook herself under the table; dragging the table cloth and her meal down with her, onto her head.

It was going to be one of those nights!

Bants at my expense, even if the meal wasn't.

A fair trade I guess and I had it coming. It's not often a colleague gets arrested or has to report a person as missing.

When it came to the storytelling, they did listen to me intently, like a class of toddlers being told about Noah's ark for the first time. Disbelief, tinged with a hint of sick jealousy that nothing *that* exciting ever happens to them.

Anyway I refuse to go over everything from last night on these pages. It was amusing in parts, especially when Jo almost accidentally set fire to someone's dress by knocking the candle on the floor. It rolled over to the next table and landed right on a young girl's floaty nylon number.

Well, it started to smoke and luckily Spencer soon became Fireman Spencer when he tossed a glass of white wine over it.

Poor Lucy was mortified, as it was her glass!

I thought she was going to literally suck the wine out from the girl's dress, she seemed that desperate.

Anyway Spence subsequently received fire related gags for the rest of the evening and not wanting to pour water on his efforts, it did get a little beyond the pail.

Right time for bed you, me, whoever *you* are...

7.45am

Despite not drinking much, it's the lack of sleep that's my real killer! Hopefully I'll hear back from the police today, as I've still had no reply to emails or texts from Steve. I just want him back now so badly.

I miss that face...

8.00pm

Well I was busy at work today, which was good, as it took my mind off Steve – well sort of.

Luckily the girls seemed to have got my arrest out of their system last night and it was Spencer, Jo and Lucy that bore the brunt of office banter today.

You couldn't write this, but there was only a fire drill at 9.15am this morning and Spence went into overdrive, donning a high visibility vest, even though Laura is actually the nominated fire warden for our floor.

'Follow me ladies!' he shouted, leading a bunch of gaggling women on a merry dance out of the fire exit and up the road like the pink Pied Piper.

I love Spencer; he has no pretence, calls a spade a spade and has a heart of gold. He loves a hint of melodrama like myself, but isn't annoyingly flouncy and in your face with his sexuality. He's just right; he's my little mate!

Right enough of the faff. Rees called me today.

Basically he said that they've CCTV footage that's tracked the American's car onto the M20 towards London onto the M25 at junction 4 for Orpington and then it loses him in country lanes around the village of Downe.

They've checked the map for possible destinations and extrapolated the sort of time it may take to get to the most obvious one – the local Biggin Hill airport.

And sure as eggs are eggs, about five minutes later than they expected, CCTV at the gates shows the car pulling into the airport. Bingo!

They're still trying to get access to Biggin Hill's internal CCTV and flight manifests, but are happy that they've tracked him that far and obviously he'll have left the country by now, but a lead is a lead.

I then asked Rees what was happening about the American Embassy and if they could shed any light on it?

'Well we've tried calling them. Well I say we, it was Scotland Yard, as I've a contact there running some checks for me with Whitehall, M15 and GCHQ as to on-going enquiries. They said the Embassy is still coming up zero.'

I was exasperated as one would imagine: 'Seeing as the car has diplomatic plates, they must know who's in it and where the car is scheduled to be at any given time.'

Rees sucked in breath: 'Well of course they do, but they aren't telling us. Why is it they went to so much effort to create a job for your boyfriend and pull him from his old one? What do they want with him? He comes up clean on our database and MI5 assures me he's not being 'run' by them.'

'Run? What are you saying, he is some sort of agent?'

'Well I don't really know Miss Sophia, but we can't rule out anything at the moment. Better he's with the US, rather than the Russians, Mossad or someone or something else that we've no leverage over. The US Embassy isn't spilling anything though. The CIA apparently "cannot confirm or deny" that they have our man. We are applying pressure higher up the food chain and we'll see what happens. If we can get evidence of a flight out of Biggin Hill to US soil, that would help our cause, but I'll let you know if and when I hear back.'

With that he was gone.

This has all got into a strange world of espionage, except I'm just caught in the middle, simply on the end of a phone and not able to see what's actually going on behind the scenes, as you would on TV. It's so frustrating, for a control freak like me to be; well, so out of control...

I just want to do something - be that girl who gets the guy, but I can't. I've got to be the one that goes to work each day, stays strong and probably gets a call to say that her boyfriend has been found at the bottom of the Grand Canyon.

Meanwhile, I'm nowhere solving my own dream riddle. My partner's not here and life's not the same without him!

I'm going to watch a film, as escapism and red wine is my self-medication for on-going melancholy.

Scientists do say that alcohol is a solution after all…

Friday January 29th 2016 – 11.10am

Weather: Sunny, clear and cold – the news hinted at even more snow tonight, so we may all leave work early - yay!

Travel: Slow going on the train due to icy rails or some such story – probably the wrong sort of ice...

Well, here I am at work typing on my tablet – again!

I've given up hiding in the loo, nobody notices anyway and being Friday, most other people are on *Facebook*. I've also had my daily update call from Rees though.

It was news, but odd news.

Get this diary, the CIA is apparently unable to comment as to whether they *know* or *have* a Steven Cartwright in their custody. But as Rees puts it, they are: "proffering an olive branch of hope my lovely", after MI5 applied some pressure. However, all they've come back with is that I should expect to receive an email. Just where and when and from whom, we don't know...

How woolly is that?!?

Rees explained that it'd been confirmed that 15 minutes after arriving at Biggin Hill, the CCTV shows Steve entering Gate One and getting into a golf cart across the tarmac to a small white executive airplane with a continuous red stripe around the outside.

Records don't show a manifest of passengers, as it was a private scheduled flight, but Air Traffic Control recorded the destination as being Teterboro Airport.

This is a small strip in New Jersey, something akin to the size of Biggin Hill, but basically US soil, which I thought should work in our favour.

MI5 has leveraged this information and evidence to lean on the CIA, who have now come up with this cock and bull hint that an email may be coming.

It's like getting a press release that announces that another press release may be released at a date unknown and by an unknown person – all that we can say is press release may or may not be coming at some time...

I'm so glad I don't have to work in this bullshit environment. It *has* to have been created by men!

A crappy code of conduct that awards the side that outwits the other, like chess on the world stage. Yet this time with cocks instead of rooks. Yet again, I'm just a pawn and the feeling of futility is completely overwhelming.

I'm sure if women ran the world we'd be far more efficient, to the point and peaceful. Not so much subterfuge, just suffragettes come good!

'That's all I have for you my lovely, but good news nonetheless!' said Rees calmly, his voice smiling that nice smile of his.

I *was* however, livid:

'What, that I may get an email to supposedly prove he's alive, when *anyone* can write an email? I want to *see* him for goodness sake!'

'Yes but I'm sure he'll write something pertinent in there, so you know it's *really* him. Plus we've narrowed down the search a little.'

'Oh yes. To a friggin continent...well done you!'

I'm afraid to say I then did something rather rash.

I hung up on him!

It was a heat of the moment thing, I'm not proud of it and I'm not sure you're allowed to hang up on the police, but as I say, this is so frustrating.

Control out.

9.25pm

Well the CIA may be woolly, but their wool is of the highest quality, as is their word!

I got home early due to the snow, popped in to see my aged neighbour and do my bit for Cameron's "Big Society".

So where the hell do I start?

I've not had any word from the Police or an agency, but I get back home and sat in my inbox is an email from Steve.

From Steve's actual *Hotmail* account!

My immediate impression was that of surprise, then elation, but finally scepticism. So has someone water boarded his log in details out of him, or was it really him? The next impression was; I'm struggling to find the words.

Absolute confusion, I guess.

Email verbatim, but as I say, absolute gobbledygook:

Brilliant to finally be able to email you my love
Quatrains were your thing, but do trios work for you?
Hell it's no iambic pentameter 'I know'

The weather is cold, but the sun cream is helping
Even The Company is nice, and they find me friendly
Back soon, I'll appear at night as a spectre?

Every day is fast paced with lots of Rushin'
Writing up my report as I watch the research
Reuters has not laid on a credit card facility!

Love you all, you are my world
Assume you know the length of may break?
Seth must be worried to be so long apart

Xavier the cat is with my neighbour Janet
Tell mum I hope she doesn't miss her flight
And thank Pa for the lovely bunch of oconus

Tried - seven to plus six Times to call your phone
Know Operator High Jump's it to voicemail
Make sure you take care of the flat!

Is he taking the piss or what?

Just his sort of humour to take off our own research and parody the quatrains!

Sounds like he's ok, even enjoying his 'break', as he calls it. That's fine you just jet off on an expenses paid trip and don't worry about us or the taxpayer's bill for wasted police time. So long as you have sun cream, for pity sake!

No, that's fine; a postcard won't be necessary, or a leaving note of any kind. We'll just play "guess where the hell Steve is today" and hope that you're not just gone 'til November!

In fact, the more I read this rubbish, the more I can pick holes in it. Bad grammar and bizarre spelling in places; I guess he must have been rushing or "*Rushin*" as he says - nobody even says that. Not even in Croydon.

He's definitely not left me six or seven voicemails, I've no missed calls on either phone and how can I take care of the flat if I don't even have a key? He knows I don't have a key! In fact, it's a wonder he still has a door left after Roger's recent visit!

What a ramble! I thought I was bad.

It makes less sense than Nostradamus' work himself...

He doesn't have a cat called Xavier or a neighbour called Janet. His mum's not going away, in fact she's afraid of flying and how the hell can his dad have sent him some coconuts, no matter how badly spelt they are.

And as much as Seth may miss him, they're not *that* close as brothers, so why mention Seth specifically.

What about me you selfish sod?

Just bizarre and my poor brain is shot!

10.45pm

I've decided, in my infinite wisdom and new sense of openness, to email this waffling piece of waffle to Rees and blind cc in Seth for his info. If only to pass on the good tidings to him directly!

We'll see if either of them knows what Steve's going on about, cos I'm too busy worrying to think straight.

Maybe by including all the false things, he's trying to prove that he's not actually in control. They may be his words, but what if he's deliberately trying to make it obvious to me that something at his end is markedly wrong?

I presume that this was read by the CIA before it came to me, so why would he spell things so badly and they not be spotted and put right – a positive redaction if you like, or what I like to call, a correction?

Why are some bits in capitals and others not?

There's inverted commas and odd slang that he just wouldn't normally say. He's an intelligent guy, a trained journalist for goodness sake. It's his job to get it right first time. It just doesn't sound like him, so it must be some sort of warning, or code, or something.

Yes that's it.

He always boasted that he was a walking enigma. Not entirely sure he was referring to the code breaking side of things at that time though...

Right done, sent.

Let's see what happens and what the others think...

Seth will know what I mean in terms of how odd it all is and Rees may look at it from a completely different perspective. Who knows how a detective thinks? They must be trained to think outside the box, laterally, literally and all things 'ally'.

Except maybe sporadically... as that wouldn't help the cause much.

Good grief – time for bed me thinks!

Saturday January 30th 2016 – 9.15am

I'm sitting up in bed, coffee in hand and no decadent croissant today thanks for asking – I'm not *that* organised!

The news headlines are alarming to say the least. If ever proof of Trident's necessity was needed at a time of renewal; then now could be that time.

Not content with a previous war with Georgia, invading Ukraine and annexing the Crimea, Russia's now sent tanks to the border of Belarus!

What's going on here? Are we back in the 40s when it was in vogue to invade? Are we back in the 80s and the Cold War? Hello, have we not moved on as a race?

Some young upstart is reporting from there now, wearing a blue helmet and a dark flack jacket over a white vest. Must be Kate Adie and Bruce Willis' love child working freelance or something...

They're filming from the air and I've heard of a tank column, but not a tank cobra. This line goes on for days. It's like when you're at the station and a goods train comes past and you can't see the end and keep thinking, *right it'll be gone in a minute. In a minute. Any second now...* And it just keeps coming and coming. Clatter, whoosh, clatter, whoosh - as truck after truck hurtles past.

The tanks are literally flooding down the hillside track, like a green metallic lava flow and then branching off into a cleverly choreographed formation. Needless to say there's nothing on the other side of the border. No official wall or fence. No defence. Nothing.

It's almost as if it's purely for the visual spectacle. Yet another overt show of power from the Kremlin that forces the West to sit up and think, and arguably take its eyes off the crisis in the Middle East.

Yep, it's on *ITV* as well. A live feed that's interrupted children's TV and the *Sooty Show* of all things sacrosanct. Well that's good for little Johnny then isn't it? He gets up, has his flakes of corn and settles down to watch *Care Bears* and he sees a potential live invasion.

They've just got no scruples these days - Russia I mean, not *ITV*. No comment or denunciation from the powers of the Western world as yet I note.

Ping – I just got an audible email from Seth in reply to Steve's message that I forwarded on.

LOL, it simply says: '*WTF??*'

Well Seth, that's two of us in the dark then...

2.35pm

Rees just called me. Does this man have a day off?

He noted my concerns from the email to him and asked me to talk through each point, or 'sticking point' as he called it.

He agreed that the composition of the entire piece was strange, albeit the message looked normal. Well wishing, gripes, a few questions. It was a newsy email intended to look like a newsy email, but Rees smelled a rat. He didn't see the point in someone else writing it for Steve, as it'd be obvious that it wasn't from him.

Yet this was something else. The references were *so* wrong, that it was obvious to him that Steve was feeding misinformation so as to flag 'a situation' in Rees' words.

'What sort of situation?'

'Well, Miss Sophia, I can't say to be sure, but the fact that he refers to a cat that he does own, but gets the name wrong on purpose would be for us to read between the lines as it were. The CIA wouldn't know his cat's name, or a neighbour's name, so he's been clever enough to pick facts that the CIA couldn't disprove or notice as being an immediate false flag.'

I was getting increasingly exasperated now: 'I see, so what can we do? Can we ask the CIA what they're playing at?'

'Well we can, but that might compromise Steve's position. What if it's not lies for a flag's sake, but some sort of code? I've got a team at GCHQ looking at it now for you. Their software will be able to detect any patterns, inconsistencies or nuances that the human eye may not uncover. Plus they're trained at spotting and decoding these sorts of things themselves, much more so than me. For me it's the fact that he's written it in trios, like some sort of sonnet. That just doesn't make any sense. If he'd just taken the time to make it rhyme?' Rees laughed inappropriately: 'See what I did there?'

'I hardly think this is the time for flippancy!'

'Yes. Apologies, got a little carried away there so I did. Anyway, where was I? Oh yes trios. Yes, even he admits he's not writing in a meter, iambic or otherwise. Then as you say, the many inconsistencies and irrelevances of the capital letters and inverted commas for example are at odds with his training. But maybe they're *wholly* relevant. Steve's a hack as you say, so he'd know exactly what he's writing. One or two mistakes would be expected, especially if he was under duress, but to have a raft of errors is tantamount to journalistic treason.'

'The reason is in the treason...' I muttered absentmindedly, reminded of the old *Kasabian* track.

'I tell you what. You may be onto something there Miss Sophia. Very interesting. Let's just think about that again. Reason in the treason. I like it. I think that he's definitely being deliberately dreadful. I'll report this back to GCHQ and tell them all of the items that don't add up and see if they can make head or tail from it.'

'Yes it has to be deliberate. It also has to be his words. Albeit, he wouldn't clip Rushin'. Not sure if that is an Americanism that the CIA has added, if he were perhaps dictating the message to them?'

'Could be or could be another oddity designed to stand out and direct us. Let me reflect on this too please. I'll shut myself away and have another look, now I know exactly what's out of place. We'll solve this, don't you worry Miss Sophia.'

I went silent for a second, trying to recall my previous line of questioning: 'Ok, but as I asked before, what next? Technically I've not even replied to his email, which may seem odd to whoever is watching or waiting.'

'Hmm, true enough. Yes best to reply, but reply as *you*. Don't think too much about your response and over analyse it, or it'll look too contrived. Also let's not let on that we don't know where he is, as he refers to the weather and the length of his break, as if it were a pre-planned trip. Odd I know, but there may be more to this than we think, so best to plead the fifth and act dumb. So please don't rant at him for being missing. Play him at his own game so he knows we are on the same wavelength. Say Janet sends her regards and the cat is staying somewhere only he would know, so again he knows it's you and you understand the code. That should do it. It'll be a holding email, until we can figure out all of this mess.'

So here I am pen in hand, figuratively speaking, but at a loss as to what to actually write. I've got this far:

"Hello you,

Not sure about your trios. We all miss you so much and hope you're back soon. I've spoken to Reuters and they said you've exceeded your credit limit. I think this is code for them saying that you've mucked about too much in the past and you need to prove yourself trustworthy in order to get back on their credit list. Janet says hi and thanks for your concern. Your mum got her flight and the cat is staying at Lea's.

Keep in touch love

Soph"

Well I think it's *me*. Friendly and a few hints in there that I don't know what he's going on about with his code and that he needs to prove that it's definitely him.

I confirmed, as Rees suggested, a few of his fallacies and I was particularly pleased with where the cat was staying. We love walking around the Leas in Folkestone, so he must spot that one and know it's me! Particularly as we don't know anyone called Lea, but hey, the CIA don't know that. Hee hee!

I'm not going to send it to Rees to proofread and I'm not convinced I can make it more authentic. Right let's send it and see what happens. Hopefully Steve will respond...

10.50pm

Just finished watching the news and the UK Government is one of many, as one would imagine, that have poured scorn on Russia's aggression towards Belarus.

The US President was coy with his statement and intimated that his hands were tied, not only because his administration was in limbo before his term ends, but because US relations with Belarus were already poor at best.

The country became independent in 1990 after the breakup of the former Soviet Union and as such Belarusian is the second language there with over 70% of the population speaking Russian. There have been many reports of diminishing freedom of the press, falling rights of freedom in this supposedly democratically elected country, as well as reports of political opposition being suppressed.

Following the signing of a treaty with Russia back in 2000 and talk of creating a framework of a new state to merge the two countries in 2007, some commentators are questioning whether it's an invasion at all, but simply Russia arming Belarus as a key ally on the NATO borders.

But an ally for what exactly?

They do border Ukraine, so maybe it's a way of Russia attacking on two fronts to finally claim Ukraine.

Belarus also has strong ties with Syria of all countries, after signing trade agreements with them in the late 90s. Everything seems to have some bloody link to the Middle East... let's just hope it's not literally bloody.

Well whatever Russia's doing, they're not commenting on it to the media. Yet.

Anyway, back to domestic issues, still nothing back from Steve and I just keep re-reading his email.

Again and again and it doesn't get any easier to understand or post rationalise. Maybe I should share it with an outsider? Mind you Seth didn't offer anything overly valuable as feedback and Beth already thinks I'm bonkers, so it'll be hard to get an impartial view from her.

'Writing up my report'. That's what he said. And he mentions *Reuters* by name. Why would you say these things if you are in CIA custody? But he met with them at an agreed time and is on CCTV getting into a car and a plane seemingly with no struggle.

No hessian sacks or being bundled into the back of a black *Sedan*. Maybe he *is* helping them. Maybe they picked up on his thoughts for the *Reuters* report on General Mabus from the bug and used that as a cover. But he already said they'd created the job for him. Why would they create a job for someone they're going to incarcerate?

It does *sound* like he's on a job. Writing a report on research. What research? It has to be so obvious. Am I just missing it? Ok, sleep on it! Brain, engage and do what you do best please.

2.55am

No, my brain hasn't worked yet, but I've just been rudely awoken by Rees, not the dustman!

He's on his way over and we're then going to bloody Cheltenham of all places!

Now and don't spare the horses!

Sunday January 31st 2016 – 5.30am

I should feel tired, but instead, I'm wired!

It's not often you get a call from the police in the dead of night enlisting your help for further immediate enquiries at GCHQ. Well *never* really!

So that's where we're off to, down the M4 to the Government Communications Hcad Quarters.

We're at Reading services at the moment for a quick break and then on the final leg of our journey into deepest, darkest Gloucestershire.

I'm quite excited, despite a little anxiety as to why we're going there. I trust they've not heard that something awful has happened? Rees said that even *he* didn't know why we're going. He just got the call from above and has suddenly turned from a Detective Inspector to just a simple handler come chauffeur.

He really is quite the wit and raconteur is old Rees. I say old, he's not that old, just old enough to be of interest! He wears no ring I note, but seeing as he's helping to look for my impending fiancé, I can merely admire from afar, LOL.

Part of the journey was a little awkward to say the least: 'So Miss Sophia.' His eyes darting towards mine to check I was still awake I presume and then back to the empty road ahead. I replied with a smile, which he must have caught out of the side of his peripheral vision as he immediately continued: 'This er, admission you gave to Carter. The full picture as it were. Did it not seem appropriate to tell me and save all that trouble?' he visibly exhaled, feeling a relief I guess at finally getting it off his chest.

'You put me in an awkward position Rees, what can I say? Truth. At the time, I didn't know what was going on. I didn't know if anything I might say could actually put Steve in danger, hell he was missing, already *in* danger. It's complicated alright, it was nothing against you, it just felt the best course of action at the time and when Campbell started to probe, he seemed to be onto something and almost needed to know the full picture so as to extricate myself from danger, or at least impending incarceration.'

My excuses were met by silence. Then a nod and a suck of his bottom lip as he audibly contemplated my predicament: 'Alright. I see. It's tough to take seeing as I'm here to help, but I understand your confusion and need for self preservation.'

Rees looked at me again, this time holding his gaze, to the point where I started to watch the road for him.

'If we're going to figure this out and find Steve, then you're going to have to trust me. What we're driving into now, I'm not so sure. I can't make any promises of how this is going to go either way, but I'm here for you. Understand?'

I felt bad, my stomach knotted. I felt like I'd somehow betrayed him, yet I hardly even know him. I could feel myself welling up for goodness sake. I looked left to the passenger side window to hide my eyes as they filled up like a scolded schoolgirl. I sniffed, breathed in to compose myself and smiled back at him, as if nothing was wrong.

'I understand Rees. I understand.'

6.35am

Ok, so we're here. Rees is off speaking to someone about parking. This place looks massive, like a huge titanium donut. It's a mixture of the glass-fronted Ascot racecourse grandstand, crossed with Centre Court at Wimbledon.

Even at this time of day the car park's jammed and no, that wasn't an overt counter communication joke.

Right, Rees is coming back now. Time to log off.

1.10pm

Well next in line on my glamorous tour of toilet cubicles is GCHQ Room 0.0.2, cubicle two, to be precise. What a place they have here! The building as a whole you understand, not just the toilets, but come to think of it, they are quite swish.

From what you can see when entering the building, there's a lot of glass, open meeting areas with stylish shaped light brown leather seats and pot plants dotted around, as if to break up the feeling of space and the brooding, dark stone flooring.

It's not new, but it smells new. Clean. No bugs in here I doubt, albeit there's a chap mopping up now.

There were people milling around, entering the building, even at this hour and speaking in hushed tones - as you would imagine. What was also nice is I could see into the green open space within the inside of the circular donut shaped building.

There were even people outside, at half six in the morning on a Sunday, or whenever it was. I got thc feeling this was definitely a 24/7 operation, a bit like Las Vegas and with just as many poker faces.

The entrance area had a real hotel foyer feel, mixed with the reception of a big blue chip company in London.

The dark stone flooring looked expensive. Open voids left me craning my neck, my mouth agog, as I traced the many balconies and bridges crossing from point to point in the upper levels above.

Not exactly what I was expecting, but I guess I've only seen like 1/1000th of the building, so pretty hard to judge.

First impressions though and I was suitably impressed, if not a little intimidated.

There was a large wooden slatted edifice rising, ever upwards from the left side of the main foyer and this, as it turned out, was the lift shaft.

Once through the relatively understated security, Rees and I were met by a Mr Glover. It sounds formal when I write it like that. He did qualify his name with: 'Call me Callum,' when we arrived, so I did.

There seemed to be no formalities or cloak and dagger here, which wasn't as I'd expected. No shades, no overcoats, no earpieces hooked up to the central intelligence chamber. Just deli's, a social network like any other office and flexible working hours apparently, which explains why it was so busy.

Callum took Rees and I to a large lift and what I found most fascinating was how he had to scan his eye to allow him to access the floor we required.

So cool.

'Retinal functionality,' he quipped, as if it were the norm.

We're lucky if the lift works at my office, let alone having security. More of a 'rectal functionality' there!

What I also LOVED was the lift buttons were arranged in two columns and went from 0 to 5 and then 0 to 0.1 and down sequentially to 0.5.

'We're going to 0.4,' said Callum, looking me in the eyes. He then winked: 'Subterranean.'

Hell yeah, I thought!

Callum's not a day older than 25, I swear – I think I may be getting better at this guessing malarkey…

A manicured side parting gelled up with product that accentuated the blonde highlights within his light brown hair. He wore a tight fitting plain white shirt with navy blue trim to the cuffs and the inside of his collar, as well as the line running down parallel with his shirt buttons. It was stylish, without being too over the top.

Smart dark blue slacks, black shoes – slip on winkle pickers. No glasses, no facial hair and I also note, no ring!

Good grief! I'm turning into some kind of sex-starved spinster, eyeing up men of all ages! I blinked heavily to return my subconscious to the present moment and the case in hand.

Callum explained that he's a Cryptologist with a First in Mathematics from Cambridge and a year at MIT studying Advanced Quantum Algorithms. I duly nodded my approval, almost studiously, as if I'd opted out of that course at the very last minute, but actually feeling more in the dark than the dark matter he'd have studied there.

Clever kid! Probably one of those who got their A* GCSE Maths aged 11 just to make my C, at the second attempt in Secondary school, look bad!

For all his intellectual nous, it was his thick Mancunian accent that belied his vast intelligence – the only wally not in Whalley Range I thought... Blimey I'm judgemental! Katie Hopkins has nothing on me.

'We're going down to meet up with my colleague Katarina Rebane. She's an Estonian language analyst and between us and a few programmes that we've run your boyfriend's email through, we've a few things to share.'

I did wonder if this was not something that couldn't just be done over the phone, but I wasn't complaining.

I was in a lift, going *down* at GCHQ!

Also I wondered why we needed an Estonian language analyst, if Steve was with the Americans. Then I realised that he must have meant that she *is* Estonian and a language analyst by trade – quick on the uptake aren't I?

Maybe I should do a PhD in Quantum Linguistic Understanding, or just plain *listening* to the layman.

I think Callum could sense my excitement, mixed with the anticipation of any news to come, as I bounced nervously on the tips of my toes.

'Nothing bad,' he smiled to put me at ease, giving a slight wink: 'Even *we* don't have all the answers. We hope you might just be able to shed some light on a few areas and quicker this way than coming to you or speaking on the phone. More secure too.' he added, nodding to himself, as if to verify his decision to pull us 175 miles at a moment's notice.

Anyway, back in the room, or the toilet cubicle at least. I'll have to get back to the open plan, glass sided canteen now, so I don't look too conspicuous by my absence. It's like being in the café at *John Lewis* at *Bluewater* in Kent. Very light and again with a void above, so as to see the amount of space in the glass fronted offices above.

I'll report back in full later, assuming I'm allowed and I don't have to sign something to say I won't write anything down, even if it is just for my own personal consumption...

9.45pm

Well if the Government is looking for ways to make cut backs, it could be overnight stays for me and Rees at a rather swanky hotel on Gloucester Road. Separate rooms of course, but dinner, bed and breakfast at £220 and then the petrol money back tomorrow...

Pro that up nationwide, across all of the Government departments and surely half of the national debt is purely down to travel and subsistence?

Anyway, nothing was said to say that I couldn't record this all in my diary and, to be fair, I wasn't exposed to much information that would be saleable on the black market, on Clapham Common, Silk Road or on the back of the 208 bus.

It was, as Callum said, simply a case of us getting to them quick smart, working on their shoulder and bouncing some ideas around. That's as nitty gritty and real as detective work gets I guess. It's not all Hollywood glitz, glamour, fast cars and even faster women – albeit I was pretty fast getting ready this morning!

We exited the lift on what I would normally class as level minus four rather than the 0.4 that they refer to it as. We turned into a corridor of doors. Gone was the glass. Gone was the style over substance. Gone was the light and space of this decadent cathedral of post modernity.

Out of sight, was definitely out of mind, when it came to design in the depths. Functionality and space saving was suddenly the order of the day. It reminded me of the Government offices in the film *Brazil*, maybe just slightly less autocratic or dystopian. Maybe it was just this section of the building and it was a *Section* that Rees and I were now attached to.

Section 4 dealt with counter espionage and cryptology and I hoped and assumed, for their own personal wellbeing that behind each closed door of this impersonal thoroughfare, they would have more than a broom cupboard in which to work, unlike in Terry Gilliam's vision for *Brazil*.

Callum Glover turned right out of the lift, walked down the hallway and opened door 0.4.4, this time using a finger print scanner, followed by voice recognition:

'Until death do us part.' he recited nasally, which seemed an odd mantra to either follow in a work capacity or simply an ironic sense of humour.

Maybe you need that working down here...

Access was obviously granted, as the door shifted to the side with the hiss of hydraulic pressure. Its entire form was then hidden within a recess within the wall. A nice touch, for an otherwise drab design scheme I thought.

We walked into the small, artificially lit room and Callum punched a wall plate to our left that promptly released the pressure and the door shunted closed behind us.

No going back now then...

A blonde lady, mid thirties like me, with hair tied back in a long ponytail, was standing over an older bald chap, who was typing on his workstation computer. She turned to face us, pushing her stylish horn rimmed glasses atop her head.

Long sighted, I surmised and from the strong jaw line, svelte figure and light complexion, I was also able to hazard a guess that this was in fact Katarina Rebane.

She extended her delicate and manicured hand in immediate friendship, backing it up with a wide grin to reveal perfectly white teeth.

Callum stepped in to break my view, hand proffered forth: 'Sophia Sinclair, DI Rees, I give you Miss Katarina Rebane.' he stepped aside; arm still extended, as if introducing the first act at the Hippodrome or the circus.

Rees' eyes visibly widened and he boldly took her hand and kissed it: 'The pleasure is mine.' he fawned. The word 'Miss' must have stirred something inside him.

He certainly never kissed my hand like that!

My main curiosity was that Katarina's accent belied her physical allure, as it was in fact disappointing and more East Midlands than Eastern Block - A child of migrant workers doing the jobs we didn't want apparently.

They settled in Boston, Lincolnshire and saved everything to put their daughter through schooling and University. Her prize for a high IQ and an ear for languages was a job in Whitehall before being re-located to Cheltenham last year.

She speaks six languages, so she says. Estonian, Russian, German, Polish, Good English and Bad English; so no need to worry if she'd understand my somewhat clipped Estuary accent, but I wondered if she'd pick out Rees' broad brogue.

The room we now found ourselves in was understated to say the least. Dimly lit, a large grey table in the centre of the room, with six work stations all facing into each other and a glass wall with a white board to the left of the three glazed panelled sections. Some ridiculous looking equation or algorithm was written upon it, as if to impress us on arrival.

Intimidate me, more like.

The centre section of the glass wall was, what looked like a large touch screen, definitely like something from the movies and the last section was a pane of glass giving a glimpse into the empty meeting room next door. The other three sides of the room were gunmetal grey in colour and apart from a white square clock on the wall facing the entrance, there was no other decoration.

It was all business.

Other than the bald technician that was sitting next to Katarina – he never was formally introduced – it was just the five of us in the room.

Katarina took up the baton straight away: 'I won't bore you with the ins and outs of what we've done, but suffice to say, we've a few watch words that we want to put to you. Also a few scenarios and inconsistencies that need clarity.'

'You're telling me.' I replied, disappointed not to get the finer details as to what they *had* been doing. Maybe that's why I didn't have to sign anything.

'Now if we can just put the email up on the wall, then we can refer to each line.' she said proffering to her technician with a sweeping gesture towards the touch screen section.

With that, the email appeared on the wall and Katarina strolled over to it, her slender arms swaying by her side: 'As I say line by line, but first a few holistic discoveries and consistencies. The computer's recognised and reported that the first letter of each word is exactly and consistently one point size larger than the rest of the sentence. Why should this be?'

We all stood there silent. Rees and I looked at each other and then at Callum, who gave a wry smile and a nodding wink.

Katarina put us out of our misery; well tried to anyway: 'This is in fact a simple clue as to why we have trios of statements, as opposed to straight sentences or the 'quatrains' that Steve refers to. They have to be in threes for the code to work you see. You may not have noticed the importance of the layout of the sections as threes, unless Steve had pointed it out.

And these larger first letters are also highlighted for us, so we don't miss their relevance.'

I shrugged at Rees, still in the dark as to what was going on and any relevance of these trios. He pulled an equally clueless expression back, which put me at ease!

Katarina pointed at the first letters, one at a time: 'They have to be in sections of three for the larger first letters to marry up in sequence. The clue being the larger first letter.'

I squinted to see the first three trios, as being coded "BQH", followed by "TEB" and "EWR": 'Right, so why's he done that. These mean nothing to me, what do they stand for? Does BQH stand for British Queen's Head? Oh, blimey. Is it a threat on the monarchy?' it was a stab in the dark at best and almost the first thing that popped in my befuddled head.

'Nice,' nodded Rees: 'Looks like we'll make a case officer out of you, after all.'

Callum smiled warmly, admiring my game efforts: 'Yeah good try. Alas a country mile away from the truth. We could've simply typed all of the sequenced codes into the Internet to get the answer straight away. However our computer software flagged up this pattern for us and automatically cross-referenced the Internet in each case to ascertain any obvious meanings. Steve is no cryptologist, but his feeling for the dark art and his nuance for a novice are quite impressive really. By using this coded system, he's basically mapped out his route for us.'

Again, Rees' eyes met mine, we smiled at each other and this time he shrugged selflessly, to share a burden of stupidity.

Katarina brought up a search engine on the wall to make her point: 'If you punch BQH, TEB and EWR into any search engine. First up each time, every time is...' she continued with a pregnant pause, as if for effect.

'An airport's booking code.'

I laughed out loud and shook my head: 'Bloody hell, he really isn't just a pretty face. Who'd of thought Steve, the super sleuth? Laying breadcrumbs for us to pick up and follow his scent. I love it! So where is he?'

‘Well it’s a bit of a convoluted route.’ said Callum stepping up to the touch screen. He tapped each of the first letters in isolation so they all showed up in bold: ‘Listen, he starts at Biggin Hill, as we know, which is abbreviated to an international flight code of BQH. Then he’s off to Teterboro, again as we know, which is known as TEB as its code.’

‘Superb. He is a clever old stick isn’t he!’ said Rees, his reverent tone tinged with amusement.

This whole process was clearly a learning curve even for him. It’s not often the parochial DIs get a chance to mix with the big boys.

Rees later told me that he once had machinations on working at Scotland Yard, but family life precluded his move, settling for an ‘easier’ and arguably safer life in Kent. The lack of ring on his finger masks his former marriage and two young children that he sees at weekends when he can, and now he also has to fit in time to see his new girlfriend. More’s the pity.

‘It seems that he *is* a ‘clever stick’, as you say DI Rees.’ confirmed Callum: ‘Now he’s in the US then. So we presume they got a car to Newark airport, which is coded as EWR, and an internal flight west to Las Vegas, which of course is LAS. XTA is an odd one though. It’s Homey Airport, a military airbase on the edge of Vegas airport, which runs Government flights to other military bases. One of which is classified and denoted as TKM. Any guesses folks?’

Callum eyed his captive audience, again that wry, knowing smile etched on his young handsome face: ‘No takers? Ladies and Gentlemen, welcome to Dreamland. Or for the film buffs among you, Area 51 to be precise.’

‘Shit the bed!’ I immediately spluttered out.

Well, my honed potty filter obviously doesn’t work underground, or so it seems! ‘So let me get this straight. The CIA have kidnapped my Steve and taken him to Area 51. What the hell are they going to do? Probe him?’

Katarina laughed: ‘Well yes, the “official”, unofficial line for Area 51, is that it’s a hide out for the fuselage of the extra terrestrial crash landing at Roswell in the 1940s. That's what they'd like you to believe, or wrestle your conscious waking hours with. It's created a tourism boom for an area that would otherwise have none and that has in part helped to fund the black ops going on within the Groom Lake compound.'

'For all its infamy, I'm not entirely sure where Area 51 actually is? Arizona?' questioned Rees, looking innocently at the two agents.

Callum coolly brought up a localised map on the wall within an instant: 'Nevada and about 100 miles outside of Vegas, to the North West. It's not *that* secret, you can zoom in on the base on Google Maps for instance, albeit the NSA may have doctored it.'

He pointed like a bus tour guide hosting a charabanc of Eastenders going down to Margate: 'See, Groom Lake here, this is all Edwards Air Force Base and around here is the Nevada Test and Training Range.' his finger swept around the periphery of each geographic area in turn as if locating high pressure systems on the weather update.

Katarina chipped in assertively: 'Historically, it's believed the base would've been used for the testing and development of experimental aircraft and weaponry systems. This may still be the case, but there's been a sudden increase in air traffic to and from the base over the last few months that have come to our attention. So it's fortuitous that of all places Steve could've been taken, it's here.'

'Fortuitous? How the hell can kidnap be viewed as such?' I demanded, almost choking on my glass of water.

'So we can find out exactly *what* else they're doing there now.' She replied matter of factly, as the lights above us momentarily flickered.

Super. Steve was now being used as bait to find out what our allies are doing on a secret base. Lord *knows* what they're doing to infiltrate our enemies!?!

Callum sat down and put his feet up on the table. He was confident and a cocksure kind of a lad. A typical Mancunian I thought at the time.

I could imagine he turned up for his job interview all chilled out and dressed down, full of bravado and that impressed the panel of judges to the point that out of all the Oxbridge entrants, they hired the one Mancunian candidate.

'There's an old mine around there. Mountains to burrow into and it's in the middle of nowhere, so quite a handy place to carry out anything, off the books.' he ended, sheepishly.

I walked over to one of the spare chairs facing the touch screen, so as to take the load off. Well, I'd waited long enough to be asked: 'So we know where he is then? Just not what they're doing with him.'

'Oh, he's not there anymore.' said Katarina, flicking her hair nonchalantly and also sitting down to join us.

Rees piped up: 'And we know this how?'

Katarina pointed to the screen: 'Well Steve says it's cold and sunny. Nevada's not cold. Plus he says they fly somewhere else.'

They all stared at the screen. Katarina and Callum waiting for us to see it: 'No?' said Katarina impatiently.

Rees and I both shook our heads.

'Let me show you.' She stood once more and pointed to the penultimate trio.

Xavier the cat is with my neighbour Janet
Tell mum I hope she does not miss her flight
And thank Pa for the lovely bunch of oconus

I looked up as they zoomed in on the trio on-screen: 'Yes, this *is* an odd one. His cat is called Shelley and his neighbour is definitely not Janet, Olive I think, from memory. His mum's not taking a flight and what's that spelling all about?' I said, almost dismissing this as being a series of key errors.

'Ah yes. Bear in mind the code. The first letters of each line have to denote the airport first and foremost. The message is arguably secondary. Well except for the last word.' said Katarina, provocatively.

Steve always did like to have the last word, but I wasn't sure what she meant in this instance. Then it struck me. The last words of each line in the first trio that were still on screen:

Brilliant to finally be able to email you my love
Quatrains were your thing, but do trios work for you?
Hell it's no iambic pentameter 'I know'

'That was the conversation that we'd had on text. "I know" was his answer to me. That's the sign. It is him! This is his message and this is his code for telling me.'

Rees looked at me baffled. The two agents smiled, as if they got a kick out of me unravelling the mystery myself, in my own time and on my own terms.

'Yes, I see it now. So he has a code at the start of each letter and a running code being the last word of each line. So what else do we have then? "Helping friendly spectre". Well that doesn't make sense for a start.' I said defiantly, frowning at the others in the room.

'What's another word for a spectre? What are they?' asked Katarina, like a primary school teacher, gradually teasing the answer from a distracted child, who'd rather be at break time.

I audibly puffed out from my cheeks: 'A ghost, a ghoul?'

Rees laughed out loud: 'It's a spook isn't it!' he said striding over to where I sat and putting his hand on my shoulder, stroking it down my forearm with a final grip of his fingers for reassurance: "Helping friendly spooks."

Callum slow hand clapped: 'You got it Rees. And so it goes on. He refers to being at a "Rushin' research facility". Then we have "world' break apart", then as you see here, "Janet' flight oconus", got it?' his hand again, pointing to the zoomed in section on the backlit screen.

'Yes, but this one makes no sense to me.' still at a loss and on tenterhooks for an answer.

Callum then typed "Janet flight" into a search engine and continued: 'Well we think that the word Xavier was just a flag to show that he was using code and prove that we couldn't take the words at face value. But of course it had to fit with the

XTA airport code and there aren't exactly a host of words that come to mind that start with the letter X that he could work with, right.'

True enough, not many sentences have the word xylophone or xenophobe randomly thrown in for posterity...

The military flights that fly out of Homey and also the red stripped plane that left Biggin Hill are run by a company called *JANET*. So he took a Janet flight, not to an island with coconuts, but if you search the word or happen to know that 'oconus' is actually an acronym, it stands for 'Off Continental US'. So basically, off the US soil to somewhere else, possibly unknown by him.'

Rees mimicked Callum's handclap: 'Very clever.'

It wasn't clear whether he meant Steve for thinking it all up, or the two agents for actually cracking it.

Possibly both.

'Ok, so where is he now?' I asked quietly, hoping they'd got that far.

Katarina duly obliged: 'Well, there aren't many lines left to unravel.' she swept her hand down the wall and pinched the last trio to enlarge it for us all:

Tried - seven to plus six Times to call your phone
Know Operator High Jump's it to voicemail
Make sure you take care of the flat!

'The computer highlighted the word "Times" as being capitalised and yes, I could've told you that, but it's merely a pointer for us to reveal the truth. So the underlying message is that you should 'phone the voicemail for the flat' or check it. Have you done that?'

Katarina looked more expectantly at Rees than at me. Rees and I then looked at each other. I shrugged and he jumped in: 'To my knowledge Katarina that has not been done. No.'

Katarina nodded to the technician who looked to immediately 'get on it', as his pale, polished dome went down and he typed feverishly on his work worn keypad.

Katarina stood back from the wall, as if to ensure she had read the verse correctly: 'It's the "seven to plus six Times" that had me stumped. He's leading us to the word "Times" by capitalising it. Then I realised that the dash before seven, could in fact, also be read as a minus symbol.'

Rees sat down and as a detective; he must've secretly been in awe of his counterparts and at the same time, beating himself up for not spotting any of the signs. He rubbed his chin thoughtfully: 'So we've got minus seven to plus six times. Could it be, I don't know. Flight times?' he chipped in, trying to earn his corn, if not just rebuilding his own sense of pride.

Callum pulled an approving face and half nodded in Rees' direction: 'Close. We think it's actually time zones. Groom Lake is PDT, Pacific Daylight Time, or minus seven hours off GMT. We therefore think Steve's destination, is plus six hours over GMT, so heading east to somewhere that's cold, but sunny and also houses a Russian research facility.'

'So it could be, Russia for example?' proposed Rees.

'Ah, so it's "Russian" around then.' finally getting the clipped code and face palming myself for being so slow.

Callum smiled, pleased that we were both keeping up with the professionals: 'Well, maybe he had to be careful of who might be listening in. He refers to "The Company", again capitalised, which is in fact a colloquial reference to the CIA, who are supposedly being friendly to him. In the last line of that trio, he also uses the two words in succession "under cover". Sophia, we think he's gone under cover for the CIA to a Russian research facility to write a report, not actually on behalf of *Reuters*, but the American Government.'

I put my hands to my face, rubbed my eyes and poured another glass of water from the nearby jug on the centre of the workstation table: 'How the hell can someone get so involved, so quickly and be helping secret service when they've no formal training? One minute he's having his lunch and then suddenly, he's being groomed for a trip to Groom Lake!'

Callum slowly shook his head at me and wagged his index finger: 'What do you think you're doing here yourself then? Work experience? You don't have to be on the payroll, to be of service. I think the CIA's using his skills and training. Just as an undercover journalist and I presume his lack of knowledge as to exactly what they're looking for, gives him an alibi and them plausible denial.'

Rees finally sat down, leaving just Katarina standing by the screen. He took out his notepad, as if to crystallise the goings on: 'Sounds like quite a few assumptions going on here. But in this spirit of looking at this line by line, as you suggested, do we therefore presume that where Steve says he is "finally being able to email you", that in itself refers to his long journey and a possible period of no email or internet access, whilst he travels to meets his new hosts?'

Katarina zoomed in on the first trio for the benefit of the group: 'I think so, yes and then he makes the point that he *has* to use trios and mentions quatrains for some reason, but I'm not sure if that's an 'in joke' or has any particular relevance?' her eyes passing from Rees' directly to mine.

'Yes. It's a thing we've spoken about together and an in joke.' I clarified, wanting to move the conversation away from our own crude research into my seemingly crazy dreams.

Rees began noting down in short hand. I could see the abbreviated items, squiggles and curls that I recognised from Steve's own notebooks. He'd tried to teach me once, but seeing as I can touch type, I felt it was a waste of my time.

Katarina brought up the next trio and stood back behind the technician: 'This is where he says the weather is cold, but it's sunny. Sam, can you look for areas six hours east from here that have a similar weather pattern this time of year. I would imagine it's quite far to the east. Maybe we'll bring up a map in a moment and have a look. As we said, he hints at the CIA being friendly and most importantly, he's trying to reassure us that he'll be back soon. This again makes me think he's on some sort of undercover assignment with a sunset date, rather than say, deep cover and trying to infiltrate over time.'

Callum then stood and walked to the screen and pinched the next trio to enlarge it: 'Here, he refers to writing up a report whilst watching the research. So he has a watching brief and the fact that he overtly name drops *Reuters* so close to this, makes us think he's definitely in there in some sort of capacity as a freelance feature writer, or so *he* believes anyway. Perhaps the facility is working on something that would be of interest to his readers and he's getting first hand insight.'

'Yes whilst taking notes for the Americans too.' said Rees, sucking the end of his well-bitten *Biro*.

Callum turned to Rees, touching the side of his nose with his index finger, so as to confirm his correct assertion: 'It appears so. We think the words "credit card" are a red herring, simply to allow the end of the sentence coding to work. Maybe, perhaps he's somewhere so remote that the use of a credit card isn't even possible, as there's nothing to buy. It was the next trio that we specifically wanted to see if there's anything we were missing Sophia.'

Callum zoomed in on the next trio, which he had assumed to be a statement of Steve missing Sophia and the family:

Love you all, you are my world
Assume you know the length of may break?
Seth must be worried to be so long apart

'Well, I'll help if I can. "You are my world", he's not specifically said that to me before, it's not a pet catchphrase, if that's what you're asking. Not sure how he can assume I knew the length his break and as to why he's put "may" instead of "my". Also, it's not his birthday. That's in March.'

Callum look pensively at the screen: 'So maybe the first line does look after itself and is a simple heartfelt message to you as he needed the word "world" at the end.'

'Oh yes', I interrupted: 'I forgot about that part of the coding; so this one says what? "World break apart", or it "may break apart" even, if you flex the rules.'

It was at *that* point I had a shiver down my spine. That phrase about the world breaking apart seemed so familiar and quite coincidental to come up again. I was sure that Steve had actually said something similar to me not that long ago and it evoked the same physical reaction as the word Mabus did. Why could that be?

‘You ok my lovely?’ asked Rees, who seemed to be able to read my anxiety better than the experts: ‘You look like you’ve seen a ghost. Or a “spectre” should I say.’

‘Yes fine, it’s nothing, I just recognise that part of the code, but can’t put my finger on it. I think Steve said something like that to me before. Not in this context, but it made me feel funny then too.’

Callum poured me some more water and looked kindly into my eyes without speaking. He realised that despite this all being exciting for me, this was still an ordeal that had seen my boyfriend disappear. Even if we did have an inkling as to where he may now be.

He pursed his lips in thought: ‘I may be looking at it too closely, but May is the fifth month of the year, is that some sort of reference to how long he may be away? Five days, weeks, months? Which would take us into, May as it goes.’

‘Five months! That’s not an assignment, that’s a bloody secondment!’ I shouted at no one in particular.

Rees now stood, looking to get in on the action and basically play with the touchscreen wall. Callum stood aside and took his seat, again looking at me for reassurance: ‘Here he goes then. The old Welsh wizard.’ he said mockingly, under his breath.

Rees pinched the penultimate trio and they disappeared: ‘Oh shit, what I do?’

Sam bobbed his head up, tutted and resurrected the screen.

Rees looked somewhat relieved at not having to pick up a repair bill: ‘Well I think Callum’s just trying to look at every angle. No one’s suggesting he’ll be away for five months. It might be five years!’

He turned to smile at me broadly. The shit.

I was NOT impressed!

Rees then continued, whilst daring to play with the screen again - such a boy: ‘Right then, so we’ve spoken about the cat, I assume the line about his mum’s flight was just to facilitate the ‘T’ on “tell” and the word “flight”, as well as to be a flag again. Whilst the last line was a nod to his father and a play on words to allow for the seemingly misspelt coconuts, which you've subsequently decoded.'

Katarina nodded and zoomed in the last trio: 'Sam, any news on the voicemail for the flat?'

The once dark haired technician looked up, nice geeky looking spectacles that fitted his learned persona to a tee, sat below his dark eyebrows: 'Good timing, just saving it off for you now. Give me a sec whilst I pop it on the 'S' drive and I'll allow you access to play, pause, etc, on the screen.'

Sam's head tilted back down and his hurried two finger typing was an art to behold.

Katarina's lips parted to reveal those white pearlers once more and then she turned to me: 'So any other little gems in the last trio? Did you have any other interpretation on the six or seven that comes to mind and are we missing anything in the last two lines?'

No pressure then: 'Er, well I think I agree with where you are coming from on the time zone aspect. I guess to have written "minus seven to plus six" would seem odd to any other reader, so the minus symbol does act as a handy dash. I think the trio is also there just to facilitate the TKM code and the 'phone voicemail flat'. I note he also adds the words "take care" in there – which is nice. Not sure what the line "Know Operator High Jump's it to voicemail" is all about, presume it's something to do with him sending a message via an operator to the flat's voicemail, which seems odd.'

'Yes.' said Katarina, her brevity somewhat out of sorts and I'm sure I caught a strained look between her and Callum. Yet just as I went to question her on this further, I heard Steve's voice and it made me jump.

Subliminal tears appeared at the edges of my eyes, as I immediately span around to see where he was.

Disappointingly, it was just a recording. The speakers in the ceiling piped his dulcet tones around the room and the message was short and sweet.

Bitter sweet to hear him in fact.

'Is that it? Play it again Sam!' I demanded, wincing at how cheesy the line sounded in the circumstances.

'Soph. The name on your phone is a drum and bass and the tune I'm dancing to.'

Katarina listened again and asked Sam for an on-screen transcript, which to his credit, he was already preparing: 'Steve likes a riddle doesn't he. And the name on your phone?'

Katarina looked me in the eyes expecting an immediate answer, but I didn't have one: 'I have a Samsung *and* a Nokia. Nothing to do with drum and bass, let alone music? I don't have music on there either. We don't like drum and bass. Well, Steve had a *Brown Paper Bag* phase in the 90s, but we all like a bit of Roni right?'

Callum nodded vociferously, which surprised me a little due to his age: 'Sam, can you please run DNB through the computer, all connotations. What strikes me first is the last bit. If you are dancing to a tune, it's usually someone else's, i.e. someone else's instruction. Could be limited hangout?'

Katarina nodded in agreement, as did Rees, but I think he was just going along with the others, as I'm sure neither of us knew what that term referred to.

However, just as I'd done him an injustice in my mind, he came up with a corker: 'Miss Sophia, the name on your phone, it's not just the brand I don't think. Don't you have a phone with just one contact name on it?' he asked, knowingly.

The two agents looked at each other and then to me for verification: 'Yes that's right Rees, thank you for reminding me. It's, Mabus.' I said slowly, if not just warily.

'Mabus?!?' asked Katarina incredulously: 'Why would you have such a God forsaken name on your phone.'

It turns out that Katarina is Orthodox Christian and well read. She knew of the link to the third Antichrist, but nothing more than that.

I shrugged and looked at Rees pitifully: 'It's a long story. I had a couple of funny dreams and the name keeps cropping up that's all.'

'Dreamt the end of the world, so she did.' said Rees perversely proud to be the bearer of such bad news.

Callum looked intrigued and leaned in, ears pricking up: 'Oh yes? What's all this about then?'

I briefly, and I mean briefly, filled them in on my dreams, my subsequent research with Steve and how that had lead to his meeting with the CIA and being warned off. I'd assumed Rees would've filled them in, or at least allowed them access to my file, but it seems they were only interested in or tasked with the content of Steve's email, rather than its actual context.

Sam suddenly popped his head up: 'Yep, been onto my mate Jack at RIPA and the girl's internet searches check out.'

He looked me in the eye, wickedly: 'Was there a conspiracy site you *didn't* go on by the way?'

All that talk had left me dry and I went to my handbag to get some lip balm when I noticed I'd had an email notification. I surreptitiously looked at it with the phone still inside my bag.

It was Steve!

'Wo, he's emailed me back!' I scrambled to get the phone out of my bag and everyone sat up waiting on my words.

'Hold up, I'll just get into your phone and bring it up on screen.' said Sam, as if it was as easy as that.

It was as easy as that.

Within seconds my email appeared on the big screen, along with the original:

On 31 Jan 2016, at 18.00 'Cartwright, Steven' wrote

Hi

Glad you liked the trios, I've ditched them this time for speed. Did you get each letter? The first letter I sent was bigger. Good to hear Reuters hasn't forgotten me. The Company should be trusted and to their credit, this assignment will be a success. Must go, the days just go on and on.

x

------Original Message----
From: 'Sinclair, Sophia'
[mailto:Sophia.Sinclair@tk421.com]
Sent: Saturday, January 30, 2016 14.55
To: Cartwright, Steven
Subject: Hello stranger

Hello

Not sure about your trios. We all miss you so much and hope you are back soon. I've spoken to Reuters and they said you exceeded your credit limit. Which I think is code for them saying that you have mucked about too much in the past and you need to prove yourself trustworthy in order to get back on their credit list.

Janet says hi and thanks for your concern. Your mum got her flight and the cat is staying at Lea's.

Keep in touch love

Soph

The room was quiet whilst everyone thought.

Again, surprisingly it was Rees who first came to the fore: 'Here look, the reply shows the time the email was sent by Sophia at 2.55pm. And Steve has been deliberate to send the email at 6pm on the dot, I think.'

I checked my watch: 'It's now 12.04pm by my watch, and the email on my phone came in at Midday on the dot. Yes on the dot. So what?'

'Well it goes some way to proving Callum's theory about the six hour time difference. He's trying to be found. Well located for his own peace of mind, I guess and yours.' said Rees stretching his arms in the air.

It felt like it'd been a long day already.

'Yes he can't assume that you've been in touch with the police, let alone us. So plus six hours time zone is where? Sam you there yet mate?' asked Callum excitedly.

Sam brought up a map on screen: 'Yes of course! As you guessed, it could be Russia, or Kazakhstan, Bangladesh or Bhutan. Russian Siberia looks the safest bet, I'll look into the weather for those places, see if it's cold and sunny.'

Katarina then spoke up: 'Ok, let's look at this. "Did you get each letter? The first letter I sent was bigger." I think he's confirming what we already know here about the point size on the first letter of each line. Sophia you asked for a demonstration of trust from him and he again refers to The

Company, so I read that as a message of calm for you and that we should all just keep the faith. He also mentions the word "assignment", as well as *Reuters* again, so it does look to be his cover story. He must be bored if the days go so slowly though. On and on he says!'

Sam stuck his hand in the air: 'Got some news back on drum and bass. Most things point to a fast paced heavy drum beat, but according to the *Urban Dictionary*, which obviously I frequent all the time, it's also slang, or rhyming slang to be specific, for the word *place*. Any good?'

Katarina pulled up the instruction from the voicemail as a transcript on the screen again: *'Soph. The name on your phone is a drum and bass and the tune I'm dancing to.'*

She tapped her finger on the line of text repeatedly, her nail echoing on the screen: 'So the name Mabus could in fact be a place and it's where he's being told to investigate.'

We all nodded, quietly trying to read a different interpretation of the message.

Nothing else was as clear.

'I've not heard of anywhere by that name and it certainly doesn't sound Russian. Sam, anything on the Internet search or on our files?' asked Callum, now standing behind him and leaning over his shoulder.

'Yep already on it. Search for the word "Mabus" and it just brings up General Mabus and Nostradamus stuff. Just searched "Mabus location" and... bingo.'

'Yes where?' I asked cutting him off in his prime.

Sam looked over at me and then carried on undisturbed: 'Good old Wiki. First up on the Internet search is a Mabus Point. It's on the east coast of Antarctica near McDonald Bay. Named after Howard Mabus; a US naval officer who was instrumental in supporting the set up of the original US astronomical control stations along the coast there.'

'Sounds intriguing. What's there now?' queried Callum, stroking his smooth chin in anticipation.

Sam laughed out loud: 'It says here that Mabus Point subsequently became the site of the Soviet scientific station Mirny. Which itself has its own website link. Bear with. Hmm,

Mirny translates into Russian as the word *Peaceful* – which could always be nefarious activity, hiding in plain sight. It's situated in Australian territory within Antarctica and first opened in the 1950s. In summer it hosts 169 people in 30 buildings and just 60 people in the bleak winters. And Callum, before you ask what they're doing there, the main research is to do with glaciology, seismology and meteorology.'

Sam shared his screen onto the main wall, so we could all see the old black and white grainy images of the station being built. He then clicked on an external link to the Mirny Observatory's own website.

This gave chapter and verse information about the topography, conditions and local environment, as well as weather patterns and site-specific activities. It was also handy that it was in English with an option for a Russian translation.

Too handy perhaps…

Sam was noticeably busy, whilst we all read the fine print about Mirny: 'Right then, I just cross checked and this part of eastern Antarctica is GMT+6. The longitudinal lines of the map we first looked at stretch down to include this continent. Antarctica is cold, surprise, surprise, but also sunny at this time of the year, which is nice. An Antarctic day can last a whole month you know?'

We didn't. Well I didn't anyway: 'So we think he's in the Antarctic then?'

'Well it's a starting place to look.' said Rees, safe in the knowledge that he'd be able to return to Folkestone, rather than explore the freezing tundra on a futile manhunt.

Callum clicked his knuckles as if to gain attention: 'Kat we need to take this upstairs. If we confront Langley with this new information, they may fold and let us in on exactly what they're up to with Steve. Sending a civi to Antarctica undercover is not exactly cricket is it? Otherwise, I'm not sure? Plus there's that line you noticed, pretty much checks out right? Are we duty bound to get Section 20 in there and extract him? Let's rattle their cage a little and see how much old Tweetie Pie actually tweets.'

Katarina nodded, she looked distracted. What line checks out I wondered? She then went within herself and breathed coldly: 'Steve does has a tongue in his head. He didn't *have* to go with the Americans.'

'Yeah he had to go,' I said unflinchingly:

'Steve being Steve. He had to go.'

*

And that's where we are then.

We broke for lunch and after the fast paced start to the day, I was just left on hand in case they needed me. Then come 4pm, I was ushered out with Rees to the local hotel. Our work done and I guess just made the place look untidy.

So Steve, you cheeky monkey.

There's me doing my pieces and you've been jetting around to Area 51 and then off to the South Pole.

Just crazy.

Well I'm jet lagged just thinking about it.

Time for bed and I think I can safely say that this end of January limit for my OCD epic diary writing has gone right out of the window.

Bring it on!

Monday February 1st 2016 – 6.30am

As we left, Callum assured me he'd speak to my boss and pave the way for my absence from work today, whilst we wend our way back. This is due to it being a matter of National Security, he confided.

He laid it on a bit thick. What must they think of me at the office? One minute I'm off ill, then arrested and now helping a bunch of Spooks – and all in a month!

I'm up with the lark today, more out of habit I guess, so let's see what's on the news.

Clinton and Johnston have both made statements about the Russian aggression, as if to help their respective campaigns and give their Presidential perception a shot in the arm.

I must say, OJ does look the part of a statesman.

Passionate, animated and a good orator.

He just spoke about his grave concerns for the lives and livelihoods of people in the states of the former Eastern Bloc. He cites the supposedly democratic countries of Belarus and Kazakhstan as being less than free, despite unrealistically high levels of turnout in their elections.

'Where's the healthy opposition? What happened to the marches, the banners on the streets and the not so quiet voice of dissatisfaction? What happened to the freedom of the press?' he was quoted as saying.

OJ has a point. I remember Russian journalists being forced to base their operations in Estonia, for fear of downward pressure from the Kremlin on their investors; or worse a knock at the door from a masked FSB man.

It's amazing how so often those who speak out about the incumbent of a nation, autocratic or otherwise, then suddenly find themselves accidentally falling down the stairs or with an unaccounted bullet in their head.

Johnston then went on to underline that the: '*Proliferation of Russian hardware at another nation's border, should not and would not be tolerated.*'

A hollow threat maybe seeing as it's from someone not even in power, let alone won the party nomination. Yet...

Yet maybe he's simply the mouthpiece of the bureaucrats in the West Wing, in the absence of any significant leadership from the fading POTUS? He has after all, appealed to voters across the political spectrum.

The current leader may be toothless, but the underlying administration; who it seems actually run Capitol Hill, are obviously getting increasingly vexed by the Kremlin.

8.15am

Rees knocked me up at around 7.30am – hmm bad turn of phrase, but I'll keep it I think... we can, but look when our beloved is away.

'Ah, Miss Sophia, you're looking radiant as ever. You ready for breakie and the off?'

He had certainly become less and less professional over dinner last night and as the wine flowed and the inhibitions dissipated, so his informality and pally nature came to the fore.

This was fine. As I say, it was less professional, but never unprofessional. Never once did I feel that he was actually coming onto me. He's just very friendly and very tactile. It just felt nice and we had an instant connection, not just about Steve. We actually became sort of friends.

I did end up telling him about my mum in Rhondda and that was it, the floodgates were opened forever...!

'Well why didn't you tell me? My Great Auntie Brenda lived in Pontypridd. Everyone knew her! Does your mother ever frequent the Ship Inn? She used to be the landlady you know, a proper Barbara Windsor sort of character, except Welsh and slightly darker hair. But also taller, more flat chested and with a Welsh accent too.'

And so it went on.

Rees, which I am simply used to calling him, has that beautiful rhythmic kind of voice that melts butter. He's funny and never stops talking, which is good on what could have been an "awks" meal for two on an away day with the police!

He also covered old ground, with the aid of a drink inside him, and berated me for not coming completely clean with him over Steve's involvement with the CIA. That I should not confess to him, but to some jumped up DI from London.

I think it hurt him more than I'd realised.

He asked about how Steve and I met, how our relationship was, not in any sort of interrogation, but out of genuine interest and empathy for my plight.

This whole situation is just surreal. One minute, I don't have a problem in the world. Well, other than the usual First World problems we tend to moan about like the Internet order not arriving when it should.

Now my world's spun on its head. Momentarily torn apart and I find myself in extraordinary circumstances, trying to come to terms with something that I swear I don't have the cognitive ability to truly comprehend.

Back on a lighter note, Rees' bad jokes were a constant source of amusement. For pudding, he ordered spotted dick and custard and immediately, I was expecting some sort of lame "spotted dick" kind of gag, but instead it was much more subtle and sophisticated humour:

'Right then Miss Sophia, see this here spotted dick. I'm about to take it into custardy.'

Rees reassured me that we'd find Steve and having slept on it, I decided it was time to take him up on these assurances:

'Good morning Mr Rees, dapper as usual. I certainly am ready for breakfast, but *about* the off...'

Over breakfast I somehow managed to convince him that we should be on hand and close to the horse's mouth for any updates. That he should contact Callum Glover again and insist that we stay at least another day.

I'd been thinking about that reoccurring line, about the world breaking apart. It was like the word Mabus; it had the same affect on me emotionally. I was laying in the roll top bath after dinner, the wine aiding the access to my subconscious and it was then that I started to recall my dreams.

As I've hinted previously, they're still with me.

Like a piece of baggage, I can never return. They're still the first thing I think of in the morning and the last thing at night. And there I was in the bath and it came to me.

Like the word Mabus, the phrase must've been in my subconscious. As I re-imagined the dreams, I became more and more certain it was the more recent of the two and as I pictured myself in the park, watching the young child and it hit me, like a flashback to actually being there.

The newspaper headline.

I hadn't remembered it until now. I knew there was a newspaper, but its contents were still a mystery. Enough to make me run off though, but if the headline was about the world or my world breaking apart, how does that tie in with everything?

Granted my world has been turned on its head since the dreams and particularly since Steve's been away, but broken?

Does that mean there's worse news to come?

I decided to sleep on it and this morning, with a new clarity and confidence, I knew that this information could be enough to prise open the doors at GCHQ once more.

Callum had been intrigued by my story, fanciful as it may have sounded. Yet linking the dreams to this current case could be a tipping point and give him something else to think about.

Rees grudgingly agreed to call him, although I think he was secretly hoping to continue the adventure too!

9.15am

YES! We're in the car heading back towards the metal donut, as I now like to call it.

Callum was on speakerphone when Rees called from my room and he was surprisingly open to it. I had convinced myself that he'd quote procedure of some sort, but he agreed to meet up in one of the unsecured meeting spaces on the ground floor for just a half an hour.

That was good enough for me!

I'm now tapping away on my tablet in the car; Rees has the radio on for the local traffic news. His black Ford Mondeo provided a smooth and comfortable ride and the heated seats were a distraction from the new flurries of snow.

Rees just looked over. Craning his neck to get a look at my tablet: ‘What you up to there Miss Sophia?’ Luckily he’s too wary of keeping his eyes on the road in these increasingly appalling conditions.

‘It’s just my shopping list. Life goes on eh?’ I replied innocently, a wry smile fleetingly visible on my lips.

Best I close down now then!

11.15am

Ok, so we’ve been in and I’m not in the loo, for a change, but still waiting in the open meeting space.

Rees and Callum are speaking by the main reception desk area. Doing what exactly I don’t know. Swapping business cards or football stickers for all I can see.

It’s been a fruitful exercise and although I’ve not witnessed the entire goings on, I’ve been kept in the loop on most things, as far as I am aware.

I explained my sudden bath time revelation to Callum and reminded him of my dream. He agreed, he wasn’t sure how the two themes of Mabus and the newspaper headline were linked, but seeing as I’d dreamt the name Mabus in the *same* dream, it was too much of a coincidence to just be chance.

I tried to help and verify our decision to return: ‘I don’t know what, but there has to be some sort of link between the dream and Steve’s location – surely?’

Short of ice breaking off a glacier in the Antarctic, I wasn’t certain what else might break apart down there.

I wasn’t allowed to sit in on the conference call with Langley, more’s the pity and neither was Rees. It was just Callum, Katarina and their direct superior Harry Bradley.

Rees and I sat in the canteen sipping piping hot coffee and chewing the cud, as to whether the Americans would finally talk or not.

‘Well I think they should. Taking my Steve like that. Mr Lennox and his heavy-handed friend! What on Earth is Steve doing down there. Why would the CIA be so interested in a research base in the South Pole, albeit a Russian one?'

I sat back to ponder and Rees didn't answer. Well not straight away.

'Suppose they think the Russians are looking for oil down there? You remember some time back, I don't know, mid 2000s, and they sent a submersible down to the bottom of the Arctic at the North Pole and claimed it as their own? They planted a piffling little flag on the bottom of the seabed.'

Rees' kind eyes enlarged as he awaited my answer, his face slightly unshaven and rugged today.

I nodded, squinting slightly as I tried to recall it in full: 'Yes rings a slight bell.'

'Well what if they're trying to pull the same stunt, but this time in the south with a polar opposite strategy?'

I simply shrugged at him with a 'who knows' gesture.

He smiled that smile and I was immediately at ease.

Well, maybe the Americans do, or maybe they don't know and they are just sniffing around. Using Steve as a human listening device or worse still, some sort of bait.

Time passed and Callum entered the canteen briskly: 'Right! You's two, on me now!'

5.05pm

So much has happened today and now is the first opportunity I've had to catch up. I just need to get it all down whilst it's still relatively fresh, for fear of losing the plot.

Literally.

Callum turned sharply and walked apace back to where he'd emerged close to the lifts.

Rees and I quickly downed the rest of our drinks, gathered our coats and bags and scampered after him, knocking into a few chairs of those sitting around us, in our haste to keep up.

By the time we reached the lift, the doors were open. We stepped in and Callum pressed the number two. Not quite to the top I thought, but a promotion on minus four.

The lift came to a steady halt and the doors opened to unveil the myriad of glass-fronted offices and meeting rooms that we'd already seen, albeit from the void below.

This was a real hive of activity.

Impromptu stand up meetings here, people leaning over colleagues' workstations there.

The ambient noise was a buzz of chatter. No radio or music like I'd have in my office. The odd person wore headphones, but I assumed it was to listen to something or *someone,* rather than *S-Club Seven*'s Greatest Hits.

We were then led into a meeting room. Room 47.

There was glass on three sides of the walls, a long light wooden lacquered table in the centre of the room with six stylish moulded and matching chairs around the outside. An LCD television was affixed to the one white wall and a projector on the ceiling pointed to the glass wall overlooking the void and the busy pedestrian bridges below.

Callum didn't speak, but proffered his outstretched hand towards two chairs for Rees and myself. Moments later Katarina strode in silently and took a seat next to me.

She simply nodded a greeting. No smiles, no words.

Next a rather portly gentleman shuffled in, struggling under his own weight. His grey receding hairline was offset by silver rimmed round glasses and shiny grey slacks. He had a bushy grey moustache, matching eyebrows, but no beard and a white pin striped shirt, protesting to open at his jowly neck.

I also noted *distinct* sweat patches under each arm – stinc being the operative part of that word! It was obviously not a good start to the day for him, which is what got me worried, such was the speed in which we were brought up there.

'Good morning gentlemen and ladies, thank you for coming up. Most unorthodox this meeting is, but we find ourselves in changing and challenging times, what?'

I shot a look at Rees, who flexed an eyebrow skyward. How the hell did I find myself in this situation?

A situation *room* no less.

His voice was Bullingdon, Bletchly and British Empire rolled into one. He could've presented the news on the BBC in the 1940s or voiced a Pathé newsreel: 'Miss Sinclair, Mr Rees; my name is Harry. Harry Bradley, Section Chief and whilst it's not the norm to invite civis up here; let alone *inside* this institution, we've had to make certain exceptions in what seems to be exceptional circumstances.'

Bradley leaned forward conjoining his fingers as if praying and propping them up under his nose with his elbows on the table top for effect.

I remember just looking at him blank. Obviously unaware of all that had been going on in the background and simply blinked and replied: 'Hi. Thanks, I think. Oh, Rees is a DI, not a civilian by the way.'

Rees smiled at me for noticing Harry's faux pas.

'Good for him!' barked Bradley in his 'tally ho!' accent and thumped his balled hand onto the table for added effect: 'Let me bring you good people up to speed. Langley's been tight lipped on this one, but the fact that they've got a Brit under their control, the fact that we have mentioned a few key words and the fact that we've such a "special" relationship, I've been able to open them up a little. Yes!' he nodded.

Bradley mocked the inverted commas around the word "special", an irony in his voice that presumed "previous" as Rees would say, on the American's behalf.

He then nodded to Callum, who promptly picked up a remote, pressed a series of buttons and the otherwise plain room suddenly morphed into something that I *would* have expected to see in this building.

The glass seemed to blacken on two sides and fade on the far wall opposite the projector.

With that, a map of the world appeared on that faded wall. It was projected by a series of fine beams of light, emanating from six points either side of the partition, rather than the projector on the ceiling, which I'd wrongly assumed would be in operation.

Callum stood and used two fingers to pinch and zoom the map into position.

Harry Bradley stood and pointed at the screen from his position at the head of the table: 'Right then. We know Steve's movements, which we challenged Langley on. They have now confirmed that they have him in Antarctica working on some undercover reconnaissance under the guise of a freelance journalist from *Reuters*. They have assured me that he is in no immanent danger and that he'll be returned within the week. Suffice to say, he has no knowledge of why he's actually there, other than his findings will be subsequently considered Above Top Secret.'

Bradley sat down and assessed his notes before him, so I took my opportunity to strike.

'Eh, pardon me Mr Bradley.'

'Oh, just Harry please, my dear.'

'Pardon me Harry, you mentioned the word danger in your succinct synopsis there, as well as working for Langley and the slightly alarming word "undercover". These are all valid points I'm sure to someone who knows what the hell is going on. As a layperson, I'd just like to know what the hell the Americans are doing with my boyfriend for Christ's sake!' my tone raised as if to emphasis that my eloquent way of speaking and perhaps mocking his own, rather than out of respect.

'Madam, I have invited you into the sanctuary and sanctity of this place. I'd implore you to have the common decency to remember whom exactly you are dealing with here. After all, who are you?'

It was at this point I almost lost it, but managed to stay professional and courteous. I breathed a silent sigh through my pursed lips and stared him one of my specials across the table:

'Who am I?

'Yes. Who are you to come in here calling the shots?

'Who am I?'

'Yes, you heard me madam!'

'Just who in the world do I have to be?'

In one movement I pushed against the table with both hands, levering my calves against the chair until it tipped backwards against the floor and I stood in a rage. Rees reached instantly to contain my anger with a strong arm across my chest, blocking my way towards the cantankerous old man.

Bradley shuffled in his chair, his pigging eyes averting my glacial glare. This misogynistic, dinosaur epitomises everything that's wrong with the Establishment, the jumped up, self-righteous little prick!

Callum looked to thaw the increasing frost in the room and quickly manhandled the screen to zoom in on the Antarctic region. It was at this point I realised that the map of the world was actually a live feed from a satellite. I then mellowed a little following this distraction and Rees nodded to me, as if to reassure that I was right in my response. I decided that for the benefit of Steve, I'd have to keep my reactions in check, but I remember thinking, if that man just so much as blinked at me the wrong way, I'd punch him in the throat!

Glover zoomed in on the Mirny research base and I could see live action movement, in and around the area: 'Welcome to Mabus Point Miss Sinclair. All Langley would confirm is that the comings and goings to this base had increased 1,500% in the past two months alone. Heavy materials are being transported in icebreakers and craned off all hours of the day. Transport helicopters are braving the elements to bring in additional supplies. You'll notice these black lines against the white snow here. A fleet of snow speeders at the ready.'

A red circle suddenly appeared around the rough outlines of the lines of skidoos. There must have been about fifty of them all told, but they were hard to distinguish in any detail.

Bradley clapped and with that, the circle disappeared. His aristocratic, husky voice took over the proceedings: 'When it comes to the Russians, investment in remote regions like this at a time when their own people at home are starving in places, doesn't really add up. The base may be Russian, but it's in Australian territory and we've been onto ASIS, and my counterpart there, and made them aware of the situation. The base is a research facility, but Langley suspects that this is now just a cover story and they may actually be investigating exploratory mining opportunities down there on the quiet.'

'I knew it!' exclaimed Rees excitedly. A grin from ear to ear and he was obviously pleased with himself that he was able to crack the operations down there, albeit it was with a bit of an earlier throwaway line.

'So why Steve?' I ventured: 'They could've used any old spy to run as a journalist down there and would the Russians not think this was a bit suspect; a journalist suddenly going down there, just as they increase activity in their operations?'

Harry nodded, agreeing with the basis of my questions and concerns: 'Steve's cred's check out. He knows nothing, so he'd not act suspiciously. They get journalists and visiting researchers down there all the time, so that *is* the norm, but these normal visitors just have tunnel vision. They only concentrate on the job at hand and don't go counting and questioning as to why the sudden influx of speeders and deliveries. I believe the CIA's banking that Steve's inquisitiveness and affable nature will stand him in good stead. Also it seems that from his Internet search history, he has inadvertently de-bunked a bunker or two.'

I looked quizzically at Bradley, at which point Katarina cut in: 'It seems the word "Mabus" resonated more with Langley than we'd have imagined. As did Steve's searches for two areas, which they are particularly coy about, namely Area 51 and Denver airport. Thirdly he was also researching an article on fracking and lastly he searched about the acoustic attributes of granite.'

I remember laughing out loud at that point: 'How do you go about debunking a bunker exactly and since when can a solid rock sing?'

I shook my head. What a load of garbage.

Callum called on another set of images that scattered across the touch screen, as if thrown down by an invisible hand. He quickly pulled them into some sense of order with his fingers and explained: 'The mountain ranges in Antarctica are granite based, which as Harry alluded to there, means they've intrinsic acoustic properties. The mountain ranges in Nevada and Denver also share these properties. And this is where unfortunately; I will need you both to sign the Official Secrets Act. Not so much to protect Langley's secrets, but to protect my ass from Langley.'

Cool! Steve would be sooo gutted to be missing this!

Katarina pulled up a satellite photograph of Denver airport, similar to the one that Steve and I had viewed online in my flat, which now, seemed like absolutely aeons ago:

'According to Langley, it's at these two points that they can effectively monitor tectonic vibrations. The granite mountain range acts as a giant seismograph for large global activity and there've been reports from Denver about peaks or 'turbulence', coming from the granite in the Antarctic region. They didn't say as much, but it seems that one of the many uses for Area 51 is as a tectonic listening station. I believe that it's just got a little out-dated, as technology has progressed and the *cost* of flying staff in and out of Homey Airport every day on the Janet flights, is unfortunately in staff retention, as opposed to dollars and cents.' she said, zooming in on the live satellite footage, as the tiny looking planes came and went.

'In this age of working from home, working on the hoof and a work/life balance, it seems that some of the best scientists living in Vegas and Nevada that commute by car and then by plane to Area 51, start to get fed up with the journey and drop out. Who'd have thought, Area 51 being brought down from within by an HR disaster?' Katarina smiled.

I nodded. I can relate to that. At least my commute is just a walk, high-speed train and then a tube. I don't have to sit on the freeway in a taxi, before taxiing on the runway.

In order to get to the core of the explanation, Callum then took up the mantle: 'They've therefore 'used' a balls up in the construction of Denver airport to their advantage. It seems that the plans were somehow transposed in the wrong place. Whether it was a CAD software problem, or a pissed off employee dicking about during a round of redundancies, they're not so sure, but suffice to say a batch of buildings were 'manufactured in error'. Langley caught wind of it and requisitioned them, receiving funding from the State Department to sink them into the ground and use them as an op's room for monitoring positions within the nearby mountain range. For them, *Denver* is the new Dreamland and an easy commute for those living in the city.'

I leaned back in my chair, unaware it was on castors and flew back suddenly, which took my breath away. Rees reacted first and caught me before I hit the wall. Luckily he was there for me once again!

Having composed myself, I quickly tried to look learned: 'So the fact that the US Government doesn't ever rebut the conspiracy theories about the UFOs in Area 51 or the secret bunker housing the Glitterati in Denver, it's because they're both convenient untruths.'

'Exactly!' said Harry: 'You couldn't make up such great propaganda, even if you tried, so they simply dangled a germ of an idea as a carrot and watched it explode over the Internet, as the next big cover up on Info Wars. It's the perfect personification of plausible denial.'

'What else are they doing at these sites then?' asked Rees, ever hopeful of putting to bed yet another urban myth.

Harry laughed: 'Well quid pro quo, my dear Rees. We don't tell the US what we're *really* doing at our Porton Down or Watchfield sites, now do we old boy?'

'What *are* we really doing there?' asked Rees part innocently, part speculatively and wholly surreptitiously.

Harry laughed again, this time causing himself into a wheezing, coughing fit. He slowly and deliberately put his index finger to his nose: 'Now that, my dear old thing, *would* be telling. Nullius in verba, indeed.'

His bushy grey eyebrows raised and his mouth started to break into a sinister smile: 'Let's just say, there's more than just a wind farm on the old RAF Watchfield site and leave it at that shall we? Always think and ask the next logical question DI Rees. If I were you, I wouldn't ask what we're doing there, but what the wind farm is actually powering.' He laughed again, smug at his own personal intelligence.

Rees looked thoughtful and caught his breath. He thought some more and resumed his fishing expedition: 'Ok, I just thought it was worth asking. But do we have similar sites then, for listening, not just for UFO storage?'

Harry smiled sanguine and nodded slowly: 'We do, yes thank you. There are large deposits of granite in Bodmin and

Dartmoor, but these don't seem to conduct sound like a proper mountain range does. Our largest and newest facility is within the Mourne Mountain range in County Down, Northern Ireland. Why do you think we fought so hard to keep control of the wretched place? Let me just say that there's a reason, the mountain called Pollaphuca has its name.'

Again, that same smug look, I could really wipe it off his face. There's insider knowledge and then there's just plain school ground teasing!

I've since searched this name and it means 'hole of the fairies'...seems like we have our *own* convenient untruth!

I was still confused about these listening stations, so I put my hand up like the class dunce: 'I'm still confused about these listening stations.' See. I told you I was.

Callum sat back down and somehow brought up a photograph of the Great Pyramid in Giza onto the screen: 'Like the Americans, we use old "Polly", as I like to call her, as a giant amplifier. We can hear space rockets launching for example. Not literally hear them, just see the readings on the modern seismograph. It was apparently used back in the Cold War as an early warning indicator of a rocket launch and we can still to this day track rocket testing in North Korea and the Crimea through the tell-tale tectonic vibrations. Tsunamis, earthquakes, volcanic eruptions, we can see them all as they happen. The trick is trying to predict *when* they're going to happen. All clever stuff kids!'

'So why the pyramid?' I asked, pointing at the screen.

Callum turned to the wall, as if reminded that it was even there: 'Ah, yes, Giza. Well it turns out that this technology or ability to hear the Earth is not as new as we'd thought. The Egyptians were exploiting the Earth's ability to "sing" or at least hum, some 2,000 years ago.'

Katarina had obviously attended the same briefing session: 'The Great Pyramid is built in such a way as to amplify the Earth's vibrations upwards, using strategically placed acoustic chambers and a network of shafts to echo and resonate this sound upwards and outwards. That's why the old images of the Pyramid always depicted lines coming out of it. Not as many have thought, depicting light shining off its once limestone rendered surface; but instead a great sound emanating from within and stretching across the desert plain.' Her long arms were outstretched, as if to emphasise its range.

Katarina stood and strolled languidly to the screen once more: 'How the hell *they* worked it all out *and* built the thing, Lord only knows, but for any traveller visiting Giza, they would've been welcomed or warned off by an almighty sound. The Egyptians had harnessed the power of the Earth as the ultimate defence. Who would attack Giza if they had Mother Earth on their side? Who would question the Pharaoh's authority if he could make the Earth roar or sing? The power of each preceding dynasty leveraged this ability to conjure the Earth's most natural pulse and that's why they were truly looked upon as Gods by the population.'

'I've never heard this before.' I questioned innocently.

Callum grinned: 'Not, the kind of thing they teach in school these days I'm afraid. Call me a cynic, but society is slowly beating the spirituality out of all of us. Anyway, the Egyptians were all about celebrating the Earth's creation. The original Creationists if you will, and what better way to celebrate the Earth's power than to amplify its own engine room? They soon realised it was specifically the granite that allowed them to do this. You remember the image of an American Indian with his head pressed to the ground in the old Westerns, listening for incoming cowboys?' he asked, cupping his hand to his right ear.

I nodded.

'Granite vibrations.'

'Wow.' I said simply stunned: 'How'd they know what to do and why don't we hear the sound now?'

Harry interjected, putting down his papers: 'It's all just smoke and mirrors in the end. What caused the fall of the Egyptian Empire? Well, the masses debunked the pyramid, that's all. They realised what it was, how it worked and it wasn't a place to bury the Pharaoh after all. They were not shafts to allow the soul to the heavens and once word got out, all hell broke loose. Many had died building it and then it suddenly transpires they'd all been shafted! Much of it was sealed, that's why it's silent now. What's more, similar things explain the rapid collapse of the Mayan Empire too, who shared many similar technologies. How two empires on opposite sides of the world got to hear about this and build pyramids is anyone's guess. There's a fine line between Quetzalcoatl and coincidence.'

I got the feeling that was a tried and tested line, not so much off the cuff.

Katarina had pulled up an image of a Mayan stepped pyramid: 'This technology or ability, was lost for aeons and it's only in more recent times that we've come to realise the true purpose and power of the Great Pyramid.' She said.

Rees was obviously in a curious mood: 'Is that why the Americans have one on their Great Seal and on their currency? To denote absolute power over the Earth?'

Harry pointed at him knowingly: 'Exactly *my* thoughts, my dear old thing. As an aside, the mottos on the dollar bill are?'

Rees shook his head. American studies were not his Major at University.

'*Annuit Coeptis*, or loosely translated from Latin as "he, she or *it*, favours our undertakings". Those undertakings refer to those that took place on 4th July 1776 at the time of their independence. Many presume that the all seeing "Eye of Providence" atop of the pyramid on the Great Seal refers to God favouring their undertakings, but in fact the use of the Pyramid in this case, is to signify that "it" is not actually God, but "The Earth". The rays of light radiating from the pyramid that surrounds the Eye, depict sound rather than any divine notions of light from a God.'

I looked even more confused: 'How or why would the Earth favour the independence of America?'

Harry sighed, aware that we'd got slightly off track, but it was still relevant to the Americans' vested interest in the subject that had brought us all together: 'It's not that the Earth would specifically approve of *them*, it's more *they* are the new world power to appreciate and harness the power of the Earth.'

Rees looked at me, vexed to say the least.

The vile Harry smiled, cutely aware that he was cracking opening an esoteric box that we could briefly glimpse, but not fully explore: 'The second motto on the note is the clue you see; "*Nouvus Ordo Seclorum*", a new order of the ages in literal translation, but the Great Seal's original designer said it was to signify the beginning of the new American era.'

I picked up on this and hopefully sounded like I too was enlightened myself: 'Was that the foundation of the New World Order then? The "*Illuminati*" as some might call them. Were they some sort of brotherhood of the Earth?'

Harry's eyes widened, the glimmer of a wry smile just itching to break out into a full-blown antagonising laugh: 'I see where you're going with this puerile line of questioning Miss Sinclair and I don't appreciate this sort of supposition or tittle tattle. "A new order of the ages", so just think about what that actually means. It's the 1700s and a new formation of liberal philosophy. They were anti-Royalist and Republican, as well as self-governing, self-sustaining, self-enlightened and basically; selfish. Nothing would stand in their way of the new imperialism, not least the indigenous Native American Indians. They were looking to create a new empire to annex the English, supposedly endorsed by God, but ultimately inspired by the Egyptians with a federal state run by elected leaders, rather than a royal lineage. This was the birthplace of Manifest Destiny and a mission of expansion in the name of God.'

'You make *them* sound like the bad guys' said Rees drolly: 'They learnt imperialism from the masters after all – and now we're just a lonely collection of islands, especially if we come out of Europe.'

Ha, glorified triangle shot across my brain and old Patrick sitting on my shoulder digging at me, telling me so.

I looked on the proceedings fascinated by the insight, but wary that Harry seemed to be revealing a lot and wandered if there would be a price to pay? A sacrifice for knowledge, or was it just his opinions, rather than the *actual* truth?

At the time, I didn't have it in me to ask such a direct question of a man in his high level of authority. On reflection,

I see that is exactly how the system is supposed to work then - simply don't question authority.

Harry stood and walked to one of the opaque windows; touched it twice and it turned back to a transparent state of glass, revealing the void below. He looked at the scurrying people below, like some kind of overlord watching his drones: 'Freemasonic principles and the spiritual essence of the Egyptian civilisation are everywhere in the District of Columbia; if you know where to look that is.'

I glanced over at Rees, catching his eye and he shrugged, both of us equally perplexed by this crazy character before us.

'The layout and geometry of Washington DC's plan has diametric links to the Nile River basin and you should check out the use of Egyptian symbolism when you can. Those above the carving of George Washington and within the Washington Monument itself, a notable edifice in perfect alignment to the heavens and their very own Cleopatra's Needle.'

'Is this not a little overt for a not so secret society?' asked Rees quietly.

Harry shrugged. It seemed that his information had hit a wall and perhaps it *was* all speculation after all: 'That's the question. Is it a front, a self-perpetuating myth or a celebration of the inspiration for a new society? Either way the word Mabus certainly struck a chord with the Americans mainly because Nostradamus' maze of jumbled quatrains were actually reconstructed for popular culture by the OSS.'

I looked into his eyes. Where was he getting this all from? How much more does he know and could it help solve the riddle of my dreams? I had to look it up, but the OSS was the forerunner to the CIA, started during the Second World War.

Harry caught my look and raised his eyebrows, as if to acknowledge his superior knowledge: 'My dear, the notion of Nostradamus' third Antichrist was simply "created" by the Office of Strategic Services in order to perpetrate the original doctrine from the Bible. This then allows the Establishment to preserve control on the God and Satan fearing populous, so they do just that – live in a perpetual state of fear and servitude. Nostradamus' texts were popularised in those days and since then, a strategic campaign has worn them down to nothing much more than a conspiracy or fantasy at best.'

Callum's young and he didn't strike me as being the sort to frequent Sunday school. However, it was *he* that called his superior out, on the subject of religion:

'So if Nostradamus' readings were manipulated to say something other than what they may have originally implied, what's to say that the Bible's not been cut and shut to bits over the ages? Those that take the Bible at face value; that every word is sacred or sacrosanct are surely just following a fabricated storybook?'

Harry was not being drawn on the wider implications: 'You'd have to ask the Vatican or wherever the Christian church has its secrets locked up to find that one out my boy. That's above my security clearance I'm afraid.' He smiled, but looked glad of Callum's questioning mind.

'Where was I anyway? Ah yes Mabus.' said Harry with glee, grabbing a coloured pen from a drawer in the side of the table and writing on the glass wall: 'An anagram of the word Mabus with one of Nostradamus' fabled letter changes is of course "Damus", short for – Nostradamus himself.'

I remember frowning at Harry. With all the political and terrorist leaders in the world that have conveniently similar sounding names to Mabus, so as to create conspiracy from, it never dawned on me the answer may lie much closer to home.

'We believe Mabus is a self-reflexive code and the third Antichrist in this instance, is in fact the author – or should I say the publisher that put the Quatrains together. It's the final ironic twist to Nostradamus' writings. It's *his* writings that have mislead so many people across the world into this end of days obsession that has allowed the powers that be, to take people's minds off the real catalyst for the apocalypse – capitalism, or the ruling corporatocracy, as well as the people themselves!' said Harry, pausing to drink some water before half heartedly offering the jug to the rest of us.

We declined, almost out or principle and he slurped through pursed lips before continuing on: 'Yes, the people themselves. The fall of coercive control will bring about the end of the world because in time, like the Egyptian populous, as people wake up and begin to realise the true filtered reality in which they live, rather than the reality shows that they are primed with, there will be an uprising. If control ceases to exist, we revert to our roots. We simply revert to chaos and hell on Earth.'

'The peasants are revolting eh? So, is this your own chaos theory Harry, or all just guesswork?' asked Rees playfully, trying to lift the spirit in the room.

This was all getting too deep for me and suddenly I liked the idea of Big Government, draconian laws and tight controls! 'So is Nostradamus just BS then?' I asked, befuddled.

'Afraid so. Well it *was* all written by him, but the order that it's taken and the meanings attributed to it have been engineered somewhat. As Callum speculated, it's probably much like the Book of Revelations by John the Apostle. Everything in life has a reason and mostly the reason is beyond the wit of normal man. In some cases conspiracy and controls are created for a reason. The Book of Enoch, for example, was removed as it didn't fit the official doctrine. What's in it, I'll leave to you to decide if it holds water.'

Even Callum and Katrina looked at each other confused by Harry's waffling.

He continued unabashed: 'The 9/11 conspiracies were started as Islamic propaganda that then became main-stream via the internet. The fact that the 7/7 London bombings happened in Oval and Shepherd's Bush is just pure coincidence that they both relate to President Bush who resided in the Oval office at the time. It was however convenient and this sort of thing is put out there by those with an anti authority agenda so *we,* who drive the machinery, get it in the neck from those who think that we actually created the mess in the first place. Which we did not by the way!'

I shook my head: 'So it's all about power and coercion. Keeping everyone ticking along, feeding the machine. That is until we wake up and rage against it? But to what end? You mention capitalism, how will that bring about change?'

‘Ah yes our beloved democracy and capitalism. Well if you ask me the whole corporate system’s based on fascist ideals, nations bend over backwards to corporate giants and it’s no coincidence that the Central Banks are not tied to Government. A greater man than me once said: “It’s easier to imagine the end of the world, than the end of capitalism.” I just fear this system might actually tip us over the edge if we’re not too careful. Nationalism’s rife in politics again and that’s the start of taking back control to a central autocratic figurehead.’

Harry puffed out his cheeks: ‘I just inherited this mess. I’m paid to maintain the status quo, not *really* question it. What would happen if there were no state and no control? I very much doubt we’d all become self sufficient and swap goods and services like a Neolithic commune.’

‘Well they didn’t in Tottenham or Croydon during the riots, did they.’ joked Callum: ‘That’s how I imagined your idea of social chaos would ensue. Looting, burning. Rape and pillage every village and we’d be no better than those who we fight in ISIS.’

Katarina then acted as balance, like a BBC news reporter: ‘At least ISIS has a cause, which they see as just. Their agenda is far bigger than simply looting the latest *Blu-Ray* player.’

Harry nodded his agreement: ‘Imagine a society without currency or corruption. The Founding Fathers thought they were building a better life, free from royalty and subversion of religion, yet they were all predominantly Freemasons, and a subversive, esoteric cabal is exactly what they started to build. The American Eagle is inspired by the double headed Phoenix from Freemasonry, which is itself, a Lucerferian symbol.’

‘No wonder ISIS call the Americans Satan.’ said Rees.

‘Wait, how’d you know all this?’ I asked.

Harry laughed and flexed his interlocking fingers out in front of him in a stretch: ‘Classics and Political History at Cambridge my dear - that and a not so secret obsession of demystifying the mystics. Listen, there are so many links to Freemasonry, Ancient Egypt and some sort of Islamic or Israeli destiny, that I could spend a week going through it all. As *he* says, why do you think the supposed “bad guys” call

America "Iblis" or the "Great Satan"? No smoke without fire I say. I think that Steve ruffled a few Phoenix feathers without knowing it and rather than incarcerate him, the CIA is *using* him for some sort of plausible denial.'

Callum and Katarina looked at each other again, this time more furtively throughout this exchange and I knew that Harry's candid conversation was now news to them too.

'The symbolic nature of the phoenix goes back to Assyrian times, which is why ISIS was in such a hurry to tear down the ancient site of Nimrud. It was a message to the US; to the fascist New World Order and to the Freemasonic cliques that hold power and political sway.' said Harry, leaning back in his chair, as a visible conclusion to his own theory of everything.

'Assyrian? I'm sure Nostradamus mentions Assyria, I remember looking into it and finding a bunch of them hanging out on the Gold Coast.' I said, tempted to check my diary.

Harry shrugged: 'What can I say? Sun, sea, sand, what's not to love my dear? The Assyrians were even assimilated into popular culture, including Joseph Heller's John Yossarian.'

We were ushered out shortly after this exchange and I'm still none the wiser as to why we were called in. Perhaps Harry was probing on a level far too nuanced for me to notice. Callum saw us to the car and had a word with Rees whilst I was getting into the car.

On reflection, I can't see how Harry, "The Establishment" Bradley can be so damning about a political and financial framework that's seemingly served him so well? Maybe he's one of those Marxist Corbynista types and remembers the original 9/11 in Chile. Many political ideologies work on paper, but as we know; history shows that absolute power corrupts absolutely. How many communist or military run states have proved this over time?

As a race, we obviously can't be trusted to lead or rule on our own, but as a brotherhood, totally aligned to the original spirit of altruism and empathy; is there in fact a true inner power that transcends us all - to believe in or fear? Maybe it's simply the concept of connection or love being the resistance. Either way, it's in the ether and not just in the air.

Wo, stop now Sinclair! This is Harry getting into my head, with his fears of fascism and a different kind of chaos theory.

Maybe the third Antichrist isn't a person, a ruler or a state. Maybe the Publisher who created the quatrains represents capitalism and control. Perhaps they're just the messenger and it's a collective of united nations, steered by autonomous orders for their own good and the continuation of mankind in their own image.

Like the famous poem, it hadda be Soros and Bilderberg right? Hadda be The Tri-Lateral Commission, a modern offshoot of the Holy Roman Empire, the CIA, the Mafia and Ginsberg in cahoots. Hadda be Harry, who's probably in on it after all, self-perpetuating the myth, by being so quick to dismiss the role of the *Illuminati*???

Is life simply futility? A lottery as to where you're born and once you're here, enjoy the ride, as there'll only be certain people that can control the pace and direction of the action. Is that why "Spin Doctors" are called as such, as they control the "spin" of the Earth in a literal sense, as well as the path we all lead in metaphysical terms?

When you start to think about things deeply and question them as I am now, it becomes dangerous. We're all therefore a potential danger to society with our naturally incendiary and pernicious minds. So, is that why we *need* to have control exerted over us, to keep us from harming ourselves and ending the human race? The Hobbesian bargain of a state of love and trust, doesn't quite sound like such as great deal after all.

I've heard evidence of Polonium-210 in Mars' atmosphere, which points to a nuclear explosion there. Maybe we're being protected from making a similar mistake…

Yet if this is true, why's there still so much war in the world? Are the differing levels of powers across the continents playing out their own power struggle? Are the "powers that be" not necessarily the powers that we voted for, but a secret society that's self-governing, self-propagating and the core founders of all state propaganda?

And if so, are the Georgia Guide Stones, Denver Airport and the United Nations all hiding their depopulation agenda in plain sight?

The mind boggles and as such, our tiny conspiratorial noggins should just stick to soaking up soap operas - that is unless, you're sat in the GCHQ canteen and your poor mind boggling off the table, like mine currently is. To have so many seeds surreptitiously planted in my mind, without any of the surrounding context, history or conclusions, is only serving to confuse me even more.

For me, that's where we are, the place we all permanently reside. Not the Matrix, but a permanent state of confusion.

Who am I to presume a higher and hidden authority, but equally, who am I to deny its possible existence either?

Harry said it first. Who am I?

My head's truly reeling and my stream of consciousness is simply an outpouring to try and decode or decalcify my brain. It's also so I can share my innermost thought with Steve on his return, as being the most conspiratorial person I know, there's something fishy going on here and just too many coincidences.

"Trust no one," said Mulder and food for thought indeed.

10.55pm

I'm home. It's late and I've forgotten which day it is. I've got myself so caught up in political intrigue, that I've almost forgotten what got me there in the first place - Steve.

Rees and I left Cheltenham and we drove mostly in silence, as both our heads ached from informational overload.

It was never an awkward silence, as I think we were both glad of each other's company, even if we weren't overtly interacting. I just felt so small and so insignificant within what is patently such the bigger picture that we have no clue about.

We ate at a seventies service station and it was at this point that I realised; unfortunately, I have to go to work tomorrow.

Normality. Futility. Indifference.

Blimey, that sounds more like a postmodern positioning statement for the NHS than a guileless fear of reality.

As I reflect on today, I still can't decide if Harry was speaking the truth or not. I've now been able to sense check much of what he was saying.

The layout of DC, the Egyptian links, the Founding Fathers being Freemasons. It all checks out, I'll give him that, but how true it is, I don't know. Can I even trust the Interweb?

Yet, if the US and other parts of the Western world *are* run by a secret New World Order, would they really be so brazen as to leave not so secret clues on bank notes or Denver Airport for example? Would they allow books that link them to Satan or would they consent to conspiracy at all?

Logic says that they shouldn't, as that would be self-defeating, but that in itself is far too obvious. Like God supposedly allows free will, does this supposed strata of political power allow us to postulate and predict within reason?

However, if you do get too close to the truth, do you then suddenly disappear to a form of limbo or purgatory? Like *Lost*.

Maybe that's what the Isle of Sheppey's really for...

You can't take the effect and make it the cause, but how else do we prejudge hindsight?

Ok, I really should go to bed and face up to my responsibilities in life, as I can't see Valentine signing on for housing benefit, if I don't go to work anymore.

Tuesday February 2nd 2016 – 7.30am

A blindingly good sleep - I can't usually sleep when I'm wired and been thinking; but tonight I slept with an almost social resignation that all I can do, is "my bit".

Every way, every day, I'm getting closer to being back with Steve. Blimey, that sounded like a Bono lyric. Or was it just *Wet Wet Wet*?

I think I've officially been institutionalised. I feel a certain familiarity and comfort in being back in a routine and packaged on the train, knowing that when I get on the tube I'll be herded on with less rights than afforded to common cattle.

Amazing how quickly we can turn from a state of despair and subversion to that of commuting bliss.

Today's going to be a good day! I can feel it in my water!

10.05pm

Ha, just re-read where I left off. Well the day was good until, that is until I got back to my inbox, which looked like a dystopian, post-apocalyptic battleground of messages and warnings from clients that had fallen on my deaf ears.

Despite being away on a matter of 'National Security', I never had an out of office, so they were neither redirected nor replied to in my absence.

Speaking of National Security, I did sign the Act!

It was not as formal as I'd envisaged. I was not made to sit in a darkened room with alphabetised spies such as B and Q shining a lamp in my face. It was almost more of a formality.

But I was warned verbally, as well as contractually, as part of the Act, that I should not speak of any information gleaned from the Security Services to anyone under any circumstances, otherwise I'd be locked in a darkened room and have a lamp shone in my face by someone from home base.

Well, they said not to *speak* to anyone, so I'm sure writing in a diary's fine. Famous last words…

Anyway, back to work and despite the pressures of the ensuing inbox, I kept calm in the knowledge that as much as the clients thought my absence was critical to their place in the running of the world's machine, it was in fact a piss in the proverbial winds of time, compared to what's really going on.

It was a mere drop in the ocean, with as much meaning in the infinite cosmos, as a butterfly flapping its wings.

These people really need a reality check.

I've just watched the news headlines and Russia continues to advance without actually making a final or decisive move.

It's like they're on parade and making no rebuttal as to their motives. The Western world implores them to recede and acknowledge their advances are in violation of almost every treaty since time in memoriam - yet nothing, which is odd.

It's like they've lost their phone signal or acting within a silo. I just hope it's not a nuclear one!

Talking of nuclear silos, maybe with the threats in the world today, a deterrent that we'd never want to ultimately use, due to the obvious repercussions to humanity, is not actually the best deterrent in the first place.

The futility and farce of *Dr Strangelove* is actually not too far off the mark. The Earth, or the granite would give the Doomsday Machine the early warning signal it would need and then, "in case I don't see you, good afternoon, good evening and goodnight".

With the US in a state of political flux, our Trident deterrent out-dated and the rest of Europe battling the far right, an immigration crisis or impending bankruptcy, now could be the time for a more stealthy than wealthy nation to come to the fore and flex its muscles. Take the initiative and take the power. Take the lot.

Russia would love Brexit for its financial and political chaos. The EU may be an unaudited, unaccountable, unelected gravy train of corruption and corporatocracy, but at least we're at the table, armed with a veto. That said, what a great opportunity to come out, go it alone like the Founding Fathers before us and manifest our *own* destiny.

These *are* changing and challenging times as Harry said, but unfortunately for mankind, for all the wrong reasons!

Are "End Times" among us after all?

Wednesday February 3rd 2016 – 7.30am

AMAZEBALLS!

Sorry, tried to shout as loud as possible, but realised if I do this: ***AMAZING!!*** Then it actually works even better!

I've woken to an email from Steve!

Just three words - three tiny words was all it needed!

Three words that I've always wanted to hear from him!

'Janet says hi!'

You beauty. He's flying home!

Well that's what I assume he means. Anyway in my smitten exuberance, I've forwarded the message to Rees and Callum to keep them both in the loop, as well as Seth too.

Callum, the cheeky northern monkey, then came back *immediately* to say: 'Yes thanks we know!'

'How do you know???' I replied instantly, wondering if they'd heard from the CIA before I had and if there was any more information he wasn't sharing with me.

'Because we're intercepting your emails, soz...'

Good grief. Note to self, don't email Steve any selfies of me in my pants! Especially my decorating pants...

2.15pm

Rees phoned me to "check in", as he calls it, but I think he's just madly in love with me and can't bear to go a day without hearing my seductive husky voice:

'Got your email Miss Sophia, good news!'

Maybe he just wanted to say he got my email, but there's a chance he's secretly in a loveless relationship, aching to be in my arms!

'Would you believe I totally forgot that it's my six month anniversary today! In all these months, I've never forgotten, but being away; with you, well it's just left my mind in a spin you see.'

See, told you. He's infatuated with me, the poor man!

I personally enjoyed the time we spent together as well. We've got an affinity, a real good connection, and I don't just mean broadband!

I acted coy and a little surprised: 'Well Rees what can I say, I'm sorry...'

He cut me off: 'I'm in a spin 'cos I can't believe that I've actually had to sign the National Secrets Act. I've always wanted to do that. And to think our little country has hidden "things" in mountains in Ireland. Fascinating. My mind is in a spin I tells you.'

Oh. It wasn't me then...

'I'd love to tell my Julia, but I dare not. What *else* are we going to talk about over our anniversary dinner? Anyway she doesn't know I've forgotten it. I blagged it a little. Said I had something special lined up you see, but I can't think for the life of me what it could be, seeing as we've been celebrating every month so far. A little over the top if you ask me, but hey you need a bit of give and take in a relationship, as I found out to my cost with my ex, Gwen. Now then Miss Sophia – you're a woman.'

'Thank you for noticing.' I nodded.

'What *is* it exactly women want?'

Christian Grey flashed across my mind; *Nutella* spread and being held aloft by Patrick Swayze, but I thought I'd better not tar the whole of womankind with a generic, and somewhat obvious answer.

'Oh I don't know. What about flowers? One for every month you've been together and in the most seasonal bloom.'

'And...?' he asked expectantly.

'And... a voucher...?' Now I was blagging it!

'A voucher you say. Interesting. Do you mean like a generic book voucher?'

Well I didn't mean a childcare voucher, did I!

'Yes Rees. I think a book voucher would be an excellent choice.' I reassured him.

Then she could go and buy *Fifty Shades Darker* herself!

For some reason, I didn't want Julia to be too pleased with him, a strange subliminal feeling of jealousy gripping me, but existentially, I still yearned for Steve, of course.

Anyway, obviously I'm back at work today. Having been off for a few days, some of the girls were asking what I'd been up to. My boss, Lucy, had told them I'd taken a few days off for personal reasons and even she wasn't aware of the true gravity of the situation.

I did tell Jo and Kate what had happened though, about my trip to Cheltenham, but none of the implicating bits.

They both just sat there agog, half unbelieving all the crap that keeps happening to me. They were very supportive and I have no reason to tell anyone else in the office, as I'm fully aware that give it just one lunch hour and word will've spread like foot and mouth on a blustery day.

10.55pm

I just know I'm not going to sleep tonight.

The waiting's killing me. I have Steve's mobile, and like me, he is completely unable to remember anyone else's phone number except his mums. Even *his* number's a mystery to him.

I find that too. It's like a fog envelopes me and turns what's quite an easy set of up to 11 numbers, into a complete mind blank.

I'll be in a shop and the assistant says: 'Can I take your mobile number please madam.'

'It's definitely 07 something.' I then nod to myself, proud that I do in fact know two of the 11 numbers off by heart.

'It's a new phone. Not got the gist of it yet you see.'

I've actually had the phone number for seven years, but I'm always right.

It is 07 something...

I digress, so back to this infernal insomnia. Every time I hear a noise I think that it's Steve. What's that knocking?

It's the pipe running off the boiler. No, that is a knock this time! Wait.

No, it's next door.

Maybe the more I write about the door knocking, I'll tempt fate and it'll knock. That's how it works, right?

Okay, just five more minutes.

Maybe if I don't think about it anymore and just close my mind and clear my thoughts, then the knock will come.

Stupid brain. Now it's just serving up a visual image of Steve knocking on my door!

Sod it. I'm gonna to watch the news.

11.15pm

Russia's denied all knowledge of the Belorussian advance. How can they not know? It's ridiculous!

The spokesman said that they're looking into the matter, but no official decree has come from the Kremlin.

Meanwhile, the rest of the world is waiting to hear who's given the order, as the advance is plain as the nose on my face.

Some newscasters speculate it's a training muster rather than an invasion and in direct response to America's own military training in neighbouring Baltic States. The US has apparently armed that region to the teeth, so it is no surprise Russia might feel a tad jumpy. Espionage and covert retaliation are the most obvious forms of retribution, but a massive show of force is a close second, short of all out war.

That's it. I'm prepping and stocking up on baked beans!

Thursday February 4th 2016 – 7.40am

I'm still here, alone.

Well I'm on the train, not in bed, but still on my own - figuratively speaking of course. The train is rammed!

I thought about reading the paper, but the front page put me off: "**CZECH MATE**!" it stated in large stacked capitals.

Mother Russia's sent planes over continental Europe as far West as the Czech Republic, rather than sticking to their previous offshore sordid sorties.

I can't read anymore. These tribulations all just sound like a prelude to catastrophe and my dream.

But, if WWIII does go off, I still don't have a daughter to grip hold of. So, maybe it wasn't me in the dream then - well, isn't going to be me anyway.

Russia still denies involvement and that shiver just went down my spine again. I don't even want to think about it.

1.45pm

Still no word from Steve and then I realised that I never replied to his email, such was my excitement! Not for the first time, so I have just mailed him now, but nothing back yet.

What? He's not hanging on my every word, like I do his?

I keep daydreaming at work!

I keep thinking how wonderful it would be if I got home to find all of the curtains closed, candles flickering in the dim light and the sweet smell of incense burning, whilst Beef Wellington slow roasted in the oven.

'I've been expecting you Miss Sinclair!' Steve would say, sitting in the armchair with a small brandy glass in his hand, whilst stroking a white cat on his lap.

'Take me now.' I'd swoon, like a line from a cheesy Mills and Boon book.

'My darling Sophia.' he'd say, breathlessly: 'Have you called Laura Metcalf about the Pritchard account?'

Sorry, that was my boss interrupting my moment - not Steve's bizarre seduction techniques!

9.15pm

I'm home. I even went to the gym to give Steve a little extra time to get all the candles lit and the roast on.

Alas, he's still not back in my life.

Baked beans out of the saucepan for one then...

Diaries are all well and good. Good for recording news, but what are you supposed to write about on a slow news day? I haven't even seen a cat stuck up a tree to report on.

Well, I did get the gas bill and the milk's on the turn, so I may have to go shopping tomorrow night. I didn't eat again.

I also text Seth to say that Steve's supposedly on his way back; well, hopefully anyway. He then replied to say the police had already called him yesterday, but thanked me for the "real time" updates.

Sarcastic sod. I've been busy!

Ok, so when the CIA is not chasing me and I'm not trotting off to Cheltenham, it seems that my life actually does suck like everyone else who lives alone.

With no kids, no family close by and no friends.

Sniff...

Friday February 5th 2016 – 9.30am

Bloody typical! Been in a meeting and missed a call from Steve on my work phone.

Darn, darn, darn, darny darn!

He said he didn't have my mobile number, so had tried directory enquiries to get my work number. Old school.

Anyway he's at Heathrow and was begging for a lift, the cheeky monkey.

So now he's coming here to see me.

Now!

In the *sort* of words of one of my former heroines: 'Thank you Antarctica, thank you terror, thank you consequence. Thank you nothingness, thank you providence, thank you, thank you silence!'

3.00pm

He's been!

I was standing at the photocopier and he sauntered through reception like he owned the joint. His clean-shaven and high cheek boned features replaced by a far more rugged looking beard. Seems he's the bit of rough I always wanted.

Our eyes met across the room and time just stood serenely still, like he'd never been away.

That face.

Beard aside, that face hadn't really changed, except for his contagious smile, which seemed far wider than normal.

Then it was all a blur, mainly due to my eyes welling up and the life literally being squeezed out of me from his warm and enveloping embrace.

So there we were, lost lovers now reunited in the conveniently located stationery cupboard of all places and certainly the most apt place for an enveloping embrace!

'I'm so sorry.' sobbed Steve, unabashed. The fact that he was emotional too, set me off even more!

'You're back, that's all that matters!' I breathed quietly into his left ear as we held each other again. All I could think of was the wonderful wave of pure intoxicating relief.

This was now the opportunity I'd been starved of.

I could finally appreciate the superb sense of lifting, as I shed a massive weight of guilt and apprehension. This represented a new opportunity for us to build and its importance wasn't lost on me at the time.

Unbeknownst to Steve, I'd not just been counting down to his return, but to Valentine's Day too and at that moment I'd never been so sure that I wanted to spend my life with Steve.

That moment will live with me forever!

A perfect moment! For better or worse, for richer or poorer, from this day forward, forever and ever. We are as one and he really is my 'one'. I know that now. Everything is clear.

I did manage to compose myself – eventually.

We emerged from the cupboard holding hands, red-eyed and I guess slightly dishevelled. It may have looked a little dodgy if it'd been the Christmas party, but we'd left the door open and the office staff were clapping, as if we had just made our wedding vows.

My girls had obviously blabbed to some extent about Steve's absence. Someone whistled through their teeth and my cheering colleagues started to laugh as we both blushed.

'Speech!' went up the cry from the back of the office and another goading bugger started to tap their pen on a tea mug to back up this call to order.

I smiled, holding my hands up to calm the raucous crowd: 'Unaccustomed to public speaking as I am, I would like to thank you all for coming.'

The laughing resumed as this bizarre moment started to turn into a mixture between a civil ceremony and an Academy acceptance speech.

'I'd like to thank Steve for coming back to me. I'd like to thank you all for your love and support and I'd like to have a moment to have a little cry please.'

With that my emotional levels peaked to the point that I chocked my last words, the room started to spin slightly and I ran to the toilet to hide!

I do like the spotlight on me, but only on my terms.

Now was just too much and as "well" as the wishes were from the well-wishers present, I just couldn't take it anymore.

I remember looking at myself in the mirror and thinking that the person looking back at me had changed. Yes she looked a mess, mascara streaking like wet paint in the rain, but there was a steely resolve in her eyes. I didn't recognise it. They were eyes that seemed so solemn in the circumstance, so I splashed water over her face, so as to bring myself back.

I stood there with my fingers slowly circling my sockets, whilst stooped down over the sink. When I looked up to reflect on the change, I saw a far greater cause.

Steve.

He turned to one of the girls to reassure them that I hadn't barricaded myself in a cubicle: 'It's alright, I've got this, we won't be long.' he winked, curiously.

The door closed and he just stood there, smiling and silent.

I cracked my momentary composure and continued to cry. There was a new light around him, almost angelic and undetectable, but I knew it to be there. I knew it to be true.

'It's an understatement, but I've been worried sick Steve!'

'I know babes.'

'How can you know? How can you ever fully comprehend exactly what I've been through? The waiting, the not knowing. The sheer unadulterated anguish, pulling my guts up through my mouth each day! That sick feeling at the very pit of my stomach every morning as I see you're not beside me. The most basic manifestation of need, outpouring in my every being! Constant feelings of love, loss and loneliness, compounded by guilt that I got you into all this in the first place. You left me without a bye or leave. No note, no explanation, no nothing! Just a sense of nothingness!'

Ok, so I never actually said this to him. In hindsight, it would've been wonderful to muster such dialogue, such emotive prose in the heat of the moment, but in reality, I don't think I actually answered at all…

I was simply nuzzled to his neck, the tightness of my grip unerring, if not slightly unnerving.

‘You can’t believe how I’ve felt too!’ he said, craning his neck around, so he could look me squarely in the eye. He kissed me on the forehead softly: ‘I’ve been so nervous about your reaction, whether there would even be an “us” on my return. It wasn’t my fault, they just took me!’

‘You’ve got a tongue in your head. What did they say? Why did you have to go so quickly without even a call?’

Steve looked to the floor ashamed: ‘I can’t say.’

‘Bullshit! Absolute bullshit! You tell me now, or so help me, we’re over right here, right now! I love you so much and you’ve killed me inside during this past week or so. You’ve absolutely no clue as to what’s been going on here. Fuck!’

I turned away, breathing deeply, trying to compose myself once again, before turning to face him once more.

Steve looked a little perplexed: ‘Ok, you’re right, I don’t know what you’ve been doing, how you’ve been feeling. I certainly didn’t think I’d be gone so long to be fair. The detail as to *where* exactly we were going was brief to say the least, so I decided to just go with it. I met the two CIA ops that morning, as you know. They asked me to get into the car to discuss things a little more and the next thing I know, the doors are locked and the car is pulling off and heading west!’

I winced, slightly disbelieving him: ‘Why would they just take you like that? You’ve done nothing wrong, they told you as much.’

‘Well mainly because I wasn’t prepared. No clothes, no phone, no goodbyes. They said I wouldn’t need any of that and nobody could know where I was going. It was safer that way. Then we were off, pinging up the M20 towards Biggin Hill.’

‘And then what?’

Steve’s eyes rolled. He knew he’d get the third degree from me and that he couldn’t plead the fifth, even if he wanted to: ‘Ok fine. What’s the worst that can happen, but we need to go out. I can’t tell you in here.’

So that was that. We went out.

Not to a nice pub, café or restaurant mind, but to the not so salubrious *NCT* car park - Steve was obviously immersing himself in this game of underground espionage!

‘And why are we in here?’ I asked as we walked down the ramp, knowing full well what he’d say.

‘They may be watching me.’ he replied, eyes darting around, trying to accustom to the light, or lack thereof.

‘And on the presumption that they’re watching to ensure you don’t give up any international secrets, don’t you think us entering an underground car park, might look just the slightest circumspect?’ my eyebrows were raised in anticipation.

I’d missed him talking himself into a corner!

Steve looked at me. I could hear him thinking, if not a little too late: ‘Point taken, but we’re here now. I’m just paranoid they might have listening equipment you know? So, if we go underground that’ll stop them penetrating our conversation.’

‘If you say so, Agent Cartwright.’ I shrugged.

‘Right, good, we’ll have to be quick then. So they get me on this plane and my brief is, I’m going to write a report as a freelance journalist for a trade geology magazine. But in fact, I was undercover, noting down all the wider activity at the research facility. I’m not sure exactly what they were looking for, but the CIA guys were pretty specific in their questioning as part of the wash up, back at Edwards Air Force Base.’

‘Yeah, we guessed that much.’

‘Eh? How can you guess that? Who’s *we* anyway? Seth?’

‘Oh just the police and some of my new BFF’s down at GCHQ.’ I replied nonchalantly, whilst realigning my eyeliner with my finger.

‘What the hell?’ Steve’s face retracted in confusion.

‘Yeah, I got a little impatient, nay worried to my wit’s end. So I just thought best to report you as missing.’

Steve burst out laughing: ‘Shit a brick! What you do that for? That’s hilarious!’

I just looked at him.

You know, one of *those* looks.

The kind that reels you in like a trebuchet catapult, straining under its own weight, ropes all taught and groaning; that is until I let loose, propelling the useless pile of a projectile across the car park and onto the bonnet of a *Bugatti*.

Steve metaphorically got up, dusted himself down and gave me a look of bemusement.

I shook my head: 'Why'd I report you as missing? Well my darling sweetheart, because technically, I didn't know where in the world you were and neither did your family or friends. Your old work colleagues were surprised you'd left so soon and your new work didn't even know who you are. So, with a little deduction and a brief cross reference of the word "disappeared" with the good old Oxford English Dictionary, I was then subsequently able to conclude that you were indeed, a *missing* person.'

Steve went to speak and then stopped short. He tried again, brain obviously re-engaged this time: 'Oh. I see.'

'Yes so the police escalated the case to frigging Interpol and following your cryptic email, I was referred to the services of those most secret.'

Steve frowned, as he comprehended what I'd just said: 'Hang on. *You* were with the British Secret Service, whilst I was working for the US Secret Service? That's the shit!'

'I could think of other ways of putting it, but it does the job I guess.'

I then quickly and briefly brought him up to speed on how we deduced his email code and second-guessed many ideas as to why he may have been where he was.

'Listen I've got it all down in my diary, I'll share it with you some day.'

Steve looked shocked by it all, if a little mortified: 'I didn't know you had a diary. I also didn't know who I could trust down there and whether they or the CIA would be intercepting my emails, so I just made up a few coding systems, whilst also trying to get you a message that made sense. It wasn't easy you know! Took me friggin' ages.'

Bless: 'I can imagine it was no small task for a bear of very little brain.' I mocked.

Despite our absence, we were soon back into our old ways.

'So I'm on the plane and I'm like, where are we going? And then Lennox says we're going to Nevada via New Jersey. So I joked to him, asking if we were going to Area 51 and he only bloody nodded! Can you believe that! So I've been there! Ok, so it was just to catch a connecting flight out again, but still, something to tell the grandkids and pop on your CV?'

'Oh yes, I'd expect any professional company these days has visiting Area 51 as a pre-requisite. Right up there with an honours degree and clean driving licence for sure.'

He nodded excitedly: 'You know right!'

I think he was actually serious and he's probably updated his LinkedIn profile already! 'Anyway so next thing I know I'm on a flight to bloody Antarctica and we land at some place in the north and I have to get on a ship around the coast and then into Mabus Point. You figured that out too right? Mabus being a place and all?'

'Yep.'

'Cool. So it was fricking freezing down there *Mrs Biggleswort*h. I had icicles hanging off my nose and the wind chill was just out of this world. I can't attempt to describe those conditions, but you know when it gets really blustery up on the Leas?'

'Aha.'

'Well imagine that, but like ten times. No twenty times. I was almost blown away!'

'Sounds like it. In more ways than one.'

'Yeah, and I had to live in this hut thing. The food was ok and sugary cups of weak tea kept me sane. I had to interview and shadow various scientists. I've no clue what they were talking about and what specifically they're researching, which is handy, as I don't actually have to write this up as an article, but they were hard to understand, as they were all Russian.'

'What, always on the move?' I smiled.

Steve rolled his eyes, as he does: 'I've missed you! They're researching geology and climate change down there, but the Americans think this is BS and they're up to something more menacing, as someone said they could "hear" them down there, underground or something like that.'

'Yes GCHQ said that they've some fandangled listening station to track and trace movements within the Earth and that's what's at Area 51 and under Denver Airport!'

‘Shut the back door!’

‘Yes and the front.’ I nodded

‘They admitted that? They said there’s something under Denver airport?’

‘Yeah they told me all sorts of stuff and made me sign the Official Secrets Act! That’s how I roll now, boyo.’

Fitted it all into my Beyoncé time, didn’t I, boyfriend!

Steve looked amazed: ‘Jesus, that sounds way better than what I got to do. A few in flight movies and frostbite to boot.’

‘So did you find what they were looking for?’

‘Well I honestly don’t know. We got back to Edwards Airbase and a few people interviewed me. They took copious notes and there was nothing too out of the ordinary, not that I really knew what I was looking for.’

‘Did they have any heavy materials coming in or out? Drills, or earth moving equipment?’ I quizzed, casually.

‘Bloody hell, that’s pretty much what they asked me? What else do you know that I don’t?’ he inquired, noticeably hurt that despite his own adventures, he was as much in the dark as an Inuit in the deep mid winter.

‘Well my chaps in Cheltenham think the Americans have got wind through these listening bases that the Russians are mining down there. It’s in Australian territory and as far as I know, not able to be mined due to some old treaty or something, but they seem to be up to something fishy.’

Steve coughed: ‘Up to something? Have you *seen* the news? They’re up to their necks in it! There’s no one left in the UN to sanction any more sanctions. They’ve maxed out and the next step is “indirect diplomacy” or worse. One thing the Americans did mention, is that they’re concerned. They’re worried that someone in the Russian army, who exerts a high level of power and autonomy, may have gone rogue.’

‘Rogue? As in corrupted or mad? So do you think this is all hotting up to fulfil my dream then? Seems a little coincidental does it not?’

He looked at me: ‘Shit! What if you’re right? What if this *is* all leading in one direction? Oblivion.’

‘So was there any machinery down there?’

'Tonnes of the stuff! There were deliveries every day, which at the time I didn't think too much about as I don't know any different. The scientist told me they were merging two bases due to austere times back home in Russia, which seemed plausible and it was so cold, I didn't get out much to see the action on the ground. They had a boat load of snow scooters, which was cool, not that I got to play on them.'

'Yeah saw those, shed loads of 'em.'

'No I *literally* mean a boatload. It docked whilst I was there and craned them off in containers. Wicked little bastards that go like the clappers in the snow.'

'I know, we were watching the base on a live satellite feed. There's like a fleet of them right?'

Steve just shook his head: 'Show off. Why'd I miss out on all this cool stuff? Did you zap your retina to get in that place?'

I nodded and then shook my head somewhat exacerbated: 'Steve, if you *had* been here, we wouldn't have needed to be there in the first place! But now you're back and I can reflect, it *was* quite exciting to be fair and I made a really good new friend in the police. He's Welsh!'

'He? He?' Steve looked at me jealously.

'He wasn't that funny, but don't worry, he's just a friend. Anyway what else did you see down there? And remind me exactly why they needed you to do this job.'

'Well apparently I hit upon a few things when we were searching for your mate Mabus and that, combined with some research I was doing for an article on fracking, led them to speak to me. One to warn me off writing about General Mabus, who's a thoroughly nice chap apparently; and also the fracking searches and those hits for acoustic properties in geology, combined with all those other crazy sites you went on, must have pinged up some flag somewhere. But if what you're telling me about Denver airport is true, that specific search must have proper freaked them out!'

'Any amount of flag waving couldn't stop us right? They did mention fracking when I was in Cheltenham, but no one actually elaborated on it and its relevance.'

'I think the CIA are on to the Russians for shale gas fracking in Antarctica, possibly not the kind of mining covered by the Antarctic Treaty.'

I frowned: 'How'd you know this?'

'Well some of the equipment that was coming in had the brand *UMS* on the side. The CIA was very interested to hear about this, as UMS is apparently a US company called Unconventional Mining Solutions. And from my previous research, unconventional mining usually points to fracking.'

The plot thickens, I thought...

'Apparently as part of sanctions imposed back in 2014, the US banned Russia from having access to fracking technology. So the FBI's investigating as to why UMS is contravening this sanction and selling them hardware - assuming it's not been sold on the basis of it being located in Australian land and so a total administrative and jurisdictional balls up.'

'Blimey, convoluted or what? So they were just using you as the idiot abroad then?'

'Pretty much. The base would've run checks on me and I'd come up clean and working for Reuters of course. Despite looking a little green on some of the terms they were using down there, I quite enjoyed following them around, asking questions more out of curiosity than anything else. I think my background and lack of knowledge about the 'bigger picture' helped me.'

'Ding ding ding! Exactly what the team in Cheltenham deduced. Damn they're good! And they solved your code.'

'Oh, I assumed *you'd* have worked all that out yourself.' he said surprised.

'Er, no. It's easy when you know what you're looking for, but when you're just looking at it with no clues to work with, it was just a load of old twaddle.'

'Well I assumed you might ask for help if you got stuck, but I certainly didn't think you'd end up at GCHQ. Classic!'

So much for the idiot abroad. The idiot just got home!

'Glad this amuses you so much. You're gone for days and I'm the one to get dragged into an international dispute over feckin' fracking. I've got *no* work done, I'm massively behind on the housework and if I was in a bad mental state before you left because of my dreams, how'd you think I'm feeling now?'

Steve seemed to strategically ponder his answer and then smiled mischievously: 'A bad menstrual state more like, same old mardy cow.'

'We'll talk later, I need to get back to work.'

And with that I left the car park, narrowly avoiding yet another silent assassin, in the form of a purring *Prius,* as I inadvertently stepped into its furtive path.

10.35pm

We did talk later too!

It's amazing that despite how much we missed each other, how quickly one can slip back into the bickering. So I'm going to make a conscious effort to be nice, well *nicer* anyway, this may be prudent, seeing as I'm going to propose to him soon!

Steve starts at *Thomson Reuters* for real next Monday. I found out, it's the Blackfriars office, just in case I need it...

We went out for dinner, for fear of the flats still being bugged and over the starter; he enlightened me as to the wonders of the Antarctic. All about its long, harsh and dark winters, its long, harsh and light summers, as well as all of the long, harsh and gritty bits in between.

I learnt how hard it is to get a shower there. How hard it is to stay warm and not use up too much power. How hard it is to find something to do every evening, except make up codes, read what limited printed material there was available in English and search for the intermittent Wi-Fi access.

The terrain is apparently striking in its barren nature. Miles upon miles of open tundra, unblemished snow and cavernous ice sculptures as far as the eye can see, framed by distant mountains and glaciers that reflect the glinting sun tenfold.

He described the green southern lights chasing across the endless night's sky. He also waxed lyrical about the supreme blackness, where, due to the apparent lack of light pollution we're all used to, it produces an amazing view of the cosmos.

I then remember completely losing him, as I had a sudden craving for a *Galaxy* or *Milky Way*!

Steve was so captivated by the ocean and the simple naturalistic pleasures of watching the local penguins diving off rocks into the freezing cold water below. I think if it were not for the temperatures and the job of work that he had to do, Steve would have spent more time exploring.

The Mirny base itself was basically three sets of stacked up Portacabins in a row, maybe 50m long by 10m wide. One had a communications dome on its roof and there were generators, back-up generators and various out buildings, but Steve was unsure what purpose they served.

He said there was a constant rumbling noise, which at the time he assumed was something to do with the generators, as well as various materials being dumped into the sea. The rumblings, it transpires, may have been the Russians trying to get at what lies beneath...

Saturday February 6th 2016 – 11.30am

I've missed the common or garden Saturday morning lay in. Cooking shows, lazy chat and easy listening on Radio 2, followed by tea and toast in bed with only the ensuing crumbs to moan about. First world problems eh? Sheer bloody bliss!

We're going to spend the day doing what we do best. We'll be walking hand in hand around town, taking in the sea air and a few half pints on the way. I need this.

It feels like a holiday - well, a break from the abnormal anyway and a chance to spend quality time and reconnect.

I slept so much better with Steve beside me.

My head hit the pillow and I didn't give a second thought to sending myself into an instant state of slumber. I think Steve may have had other items on the agenda, but I had no choice in the matter - my body ruled out, before it could ever put out…

The radio reports that The UN is threatening Russia with military pressure and calling for its leaders to meet for an open dialogue. Despite Russia still denying all knowledge of the "so called" invasion, thank goodness diplomacy will prevail, but in the current economic climate, I doubt anyone can actually *afford* a full-scale war.

There was a worry that if we pushed Russia too far, they'd simply turn off the lights in London and pull the plug on our energy supply. But I think they need the cash too badly; so despite the frosting relationship, we all need each other too much to fall out completely. Well, I hope so anyway!

We both continued conversations about the house move last night, which is now totally on! As payment for doing the CIA's dirty work Steve has been notified that he'll be given three months *Reuters'* pay in advance and he negotiated with them that they issue separate payslips for the preceding months from the back end of last year, even though he wasn't actually working for them at the time.

He's arranged all this just to ensure that we can get around the mortgage rules and regulations, which will require proof of earnings and so not slow the conveyance process any further.

So fortuitous having the CIA pulling strings for us and it's turned out to be a nice little tax free earner that now helps cover our deposit and moving fees!

So later today we're serving notice on our respective flats, as the lease is up on both of them soon, which is handy and tomorrow we're going bloomin' house-hunting!

I suppose I'd better winch myself up and get showered now that Steve has just come out of the bathroom.

I'm not actually convinced he remembers that I'm writing this diary, seeing as I told him I'd share it at some point, so as to fill in the blanks. I don't think I've painted too bad a picture of him - Steve, my man, my love!

Sunday February 7th 2016 – 12.30pm

There's a theme returning here - another Sunday, so another lay in.

I'm now at Steve's flat and having woken up hanging like a monkey with a hung over hangover; I think I've pretty much slept it off now. Well, Steve helped to blow away some of the cobwebs anyway!

I've missed him so much!

Yesterday was great. Far too busy for diary entries and by mid afternoon, I was half cut, so probably wise not to start rambling on here anymore than I've already done to date!

Needless to say I recall ranting about politics and state control, as well as religion versus spirituality in the pub and the collective futility of it all...whoops...

The weather was cold, but the snow had finally abated. Steve assured me that this is comparatively tropical to some places he's recently frequented that average around minus 11 degrees in the shade and that's on a good day.

I assumed he meant Centigrade and not Fahrenheit?

It was superb to walk without a care in the world. We held hands and we just had the future to think about, which was ours for the shaping. A new home, a new life together and not long to wait either. What's more, maybe we'll have a wedding to plan for in the not too distant future! Fingers crossed!

I can't wait for Valentine's Day!

I've been carefully planning how I'm going to do it. I can't decide if we should walk out onto the rocky pier at Dolphin Bay at sundown and I pop the question; or if that's a little too clichéd and I should just do it at home over a candle lit supper - away from public eyes, in case he says no...!

Either way, it's just a week to go and no work to get in the way of the celebrations, assuming he says 'yes'.

I think I'll do it early on, so we can really enjoy the whole day of good news. Or on the other hand, should I do it later, so I don't have a whole day of awkward misery to contend with?

Maybe I'm over thinking this one.

Maybe I'll just hedge my bets and do it at lunchtime...

We stopped in numerous pubs, had a nice Ploughman's lunch overlooking the sea and generally pottered around aimlessly, talking about nothing more than the price of fish.

We popped into the High Street and did that thing that young couples do and peered, arm in arm, into estate agent's windows saying things like: 'How much? Blimey, imagine the repayments on that place,' or 'You'd be better off demolishing that one and starting again, rather than spending a pot on polishing *that* proverbial pile.'

Oh, and finally my favourite new house-hunting saying: 'My goodness Steve, that house is perfect. This is a place where I'd feel at home.'

And I did get to say that too, for I knew there and then that the cottage we were looking at in the window had to be ours.

It's a Victorian mid terrace property dating back to the late 1800s. It has a fire engine red front door, original tiled entrance path, a white painted picket fence and all original features within. There's cornicing, coving, ornate fireplaces downstairs, as well as wrought iron fireplaces in both of the two bedrooms. It has a small, but manageable garden with a shed and roses growing under the front living room window.

As I say - Perfect!

We went into the agent's office and we have a viewing at 2.30pm today – is it just fate stepping in, or is it so good to be true that I need to mentally prepare myself to be gazumped? It's been on the market for a while, as it's quite close to the train station, but that suits us!

So for a world that was breaking apart, it seems to all be coming together for us now!

Best get dressed then...

5.30pm

Well they say: "*when you know, you know*". You know in a blink of an eye, through a unconscious gut instinct. You can thin slice people, things and situations and in this case we were able to envisage a house as our home.

Yes it's close to the station, the décor's dated and there's a bit of damp under that front window. But you know what? It comes in on budget, it's chain free as the old lady owner is moving into a old people's home and there's nothing else around as perfect as this. It has loads of character and it just 'feels' right.

So we did it.

We visited at 2.30pm, had a drink in the station pub, talked it over and called the agent to make a cheeky offer. We went in £20,000 under asking price, leveraging the fact that it had been on the market for a while and we were first time buyers with no chain. A little bit of drawn out haggling later and we had our second bid for just £5,000 more accepted. Boom!

If you'd told me this time last week, when I was out searching for Steve, as well as searching my soul, that just one week on and he'd be back and we'd have bought a house, I'd have said you were a fool!

Well as much as a fool as an inanimate diary can be…

One week further on again and we may be getting engaged too – let's just see eh, as I don't want to tempt fate!

I'm so happy. Steve loves the place too and what's more, we can both commute on the same train into London.

As I say – perfect!

As frustrating and demoralising as life is at times, it's the days like today that I live for. We have to experience bad or bitter times so we can appreciate how sweet life can be when it finally comes good!

So despite the omens of *Apocalypse Now* being on *ITV3* tonight combined with reports of a North Korean ballistic missile test on the news, today was in fact a perfect day.

Monday February 8th 2016 – 7.40am

I stayed on my own last night, so as to prepare for the world of work once more. The state of euphoria has calmed somewhat, but I do catch myself smiling sometimes, as I think about the last few days. So much so that I think the guy opposite me on the train thought I was coming onto him...

Steve starts his new job today too, albeit at 10am, the lucky thing. First day butterflies I expect, so I'll text him good luck, but knowing him, he's probably still in bed.

12.15pm

I've just had a text back from Steve. Not sure what this means and what they want him for exactly, but: *'Lennox text to say I need to meet him asap... x'*

Superb! Just as you think all's back to normal, the Secret Service wants to speak to your boyfriend again!

After everything that's happened over the past few weeks, this actually now sounds like a perfectly normal thing for me to write in my diary! Who'd 'ave thunk it?

'Great... when and where?' I replied, thinking maybe next weekend and it'd be sod's law it would be on Valentine's Day around lunchtime! The text came back immediately: *'One hour at Smithfield Market!!!'*

I scoffed; completely unsurprised at their efficiency, but still apprehensive all the same. So long as he doesn't do his Houdini act, I don't mind what they ask him, within reason…

8.30pm

I just met Steve for a drink in the pub by the station – our new local to be, in fact! His first day in the new job was good, having spent most of it being shown around by his new mentor Jennifer, followed by the reading and signing of various policy documents and intellectual property waivers. Apparently his ideas are in fact *their* ideas and he's unable to write freelance without being sued. At least he knows where he stands! So, I guess the CIA doesn't care though and bend their rules to suit.

He then of course had to pop on the train to Farringdon for his meeting at Smithfield Market. As it turns out, that in itself was a red herring and Lennox was instead waiting outside the Victorian tiled façade of the tube station opposite Farringdon, lurking, cigarette in hand, next to a bakery.

People milled about and Lennox watched and waited for a few seconds before nodding and leading Steve along the claustrophobic Crossrail hoarding to the diamond district.

Steve then regaled how he was worried by Lennox steering him down a dodgy looking alleyway and then, surprisingly into *Ye Olde Mitre*, a tucked away pub with wood panelled walls and many dusty old trinkets. They sat in an anti room off the quieter public side of the bar and luckily there weren't too many punters, despite it being lunchtime.

Now, I've paraphrased Steve's conversation with Lennox for posterity, seeing as it ties into my own esoteric story so far.

Lennox was dressed in a black suit and dark black overcoat. He'd obviously lost his matching shades.

'Funeral, interview or CCJ?' asked Steve, with a tone of sarcasm that the American didn't pick up on.

Lennox looked at his attire and brushed the statement off merely as impenetrable "English humour".

'Mr Cartwright, good to see you again.' This was the first time he spoke and it was in a hushed tone.

'So soon Lennox? You guys must've really missed my quick wit and dashing good looks.'

'I thought you'd like some feedback Mr Cartwright. Your "work" has proved extremely enlightening for my colleagues at Langley. Do you know who or what UMS is?' Lennox peered at Steve through his rounded glasses.

'Too fracking right I do. They caught me out on that in the debriefing, so I looked them up on my return. A fracking company right? American outfit, what they doing down there?'

'You go top of the class for your extracurricular activities Mr Cartwright, but I'll be the one asking the questions today.' Lennox replied, surprised and impressed in equal measure.

With that, the landlady came into their side room and took their lunch orders, limited as the menu was. They ordered the guest ale and a plate of pork pies with an assortment of pickles much to Steve's amusement as he told me the graphic story. Apparently, he couldn't wait to see Lennox's face when he finally bit into the gelatine interior of the pie!

Lennox leaned into Steve and spoke just a few decibels above a whisper: 'We've looked into sales from UMS and the machine that you described sounds like a hydraulic fracking pump. Only one of these models has been sold in the world to date by UMS to the size and specification that you described, and that was sold to the Iranians last year. So all above board as far as UMS's concerned, but now Tehran's doing deals with Russia again, despite our efforts of deep sixing the Russian defence system they were trying to sell to Iran last year.'

'Ok, so you meddle in other countries' affairs, tell me something I don't already know.' Steve was still waiting for the point of this hastily arranged visit to materialise.

'Well who in the world is making the most noise at the moment?' hissed Lennox against the supposed subordination.

'I don't know? Physically or hypothetically?'

'Intelligent question,' he nodded admiringly: "Both in this case!' Lennox removed his glasses to clean the lens.

'Russia?' Steve wasn't overly convinced, but was fairly confident that Russia would have some part to play.

'*And* Iran. Just in their very own different ways. Iran seems to be doing their level best to play most of the countries in the Middle East against each other, whilst Russia makes noises on the flanks of the Baltic States.'

'Right.'

'However, Russia is making a hell of a racket not just at its neighbours' borders, but also underground – physically. And that's where you've come in Mr Cartwright. It seems that you've unearthed one of the biggest risks to mankind there could actually be.'

Steve looked at Lennox, unable to follow exactly where he was going with this. One minute he thought that he'd be sent on another mission, or bumped off down a dark alley and yet here he was being lauded as the Earth's preeminent saviour. Was a Congressional Medal of Honour stuck in the Second-Class post too, he wondered?

'A risk to mankind in Antarctica? What is it this time? Climate change, the ozone layer, or is fracking as bad as *Green Peace* is making out?'

Lennox nodded: 'Hydraulic fracturing is temperamental at the best of timcs. As you will know from your own recent research, the process involves drilling and injecting water mixed with acid and a slurry of poison into the ground at high pressures, so as to fracture the shale rocks below and release the natural gases. We believe that Russia's unearthed massive deposits of shale gas around Mirny and despite being based on foreign independent soil, is about to illegally help herself to Antarctica's abundance of riches.'

'Jeez, they must be really pissed that they sold you Alaska all those years ago eh?' japed Steve.

'You could say that. Anyway they've already been busy in the northern Arctic, with deep-sea exploration, but now the granite landmass below the frozen tundra in Antarctica seems to be the latest discovery. They're pumping water from the sea through a network of newly laid pipes that you saw first-hand.'

'I did. They're putting the finishing touches to them now and the Professor at Mirny said they were part of the base's expansion and being used for a water purification plant, which seemed to make sense to an outsider.'

Lennox shook his head and smiled at their porous cover story: 'They are actually shipping in the sand and a concoction of chemicals to create the slurry on site and any waste is being dumped at sea. Not only does this contaminate the sea, but the local ecosystem; all of your little penguin friends would be wiped out. The waste is also pumped out at extremely high temperatures, so that will in turn have the knock on effect of raising the water temperature in the vicinity and so melt the ice sheet quicker. This will of course raise water levels, but will also make the transport of sand to the frozen continent even more efficient, as icebreakers wouldn't be required. The whole process therefore produces cost efficiencies over time!'

Steve looked shocked: 'There's up to 600 chemicals in fracking fluid, they'll decimate the whole ecosystem if they release that stuff. They can't get away with this! The slurry makes the rock fracture and then the gas comes out into the well and up again for collection. Lord only knows what goes down in terms of the chemicals, once the fracking is over. That slurry runoff will even seep into the underlying aquifers!'

Steve pulled back from their close, head to head conversation, as the barmaid brought their order over.

Lennox took a bite into the pork pie and Steve recalled his eyes widening, as he wasn't prepared for the gelatine filling: 'What is this shit?' he mumbled with his mouth stuffed full.

Steve laughed: 'Put the pickles on it, it'll hide the taste!'

'But the pickles are just as bad!' said Lennox, trying to stave off his gag reflex.

'Ah, but that's what the ale's for!' replied Steve, a mercurial food scientist, or so it seemed.

Lennox leaned back in, eyes darting around the bar area hoping no one would see him spit out the food into his napkin: 'There's over half a million active shale gas wells back home in the US and we've got cases of sinkholes appearing, of homes completely disappearing, chronic water pollution and flooding; so technically we're not exactly ones to judge.'

Steve replied, not so politely with a mouthful of pie: 'We never are. We just like to let others learn from our mistakes, like getting the Chinese into renewable energy early, before they burn off every fossil fuel left in existence, right?'

'Exactly,' said Lennox, supping his ale to take away the taste of the napkin: 'For us, fracking all started in the 1950's and it's never been proved, but it does feel like Cancer is more prevalent in the last half a century than before. Maybe that's because it was never reported or diagnosed as much before, but maybe it could be that the drinking water was never contaminated so widely with such a cocktail of carcinogenic. That's just my take on it anyways. Can I light up in here?'

Steve was stunned. Not by Lennox's lack of social awareness, but the fact that he'd apparently found evidence of arguably the biggest untapped well of natural shale gas in the world, and it was now being tapped.

'Mr Cartwright, if I may be so bold, we've learned about your partner's dream. About the disaster she saw.'

'Yes she's particularly paranoid about that dream at the moment, what with Russia seemingly on the brink of nuclear war and North Korea just warming up in the wings.'

'Agreed, we all hope that's the case, but on reflection we don't actually think that nuclear war is the issue here.'

Steve started to get animated and drew unwanted attention from the main public bar: 'Not an issue? Christ our Trident subs have rust on the rudders, you're rudderless until the new administration is in office and Iran is desperately trying to weaponise itself, despite your best efforts to sanction them in Vienna last year. How can 'nuclear' *not* be the issue?'

'Mr Cartwright, your subtlety would be appreciated if you don't mind. I agree, the world does seem to be coming to an impending conflagration, but we think that it's all a front.'

'Yeah the Eastern front from my point of view. Have you seen the amount of tanks along the Belo-Russian border?'

'The wrong kind of front. Sheer bravado and bluster for the benefit of Bloomberg and CNN. The more they show images of Russian expansion, the more our eyes are diverted away from the real show in Antarctica. They're getting away with it because it's underground, out of sight, out of mind. We need your help again and there's a chance of making you extremely popular, or conversely, extremely unpopular.'

'Speak English man!' roasted Steve across the table: 'Stop dancing around the subject, what do you want me to do? Have I not done enough for your guys already? This is ridiculous, I'm no trained envoy or Spook and I'm not even an American, so why should I do all your damn donkey work?'

Lennox smiled: 'I don't need your body this time, just your brain and your passion. I want you to simply do what you do best. Write me an article Steve, just write me an article.'

'But I thought we agreed that I wasn't really going to write an article for that trade rag, besides I don't know all the technical mumbo jumbo they're spouting. To be honest, I didn't really take any notes as such, no quotes anyway.'

Lennox pre-empted this response. Plucky, but predictable was Steve: 'Write an article about the end of the world.' he added softly, his palms placed together at his lips, as if imploring Steve to take heed.

Steve's face turned from that of worry to total confusion: 'But if nuclear isn't the issue, why the end of the world?'

Lennox smiled again, it really didn't suit him: 'This, Mr Cartwright, is where your partner can help us all.'

'She does have a name you know!'

'We know. We *all* know.'

With that Lennox rose to his feet, finished his drink with a wince and popped a gum to take away the taste of the ale. He then put on his woollen trench coat: 'We'll be in touch.'

Steve was too perplexed to question him as to why I should be involved in all of this and the true interpretation of my dream, if it was not to be a nuclear strike or the end times.

Lennox's rapid retreat took Steve aback and he was left alone, with just his thoughts, a half eaten pork pie and the bill still to pay. Yet another debt the CIA seemed to adding to their growing slate.

Steve then returned to work, late on his first day's lunch break, but apparently an unnamed man with an American accent had been in touch to warn his boss of his late arrival. Steve apologised, but his boss was fine with him and said it was all part of his research. After all, they knew a big story was about to break!

Tuesday February 9th 2016 – 8.00am

I know nothing about fracking. You hear it on the news sometimes, seeing people demonstrating and it's weird how the media just treat it as though everyone already knows exactly what it is and the supposed dangers involved.

However these protesters are often portrayed as a nuisance and are further demonised by their clashes with the police, so as to give the impression that they're the main perpetrators of perjury and it's not the megalomaniac multinationals of mining and manufacturing.

I've been increasingly concerned as to why the US Government seems to be leaning on us so much - a simple couple from a simple town, so what gives?

Did Steve's Internet searches *really* screw them up that much, or are they *really* giving him this opportunity to save the world through the media? Surely they have *some* fact-based journalists over there that they can rely on?

We got to the bottom of Lennox's cryptic comment. We assume that Steve would be 'popular' as his report would blow the whistle on a major potential contamination of the Earth's water and show Russia to be illegally mining on independent land. The Antarctic Treaty, signed in Madrid in 1959, banned any mining on the continent and yet the more malevolent states obviously seem to think that there may be a loophole when it comes to fracking and unconventional mining.

It's this sort of state that would view Steve as being 'unpopular', and so in turn, may put his life in danger.

Save a life or save the world.

There's no way that's fair for a civilian to make that kind of decision, especially one that's not even from either of the two protagonist nations involved.

So, we wait to be informed as to the CIA's next move.

Feeling out of control, as is now usual...

Control Out.

3.25pm

Our lives get stranger by the day!

Steve went out for lunch earlier and sat in the local park, only to be joined in time by two women. One was walking a dog and was seemingly resting up, whilst the other started to read her paper.

'Just imagine Mr Cartwright. Your name on the front page. Breaking news with a by line.' the agent looked towards Steve who was caught mid-bite in his standard daily sandwich.

'I'm sorry do I know you?' he asked politely, as he munched down on his ham and cheese snack.

'My name's Claire Bradbury, MI6. Listen, I'll cut to the chase. A certain Mr Lennox, who I believe you already know, is trying to set up a meeting with you and your partner Sophia and we're simply going to facilitate a venue.'

Steve laughed as the situation got to the level of ridiculous: 'Ah, jolly good show. I wondered when "Six" was going to turn up. What about her and the dog? Are they in on it too? Lennox doesn't usually go for anything this formal, so where are we going? A speak easy in Mayfair, or a safe house in Dolphin Square, Pimlico?'

Bradbury closed her newspaper and returned it to her lap. Steve described her to me as being in her late 20s, brunette and "quite pretty", which I then translated from him as probably being "well fit", as he might have said to the lads.

She wore a trouser suit, high heels, dark sunglasses that she removed when talking to him, her hair was long, dark and flowing, like she'd just stepped out of a salon.

'Nowhere with quite so much notoriety Mr Cartwright, so meet us tonight at 85 Albert Embankment, 7pm sharp please and can you also bring Sophia.' It was framed more as a directive, rather than a question. Good job I didn't have plans!

I've made my excuses from work, part timer that I now seem to be and Albert Embankment's where we shall meet.

Wherever that is...

01.15am

Good grief. We've just got home in a cab paid for by the SIS (Secret Intelligence Service), or MI6 for short.

Jolly dash decent of them too, seeing as it would've been a crazy long walk after the last train had gone!

Steve and I met at Vauxhall station and walked around to Albert Embankment.

'You *do* know where we're going, right?' I asked, following a map on my phone, albeit upside down.

'Yep.' said Steve, striding purposefully.

'You sound sure of yourself! Your sense of direction is notoriously bad. When have you ever been here before?'

He looked at me with a silly looking smile: 'I haven't, but I've watched *James Bond*, so I think I know where it is, it should be right by that bridge.' he said pointing.

'You watched it on...? Oh well, that's ok then. You may as well chair the meeting. Should I call you "S" or "C" for your codename, or do you have a "Double O" number after all?'

'No, but I've got a double entendre name for you Miss Funnyfanny.' he sniggered.

'Charming to the last.' Despite missing that now clean shaven face, he could've done me a favour and left his sense of humour in the tundra!

Steve then quickened his pace again, like an expectant child wanting to hasten his arrival at the gates of Disneyland: 'We need to turn right here and we should be pretty much on top of it.'

As we turned the corner I was suddenly faced with a great monolithic structure. I craned my neck up to take in its mass, with its bottle greenish glass at the top of the building and bits of the design jutting out all over the place: 'Where the hell are we?' I asked, kneading my poor neck.

'This babes, is MI6 headquarters and it reminds me of you.' said Steve playfully.

I just looked at him questioningly.

'It looks better from the back.' at which point he slapped me on my arse and ran off giggling like a wayward schoolgirl!

I won't say in here exactly what I shouted at him down the street, but suffice to say, it turned a few heads!

We arrived in reception to be greeted by security.

'Hi. I've got a meeting with Miss Bradbury and Agent Lennox, who's actually from the CIA, you know, the Central Intelligence Agency?' said Steve coolly, name dropping agents willy nilly, just because he could and revelling in his new action hero persona.

The burly doorman looked us both up and down and then his eyes diverted to a palm sized tablet in his hand: 'Yes, I have heard of the CIA thank you. One moment sir.' he said, nodding an emotionless acknowledgement.

The guard was a good six foot six and climbing, built like the proverbial outhouse and sported arms like oak trees. The guy spoke into a small microphone, surreptitiously tucked into his dark suited jacket lapel, and he turned his bulk away from us while he waited for the go ahead.

Finally, after an audible crackling sound, he held his finger to his earpiece and pushed it further into his ear canal, so as to hear the reply with greater clarity.

He raised his large index finger to us, as if to plead for patience. I wasn't about to argue! The big digit was then lowered and he finally boomed an official welcome that echoed within the cavernous reception: 'Walk this way Miss Sinclair, Mr Cartwright if you will. Our Mr Thomas will be with you soon.'

The guard had gone from officious to official and then to welcoming host in a matter of seconds.

We walked through the security scanner. My handbag and Steve's boy bag went one way and we were lead in the opposite direction. Then after a quick frisk, suits you sir, we were reunited with our baggage.

The high vaulted ceiling was more ecclesiastical than you'd have imagined for such a modern looking building, with the massive glass windows letting natural light flood into the vast reception area. We were then led across the light polished Travertine floor to some striking black leather Barcelona style chairs within the guest area. Nice to know where our tax goes.

There was an array of daily newspapers, spread out on the low-level designer glass table before us, as well as an

Economist and a *Spectator* magazine for added political effect. Each had a version of a Russian flag characterised as a red missile, pointing at Obama, depicted knocked kneed with his pants around his ankles, holding his naked modesty.

Just as we'd got comfortable and Steve had picked up a tabloid to check the football scores, we were approached by a youngish chap of West Indian extract.

He had short dreadlocks, a tight, but sharp fitting navy coloured suit with a pristine white shirt and no tie: 'Welcome to Vauxhall Cross folks. My name's Devon Thomas and we've quite a lot to get through tonight.'

Steve beamed and extended his hand in friendship: 'Ah, we used to holiday in Devon, is that where your parents took the inspiration for your name?' he asked innocently.

Devon's thick and relaxed pace to his accent was the sort of reminder that *we* really needed a tropical beach holiday: 'Mr Cartwright. My parents were born and raised in Antigua. Unfortunately for them, they had no opportunity to visit Branscombe beach. No, my name is simply inspired by the three great pillars of civil society.'

Steve looked embarrassed: 'Ah, I see, apologies. Let me guess then. Justice, freedom and social mobility?'

Devon laughed heartily: 'No my man. They are simply Off, Middle and Leg. My name is inspired by the great Devon Malcolm and trust me, life at MI6 is just as fast paced!'

Steve smiled at Devon's joke, but unfortunately the whole routine had me stumped.

Devon then turned away, beckoning us to follow with a lazy arm action. We duly followed, and I was excited to be in yet another great British institution.

We were led to the lift and up to level six. We turned right out of the lift and down a corridor, passing meeting room after meeting room. Some full, some empty. Some lit, others not, but all glazed with the doors closed.

Then we finally reached the end of the artificially lit corridor, the grey unobtrusive carpets adding a sense of visual perspective to the corridor length, with its darker stripes hugging the walls either side, accentuating the distance.

Devon ushered us into Room 47, which was also plainly decorated and already housed Claire Bradbury and Agent Lennox around a large glass table for eight. There were just six high backed ergonomic looking black chairs and on the wall facing the entrance, a landscape modernist painting of what looked like two giant statuesque legs, hacked at the knees and sunk within the sand within the desert scene, entitled "*Hubris*."

Claire rose first: 'Pleased to meet you. You must be Sophia.' She greeted me in a very well spoken tone and with an outstretched hand. If nothing else, Steve had good taste in women and to his credit and hers, she was in fact *very* pretty.

I did then wonder if that meant that seeing as Steve had 'chosen' me, he therefore thought I too was pretty, but now was not the time or place for self assessment. Far too taxing!

'Hello, and you must be Agent Bradbury and Agent Lennox?' I guessed, turning to the American.

'The one and the same. Pleasure.' He shook my hand. Limp and loose. Yuck.

Devon called the meeting to order. Welcome one and all, I'm the MI6 Grade Six facilitating the meeting and overseeing proceedings this evening. Agent Lennox will be leading the meeting and Miss Bradbury here, is the SIS representative responsible for your on-going safety and tactical recall.'

'Yes,' said Steve, quickly jumping in: 'About my safety. I've had time to ponder this and Lennox; you said I'd be popular with some and unpopular with others. I presume this popularity would warrant a knighthood and the unpopularity; well, more of a nightmare?'

'If you're named on the press report to receive the kudos that you so rightly deserve, yes, you may well encounter hostility from those you have attempted to unveil.' he replied, relaxing into his executive chair, his dull accent unwavering.

'And from "hostility", do I take that as being a few choice words and a hand slap; the odd shake down and a Chinese burn, or just a bullet in the head?' said Steve pointedly and adding inverted commas in the airspace as appropriate.

'I'd hope not the latter, but that's where Agent Bradbury and her team should be able to help you.' Lennox retorted, face devoid of emotion. He was all business.

Claire joined the conversation: 'We can of course detail protection to you 24 hours a day. We can move you both to a short-term safe house, from where you can work remotely for a sense of normality. Once the dust settles, we can reassess the situation and gradually "bleed" you back into society. Only when the time is right of course.'

'Sounds delightful, if a little messy,' I said: 'Do I get any say in this matter? Why exactly does Steve have to write the article? Why does he have to take the pressure, the plaudits *and* the pain? And what do *I* have to do with all of this?'

'Miss,' Lennox looked down to review his notes: 'Sinclair. Your partner was kind enough to go to Antarctica for us and it's only right that as a journalist, he writes the article and it's up to him whether he wants the associated trappings.'

'Depends what sort of trap it is.' I snapped back.

This American was short. Not in stature, but in his curt nature. I can however, always go shorter for the long game! Inappropriate opprobrium is my strong suit.

Devon could feel the building tension in the room and looked to defuse it immediately: 'Let's move on shall we? Agent Lennox, perhaps you can fill us in on why Sophia *is* required here tonight?'

All eyes turned to Lennox: 'Your dream, Miss Sinclair. As I said to Steve, we're aware of it and its content. However I need to hear chapter and verse every detail from the horse's mouth, as it were, to ascertain if this is something we need to worry about.'

I looked at him, assessing his face, his eyes and expression. This time he looked genuine, no sense of spite in his tone, *or* his eyes: 'Ok Lennox, which one?'

'The first. The destruction dream.'

'Well it was more of an explosion, a blast in fact. I've always assumed that it was caused by a nuclear strike, due to the light in the night sky and the ensuing chaos.'

Lennox looked back at his notes, as an aide memoire: 'Your police statement from early January reports the earth shaking and dust raining down on top of you, is that correct?'

'Well yes, but that wasn't the main bit. I was with a young girl you see. Well I say I, it certainly felt like me, albeit I didn't recognise the place, or the child. But the emotion of anguish was there. I felt a real connection to her you see. I felt like I loved her, like I've never loved anything or anyone before and then there was the blast and it was...'

'Scary?' questioned Claire, butting in, her brow furrowed as she listened intently to my description.

'No. It was beautiful.' I replied incredulously.

'I hardly think the end of time would be described as beautiful.' chipped in Devon sarcastically.

'It was just the sheer spectacle of it. Like one hundred New Year fireworks events, all rolled into one. You could have set it to music, it was dazzling, almost like something out of *War of the Worlds*. The heat was amazing, unlike anything you could imagine and I could smell what I could only assume was burning flesh. It was acrid, disgusting and really pongy. Then there was the sound too. It was a blast, then silence, followed by an almighty whoosh that just took us away. It had to be a bomb, right?'

Lennox filled his empty glass with sparkling water from a jug on the glass-topped table, its spindly steel supports fitted under the glass, all seemingly defied gravity and engineering.

'So, a bomb that shakes the Earth, emits dust and smells "pongy"?' he confirmed with the corner of his lip slightly upturned in his best attempt at a wry smile.

'What are you saying Lennox? That she's lying?' spat Steve defensively.

'I'm simply saying in the heat of the moment; if you pardon the expression, you may've been distracted from the essence of what was actually happening. Miss Sinclair, as you know, there are various details from your second dream that have subsequently come to pass.'

'Correct.' I answered somewhat gravely.

Lennox placed a file on the table in front of him and took an audible breath as he opened it: ‘What you don’t know Miss Sinclair, is that we collect accounts of dreams and visions all of the time.’

I smiled, mildly annoyed that I’d not found this during my original Internet searches, albeit it could just be an American service and a Black Opp to boot: ‘Makes sense, I was looking for an official channel to report mine into.’

Lennox shifted in his seat, again an intake of breath: ‘Yes, we know. However, in this instance, yours is not the only one.’

I remember looking at Steve, then back to Lennox, who just sat there stern faced, still devoid of emotion. I tilted my head: ‘Only one what?’

Lennox sucked his teeth and this time checked his watch: ‘We don’t just have *your* account of your first dream miss Sinclair. We have...’ he looked furtively towards Thomas, who visibly nodded his approval: ‘We have over 2,000 different people citing apocalyptic dreams and they were all collected around the same time period as yours.’

Steve again leapt to my defence, without actually comprehending what Lennox had just said: ‘Well with the amount of people in the world, maybe people are having these sorts of dreams all the time. Maybe not everyone has reported them in. Maybe they didn’t take them as seriously as Sophia, or have them so profound. Can you blame her for calling it in?’

‘Mr Cartwright, listen to me carefully as I’m not sure you fully understand. We’ve had exactly 2,019 other accounts of a vision so similar to Miss Sinclair’s first dream that they could’ve quite easily all been from the same person. They all describe a massive sense of loss. Sometimes a daughter, a son, an elder relative, but always a connection to someone they don’t actually recognise and always with exactly the same ground movements, the dust and the distinct smell. Is it mere coincidence Mr Cartwright or a message? A warning perhaps?’

There was then a collective silence, as we all tried to fully comprehend exactly what he was saying.

I was stunned.

For once in my life, I was stunned to absolute silence and somehow my brain seemed unable to process the information in terms of scale or correlation.

Steve looked to break the deadlock, or at least the haze clouding my own vision: 'You're not going to go all preachy on us are you?'

Lennox snorted, pre-empting his own irony: 'Heaven forbid Mr Cartwright. Heaven forbid. Each account mentions this ash in particular and seeing as parts of your second dream are starting to come to fruition, that's why I've got you in Miss Sinclair. To enlighten me, personally.'

'Ok, so was it like a nuclear winter ash?' I asked.

'No, that always comes down some time afterwards. The accounts from each visionary all recall a blast, then a black ash immediately apparent in these dreams. What we're looking at here, Miss Sinclair, is not a nuclear war, but a possible volcanic eruption. The smell you describe was not burning flesh, but simply primordial sulphur, emitting from the crater as part of the eruption.'

'So it's just a natural event? Not the end of the world after all?' asked Steve, almost disappointed on my behalf.

In hindsight, I think Lennox was surprised at our reaction to there being 2,020 of the same dreams reported. Perhaps he expected more of a shock, but after all we've been through, it just seemed par for the bizarre course of events.

Lennox continued undeterred: 'Not through nuclear causes anyway. Ladies and Gentlemen, do you know anything about induced earthquakes.' his question was rhetorical.

'We've been researching this in Nevada and at HARRP in Alaska since the 1950s, as a way of weaponising natural events, as well as the weather. However, since we've been carrying out hydraulic injection or fracking within the US, there's been a marked increase in seismicity and the amount and frequency of earthquakes that occur up to magnitude three. Occasionally, and I mean occasionally, they've got up to magnitude six. In short the increase in seismicity has been found to coincide with the injection of wastewater into deep disposal fracking wells in many locations across the Mid-Western states.'

'Your point, sir?' asked Devon politely.

'My point is that if we're willingly inducing earthquakes in our own back yard through mining and we can read their output via our Nevada and Denver listening outposts, does that mean you could weaponise or localise an earthquake by simply mining? We've run some tests based on the theory of a volcano erupting and it wouldn't take much for Russia to start fracking off their East coast, so as to deliberately cause a tectonic shift such that the seismic forces involved could cause a series of earthquakes down the Western Seaboard and/or a volcanic eruption.'

Steve laughed: 'Don't be so ridiculous, it sounds like something far fetched out of a film. I can picture the San Andreas fault opening up to swallow the hero, but volcanoes too? Please give us some credit here!'

Lennox looked at Steve pointedly, as if he'd just laughed off the existence of Nazi concentration camps: 'Does Mount Rainier ring any bells?'

Again silence from the room.

Lennox's monotone drawl continued apace: 'Washington State in the Cascade Range and the highest damn mountain in the Pacific Northwest. It last erupted back in 1894, and being what they term as a "Decade Volcano", it's slightly overdue to say the least!'

We all looked at each other and then back at Lennox: 'Yep. Officially the most dangerous volcano in the world! She's situated just a mere 50 miles from the major populous of Seattle. The danger in this case wouldn't just be from the eruption itself, but from the lahars that would flow downhill *caused* by the eruption. This is a glacial volcano with 26 major glaciers within it and two volcanic craters spanning over 300 metres in diameter. Simply put, this baby's massive! This is not just a snow-capped mountain, people. This thing has enough mud and ice to flood the whole river valley below and engulf a huge amount of innocent people.'

Lennox paused for effect, stretched his arms and then continued: 'Now, natural disasters are one thing. They happen. Shit happens. But if they're deliberately set off by another nation. Well then, that's just fucking hostile!'

Lennox sat back and waited for reaction, re-donning his glasses for a more sincere and learned look. Sinister more like.

That was quite an insinuation that another country would willingly cause incineration. Be it nuclear or otherwise. Could Russia really cause tectonic shifts and earthquakes large enough to upset the world's most dangerous volcano?

'Even if they wanted to do it, you've already said they're testing in Antarctica. What sort of timeframe are we talking about here until they are fully weaponised?' asked Devon, checking his own notes.

Lennox started cleaning his glasses once more: 'Well, with the intel we have at the moment, they're just starting out, but mining sure seems an effective "non-weapon" to us. It's the ultimate accident or an ability to create an effect without obviously being the cause. No troops on the ground, no jets in the air. Just let the Earth do what it does best. Move. They can sit back and watch the terror unfold, while the protagonist nation gets off scot-free.'

'Ok, we get that now, but how long? Next week, next year?' demanded Devon impatiently.

'Well we don't know exactly, but they could be two to three, to four years away from developing something that powerful and by the end of 2020 most certainly. It would need to be a massive hydraulic injection, much larger than is currently required and one that sends shockwaves straight across the Bering Straits once the gas subsides. Naturally it's cold there and since the influx of these crazy dreams that so consistently described a massive volcanic event, we started to listen for the signs of tell tale tremors across the globe.'

'Yes, we've been picking up signals too, but just assumed it was natural tectonic movement.' said Devon.

'That's when we accidentally hit on the increased seismic emissions coming out of the Antarctic. We think they're currently testing and training in Antarctica. Not specifically mining, but testing. Out of sight and bringing a whole heap of misinformation to the rest of the world to distract us. So, Miss Sinclair, was there anything else in your dream?' asked Lennox, peering at me expectantly.

I simply shook my head. This was half in answer to his question and half in disbelief that I'd been one of 2,020 people to have the same, or similar dream. Crazy!

Surely that can't be right?

The dream was powerful. So powerful I felt compelled to act on it, but for that many other people to do the same beggars belief. How many didn't report it? Lennox said it might be a message or a warning. But from who and how'd they do it?

'So you want me to expose the thousands of visions and this impending volcanic emergency to the world and stave off the threat from the Ruskies huh?' asked Steve in a tone that said; "*Well if that's all, I'm game if you are...*"

Lennox stroked the stubble on his chin, hearing it rasp against the grain: 'Well I wouldn't give away all the cookies from the jar. We'd expose the fallacy of the facility in Mirny. We'd also put more emphasis on pointing the finger of blame towards that of illegal mining and therefore instigate a total worldwide ban on fracking and not just as a short-term sanction. A lifetime ban if you will. We'd then build a new localised listening station in the granite at Koyuk in Alaska, just to be safe and future proofed.'

'Koy what?' said Bradbury, growing confused.

'If you ever happen to see it on a map, there is a long snowy road that meanders north of the town to a frozen lake. That would be our new Groom Lake. It would be a new base for a new era and just 300km away from the Russian mainland. Shit! The granite would sing so loud, we'd hear it coming before the Russians had even launched the attack, let alone start drilling. And that's when we'd strike!'

Bradbury cleared her throat: 'I'm not sure you should be so free with your information Agent Lennox. We have civilians in the room remember. So where did you get so many visions pooled anyway? Why are we not aware of all this via the CIA or Interpol?'

Lennox was seemingly braced for this line of questioning: 'Well, we've had 67 cases from the US come across my desk over the past few months, as 'unexplained' from the NSA and that was when I approached my Canadian counterpart. He had another 14 matching cases. I then contacted Interpol and they collated almost 600 cases from across Europe and the Far East, including 37 from the UK alone. Each case had been referred to a mixture of local police, in some cases secret service and in others shared via a public forum for debate. There's people on *Reddit* and *Gab* right now trying to debunk there meaning and in the main, coming up with a conclusion of an impending nuclear war. Conspiracies that suit us just fine for now thanks.'

Devon concurred: 'Yes I'm aware of that and there's also some conspiracy chatter linking Russia with funding ISIS, so as to try and commit US troops on the ground in the Middle East. Then there are the reports about ISIS' ability to flood Europe with refugees as a tipping point to annexe the UK from Europe and promulgate widespread populism. I presume *that*, combined with some of the work the FSB is doing on your own election, it's to divert the CIA's eyes off the South Pole. Whilst we're all fighting over Baghdad and Brussels again and spending time fending off Russian advances in the Baltic, the Kremlin can carry on quietly digging for victory.'

Steve stood up to reach for the water jug: 'So it's a no brainer then. I *have* to write the article!'

Bradbury cut in before I could protest: 'Well I think we need to fully explore your options, take some council before making any rash decisions to aid the special relationship.'

Lennox slammed his drinking glass down on the table, making us all jump: 'Special relationship? This goes far wider than that, lady. It wasn't so special when you sold us London Bridge now was it?!? This is about world peace, saving lives across the Middle East, not just in North West America. It's about saving the ecosystem in the Antarctic and about giving credence to the anti-fracking lobby groups that are trying to stop this nonsense.'

'You really are fracked off by this aren't you?' said Steve.

‘Yes. As a matter of fact, I am. Both my parents lived in Cleveland, Ohio. Both fit and well and drank the prescribed two litres of tap water a day. Within a year of each other, five years ago, they died of differing forms of cancer. The doctor said that anyone can get it at any time, but with numerous fracking wells located close to where they live, I personally have another view on things. The contamination of the aquifers has to stop. It shouldn’t be about creating a self-sufficient gas supply. This is top of Governor Orlando Johnson’s political agenda and I wish to see him in power on the back of it.’

Steve scoffed condescendingly: ‘Ah, so now we have it. It’s personal agendas and vendettas getting in the way of clarity and justice in politics yet again. Anything to see the Republicans back in power and so guarantee stopping the proposed budget cuts to the CIA in their tracks, right?’

‘You know your politics, Mr Cartwright. And like the Cartwright’s before you that died for the freedom of our fathers and our father’s fathers, you should stand up for the principles of freedom and democracy too. I may wish to see the GOP back in the White House, but purely from a moralistic and Christian standpoint. In this time of heightened terror we need someone with morals, scruples and not afraid of dishing out justice where it’s deserved. These Libtard snowflakes have gone too far!’

Devon poured scorn on Lennox, from a more British perspective: ‘So that’s why you wanted us to commit 2% of GDP to defence and renew Trident, so we can back you and NATO up on your sordid offense.’

‘It’s in your nation’s interest too Mr Thomas. If the Argentines suddenly see weakness, they’ll strike back for the Malvinas and if you keep on cutting budgets the way you are, you won’t be able to do a thing about it. What’ll be next, Gibraltar? If you give away any more of your Empire or devolve any more powers, you’ll be just another country and certainly not “united” or a “kingdom” like old.’

Devon couldn’t sound stressed in his lazy burr, but made his point vociferously all the same: ‘Let us worry about our own affairs, Lennox; you stick to the case in hand. So you feel that Steve deserves to take the credit for a discovery that you asked him to go and verify? Seems a little magnanimous, or are you just putting the blame of stopping Russia in its tracks at the other side of the Atlantic, so that we *have* to support you, whatever shit comes the way of your fan?'

Again, just the slightest tip of the head from Lennox in acknowledgment: 'Well let's see shall we? Let's see.'

Steve raised his palms and shrugged his shoulders: 'I said I'd do it already. I was there. I saw what happens there and now in context, a lot of the detail I witnessed makes more sense. I think it's an amazing story. The scoop of a lifetime – I can see it now – "The man who saved the world!" Got a kind of ring to it, huh?'

I looked at Steve sternly: 'This isn't a game babes. You. We, could both be in danger.'

Steve shrugged: 'You always said you wanted a job that saved lives. A job that mattered. Well, here's my chance to make a name for myself. Make a difference, not just to journalism, but also to mankind. The Earth too. Shit, if we can pull this off, America will be able to flex its muscles on the world stage, cut off any supposed funding to ISIS, calm things in the Middle East without having to go to war and hopefully stave off the *real* apocalyptic scenario that we researched about before. Lennox's motives may be shrouded with retribution, but on reflection they do tantamount to justice. Besides, I grew fond of those pesky little penguins.'

Lennox clapped his hands together once and rose: 'So that's settled then.' more of a statement, rather than a question.

Lennox started to slide into his overcoat: 'Mr Cartwright, if you begin working on the article, and once you're done, I can pass it through at my end for sign off and it can be released to the world's media. Our UN envoy is preparing a diplomatic meeting with the Kremlin and will have his fair share of bargaining chips to reverse Russia's challenge to Belarus.'

Bradbury caught his eye: 'Before you go, Agent Lennox, should the UN envoy not impart his knowledge of the fracking plans to his Kremlin counterpart and simply use that as leverage for Russia to stand down?'

‘Weakness!’ Lennox struck the table once more, droplets of water emanating from the top of his glass: ‘We must use the power of the media and public outcry to stop them in their tracks once and for all, not just politicking over coffee this time, sweetheart. Take the power back. If we go in half-baked, it’ll show weakness and we cannot be exploited at this time of political flux in the US. So no. We go on message, as planned and the UN envoy will have this knowledge as part of his arsenal to stop the onset of a new Soviet Union.’

‘Yes I did wonder if the reunification of the old Union was your ultimate fear,’ said Devon candidly: ‘Ok, have it your way, any form of political stability will work for the British Government. I too will report back to my superiors and I’m sure you’ll hear from the Foreign Secretary in time. Goodbye Lennox.’ Devon’s hand was outstretched across the table, but Lennox was already turned and walking away.

The American was the one calling the shots at the British table, but it was a problem for *them* in the main.

We were then led into a waiting taxi, which took us all the way to each of our respective flats. I’ve therefore had the time to write up an amazing evening’s events. Just so glad I kept this diary thing going and to think I was getting cold feet!

I just can’t get my head around so many people having the same vision and they’re a possible message or warning.

Fancy my dream being one of 2,020 reported visions.

Just plain crazy!

Wednesday February 10th 2016 – 2.00pm

Got into work late today, not that anyone noticed really. I think they assumed that I'd been in early and been to a meeting, or simply been called to 10 Downing Street this time, such is my growing reputation for international intrigue.

Close your microphone diary, I so nearly messed up!

I'd left you on and open on my last entry when Lucy came sidling over to the desk and started to read over my shoulder.

'What's all this then? "*A message or a warning*?" You writing a book Soph?' she asked innocently.

I jumped in my seat: 'Wo Lucy, you scared the living whatsits out of me.' I slapped the tablet shut within its cover: 'No this is actually my diary and not for public consumption.'

'Fair enough, but if Steve's about to get a message or warning from you, I'm glad I'm not on the receiving end! You get that email from Sam Rogers? Looks like another delay to the end date on "Project Bluebird" then.'

'No not yet, I'm about sixteen emails behind, so bear with and I'll go back to her direct and cc you in, but thanks for the heads up.' I replied, quickly composing myself.

Close! I had it open as I was going to add in there that I'd been online this morning looking for these forums that Lennox was talking about and he was right!

There they were, as plain as day on a few apocalypse related sub Reddits and who knows how many more there are on *Twitter*, *Facebook*, let alone meltdowns on *Mumsnet*.

I'm not going to get involved with other people and I'm sure as hell not going to tell them that they're not a lone voice in the dark and there are in fact so many of us!

Maybe I've been mistaken. Maybe there *is* a higher spiritual power with a just cause that can transcend space and time. Perhaps this kind of celestial intervention would be one step too far in terms of the free will of humanity, that is unless of course it *is* the prelude to the second coming??

Christ knows!

9.55pm

I just got home late from work. Cereal and toast tonight I think, as I can't be arsed to cook for one. One person that is, not me being posh...

Steve text to say he's also head down at work too and not had a chance to start work on this new "commission" to save the world - Time waits for no man, but apparently The Earth can just get in the queue at *Reuters*!

Thursday February 11th 2016 – 6.00am

Up early today to get in and fight the good fight again. I seem to be enjoying work a bit more, now that Steve's back and my head's in a slightly better place, I guess.

Think I'll instigate meeting up with him tonight, maybe try to channel his thoughts onto the planet and also to instruct a solicitor to act for us on the house move - that has also moved to the back of the queue!

2.45pm

I've just had a totes hilar call from Steve - if I thought my deadlines were ridiculous, the expectation of the American Government truly cannot be surpassed.

Lennox had called him asking him for timescales for the first draft. Steve, being Steve ventured for next week, to allow him the weekend to do it and they came back with a final demand of close of play tomorrow, so Lennox could get senior approval before issuing the press release next Monday!

Thank goodness for the five-hour time delay, or they might have wanted it Friday lunchtime...

So our plans for tonight are off, as he'll be working on the article and whether his boss has received a call, we're not sure, but suffice to say the article he was currently working on has suddenly been demoted in priority and he'll be working on the Antarctic story for the rest of today and through the night.

10.00pm

I think Steve does it just to wind me up.

He's headlong into the article and making good ground, so I asked him if his headline would be "*The Man who Saved the World*" and he laughed: 'No love, I've got something far more befitting the situation!'

"Your world is breaking apart!"

I just hung up...

Friday February 12th 2016 – 7.45am

I'm still not speaking to him! It's such a bloody liberty, taking my dream and making it a reality like that.

Ok, so he'd probably argue that I started it when I put the word Mabus into my phone, but it's my prophecy to self fulfil, not his!

I've soooo got out of bed the wrong side today!

1.05pm

I've text Steve, but still no reply - I think he may have got all hung up about me hanging up on him or something.

I thought best to make peace to pave the way for the big day on Sunday. Two days away until I pop the question.

SCARY!

I can't remember if I mentioned my engaging idea to the girls at the gig we went to. They've not brought it up, so either alcohol related brain fade wins again, or it wasn't quite as an engaging story as I'd hoped.

As far as I'm concerned, I don't need any additional pressure on me, so probably best not to talk the idea to death in the mean time.

6.05pm

I'm just on the train going home alone.

Steve has finished his final draft and sent it off for US approval, but being a journalistic perfectionist, he's stayed behind to proof it and keep close to his emails in case they come back with revisions. They did request him to be on hand.

He apologised for not texting me back, as he was busy working on the article. Fair enough I guess. Save the world or save yourself from some crazy lady on an ego trip.

I apologised for hanging up and he just laughed. I think we're fine, so much so that we'll meet for breakfast in the café.

Bring on Saturday, that was one hell of a roller-coaster week and I think I'm about ready to get off - trouble is I've got a bad feeling this ride happens to go around twice…

Saturday February 13th 2016 – 8.45am

Just got up. One day to go to V Day!

I feel like a child looking forward to Christmas, or a teenager counting down to the girls' first trip to Ibiza. Oh those were the days. Sun, sand and sangria. Nothing else mind, we're British - the only stiff thing I ever saw was an upper lip.

I wouldn't describe myself as prudish per se, just picky. And slightly prickly, which may not have helped my cause. Anyway I have a man now and soon he'll be mine, all mine.

Cue evil laugh...

Time to get ready for breakfast. The sun is shining today and it bodes well.

7.00pm

We met at the café at 10.00am, sat and perused the menu. Sausage, bacon and eggs with fried bread, black pudding and lashings of baked beans. Twice. "*Sorted mate*", as the man behind the counter said to us.

'So what time did you finish?' I asked, checking my phone for emails.

Steve looked tired and a little distracted: 'Hmm. Oh finish. Er, well, technically I haven't, but last night it was just gone ten and then I got the last train home.'

'Blimey Steve, no wonder you look like something Valentine dragged in. Talking of cats, what the hell happened to Shelley? Sorry! I forgot to ask.'

Steve laughed: 'Oh Shelley, yeah I forgot her too and she withered and perished whilst I was away and I found her emaciated body out by the bins, surrounded by flies.'

I choked on my mug of tea that had just arrived: 'Shut up! Serious? No you wouldn't have done that! Where was she?'

Steve knew how to press my buttons and this is another reason I love him: 'Sorry couldn't resist. I sent her to Seth's via a special delivery, but the Royal Mail messed it up and she ended up in Catford. Mission not accomplished!'

I just gave him a look and continued to drink my tea. He smiled and we relaxed back in our chairs.

‘So are you going to get her back from Seth’s then?’

‘Nah, the kids love her and I’ve got too much going on. Plus seeing as we’re moving in together, I’m sure one cat will be enough.’

‘Yes good call. It’s a wonder I’m allowed in sometimes, what with Valentine around. She rules the roost somewhat.’ I frowned; I’d not seen her myself for a while. Mangy moggies!

‘So yes,’ sighed Steve, stretching out his arms accompanied by a cavernous yawn: ‘Some bod at Langley came back with changes. Nothing too fundamental, just the tone in some places, putting more onus on the illegality of the fracking down there and quoting certain paragraphs from the Madrid Treaty from the 1950s. No biggie, just took me a while to finesse it.’

‘But you said you hadn’t finished yet.’

‘Well yes, now they’ve got the revised article, it’s gone to the next level up the chain. The Joint Chiefs or some crazy level of bureaucracy like that.’

I must’ve looked shocked: ‘Seriously, it’s gone that high?’

Steve laughed: ‘Yeah I know, crazy eh? It’s just nobody wants to take final responsibility for the grenade before I throw it out there and we all watch it go off. My guess is the President himself will need to have eyes on it. So there you go. My pedestrian prose makes it to the Oval Office. Not bad for the new kid on the block?’

They must have had much of the food on the hot plate or simply on the go, as our breakfast soon arrived and we sat in a comfortable silence, as we enjoyed our brunch.

I smiled at Steve across the table thinking about tomorrow’s timings and got butterflies in my stomach.

I was and still am, so excited. Did you guess?

He smiled back and gave me a wink: ‘So this time Monday, you’ll be front page news then?’ I said, half mumbling whilst munching on my fried bread.

‘Well TV news I would imagine and then front-page the following day in the press. It’ll go viral of course. It’ll be on TV across the world, websites, the global press and social. My story will be trending. I may end up with my own hashtag!’

‘There’s trendy for you. First time for everything eh? Will it be #FrackGate?’

Steve put on a deep voice, like from the American movie trailers: ‘My story around the globe. How one man risked his life for the greater good. Going deep undercover into the bleak Antarctic and putting an end to illegal mining and the potential collapse of the world’s ecosystem.’

‘Ok Spielberg, let’s not get too carried away. You’ve got to get the Presidential seal of approval yet.’

‘It’s just a matter of time babes.’

The rest of the day was spent looking up solicitors and thrilling things like that. Talking budgets and preparing to move our ‘liquid assets’, as my Financial Advisor called them.

Usually most of my wages go on liquid assets – booze in the main part!

Not anymore, we’ll have to save up for furniture as both of our current flats came furnished. We’ll need to decorate, get insurance and write a will. Basically grow up!

I’ve come back to my flat now to leave Steve, as he received an email from the White House - as you do on a lazy Saturday afternoon...

That’s given me a chance to regroup write this up and plan for tomorrow’s big day. I said that I’d have him here for lunch. I’m not sure he even realises that it’s Valentine’s Day tomorrow, as he never mentioned it.

I decided against the proposal on the rocks idea, in case the notion sent him into shock and he then fell into the sea. I’m always thinking. Always risk managing!

Sunday February 14th 2016 – 9.05am

I feel a bit sick.

The butterflies in my stomach have now turned to full on nerves and I think I need the loo!

I'm lying in bed planning how to pad out the next three hours until Steve arrives. I can't decide whether to propose over the food, pre food or after. I think if I do it after the meal, I'll just lose my appetite and not be able to eat anything.

During the meal may be a little odd. I can imagine pushing peas around my plate putting off asking the question for fear of getting an answer that puts me off the rest of my meal.

Ok, so I'll do it before we eat. Maybe I'll even do it before we raise a toast to his safe return.

Yes, done!

Right, it's time to shower, get dressed up and get peeling that veg.

12.15pm

Oh bloody blimey, he's here! On the sofa.

I'm in the bathroom pooping myself! Figuratively speaking of course, otherwise I really would be in more of a mess than I currently am!

This is such a big thing for me. The whole commitment thing's fine, but sharing my personal space with someone and even the notion of sharing in general will be alien.

The trouble with not being married at 34, is by then you have become like an only child. Quite used to all the attention, not having to share and being able to get what you want and when you want it. I'm not sure what I'm more scared of, Steve saying no, or perversely, saying yes, but not allowing me to watch my own tripe on television.

I've got my Dad's old wedding ring at the ready as a pseudo engagement ring for Steve; that is until we get me sorted with my sparkler anyway!

This is when the practicalities of a woman proposing work out a bit arse about face. He wouldn't normally have an engagement ring, but I'd feel a bit daft or tight not offering anything more than just an onion ring or a *Hoola Hoop...*

Right, it's now or never.

It's time to take the engaged sign off the bathroom and see if I can put one on his finger instead. Time to face the music and time to dish up and see if he fancies what's on the menu.

Ok that's all the analogies I've got. Get on with it!

6.15pm

Oh my God, I've never been so scared.

I've never been through so many emotions. Today's been like a rollercoaster. But a good one with a twist!

After I eventually came out of hiding and found Steve on the sofa, he looked up and I could hear his brain ticking: 'You look nice babes.' I think he noticed I was out of my jeans and probably wondered what was up there and then.

There was a pause...

'Happy Valentine's Day.' he said, as he swiftly whipped out a bottle of wine from his overnight bag.

He stood to kiss me: 'Oh you did remember then,' I said smiling: 'Happy Valentine's Day too, gorgeous man of mine.'

'Of course, how can a "Metro Man" like me in this day and age go anywhere without being bombarded by it? You don't get a card though, waste of a tree - well a twig anyway.'

That was fine. He knew the way to my heart was through good old-fashioned grape juice anyway.

'Any updates on your story?' I asked.

'Just a bit! I thought you'd never ask.' replied Steve passionately: 'Get this - the CIA's been ramping up on its Intelligence sources and the recent aggression towards Belarus, as well as the activity in Antarctica, which technically appears not to be Russia's fault. I'm not convinced that the Politbureau is actually aware of exactly what's been going on, hence the delay in them renouncing knowledge of the aggression.'

Good to know a country is unaware of its military actions, but turns a blind eye once highlighted anyway....

Steve poured a glass of my new wine for us both and continued: 'It seems there's a rogue General from the Cold

War era who still has an axe to grind with America and has been funding the purchase of the UMS machinery in association with one of the many cash rich and power hungry Oligarchs. This machinery has in turn been provided to the mining company and not only are their actions out of sight of the rest of the West, they're also under the radar of the Kremlin too.'

'What about the scientists at Mirny? Would they not blow the whistle?'

'What, and risk their own funding? And guess which Oligarch that funding comes from? Yes, the one and the same guy funding the military op. His name's Bacchus Borichevsky, a 65-year-old former Military General, who was given his wealth and assets on a plate during the fall of the USSR. Now both he and this rogue General Serpik are hell bent on Western retribution.'

'Blimey, so the UN envoy may not have as much leverage up his sleeve after all - that is other than to demand that Russia gets its own house in order.'

'That remains to be seen. We're not sure if the aggression against Belarus is part of an elaborate putsch to topple the Russian top brass, or just a smokescreen created by General Serpik to impress the Kremlin as to his own potential in the military. This is of course, whilst Borichevsky goes about his work quietly in Antarctica.'

'But how do they amass such a force on the border without it flagging up to someone in the Kremlin?'

'Well they've got about 100,000 troops and artillery down there for a training exercise, which was legit, but Serpik's taken autonomous control and evolved the exercise into a battle ready situation. Seems he's using his own propaganda about the UN putting sanctions on Russia over Ukraine and the annexe of Crimea to rally the troops to fight for real.'

Dark forces do seem to be at work and perhaps not the sort that I'd originally envisaged as being those that would accelerate the apocalypse. It's coming from all sides!

Steve passed me a glass of red and sat on the sofa: 'This is all just hot off the press, but the fact that they shared it with me leads me to wonder whether there may be in fact another seminal article to be written by the next great whistle-blower of our time. Me.'

'Yes, but unlike Snowdon, you won't be able to hide out in Russia. The closest you'll get to anything Marxist is *his* actual grave in Highgate Cemetery.'

'We'll have to wait and see what happens, but I'm expecting a call from Bradbury tonight about taking us away!'

'Wo, I totally forgot about that! I've not packed, informed work or anything. I think I thought it was all a bit tongue in cheek. So we really will be spirited away to a safe house?'

Steve nodded: 'You did say you wanted to live together as soon as possible.'

I crossed the room to check on the lunch and laughed to myself: 'Yes, but not in those sort of circumstances. So should we actually be packing rather than just chatting?'

'Nah, let's eat first, I'm famished, then I'll call Claire to assess the situation fully.'

'Oh, so it's *Claire* now is it?' I muttered, as I took the small joint of beef out of the oven. The smell was intoxicating - like coming home and we won't get that in a safe house.

'Babes, you know you're the only one for me and on that subject, seeing as you brought it up. We need to talk.'

I immediately thought the worst and quickly imagined Steve reneging on the house purchase to give us some more time and space, or wanting to use the safe house as a test of our suitability of living together. My head was awash.

Yet, it was quite the opposite in fact!

Steve reached into his pocket and knelt down in front of me. His hands prised open a small black box that he was now holding and stone me, there was a diamond ring in it! **For me**!

This all happened so fast and I was so not expecting it from Steve. I immediately squealed in delight and then in my excitement, and in an automatic motion to cover my mouth in shock, I promptly dropped the tray with the beef on!

I screamed again and Steve fell backwards off his knee in shock of the roasting tray crashing down before him, hot fat swilling over the sides onto the laminate floor and lapping up onto his bended knee.

'Pissing Nora!' he exclaimed: 'I haven't even asked you yet! Jesus, talk about a total freak out.'

'No, No!' I cried: 'I'm so sorry; you just caught me by surprise. Total surprise!' I apologised, as I quickly mopped up the fat with a handy tea towel.

'Well this wasn't exactly how I'd planned it,' laughed Steve, as he replaced the loose roast potatoes back into the metal lipped tray: 'I thought you'd appreciate it on Valentine's Day, you know, after your cat and all?'

I stood up and composed myself, removing my apron and placing the hot tray on the worktop: 'Appreciate what exactly Mr, you haven't asked me anything yet?'

I beamed at him, composure fully regained and prepared for the best moment of my life!

Steve stood and shook his head, dusted the crumbs off his knees and picked up the fallen presentation box: 'Miss Sinclair. My Sophia. Would you do me the greatest honour in the world of being Mrs, I Saved the World?'

The light glinted off the admittedly modest, but still quite beautiful rock that was set flush into the slender platinum band. Its amazing shine then suddenly seemed to blur, as my eyes began to well up.

I expected some moving words from my wordsmith, but I was actually glad of the humour to make me laugh out loud, rather than start crying.

I smiled, wiped away the last tears from my eyes and stood on my tiptoes to give him as massive a hug as I could muster. I'd never seen this coming. There was I worrying about what *I* was going to say to Steve and then suddenly his own disastrous engagement routine rolls into town.

I loved it! It's my very own disaster story that I can now take pride in sharing with anyone who cares to listen.

'Well?' he whispered in my ear, gripping me ever tighter: 'Does that sound like a plan you can manage?'

'It sounds like a bit of a project, but I believe that I'm just the gal to manage you.'

I broke away, looked him in the eye, put my hands around his beautiful face and planted a passionate kiss squarely on his lips: ‘I love you. Let’s do this!’

11.15pm

Although we’ve only just got engaged, we’ve been practising the consummation of the marriage for some years now. Too many times than I care to remember. Anyway the latest rehearsal proved to be a thoroughly good exercise, to the point that Steve is now asleep.

I can’t believe I’m going to get married!

I know that I was planning to ask him myself, so I should’ve seen it coming one way or another, but it still hasn’t sunk in yet. I’ve not told him my own plan for a proposal; not wanting to steal his thunder, bless him.

I’m so happy. He asked. I said yes. Job done...

We’ll have a new home and a new life together to enjoy and look forward to as a proper couple.

Wedding planner mode will soon be in full effect and then *Project Honeymoon* will commence with a pre-planning meeting to take place sooner, rather than later! Should we take a tour of Thailand or maybe a shorter trip to Venice and Lake Como instead? Perhaps we should avoid Moscow and on reflection, probably we should just get over the release of Steve’s “shit storm” article first.

We’re now all packed up, not for the house move, but for our Witness Protection Programme - to witness the tipping point in modern history no less.

Steve spoke to Claire and it’s on, tomorrow morning!

The suitcases are at the door with enough clothes for a week. Steve popped back to his flat to get some extra things, probably just one pair of pants, a T-Shirt and some flip flops knowing him. Unfortunately we’re not going anywhere too salubrious. Cheam, to be exact.

I’m sure it’s a lovely part of the world, but it certainly won’t be on my Honeymoon bucket list. I’ve never had cause to go to Surrey much and Cheam seems a bit of a random place. Yet thinking about it, one would hope that it serves as *the* last place anyone would look for us!

I'm told that we're not allowed to take any electrical communication devices, so no phones, or computers and there's no WI-FI, so we will be incommunicado for a week.

What am I going to do with my time? I'm allowed to take my tablet, so at least I can keep on rambling on here, albeit I might have the rein it in a bit. I've got books on my tablet too, which I never get to read, so every cloud eh?

I'm just glad I get to take my tablet; it's now an extension of me. It's the place I go to share, to rationalise and to vent steam. It's my secret retreat and to not write in here would be like losing an arm. Ok, maybe that was a little melodramatic. More like being separated from a dear friend, or a confidant.

Only now do I fully understand why people write "Dear Diary". It makes complete sense to me now - finally.

I'm set to leave at 05.00 hours, as Bradbury said. I expect a black *Sedan* with darkened windows will roll up and a man in dark sunglasses will knock at the door to take me to my car.

I'll then probably turn and look back at the flat, wondering if and when I'll be back again.

Valentine is being taken into care too.

The new and extremely happy, future Mrs Cartwright signing off for Queen and Country... See you on the other side!

Monday February 15th 2016 – 10.55am

Well, we're in and it's not quite *The Ritz*, but it's fine. More like a cheap, utilitarian *Air B&B* in fact.

The car picked me up as planned, under the cover of darkness. The black *Sedan* with darkened bulletproof windows screeched to a halt outside my block of flats, scattering gravel as it stopped. Four large men, wearing with dark suits and dark sunglasses got out of each of the four car doors, three of them training their assortment of assault weapons on unmarked enemies that could be lurking within the grassy knoll of the communal landscaping.

The fourth guy, the biggest of them all, clocked me in the lobby and ran over at full pelt: 'You on me, NOW!'

His gloved mitts grabbed me around the waist and swept me off my feet towards the waiting vehicle, which was still purring in readiness to leave at a moment's notice. The agent pushed down on my head as I was bundled and bustled into the back of the car, the three other men all clambered in at once: 'GO, GO, GO!' shouted my security detail and with that I was thrown back into my seat, such was the force that we pulled away with.

The car then reversed out of the my road at breakneck speed, the whirring noise of the reverse gear screaming in protest and the driver span the wheel in on itself so the car performed an immaculate 180 degree switchback. I'd not even had time to belt up and we were off, hurtling towards Steve's flat before the sun had even had a chance to rise.

Now this is what I'd imagined might happen as I lay not getting a wink of sleep last night. I'd imagined all sorts of scenarios, but this fitted with my new persona of international intrigue that I've worked so hard to build up.

In reality I didn't hear the car arrive. There was a ring on the bell at 4.55am as I was cleaning my teeth and a skinny small block with NHS glasses and a flat cap stood in front of me. At first I thought he was the Milkman, lost: 'You Sinclair? Sophia Sinclair?' he asked in a think Brummie accent.

Bloody cheapskates, there was no black *Sedan* after all, no bustling, no bundling and certainly no man handling me into the car. It was just a bloody taxi! He did help with my luggage, which was something, as I'd certainly not accounted for that in my daydream, and might have regretted a lack of clean clothes.

So I locked up, we pootled over to Steve's and Gumbo, the driver, got out and performed the same well honed routine of welcoming my new fiancée into the car.

'Morning darling,' he said: 'Not sure I've ever seen you up this early before.'

'That's 'cos it's obscene o'clock and you seem far too cheery considering the circumstances!'

'Ah, come on, I know you just can't wait to be alone with me for a week.'

'Alone, I expect we'll have guards in the wardrobes and bugs all over again, so I'll hardly feel alone. Anyway if we're moving in together this will be a good test.'

'Yeah, to see if I can put up with your nagging!'

I turned to look out of the window, my own selective hearing choosing to screen that last remark.

The drive was longer than I thought, despite the lack of traffic and I started to dose, whilst Steve struck up a conversation with the cabby. I'm not sure if he knew that we were going to a Safe House or not, so we never mentioned it.

Eventually, we pulled up outside a chip shop in the High Street and Gumbo jumped out to retrieve our cases from the boot: 'All paid for folks, stay safe right.' With that he pulled away and left us looking for our next meeting point.

'What did Claire say to do next?' I asked impatiently.

'She just said to wait here and oh…'

The unassuming door to the side of the chip shop cracked open and a tall man with an Afrikaans accent peered above the chain that held it so far: 'You have anything to say to me?'

I looked at Steve, confused by the situation.

'It's ok, I've got this babes. Yes sir, the thing I'd like to tell you is Mabus.'

'You're kidding me right? Jesus!' I scoffed in disbelief.

With that the door opened to reveal our first security detail Joris, a slab of a man with a face carved from granite and a patterned tattoo that ran from his ear down the right side of his exposed neck: 'Welcome, best I get the kettle on ja?'

We walked in, heaving our luggage up the stairs that led to the flat above the shop. The door opened onto an open plan living area with a modest dining table, access to the kitchen and then two tiny bedrooms and a bathroom.

Home sweet home eh?

We unpacked, freshened up and Joris, who despite being the sort of person you'd expect to see in an action movie, is actually a bit of a softy. He put on breakfast for us, bless him and we sat on the sofa and tucked in.

'You know the rules ja? No phones, you leave them with me now. You don't leave the building unless me or one of the other boys tell you to and the rest of the time is your own. Go!'

So that's it then, we're unable to make contact with anyone, least of all Devon, Agent Bradbury or Lennox for any sort of an update. Our handlers or glorified minders are Special Service operatives on a 24-hour rota. I suspect most of them will be quiet, not wanting to engage in conversation, a few may even be mute.

If ever there was a test of impending married life, it was locking up two people all day, every day for a week with no wine! I feel for those poor souls on *Big Brother*!

Steve's watching the news and I'm bored already. His revelation is supposed to break today, but we've no idea when.

3.00pm

Still bored. It must be agony for Joris, as I bet he does this all the time, but he seems quite happy reading on the sofa. Steve's dozing next to him, worn out doing nothing I guess and I'm just writing for writing's sake and mentally critiquing the choice of wall colours in the bedroom where I'm sat.

Ah, this is pointless. I'm going to read too.

8.40pm

Newsflash – no not Steve's story, which still hasn't broken yet, but Joris has been replaced. There was a knock at the door about 6.00pm and a tall, lean looking chap, whose dark leathery skin evidenced lots of time spent outside. He had a shock of dark hair, a large Roman nose and was holding what I immediately recognised as fish and chips, judging by the divine smell of vinegar.

'Anyone order dinner? I'm Rocco, Doris has gone home and I'm here all night.'

Steve laughed, saying he couldn't imagine anyone further away from the name Doris if he tried, particularly a man.

So we ate, Rocco chowing down like it was his first meal of the day and we weren't far behind, it's amazing how lolling around all day can make you peckish.

'Hmm, you got that diary I can look at Soph?' asked Steve, wiping his greasy fingers on his trousers.

'Er, yes.' I replied cautiously. I'd wanted to just extract a certain section, rather than let him have free reign over all of its content. Lord knows what he'd find: 'Yeah let me just clean up and I'll download if for you. Just the bits of when you were away mind.' tapping my finger to my nose to imply secrecy.

Steve nodded his acquiescence and waited patiently whilst I packaged the file for him to read and that's what he's been doing for the last hour or so, catching up on what he missed out. I've only just got the tablet back really, so I thought I'd catch up whilst he has a bath and we await the 9.00pm news to see if there's any updates on the story coming out.

Steve's face was a picture. Frowning, eyes widening, scoffing to himself and the occasional look in my direction and a shake of the head in disbelief.

Once he'd finished, he popped the tablet on the sofa, pulled me up off the chair and gave me a hug: 'Thank you.' he whispered in my ear.

'What for?'

'For being there. For sticking by me, for believing in me.'

'Ah, it was nothing, you know.'

'Soph you got arrested, you got taken to Cheltenham and you fell in love with a Welshman.'

'I never fucking did!'

'Steady love! Ah, come on, you thought about it.'

'Piss off!'

I stormed off into the bedroom, knowing full well he was goading me really, but I wanted to shut him down. Shit I forgot about Rees being in there! I wonder how he is. I wonder how his book voucher went down in the end, bless him.

'No, joking aside, really thank you, it sounds like a crazy time, your emotions must have been all over the place.'

'They were, your quite right.' I said, with a serious pout.

'Still can't quite believe you've been to GCHQ.'

'Twice!'

'Twice. You cracked my code with the big boys and that Harry chap sounds like a bit of an arse.'

'Meh, he's all right I guess. Just old school principles.'

'He was quite open wasn't he. You know what. Once this has all died down, you should go back into your diary and tidy it all up a bit, there's a great story in there somewhere.'

'You think? You've only read a few pages.'

'I've read enough to interest me. If you put in all that stuff about our research and the bugging, it'd be a classic spy novel, just based on fact, rather than fiction.'

'It's all in there Steve, every last detail. It's been a bit of a labour of love to be honest. I nearly quit it at the end of January, but that's when it all seemed to kick on again. Nobody wants to read my bloody diary anyway.'

'You'd be surprised, the amount of other crap out there.'

'Thanks. I think.'

'Give it a go. You've got nothing better to do whilst you're in here, why don't you just knock up a bestseller on the quiet?'

'And who's going to publish this book then? I've signed the National Secrets Act.'

'Nah, don't worry about that, if they didn't want you to know something, they wouldn't have told you. Anyway you can self publish these days. Get it out there and see what happens, you could be the next E.L. James and go viral.'

‘She couldn’t help but go viral, the amount of filth that woman wrote.’

Steve frowned at me disapprovingly.

‘Ok, so I enjoyed her book.’

Steve raised his eyebrows at me.

‘Ok, all three of them, but that’s not to say she’s going to go down in the annuls of time for great British literature.’

‘Anals of time more like.’ laughed Steve.

It was at this point we heard a stifled titter coming from the sofa as Rocco was blatantly earwigging our conversation.

So here I sit, on the bed wondering where to start on this modern day espionage epic. It makes sense to start at the beginning, but the last few days are fresher in my head.

I think I’ll start tomorrow; I’m not cut out for this really.

Tuesday February 16th 2016 – 7.35am

Holy shit, we missed it. There was nothing on the 9.00pm or 10.00pm news, so we gave up, having had an early start.

We both woke at seven this morning to Rocco beckoning us into the lounge to watch the live coverage.

Steve's article has hit the headlines and as I assumed, it's caused an absolute international shit storm.

According to the newscaster who reviewed the story, "***Your World is Breaking Apart***" appeared on the front page of *The Times* in London and New York, *Das Bild, Paris Match* and every other newspaper and website across the world. This was a truly global story for a potentially global situation.

I remember sitting on the sofa, Steve to the left of me, Rocco to the right and thinking I'm stuck in the middle of all of this. What have I let myself in for?

Not that I've actually had a chance to read it yet, but the article warned of Russian mining practices in the Antarctic, the potential for an unprecedented ecological disaster and the brazen flouting of international law. It told of melting glaciers, rising sea levels and the possibility of tectonic shattering, but didn't go into the potential weaponising of the technology, nor the links to the aggression at the Belorussian border.

Despite MI6 knowing that the article was coming, you'd assume they'd be ready for its impact.

Suddenly UK Ministers for Foreign Affairs, the Home Office and the Energy Secretary were all unavailable for comment. This meant that the story could neither be verified in the eyes of the media, nor refuted; which set them off into a catastrophic spin of endless conjecture.

The "author" of the article was unavailable for comment, 'cos he was sat here with me, and at first Steve was lauded as being some kind of ecological hero, rising up against the big mining corporations. The next great whistle-blower.

The Kremlin had already come out to deny all knowledge of the claims; as well they might, if this work at the South Pole was indeed done as a "black" or covert operation.

From the speed of their rebuttal, I'd got the impression that they were pissed!

So we wait. It's only like 7.45am on a random Tuesday and most people haven't even seen the news yet, on a global scale I mean.

Oh, hang on Steve's calling me.

1.25pm

We just watched the news and seems like the US is now awake, as Obama's Press Secretary has just made a statement condemning Russia for breaking international law, as well as amassing troops in the Baltic. They've now outed General Serpik as being the main protagonist in this potential conflict, so it will be interesting to see if Russia comes clean or not.

I can't watch anymore, it's just surreal. It's like passively observing your life story unfold from a far, unable to control the course of events, the speed or direction of travel.

I do not like this lack of control!

So how am I going to write this book then? Publish it as it is? Flower up the narrative a bit? I guess I should expand on the descriptive parts, but if I'm writing a book at one end and writing a diary at the present day at the other end, where does it stop? Does *this* paragraph make the final cut? Blimey this is doing my tree in already.

5.35pm

Rocco's just started packing up. He's been pretty silent all day and then he just stood up: 'Right kids, it's been fun and we should do this again some time. Doris will be here shortly, so I will see you both tomorrow.'

'Yep.' said Steve, flicking through a magazine.

'Yeah bye Rocco, thanks for looking after us.' I cringed.

With that the door opened and Joris walked in, stretched his large frame, as if he'd been stuck in a car for hours and patted Rocco on the back as he left the flat.

Steve was zoned out and perused the magazine, yawning.

'Hey Doris. I mean Joris!' he said, jumping up and dropping the magazine as he realised his unintentional slip up.

Joris nodded. I think he'd heard it all before and figured Rocco must have let his nickname out of the bag.

'Hey Joris. Busy day?' I asked jovially.

'Nee, so so.' He replied under his breath as he set about unpacking a bag of provisions.

'So what do we do about eating tonight?' I asked.

'In here my lady.' he replied, pointing to his duffle bag.

It seems that not only is Joris a hired muscle, he was also a sous chef in a former life and immediately set about preparing a steak dinner.

'Touch!' said Steve, when he finally realised what was sizzling on the pan: 'I could get used to this.'

'Yeah, don't go getting any ideas for when we've got our place, right. It won't be roast beef every night.'

'Yeah, once was enough I think, it ended up on the floor anyway.' he sniggered.

7.35pm

I really have nothing better to do than keep checking in on here, it's painful and it's only day two in Big Brother's house. It's snowing again, I thought we'd left all that behind, but apparently not. Ok let's not resort to talking about the weather.

3.25am

It's silly o'clock and I can't sleep. Just when you think you know someone, Jesus, this is *so* going in my book!

Steve asked me into the bedroom earlier and I thought he was a bit keen with Joris sitting in the next room, but he said he had something he needed to get off his chest.

'Ok. Something good or something bad? I asked, almost afraid to ask in case I didn't like the answer.

'Just something. Do you believe in coincidence?'

'Coincidence? Is that something you can actually *believe* in? Sure I guess, you see it all the time right?'

'Ok, let's re-phrase it for you. Do you believe in fate, or do you believe that everything happens purely by chance?'

'Ah, I see. Er, I think that everything happens for a reason. Within reason.'

‘And, what if there’s no rhyme or reason behind it?’

‘What are you getting at Steve?’

‘You weren't the only one to have had a dream.’

‘I know, there were like 2,000 of us, so what? I can only recount what I personally experienced.’

‘Ok, don’t freak out. You said in your diary that you had a meeting in Room 47 at GCHQ.’

‘If you say so, I’ve slept since then, I can’t remember.’

‘Sophia, I’ve not been completely honest with you. I too had the same dream. I’m one of the 2,020 visionaries, well one more really, as I never reported mine in.’

I almost swore at him. I almost questioned him and yet as I looked into his eyes, I somehow knew, deep down, I’ve always known. I’d never really asked him why he’d not interrogated my delusions more, or warned me off wanting to report it into the Police. He went along with it because he was in the same predicament and was too weak or confused to say anything:

‘Christ Steve, why’d you not say anything?’

‘I, I dunno. I think I thought it would all blow over and when you said you’d had your dream, I freaked out a bit and clammed up.’

‘I thought mine was a fever dream, or so you said. You never had a fever.’

‘I made it up.’

‘Well it bloody well checked out when I was searching the Internet about them. It made complete sense.’

‘Trust me, it makes no sense. None of it. Room 47, that’s in my dream. You had a headline, *my* headline. I had a room number, *your* room number.’

‘Ah come on! That’s just coincidence!’

‘Is it? Is it Sophia? I think that’s how this interwoven web or matrix of synchronicities works. People just don't see them and they hide in plain sight. Our subconscious knows full well they’re there. Five senses I ask you! There’s more to it Soph, way more. It’s the hairs on the back of the neck, the red flaring on your chest and ears. They’re all natures tells to expect the unexpected. Yet all you feel is a slightly hot ear and simply go about your business, oblivious to the signal.’

‘Wo, you’ve gone right down the rabbit hole haven’t you!’

‘Shit I’ve seen behind the looking glass Soph and it ain’t what it seems. How many artists, musicians and writers have vouched for the fact that their creative work was in fact easy? That they were simply “in the zone” and channeling something from a higher power they couldn’t describe? It just “comes natural” to them, like an “outpouring”. Really??’

‘I just assumed that was the drugs kicking in, well what else is it then? God?’

‘You know what, I’m not so sure what to believe now. There’s probably an overarching creator, but this thing’s layered, it’s complex and too interwoven. It’s like they’re messages from another space and time, trying to get through.’

‘I think you’ve been watching too much sci-fi Steve.’

‘Seriously though, how can we expect to contemplate the architecture of the universe, when we can't even understand the inner workings of our mind? We need to get to grips with reality, be more conscientious about consciousness and strive to unlock the multi-layered dimension we reside in here before we go disturbing forever the fabric of space time elsewhere.’

‘What are you talking about? Who’s disturbing what?’

‘Quantum mechanics Soph, quantum computing.’

‘Is this CERN again Steve? You know they’re just bashing particles together right?’

‘Yeah to what end? To understand the infinitesimal so they can fully exploit the infinite.’

It was at this point that our conversation was cut short by the onset of the 10.00pm news, our exciting new way of punctuating the day, so we can observe how the new world order of events is shaping up.

It seems that the British and American Governments have finally collaborated and got their stories straight. Statements were made by the Foreign Office about the truth of the allegations written in the article, whilst the White House spokeswoman laboured the illegality of the mining, the compelling nature of the evidence and Intelligence presented.

She then called on the UN to act impartially in the matter, as the Earth should not be made a political pawn in all of this.

Despite our foreknowledge about Serpik going rogue, the media seem hell bent on reporting that his actions are in fact part of a premeditated Russian attack on Belarus' sovereignty and again the UN should impose further sanctions on the state.

'What's their agenda here?' asked Steve quizzically.

'What do you mean?' asked Joris.

'Well we heard from MI6 that Serpik is acting alone, using the army training as a way of amassing a force and then launching an attack so as to either bring down Putin, or hasten US involvement in a new Cold War, leading to pretty much mutual annulation.'

'Sounds dicey.' said Joris.

'Dicey? The whole world's safety hangs in a fine nuclear balance, the Russians could set off the most dangerous volcano on the American's Eastern Seaboard and they're on the verge of ruining the planet's ecosystem in Antarctica. I think it's slightly more dicey than dicey!' I said, upping the anti and realising the full enormity of the situation we find ourselves in.

'So if they know Serpik's septic, then why are they covering for him?' Joris replied.

'I'm not convinced they are, said Steve: 'I think the media and the Establishment would like this to be the final straw and a way of nipping the conflict in the bud before it escalates too far anyway.'

Then the news changed tact to the "author" of the story and how some outlets across the globe, namely *RT* and the US Liberal media, had turned on Steve and tarnished his name as a Charlatan. They accused him of being a shill, bribed to lie by anti-fracking lobbyists, a stupid bloody story, probably put out by the pro fracking lobbyists themselves! His supposed unavailability for comment was tantamount to his guilt, even more so that the Home Office was reportedly protecting him.

So, not innocent until proven guilty, but like so many villains of the press, guilty until they can prove their own innocence or afford the libel case. It really riled me how

Steve's character was assassinated so quickly and all he was guilty of was having the balls to stand up and be counted!

Steve got up in silence: 'I'm going to bed. Night all.'

And that was that. I latterly slipped into the bed alongside him, but he was sparko and there I lay thinking, until now.

How can he have had the same dream? Was it exactly the same, he never actually said and then there's his whole tangent into the unknown, which I've no idea where that was ending up. I'm not sure he did either.

Wednesday February 17th 2016 – 8.15am

Well I tried to pries some more information out of Steve before breakfast, but after the news last night, he's really gone into himself.

'You alright babes?'

'Can't you see what they're trying to do Soph. They're positioning a play for the long game. If it all goes to shit, they can say I was a shill from the start. If it goes well, that'll be yesterday's news. I'm just a fucking pawn in yet another bloody game! I knew this would happen, but the stakes are too high not to get involved. It's the bloody planet Soph!'

I cuddled up to him to console his woes: 'It's fine babes, it's all going to be fine. They'll expose Serpik for what he is and get to the bottom of what's going on in Antarctica. Whether they come clean about the true motive for the work down there, or whether they keep pushing the mining motif, remains to be seen.'

'And what about that Bacchus chap? No mention of him! Instead, it's my name in lights and right ready for the pot shots to come raining in on.'

'Borichevsky,' said Rocco: 'Bacchus Borichevsky and you won't be hearing anything about his involvement, he's, how'd you say? Untouchable.'

We looked at each other, unaware of Rocco's wider involvement in the case and not sure as to whether we should question him further. He didn't say anymore, so we simply changed the subject.

10.35pm

Well pretty uneventful today and certainly nothing of note for a novel.

I did get a little bit more out of Steve about his dream though, which is worth sharing. He asked why I think he went off with the CIA so readily; he was trying to deflect attention from me and keep me from danger. Little did he realise in the process that he'd wind up getting me deeper into this mess than either of us could ever have imagined. Such a mess.

Thursday February 18th 2016 – 8.15am

The UN has met with the Kremlin over the Antarctic issue, which the media had interminably referred to as #PolarGate. The Kremlin came out and gave assurances that it had no knowledge of this mining work and would act accordingly, citing forces "out of its control".

Considering the global condemnation of the country for seemingly flouting the Madrid Treaty and threatening the Antarctic region as a whole, the Kremlin was suddenly very quick to clamp down on General Serpik and climb down from the Belarusian border.

We're still not sure whether the Belarus offensive was the doing of Serpik alone, but the General was duly made the convenient scapegoat and wheeled out for public censure and proof that the Russian justice system could prevail.

However, there's still never been any mention of Bacchus Borichevsky. He wasn't mentioned by Russia as being part of the problem in the Artic and deep down, I think therein lays the main problem within Russia - money talks and as such, you can buy anonymity or complete autonomy.

It's stopped snowing. I've started to write this here diary into a book, from the beginning, you might be glad to hear and that's about it. Time is going so slowly, it's almost agony. It's like being trapped on a dessert island with just *Homes Under the Hammer* and worse still, Jeremy Kyle as company.

Getting any more out of Steve about his dream is proving difficult. He just rebuffs me, saying he'd seen what *I'd* seen, but I had two dreams. Did he? Not that he's saying, but I very much doubt Room 47 made it into a vision of the apocalypse.

There must be another dream he's not letting on about and maybe that's where he's getting all this inter-dimensional stuff from, maybe his second vision was more of a visitation?

Friday February 19th 2016 – 11.15am

There's still not been any mention of the volcanic theory in the media, but Steve received a call first thing via Rocco's phone from Claire Bradbury who told him that Intelligence sources within Ukraine and Moscow are reporting "knowledge of such an opportunity".

An opportunity to weaponise fracking that is.

'Did she say anything else? Did she ask after us?'

'Not really,' said Steve: 'Just that really, I took it as the inside track, knowing that we'd only be exposed to what the news was telling us.'

'Two sides to every storey eh?'

'It seems so yes. Alternative facts.'

Meanwhile in the US, Orlando Johnson has also jumped on this entire situation, using it as a standpoint from which to campaign on. He's now promising that should he be elected, he would ensure the US would act as the rightful World Police once more, putting right the wrongs in the Middle East and presuming to keep the rest of the world in check too.

Needless to say, the public at large are lapping up his populist rhetoric and I bet old Lennox is just rubbing his limp hands for an increased budget or simply a big fat pay rise.

Here, the anti-fracking lobby has been putting pressure on the Government, what with the first fracking trials due to start in Lancashire later this year - a good opportunity to push a cause closer to home eh?

Thinking back to what Steve was saying about our place in the cosmos, the question of consciousness and the self, I often wonder why we're all here.

As a human race I mean, not why we're in Cheam.

It probably just boils down to continuing and protecting the survival of the human race right. Surely it's as simple and primeval as that?

What else is out there? What other way should we exist? What new order for the age could we create today and what new order may lurk behind the scenes, plotting and charting the course of our own pilots?

Diaries are forums for radical thought right? Getting ideas off your chest, throw them out there and see which looks the least fanciful in print. How can we be so consistent at getting everything wrong in the world, from war and geopolitics to the constant attrition of the ecosystem in which we all inhabit?

Georg Wilhelm Friedrich Hagel once said: *"We learn from history that we do not learn from history."* Now, I'm no theologian, but re-reading what I wrote earlier has got me thinking even more.

Should I pay homage to a God? Should I pledge allegiance to a flag. Or should I just stay in this safe space and hide?

I feel like more of a spare part than an actual cog in the wheel, now that I've been given a glimpse of the world outside of the engine room. I've seen behind the scenes.

I once read that "Real eyes realise real lies". I like this. Not just the sheer unadulterated beauty of the wordplay with our wonderful language, but the fact that it has true meaning for a cynic like me and particularly at a time like now.

Who am I to question?

Who am I?

Saturday February 20th 2016 – 10.10am

It's been almost a week and as Bradbury had predicted, the dust did begin to settle. Either that or the flooding disaster in Sumatra turned our story into yesterday's chip paper.

There are fewer reports about PolarGate now and certainly nothing on the news about Steve anymore, which is good and he does seem a little more, *back to himself*, shall we say.

Rocco and Joris continue to swap shifts and I've taken to staring out of the front window, watching the world go by on the High Street. Who'd have thought chips were in such demand at all times of the day?!?

So I guess we're just waiting for a call, another cab, or a screeching *Sedan* to arrive and break the monotony. I'm cracking on with this ridiculous book idea, which is keeping me from going completely insane and also reading a few books too, just basically trying to avoid any more television.

Sunday February 21st 2016 – 8.05

We're going home!

That is all and I didn't think this warranted it's own page!

Monday February 22nd 2016 – 11.11am

Steve's gone to the office today to start writing up the fracking article that he'd previously started researching when we were originally searching for Mabus.

It's topical, so in the world of journalism, there's no time like the present – despite Bradbury's advice to the contrary. This was not advice that he shouldn't write up the article; just that Steve shouldn't go back into the office just yet.

'There are plenty of people out there that don't like free speech.' she said to him on the phone. Yet, Steve being Steve had other ideas. He's his own man. I'm not his keeper; just the keeper of his counsel and this time the advice of two women wasn't enough to stop him.

So now I'm in a position whereby I feel compelled to go back to London to meet him after work, for my own personal reassurance, albeit I won't be returning to my office just yet.

4.05pm

I'm sitting in the park watching the world go by.

I'm in the delightfully named *Bernie Spain Gardens* to be precise, with its views of the Thames and just a stone's throw from Steve's new office in Blackfriars.

The weather's chilly, the wind is brisk, but the sky is blue, hence the low temperature.

When I'm not typing, I keep looking at my ring and smiling to myself.

It's been over a week now, but a weightier left hand is always what I wanted! It's simple and effective, with one diamond cut into a platinum outer ring. It's just beautiful.

The sun catches the tidal river to my right. I have my dark sunglasses and headphones on playing a dance mix, so as to escape from reality and any minor publicity.

I still have a minder detailed to me and Rocco's sat on the bench opposite, looking truly undetectable in plain clothes and pretending to play on a tablet of his own. To his credit he only occasionally looks down at it, the rest of the time, his eyes are darting around my immediate vicinity.

Whether his attention is actually necessary, I'll never know. I'm not party to the security briefing or the risks involved. I'll never know until it's too late I guess.

You can tell I'm padding whilst I wait for Steve.

It was in the usual situation whereby the train I got would get me here too early, or the next train would get me here too late. So I plumbed for the early one and a chance to reflect by the river.

Oooh, a football just hit my foot, spilt the takeaway cup of coffee that I'd placed on the floor and made me jump.

It belonged to a young girl, about seven or eight playing with her dad nearby and she spoke to me, but with my headphones on, so I didn't hear her.

'I'm sorry.' she repeated, smiling sweetly.

'That's ok lovely, no harm done; not the end of the world.'

She turned and ran back to her dad, who waved an embarrassed apology, to which I just smiled back.

Now my headphones are off, I can hear the noise of a helicopter, circling close by. Blimey that's loud; I think I'll put them back on!

There's a chap sat opposite me. He's an old guy with a newspaper - *London Evening Standard*, West End Final.

I suppose I could try and pick one up to pass the time. But that means going back to Blackfriars station. Maybe I'll just wait for him to finish reading his.

Blimey that was quick. As I write, he's just upped sticks and left the paper where he sat. Oh, hang on my handbag is vibrating now...

OMG.

I've just had a call from Julia at Vauxhall Cross. They've received a call from *Reuters* asking when Steve was coming back from his lunch break, as they assumed that he'd been seconded for a meeting with MI6 again.

Claire apologised for the delay in contacting me, but has confirmed that they'd not called Steve back in to see them and they cannot raise him or his own minder - was he with me?

No he's not bloody with me!

Therefore, both Steve and Joris have been missing since after 2.00pm and no one realised until the routine contact with Joris at 3.00pm came up blank.

Claire confirmed that they've got a team out on the streets looking for them now, a team in the office tracking CCTV and another team listening to the wires for evidence of a plot against his safety. Finally there's a helicopter out tracking for Joris' phone, which is apparently transmitting his position.

I don't bloody believe it!

My heart's just dropped through the floor!

They told me to sit tight, then changed their mind and asked me to make my way to Vauxhall Cross. I don't think they know *what* they're doing! How can they just lose them like that? They are the Secret Service for goodness sake!

They know who and where everyone is at all times right? Missing for over two hours, he could've been smuggled out of the country already. Again!

My eyes have just alighted on the newspaper opposite. It was too far away to read the headline when the old man was holding it, but I wonder if... I now have a real feeling of dread.

Not just because my fiancé is missing, but also because I'm sitting in a park with a young girl and an old man with a newspaper. I am beginning to get a little freaked out. I dare not look at the front page, but feel strangely compelled, like I'm being urged by a higher force to look. It feels like the fickle finger of fate is playing chicken with me.

Rocco's just come off his phone and it looks like he may've just had the call too and has noticed my anguish and is coming over to me.

Why am I still typing? I need to do something!

Ok, we have to get to MI6 headquarters, but I need to put my paranoia out of its misery - what does it say then?

'CARNAGE ON THE STREETS OF SOUTHWARK!'

*

9.05pm

I'm sitting in intensive care at Guy's and St Thomas' Hospital - next to Steve and we're finally alone now.

When I first arrived at 5.30pm, I didn't know exactly what to expect, or if he'd even be here.

I raced to the front reception in A&E and asked for him by name. The young girl behind the beige coloured desk seemed very low down behind the counter and my visit looked like one that she'd been dreading:

'Mrs Cartwright?' she asked slowly.

'Miss Sinclair, Steve's my fiancée. So is he here then?'

'He was admitted two hours ago via ambulance. Please can you wait over there and I'll ask a nurse to come and speak to you shortly.' My eyes followed the direction of her pointing finger and I nodded my appreciation.

'Is he ok?' I asked tentatively.

'As I say, I'll ask a nurse to speak to you, as I don't have that information to hand here.'

Fair enough, I thought, as it wouldn't be up to the junior on reception to break any bad news to me.

I say *bad* news, as the *Standard's* breaking cover story reported, one fatality and one man fighting for his life in a motorcycle accident in Southwark and somehow I just knew it had to be something to do with Steve.

On my instinct or whim, Rocco and I jumped into a cab and asked to go to the closest Accident and Emergency, which is where I find myself now.

Having spoken to the nurse, it transpires that Joris was killed by the motorcyclist outright. However, the reporter only had time to gather the bare bones of the story before the paper going to press and told of a hit and run where a man on a motorbike accidentally drove into two pedestrians, leaving one dead the other critical in hospital.

The eyewitness reported hearing the motorbike accelerate, saw the bike swerve and assumed that it hit them. Knowing what I know now, what they failed to see was the silenced revolver in the hand of the pillion passenger.

What's more, the reporter didn't have the time to gather and write before going to press, the fact that one bullet to the back of the minder's head pushed him forward, his mobile phone skidding off into a nearby bush.

Because of the bike's sudden swerve, the second silenced shot missed Steve's head and hit the back of his left shoulder, sending him spiralling forwards towards the pavement.

In the shock of the impact, his right hand must have grabbed for his aching shoulder, but as he hit the ground, his hands were not there to break his fall. His head then ricocheted off the kerbstone and knocked him out cold.

As I say, I didn't know what to expect on arrival, would he be conscious, would he be lucid or out cold? The kindly nurse was quite open with me:

'Miss Sinclair?' she asked softly. The tone of her voice immediately made me start to cry. I was braced for the worst!

I nodded at her, wiping away the first few tears.

'Please follow me.' she said, leading me down a corridor and into a lift.

'Is he ok? Is Steve ok?' I asked, whimpering now.

'I'm just taking you up to intensive care now and a doctor will see you there.'

I remember looking up in anguish and that gut wrenching feeling of not knowing what to expect taking hold.

I was led down another corridor, people passing me in wheelchairs and beds being pushed by porters. We then entered a set of double doors marked ICU and I came to rest by the busy nurse's station.

My nurse broke away and spoke to an older Asian lady in a white coat, her hand on her shoulder as if to get her attention and then both producing furtive glances in my direction.

The doctor treaded towards me and smiled grimly: 'Miss Sinclair, your fiancée has been operated on and is now in recovery. Only time will tell what happens, but the surgeon reports that the pressure on his brain has been relieved.'

I didn't know what to say, so I didn't - for once, I didn't.

As we approached the ward, I immediately recognised Steve, despite the bandages on his head.

He was hooked up to a drip, the awkward looking cannula held in his wrist with tape. There was an oversized white mask on his face to regulate his breathing, the tube going into his gullet caused a laboured breathing. He had wires going in and out of his skin, which looked painful, but he wasn't awake to feel or fear anything.

That was my job!

So here I sit, with Rocco standing by the door and I don't know what to do. I find it hard to even look at him; this isn't how I want to remember Steve should the worst happen.

I want to remember our enduring embrace after the proposal, his eyes and that face.

Yet now it was hard not to look at him.

This shell of a man covered by blankets and bandages, his face battered and bruised.

That article has got him all but killed the stupid bastard and now yet again, it's left to me to pick up the bloody pieces!

It's me whose world is breaking apart!

Rocco ventured over and put his hand on my shoulder: 'Got a call for you Sophia. It's Bradbury.'

'Thanks Rocco. Hello Sophia speaking.'

'Oh my God Sophia, are you ok? I'm so sorry this has happened, we did everything in our power to prevent exactly this sort of thing from happening and I can't understand how this has happened, the security was watertight. Watertight!'

'I don't know what to say Julia. It's happened. It shouldn't have happened, but it has. You put this sort of story out there and I guess you pay the price right? If it weren't today, it would've been next week, next year. So what happens when he's better? Do we live life looking over our shoulder? Does Rocco move in with us? Christ what about Joris' family?'

'I don't know what to say Sophia. I feel personally responsible, yet can't reconcile exactly what happened. It just doesn't make any sense.'

‘What doesn’t?’

‘Hardly anybody knew where you both were. It just doesn’t make any sense.’

‘I don’t know what to say either Julia. I should be seething with your bunch of meddling arseholes, but I seriously don’t have the energy. I should be fighting down your door looking for justice, but as I’ve been sitting here, I’ve simply come to terms that this is as much on Steve as it is you all. I just don’t know what to say, what to do. I feel so empty and alone.’

Bradbury rang off shortly after and I’m just sat in a high backed chair alongside my fiancée, waiting and writing.

That’s all I can do.

Monday June 20th 2016 – 9.10pm

It's been exactly 19 weeks since I last wrote.

A lot has happened since I last visited these pages and only now am I able to bring myself to open this once loyal friend again and make a new entry.

My last entry!

It was on the evening of Tuesday February 23rd at 8.20pm that Steve finally slipped away and left me alone.

That's the hardest thing I've ever had to write and for a cathartic conclusion on this chapter of my life, I feel that I have to get it down in order to finally get it out.

The pain that is.

He waged his battle longer than the consultant expected, considering the level of brain damage caused. The angled kerbstone had shattered his scull into his frontal lobe and even if he'd lived, he wouldn't have been Steve.

We've had the funeral.

It was the saddest day of my life, but at the same time it was beautiful. It was a celebration of *his* life. I never got to plan a wedding, be carried over the threshold or see him hold our first-born. Yet I did get to give him the send off he deserved and so did the many friends and family that attended.

That man who saved the world.

My feelings of love and loss are akin to those experienced in my dreams. As such, I'm now at an all time low.

I never went back to work on medical grounds. They called it depression, but for me it was more than that. It was a pure emptiness, an angry bitterness and a general resentment towards life. If there is a God, how can he allow my Steve to save the world and then take him from me?

Since Steve *was* taken from me, Tom has been my rock. Tom Rees that is. He was there as a friend at my darkest hour, firstly volunteering as my police liaison, which was below his station I know, and for that I will be eternally grateful.

I've been trying to make sense of everything that's happened this year. Has it happened for a reason?

To stumble on the murals at Denver and a subsequent search for fracking was what lured the CIA to Steve in the first place, but he wouldn't have been looking unless it was for me.

Or would he? He too had the same dream after all.

His killers have never been brought to justice for either his murder or that of Joris, who left behind a wife and two young children - just awful.

At the time, General Serpik was trolled out by the FSB in front of the media as a scapegoat for most of the indiscretions, but whether that's actually true remains to be seen – or not as the case may be…

There's been nothing in the press about seismic warfare, volcanic eruptions or impending nuclear war. That's a good thing and maybe the one good thing to finally come out of this saga - that my first dream doesn't fulfil its own prophecy, unlike my second.

And if my first and darkest dream and that of the other 2,019 people plus Steve that were similarly blessed or cursed, has in any way stopped any of these terrible things happening, then it's all been worth it.

Yet I'm not privy to Intelligence anymore.

I can't even hold down my old job. So I've been reading a lot over the past few months, learning more, so as to impart my knowledge when the time comes.

See one thing I've learnt over this whole process is that we have to live life to the full and live life with our eyes open.

Make sure that we have no regrets and see life's little idiosyncrasies, its nuanced coincidences and appreciate those moments that it has just for you. Appreciate them, recognise them and connect to them, because if you can do that, you'll have a better time on this Earth than most.

Nietzsche died in 1900. He wasn't alive to have seen an airport, let alone the one in Denver. His quotes that I've read recently are all thought provoking and he had a sense of foresight on so many things, not least one of his most famous conclusions, which may explain the reason why such prophetic and catastrophic murals are at Denver airport after all: *'We have art in order not to die of the truth.'*

I was so struck by this quote. To many it must seem like a profound or "cool" little saying, but to me it now means so much more. There's no way he could have known, but are the murals now a clue from the artist or some kind of anti establishment group hinting at things past or things yet to come? Are they clues hidden in plain sight?

'Plane sight, more like.' Steve would say in this instance.

Maybe Lennox was right. Maybe all these crazy dreams *were* a warning after all - a test of faith perhaps. You know what? It's not that I'm past caring; I just can't give it the headspace that it deserves any more. I'm tired! I'm tired because, as of yesterday, I can confirm that I'm officially 20 weeks pregnant.

You are reading this diary now.

Despite me previously referring to it as being 'not for public consumption', you are now reading these words because I've self-published it in memoriam of Steven Cartwright.

I've also retrospectively embellished it slightly by adding more of the conversations and visual cues, so as to allow you to picture yourself in each situation.

If I'm the next to die because of flouting the Official Secrets Act, or outing American defence plans, then so be it. But this diary; this book will remember Steve long after I'm even gone.

I've also included Steve's eloquent interpretation of my first dream that he'd previously penned for posterity.

This is in bold at the start of this book and for all I know; he may have actually been describing *his* own dream after all.

Soon afterwards, he also created an ironic and imaginative interpretation of my second dream. Ironic at the time, as he correctly projected that we'd be married. It was just the cause of the impending break up that he got slightly wrong…

Oh and the baby? Yes it's Steve's and his legacy lives on in more ways than one! Conceived on Valentine's and I had my 20-week scan yesterday, which confirmed that it's a girl.

Patrick and Pam are so thrilled that they'll have a little piece of Steve to hold onto. I told them face-to-face and even Patrick cried. They'll always be there for me and I for them!

As I say, Tom's been my rock and although he's now single, it's way too soon and too raw to even contemplate starting anything with him, but he understands. He said he'd wait for me, however long it took. Bless.

And my little girl?

I'm not going to call her Rebecca.

It'll just bring back too much pain and memories linked to those accursed dreams and I'm not about to self fulfil the last element of this appalling prophecy.

I don't have it in me.

So if not Rebecca, then what other name is befitting the daughter of someone that averted an Earth shattering event?

I'm going to call her Faith.

Inspired by the trust and loyalty I had for Steve, that we had for each other, but never actually got to exchange as vows in matrimony.

But now I can write no more.

It hurts too much and as I finesse the final chapter to this most cathartic of processes, I've finally found peace.

After all this time, I've finally been blessed with my own sense of devotion. I've had a chance to get a true perspective on life, my spirituality and at last, a true chance to start again.

After all this time, I've finally found my Faith.

Keep Connected with the Author...

If you've enjoyed this book, please engage with me via the official *Facebook* page for background information and the story of how the book was written over a six-month period in 2015 - www.facebook.com/2020visionbook

Alternatively, you can visit www.M-OwenClark.co.uk and leave your comments there. You will also find details on these pages of any future publications that are in progress, including part three of The Visionary Series – *Manifest Destiny*.

Finally, if you're not already, please follow me on *Twitter* @Owenclark77 and I'll follow you back, or on Gab at the same handle gab.ai/Owenclark77, or finally @m.owenclark on Instagram.

Reviews are increasingly hard to come by, so I'd be most grateful if you could please leave a review of the book, good or bad (but hopefully good if you made it this far...) wherever you bought it and on the *Goodreads* website.

Thank you in advance for your support and I'll see you on the next one!

Control out.

*

Here is a sneak peak at the sequel, *The Quantum Contra*, available on Amazon now.

1 – Covering Tracks

Click. Click.

A burly, raven-haired man stood shaking a yellowing stainless steel lighter with an almost desperate vigour. He longed to bring back to life this most treasured keepsake, on what was the coldest day of 2016 that he could remember for some time.

The repetitive and mildly violent action caused small flakes of white snow to fall from his full beard. He was wrapped up warm, braced for the elements, a trusted fur lined deerstalker clasped around his hairy chin by two precariously threadbare looking ties.

His heavy brown overcoat did its level best to buffet the wind, but this was almost futile, being as they were, in the most bleak and remote of places. The Siberian tundra.

The *Zippo* had an engraved insignia on the side. The fading and well-thumbed eagle's head was positioned above the motif of two spreading wings, split through the centre by a downward pointing dagger. The writing below was so well worn that it had become almost illegible over time. So much so that just three engraved letters remained visible.

K.G.B.

Click, click, click - still nothing.

'Blyad!' exclaimed the shivering smoker, furiously tossing the forsaken catalyst against the one nearby excuse for a tree, which was helping to shield them from the swirling storm.

'Hvatit!' replied his taller counterpart in frustration, holding up his palms in a questioning response. He then proceeded to lumber through the snow towards his father's only lasting legacy. It was as if his life depended on it.

Artyom was gangly in comparison, dressed in equally wintery garb and sporting a lighter, but just as impressive looking beard. This hairy appendage seemed to swing in the squall, as he exposed his face to the ferocious weather.

His eyes squinted, his left hand raised to protect his face as he knelt and scrabbled around in the low scrubby brush for his beloved family heirloom.

He stood once more; arms outstretched either side of his padded torso, two begloved hands raised towards the sky in apparent exacerbation.

'Chto?' queried Pavel innocently, his shoulders rising and his lips pursing downward on each side to protest his innocence. He was finding it increasingly difficult to see his comrade and wondering what was taking him so long.

'Net. Nichego.' replied Artyom under his breath, shaking his head to himself in the negative, as he ducked back down into the frozen undergrowth. He searched slowly, hoping for any glimmer of the lost article.

'Ya ponyal!' he exclaimed happily, standing up straight with the lighter held aloft and a toothless grin appearing on what could be seen of his red and mildly frostbitten face.

Pavel rolled his eyes and made his way back to the parked *Vaz Reka* off-roader, conscious that if they stayed too long, he may have to dig his way out of the snow.

Artyom was aware their work was only just about to begin. He punched Pavel in the arm on passing. 'Idiot!' he hissed in English, no love lost for the smaller man.

They may have been working together, but close friends they were not.

Suddenly, the howl of the wind was replaced for a second and both men's senses were heightened to the distinctive horn of the Trans-Siberian Railway train, echoing in the ever-depleting middle distance.

'Bystro!' exclaimed Pavel, thumping his rebuttal into Artyom's brittle ribs. Artyom's need for speed was not lost on him, despite the sharp pain welling inside for a few seconds, before subsiding once more.

The incongruous couple quickly set about hauling two long and heavy bags from the open back of the dark grey *Reka*. Pavel immediately set to his task and grimaced as he heaved at one end of the bag, before Artyom offered to take up the weight of the other end. Pavel ushered him away with a nod of the head and then gestured with his elbow towards the second bag, intimating that they should hurry and take a sack each.

The two men made surprisingly fast work of dragging the two bodies away from the truck, the taller man deciding to lift the cadaver over his shoulder much like a fireman rescuing a victim from a burning building. In time, both wraps were laid side by side in the barren wasteland and it was then Pavel poured on the petrol.

Artyom quizzed his colleague in Russian as to the identity of the deceased. Pavel shrugged and spat a curt answer, insinuating the boss had not told him, but he had simply overhead someone say, that they were two hit men who had both failed in their mission.

It meant nothing to either man. They had their orders and they had their lighter.

Click, click. Suddenly the effectiveness of the *Zippo* in the wailing gale was integral to Artyom's own survival and the completion of their assignment. Pavel stood watching expectantly as his partner patiently persevered.

Click, click, click, but the sound of the lighter was soon drowned out by the guttural tone of the passenger train. Its horn was longer and louder this time, hauntingly echoing across the distant wasteland. It was like an arrogant predator, patiently sounding its imminent and nihilistic arrival.

Pavel's eyes darted from the inert lighter to the trembling trackside and back again. 'Bystreye!' he exclaimed in desperation, holding back the urge to snatch the appliance that he knew full well only Artyom had the uncanny knack of striking. Just never the first time.

There it was again. The piercing sound was even longer this time, as the illustrious locomotive approached a nearby signal, its imminent presence likely to provide multiple witnesses to their plan if they did not hurry.

Artyom concentrated, his eyes burning into the pitted wick as if to ignite it by sheer will alone.

Click, click, spark.

The on looking Pavel punched the air with joy. 'Da!' he shouted with relief as his associate lit the cotton fuse tied to one end of their latent baggage. The small flame soon took hold and chased along the slender line towards the two bodies, finally engulfing them in a miniature inferno, fuelled by the foul east wind.

The train still approached rapidly from the west, pounding towards them on age-old irons and tearing through the gathering mist.

The men looked at each other, happy the flames were now subsiding, the dark hessian sacks slowly smoldering to reveal the charred human remains within.

The men covered their noses to mask the smell of the burning flesh. Yet rather than jump into the *Reka* and head back along the track that brought them out to this remote area in the first place, they could not help themselves but stay and watch the eminent old train go by, out of respect.

*

This delay was exactly what the businessman Bacchus Borichevsky had predicted. Exactly what he had envisioned when booking his envoy onto the rear carriage of that *very* train and exactly what he now hoped would allow him to cover his tracks. Tracks that led back to the death of the English civilian Steven Cartwright earlier that year.

The *Golden Eagle* sped past at almost 60mph, in a brilliant blur of blue paint, eating up the tundra and the track, whilst sounding its hostile horn at the exact moment the red star fronted engine reached the *Reka*.

Coach after coach disappeared rapidly from sight. The two mercenaries were aware of the indistinct passengers at the fogged up windows, but the speed and the height of the train made it too hard for them to focus on any features. The internal lights were on as day now turned to dusk and they could only imagine the merriment and wonder inside as the travellers passed through the seemingly undiscovered wilds of mother Russia.

*

A tall, suited man glided unannounced into the Purser's office at the rear carriage of the train. The long, slender black suitcase in his hand made it look like he was returning from a game of billiards; only it was slightly deeper in size.

The Purser simply nodded his approval of entry, as if he had been fully expecting this dapper visitor.

The man continued apace through to the end of the train. A quick check of his expensive looking timepiece and he propped the case on the side of a wooden desk.

He then unclipped the two metal fasteners and revealed the silenced long barrel of a sniper rifle.

With the confidence only a professional would exude, the weapon was snatched up to his right shoulder, its metallic hollowed out frame of a butt lodged in the natural pocket under his right clavicle. He breathed in slowly and stretched his head to the left until there was an audible click. The rifle was then nestled into his shoulder for a few more seconds until the feel was exactly right.

He had already affixed the long scope onto the catch above the gun bolt at the top of the barrel and now the marksman stretched his eyes wide open, as he then carefully set the sights of the crosshair.

The rear-sliding window of the train was then pulled down slightly and the sniper could hear the wind competing with the sound of the train. Suddenly, he was aware of the train passing a grey truck parked next to a smoldering campfire and this is what he had been specifically briefed to watch for. Now he *knew* this was his mark.

*

Pavel was impressed by the majesty of this celebrated locomotive and was honoured to have witnessed something so historic through his own eyes. He thought it was even better than the *Orient Express*, which he had once seen sat in London Victoria station some years ago, but he noted his obvious Russian bias.

He then looked at Artyom who just nodded his equal appreciation and they both smiled, content their mission was finally complete and they could retire from the cold, which was now, exactly where they headed.

With that, Pavel was abruptly aware of a shrill whizzing noise, followed by a strange sounding crack.

'Shhhh!' whispered Pavel, gripping the forearm of his partner, but suddenly all of Artyom's weight was shifting onto his outstretched and now load bearing limb.

Pavel turned to look Artyom in the eyes and through the fine mist in the air, became aware of a small black hole in the centre of his forehead. Before he had time to notice the trickle of blood emanating from within, his ears pricked up again at the briefest hint of yet another whizzing noise and then there was immediate darkness.

*

The long, elegant weapon was neatly placed back into the black foam lined case and the nickel clasps pressed confidently onto their holders. The well-groomed gunman then returned towards the Purser and nodded once more, before disappearing off towards the front of the train.

The Purser slowly lifted the antique looking telephone and dialled a number that had been written on a note, surreptitiously hidden inside his maroon, leather writing pad. He waited for three rings before hearing the call connect.

*

In a dark room within a private members club in Kaliningrad, a large, bald man sat back against a white leather sofa. Soft red spotlights scattered mood lighting onto the surrounding cushions that all struggled to retain their plumpness under the weight of the massive man sitting within them.

Bacchus Borichevsky's mobile phone vibrated within his trouser pocket, much to the surprise of the nubile blonde straddling his lap. The man's large paw, swatted the girl away in seeming annoyance, her hands clamping to her naked breasts as part of a retrospective show of indignity.

He quickly fumbled for the phone, which was still murmuring within his pocket, hoping that his slow reactions would outpace the impending voicemail. Finally two chubby fingers managed to prise the device from his tight trousers and Borichevsky mumbled an acknowledgement.

'It is done, sir.' came a whisper with the slightest hint of a Parisian accent.

'Otlichno,' was the monotone and guttural reply, a faint smirk of satisfaction appeared on his face, 'excellent.'

He sat back with his arms stretched out behind his bulbous folded neck and beckoned the blonde back with his eyes. *Her* job was not yet done.

*

Printed in Great Britain
by Amazon